ADVANCE PRAISE FOR

The Moon in the Well

"Erica Meade is not only an exquisite storyteller, but also a true wisewoman and healer who shows us just how to apply her storytelling medicine so that our lives might be healed and transformed. *The Moon in the Well* is a gem—anyone who has ever felt the power of myth should run and buy it!"

— JALAJA BONHEIM, Ph.D.
Author of *Aphrodite's Daughters* and *The Hunger for Ecstasy*

"This is a lodestar of a book, one that can help us find our way through the borderlands our civilization is crossing through now. It gives us stories that are truer than true, reminding us of the deepest human wisdom so we can laugh, and listen to each other and find the compassion to create new solutions for our time. I intend to give this wise compass to everyone on my gift list this year."

— SHERRY RUTH ANDERSON
Author of *The Feminine Face of God* and *The Cultural Creatives*

"This is a lovely conglomeration of stories—Irish, Greek, Persian, Siberian, Chilean, North American. It will be helpful for all of us looking for good stories to tell our children or someone else's children at a crucial moment of their lives."

— ROBERT BLY
Author of *Iron John*

"More than any other book in years, *The Moon in the Well* explains the rightful and useful place of myth and stories in people's lives. Erica Helm Meade does this in an engaging way, making connections between myth and story and how people are in the world— as individuals, members of families, communities, in nature, and in other larger senses of the world. Her retelling of stories—some well-known, others not—is alone worth the price of the book."

— RICK SIMONSON
   Elliott Bay Book Company and author of
   Multi-Cultural Literacy

"Erica Helm Meade has given us a valuable collection of teaching stories and many wise ways to use them. A blessing for discovering the modern power of these ancient inspirations."

— JACK KORNFIELD
   Author of *A Path with Heart*

The Moon in the Well

Wisdom Tales to Transform Your Life,
Family, and Community

RETOLD WITH REFLECTIONS AND SUGGESTED USES BY

ERICA HELM MEADE

WITH A FOREWORD BY DAVID ABRAM

OPEN COURT
Chicago and La Salle, Illinois

To order books from Open Court, call 1-800-815-2280.

Open Court Publishing Company is a division of Carus Publishing Company.

Printed and bound in the United States of America.

Library of Congress Cataloging-in-Publication Data

Meade, Erica Helm, 1954–
        The moon in the well : wisdom tales to transform your life, family, and community :
    retold with reflections and suggested uses / by Erica Helm Meade ; with a foreword by
    David Abram.
            p. cm.
        Includes bibliographical references and index.
        ISBN 0-8126-9440-6 (alk. paper)—ISBN 0-8126-9441-4 (pbk. : alk. paper)
        1. Tales   2. Tales—Indexes.   3. Folk literature—Themes, motives.   I. Title
    GR74.6 M43 2001
    398.2—dc21

                                                                            2001021600

Dedicated with love and gratitude to
my grandmother, Florence Helm,
and to her storytelling cohorts
Lillian Dodd and Maxine Thompson,
whose stories blessed my early years
and inspire me still,
and to my beloved stepchildren,
Oona, Aram, Bran, and Fionn,
who in their own artful ways
carry the story onward

Contents

Foreword

In the prosperous land where I live, at this dangerous and delicious moment on the cusp of a new millennium, a mysterious task is underway to invigorate the minds of the populace, and to vitalize the spirits of our children. In a strange and curious initiative, parents and politicians and educators of all forms are raising funds to bring computers into every household in the realm, and into every classroom from kindergarten on up through college. With the new technology, it is hoped, children will learn to read much more efficiently, and will exercise their intelligence in rich new ways. Interacting with the wealth of information available online, children's minds will be able to develop and explore much more vigorously than was possible in earlier eras—and so, we hope, they will be well prepared for the technological wonders of the coming century.

How can any child resist such a glad initiative? Indeed, few *adults* can resist the dazzle of the digital screen, with its instantaneous access to everywhere, its treasure trove of virtual amusements, and its swift capacity to locate any piece of knowledge we desire. And why *should* we resist? Digital technology is transforming every field of human endeavor, and it promises to broaden the capabilities of the human intellect far beyond its current reach. Small wonder that we wish to open and extend this dazzling dream to all our children!

It is possible, however, that we are making a grave mistake in our rush to wire every classroom, and to bring our children online as soon as possible. Our excitement about the Internet should not blind us to the fact that the astonishing linguistic and intellectual capacity of the human brain did not evolve in relation to the computer! Nor, of course, did it evolve in relation to the written word. Rather it evolved in relation to orally told stories. Indeed, we humans were telling each other stories for many, many millennia before we ever began writing our words down—whether on the page or on the screen.

Spoken stories were the living encyclopedias of our oral ancestors, dynamic and lyrical compendiums of practical knowledge. Oral tales told on special occasions carried the secrets of how to orient in the local cosmos. Hidden in the magic adventures of their characters were precise instructions for the hunting of various animals and for enacting the appropriate rituals of respect and gratitude if a hunt was successful, as well as information regarding which plants were good to eat and which were poisonous, and how to prepare certain herbs to heal cramps, or sleeplessness, or a fever. The stories carried instructions about how to construct a winter shelter, and what to do during a drought, and—more generally—how to live well in this land without destroying the land's wild vitality.

So much earthly savvy was carried in the old tales! And since there was no written medium in which to record and preserve the stories—since there were no written books like this one—the surrounding landscape itself functioned as the primary *mnemonic,* or memory trigger, for preserving the oral tales. To this end, diverse animals common to the local earth figured as prominent characters within the oral stories—whether as teachers or tricksters, as buffoons or as bearers of wisdom. A chance encounter with a particular creature as you went about your daily business (an encounter with a coyote, perhaps, or a magpie) would likely stir the memory of one or another story in which that animal played a decisive role. Moreover, crucial events in the stories were commonly associated with particular *places* in the local terrain where those events were assumed to have happened, and whenever you noticed that place in the course of your wanderings—when you came upon that particular cluster of boulders, or that sharp bend in the river—the encounter would spark the memory of the storied events that had unfolded there.

Thus, while the accumulated knowledge of our oral ancestors was carried in their stories, the stories themselves were carried by the surrounding earth. The local landscape was alive with stories! Traveling through the terrain, one felt teachings and secrets sprouting from every nook and knoll, lurking under the rocks and waiting to swoop down from the trees. The wooden planks of one's old house would laugh and whine, from time to time, when the wind leaned hard against them, and whispered wishes would pour from the windswept grasses. To the members of a traditionally oral culture, all things had the power of speech.

Indeed, when we consult indigenous, oral peoples from around the world, we commonly discover that, to them, there is no phenomenon—no stone, no mountain, no human artifact—that is definitively inert or inanimate. Each thing has its own pulse, its own interior animation, its own life! Rivers *feel* the presence of the fish that swim within them. A large boulder, its surface spreading with crinkly red and gray lichens, is able to influence the events around it, and even to influence the thoughts of those persons who lean against it—lending their thoughts a certain gravity, and a kind of stony wisdom. Particular fish, as well, are bearers of wisdom, gifting their insights to those who catch them. Everything is alive—even the stories themselves are animate beings! Among the Cree of Manitoba, for instance, it is said that the stories, when they are not being told, live off in their own villages, where they go about their own lives. Every now and then, however, a story will leave its village and go hunting for a person to inhabit. That person will abruptly be possessed by the story, and soon will find herself telling the tale out into the world, singing it back into active circulation.

There is something about this storied way of speaking—this acknowledgment of a world all alive, awake, and aware—that brings us close to our senses, and to the palpable, sensuous world that materially surrounds us. Our animal senses know nothing of the objective, mechanical, quantifiable world to which most of our civilized discourse refers. Wild and gregarious organs, our senses spontaneously experience the world not as a conglomeration of inert objects but as a field of animate presences that actively *call* our attention, *grab* our focus, or *capture* our gaze. Whenever we slip beneath the abstract assumptions of the modern world, we find ourselves drawn into relationship with a diversity of beings as inscrutable and unfathomable as ourselves. Direct, sensory perception is inherently animistic, disclosing a world wherein each thing has its own active agency and power.

When we speak of the things around us as quantifiable objects or passive "natural resources," we contradict our spontaneous sensory experience of the world, and hence our senses begin to wither and grow dim. We find ourselves living more and more in our heads, adrift in a set of abstractions, unable to feel at home in an objectified landscape that seems alien to our own dreams and emotions. But when we begin to tell stories, our imagination begins to flow out through our eyes and our ears to inhabit the breathing earth once again. Suddenly, the trees along the street are looking at us, and the clouds crouch low over the city as though they are trying to hatch something wondrous. We find ourselves back inside the same world that the squirrels and the spiders inhabit, along with the deer stealthily munching the last plants in our garden, and the wild geese honking overhead as they flap south for the winter. Linear time falls away, and we find ourselves held, once again, in the vast cycles of the cosmos—the round dance of the seasons, the sun climbing out of the ground each morning and slipping down into the earth every evening, the opening and closing of the lunar eye whose full gaze attracts the tidal waters within us and all around us.

For we are born of this animate earth, and our sensitive flesh is simply our part of the dreaming body of the world. However much we may obscure this ancestral affinity, we cannot erase it, and the persistence of the old stories is the continuance of a way of speaking that blesses the sentience of things, binding our thoughts back into the depths of an imagination much vaster than our own. To live in a storied world is to know that intelligence is not an exclusively human faculty located somewhere inside our skulls, but is rather a power of the animate earth itself, in which we humans, along with the hawks and the thrumming frogs, all participate. It is to know, further, that each land, each valley, each wild community of plants and animals and soils, has its particular *style* of intelligence, its unique mind or imagination evident in the particular patterns that play out there, in the living stories that unfold in that valley, and that are told and retold by the people of that place. Each ecology has its own psyche, and the local people bind their imaginations to the psyche of the place by letting the land dream its tales through them.

❀   ❀   ❀

How, then, can we stir our oral selves from their slumber; how might we reawaken the storied universe? Why, by carefully gathering a host of well-worn stories from different lands, tucking them into a medicine bundle, or quietly sewing them into the pages of a book and sending it out into the world! Indeed, the book you now hold is itself a sort of medicine bundle, and it carries a power both wonderful and dangerous. Dangerous, yes: for though we may think that we are *reading* these very pleasureful pages, what we are really doing is exposing ourselves to these magic tales, rendering ourselves vulnerable to their subtle solicitations. Inevitably, two or three or seven tales will choose us, leaping up off the page and entering through the pupils of our eyes, and soon they will begin telling themselves through our mouths! Such is the power and potency of stories, that each person finds herself unable to resist certain tales. And Erica Meade has fortified the transition from the page to the tongue with a rich array of clues and suggestions keyed to particular stories, and with her marvelous introductory musings on, for instance, the process of learning a story "by heart," weaving together memory and improvisation.

How basic and instinctive is the imaginative craft of telling a tale! And yet how little we exercise these skills in the modern era. Of course, we'll *read* a story to a child before sleep, but we won't take the time to really learn to tell the story ourselves (without reading it), or to improvise a fresh version of an old tale for our neighbors and friends. We have too little time for such frivolities; a world of factual information beckons, a universe of spreadsheets and stock comparisons. If we crave entertainment, we have only to click on the TV or the computer, and straightaway we can synapse ourselves to any one of the rapidly multiplying video games and virtual worlds now accessible through the glowing screen. Surely this rich and rapidly shifting realm of technological pleasures is the niftiest magic of all!

Perhaps. Yet for all their dash and dazzle, the inventions of humankind can never match the complexity and nuance of the sensuous earth, this breathing cosmos that we did not create. The many-voiced Earth remains the secret source and inspiration for all the fabricated realms that now beckon to us through the screen. Let us indeed celebrate the powers of technology, and introduce our children to the digital delights of our era. But not before we have acquainted them with the gifts of the living land, and enabled its palpable mysteries to ignite their imaginations and their thoughts. Not before we have stepped outside with our children, late at night, to gaze up at the glinting lights scattered haphazardly across the darkness, sharing a story about how the stars came to be there. Not before they've glimpsed the tracks of coyote in the mud by the supermarket, or have sat alongside us on the banks of a local stream, dangling a line in the water and pondering an old tale about the salmon of wisdom . . . "Listen—that's Raven squawking! There he is, swerving onto that high branch. Why's he so excited—is he planning to steal the sun once again? Hey, bodacious bird, black as the night: what new mischief are you up to?"

The potent stories in this book, when we make them our own and tell them aloud, wake us up to our immersion in a dreaming universe—to the vast and enigmatic story deliciously unfolding all around us. They induce us to taste the icicles dangling from the roof, and to smell the breeze, and to wonder what's going to happen next!

DAVID ABRAM

Preface

Stories go to work on you like arrows.

—BENSON LEWIS

Handed down by the village elders of old, the tales in this book have long proved their ability to go straight to the heart. They nourish and sustain us, sticking to the ribs long after they've been told. They model resilience of spirit and perseverance of character. They guide us through the twists and turns of life. When we delve into the well of these sagely old tales, our innate "elder wisdom" begins to percolate. Told to a group, these tales create commonality, spark dialogue, and help us to articulate previously unformulated truths.

The human soul, in its quest for things that endure, longs for the old stories and the wisdom called forth by old stories. Never before have our lives so powerfully been shaped and reshaped by rapidly changing technologies. More than ever we hunger for things of depth which matter, and which have lasting meaning. At a time when our minds are inundated and dulled by an excess of information, wisdom tales give us a sorely needed life-giving infusion, plasma for the imagination, food for the soul.

This book was designed for story-lovers of all kinds, but especially for those who seek to nourish themselves and others by bringing pertinent wisdom tales to life where they are needed most, in the dialogues of everyday life. In my work as a healer, and in traveling and teaching, I have worked with parents, grandparents, group leaders, teachers, therapists, environmental educators, hospice counselors, and health care professionals, all of whom have been eager to access elder wisdom through story, and to put it to work in their personal and professional lives. These people have been pleased to discover that metaphor is not beyond their grasp, and the art of storytelling is more easily mastered than they think. They find that with a bit of effort, their own authentic storytelling voices readily emerge. They are also pleasantly surprised to learn that committing stories to memory can be made simple through the enjoyable exercise described in this book.

More challenging for potential storytellers than finding their voices and learning tales by heart, is the task of finding the right tale to suit a specific occasion, person, or group. This book is designed to help. In the theme index, I list hundreds of themes which hold particular psychological, social, cultural, and environmental significance for our time. Perusing the index, and choosing a few relevant themes will lead you to clusters of applicable tales from which to choose.

Alternatively, if you use the index you'll also find that a single tale often illuminates many themes. One such example is the delightfully inspiring Irish story "Finn McCoul Learns to Run." This tale explores the loving tutelage a young hero receives from his grandmother. In the theme index you will find the tale listed under the following: **ADOPTION AND FOSTERING, ADVOCACY FOR CHILDREN, CAST-OUTS AND RUNAWAYS, COOPERATION AND DEVOTION, EARLY CHILDHOOD BONDING, EMOTIONAL RESILIENCE, HEALING TOUCH, HELP FROM WISE ELDERS, REVERENCE FOR NATURE,** and **YOUTH-ELDER ALLIANCE**.

Bearing these themes and more, "Finn McCoul Learns to Run" strikes a thematic chord for numerous occasions and groups. Read silently to oneself it heartens young and old, makes us grin, and reminds us of what truly matters. Told at home it honors grandparents, young children, and the bonds between the two. Told in schools it makes students laugh while it inspires learning. Told in senior centers it reminds elders of their worth, and encourages them to engage with the younger generation. Told at teachers' conferences it celebrates the heart of learning and inspires dedication and recommitment. Told at psychology seminars, it portrays the healing rapport between elder and youth. From the perspective of depth psychology, it reflects the dynamism between inner beings, the old wise one and the eager youth. Not all the tales have such multifaceted applicability, but many of them do. The magic of stories is that they hold multiple meanings and touch the human spirit in many ways.

In the introduction of this book, "On Stories and Storytelling," I address commonly asked questions. I speak to the origins of storytelling and the importance of storytelling in healing, teaching, and community building. I summarize the craft of learning tales by heart. I also stress respect for the sources of the tales, as well as respect for the specific needs of the listener. I illuminate the dance between innovation and preservation which keeps the art of storytelling alive.

The body of the book contains sixty-three tales from around the world. Beneath the title of each you'll find its place of origin along with an indication of its length. Short stories containing 500 words or less are easily learned by heart. Medium stories running 500 to 1000 words in length take a bit more effort, and long stories running 1000 to 1500 words in length, more yet. Extra long stories, those exceeding 1500 words, can be read aloud, or can be offered as assigned reading. But don't underestimate your capacity to learn even extra-long tales by heart. With the simple memory exercise I describe in this book, many first-time storytellers astonish themselves by learning an extra-long tale straightaway.

Scholars have extensively interpreted wisdom tales from sociological, anthropological, psychological, archetypal, and spiritual points of view, all of which open doors to a richer understanding of the human experience. These tales are at once wells of sacred wisdom, mirrors of the inner life, touchstones for relationship, and calls to environmental and social action. Following each tale are interpretive comments, suggested uses, and true-life examples of what can happen when we dive into a story and get wet. My intent here is not to further a single perspective, but to entertain many, and to share the immediacy and applicability of wisdom tales to our own blemished lives. By offering real-life examples I sacrifice theoretical elegance for the grit of the community storytelling experience.

The theme index and after-story comments are not meant to be exhaustive, for in a single volume it would be impossible to enumerate all the themes and to comment extensively on each. Themes are living, breathing entities, carriers of complex and paradoxical truths. Words can never fully do them justice. They draw us into a story, but like a flower or a sunset, they strike each person differently, and they rarely strike you the same way twice. Their meaning remains enigmatic, revelatory, and fresh. The theme index and comments reflect my personal experience in entering the tales, and the experiences of others who have entered them with me. Over the years people have called to my attention interesting themes I might not have noticed, such as "male intuition," "misguided leadership," and "reverence for nature." The list of themes given in the index grew organically out of theme-oriented storytelling work, and will continue to evolve. My words are not meant to pin down or explain the tales, but to serve as doorways and entry points into your own explorations.

Some of the tales feature prominent cultural figures such as Kuan Yin, Maui, or Coyote, who merit brief "biographies." These precede the first tale of each figure.

A few tales are too frightening, sexy, or morally complex for children. This is noted below the title and clarified in the commentary following the tales.

Before you begin, I should impart this warning: Stories can be habit forming and contagious. They get under the skin and take up residence inside you. If you take one to heart, you may ruminate on it at odd times of day, and find yourself itching to pass it on. If so, I hope it leaps to life on your tongue, igniting hearts and sparking dialogue in your clan and community.

Introduction

On Stories and Storytelling

What is a wisdom tale, and what does it take to tell one?

Wisdom tales are treasures from the ancestors. Included in this collection are myths, legends, folk and fairy tales, and fables. Though these categories commingle and overlap, we can safely give these general descriptions: *Myths* tell us who started this awesome, quirky cosmos and why. They tell how the great deities love, compete, create, and blunder and how the human race came into being. Myths satisfy our hunger to participate in what Joseph Campbell called life's "inscrutable mystery." *Legends, folk tales, and fairy tales* unravel the adventures of heroes and heroines who long ago faced the same dilemmas we face today. These tales show us that by trusting the best in ourselves and by heeding guidance from animal helpers and wise ones along the way, our life stories will unfold like unique tapestries. These tales help us sink our teeth into the dance between character and fate, for they show us that life is a collaboration between who we are, what comes to us, and what we do with both. *Fables* are juicy plums, cross-pollinated by the tree of intuition and the tree of common sense. They go down easily and are never heavy, because they put words to what we already know.

Long ago, all the ancestors belonged to tribes or clans, and each group had its tellers. Story motifs corresponded from one group to the next. First peoples around the globe shared an understanding of original chaos, the unformed mass, and the longing of creators to establish a beautiful abundant place, and to populate it with living beings. Heaven and Earth had to be pulled apart and made distinct. Heavenly downpours flooded the earth, and first beings searched for someplace to stand. The great land masses began as bits of mud dragged up from the dark sea. Later, humans were made from modest things like sea foam, dust, spit, and fingernail dirt. Mythic correspondence between groups can be attributed in part to swapping, for tales are nothing if not shared. But what about remote tribes? Why were their tales similar to the rest? Perhaps because when it all boils down, humans the world over share the same mother. Our hearts struggle with the same desires and strive toward the same ends. The streams of our imaginations are fed from a single aquifer. Perhaps our myths are the First Mother's dreams. Perhaps they are songs sung to her by the First Father.

Today, in most of the world, the oral storytelling tradition has merged with the written. As newspapers, radio, television, and now cyber-communication have taken the place of fireside telling, folklorists have scurried to take stories down and to preserve them in books. Pessimists say the real storytelling tradition is dead, and can't be revived. But I believe the essence of oral telling reincarnates easily. If you dust off a book and read a few tales, one of them is bound to spring to life in your imagination. The ancestral voice comes to life within you. If you decide to learn the tale and tell it to others, the voice will speak to them. Telling conveys distilled spirits from the ancestral mind to the living community.

Many tellers are awed and humbled by this and come to approach storytelling as a soulful task. Yet storytelling does not require a degree in divinity, psychology, or folklore, nor does it require bardic lineage. It's an art that thrives on respect for ancestors and a love of community. Imagination, humility, and wit come in handy. The art of telling calls for queenly reverence, heartily salted with Coyote irreverence. It craves Japanese grace and African understatement. It relishes Scottish pluck and Irish audacity. It flourishes with Russian verbosity, Mexican vitality, and Polynesian heat. Most of all, the art wants something authentic, a voice that will carry the ancestral song, turning a phrase, sketching a scene, drawing out a character without getting in its way. Lucky for us, wisdom tales have their own integrity. Good things happen when we take an interest and bump up against them with curiosity, a willing voice, and an open heart.

Why do we need wisdom tales in education?

Learning is at its best when the heart is aroused and the mind hums with curiosity. The judicious use of a few pertinent tales can help bring this about. I've watched many so-called "burnt-out" teachers take enormous pleasure in re-storying the learning environment in ways that recharge them and their students. Catherine Goetsch lights up her calculus classes with legends of Pythagoras, Hypatia, and other mathematicians of old. These tales amuse and motivate students. Math problems are far more intriguing when we imagine them tweaking great minds down through the ages.

Native American teachers who've remained close to ancestral stories have long understood the importance of fully engaging the learner. "We learn best while we're laughing," says Native teacher and storyteller, Terry Tefoya, who teaches serious ethics through trickster tales. Learning anchored by cultural lore becomes part of a fruitful continuum, rather than a heap of facts that begin drifting away the moment spring break begins. Like his tribal ancestors, Dr. Tefoya works with ambiance, dimming the lights, playing the drum. These heighten learners' attention, and make the learning more memorable. But such flair is not required. To add story to their lesson plans, teachers need not be showy, theatrically trained, or even flamboyant. Many teachers simply allow storytelling to unfold as a natural extension of their lectures.

Stories help to draw out our innate wisdom, natural curiosity, and enthusiasm for learning. The word *educate* comes from the root *educare, to draw out*. In addition to *instruction*, which is literally the act of *packing information into* the student, we must also draw out and honor the innate wisdom that is already there. Teachers describe this innate wisdom as a matrix for understanding—a vessel which intuits, synthesizes, integrates, interprets, and puts things together in a way that makes sense. It is drawn out by rapport, face-to-face dialogue, eye contact, nuance, gesture, warmth, and the resonance of a teacher's voice. But nothing coaxes it forth like a story.

For example: In an abuse prevention class for "at risk" teens, students started out tight-lipped and fidgety. Many of them had been sexually or physically abused by adults in authority roles, yet they insisted they had nothing to say on the subject of power and the abuse of power, or boundaries and the breaking of boundaries. But after hearing the Greek myth of young Persephone's rape and abduction and her prolonged captivity against her will, the students lost their reticence. Even shy students spoke with enthusiasm and conviction about justice and about young people struggling to have a say in their own fate. The story gave context to their experience. It helped them formulate observations and voice insights. A tone of mutual support emerged, drawing out the students, helping them to strategize and learn from each other.

Most of us learn best when love-struck by a subject. Love for learning is at its peak when the heart and intellect are awakened and fed by the imagination. In earlier times story was the heart of education. The pleasure and necessity of learning were united, since even pragmatic skills such as geography, navigation, hunting, herbology, agriculture, and astronomy were learned and passed on through story. There was no written means of capturing knowledge, so the survival of the race depended upon each generation learning these skills by heart. The love of a subject, such as astronomy, key to navigation and measuring time, was ignited and sustained through compelling stories of the Pliades, Cassiopeia, Orion, Ariadne, and various other mythical beings whose celestial bodies make up the constellations.

In more recent times we've come to rely almost wholly on written texts. Today it seems unnecessary to store knowledge within, when we can so easily turn to the encyclopedia or the Internet. But in doing away with the mythic components of education, we've drastically reduced the imaginative pleasures of learning. Students grow bored and apathetic. They lack fondness for their subjects, and we blame them for it. Today's teachers are working to rekindle academic passion. To accomplish this they are bringing story back into the classroom.

Imagine an adult education course on women and leadership. Theory and step-by-step approaches come to life when augmented with a tale such as, "How Brigit Got Lands for the Poor." Women are profoundly heartened by Brigit's strength and persistence in the face of adversity. Their love for Brigit's intrepid leadership gives passion and purpose to the course curriculum.

The current crisis in education makes story especially important now. In earlier civilizations, the architecture of educational institutions reflected the higher values of the culture. Outside school doorways stood statues of gods and goddesses of inspiration and erudition such as Apollo and Sarasvati. Students knew the stories of these deities, and following their path to knowledge was a recognized privilege. Today the architecture of public schools is frightfully similar to that of prisons, and indeed many students feel they are imprisoned or "warehoused" for the school day. Weapons checks, now commonplace at school entrances, are a sobering sight. Colleges, ever more conscious of the bottom line, are run more and more like corporations. Police control and corporate values are all too evident in our schools, and students are anything but inspired. They suffer high anxiety over soaring tuition and all-important test scores, and they often fear for their physical safety. It's alarming how often our educational system breeds fear, unhealthy competition, and depression, when what students, parents, and teachers want is for education to engender meaningful learning, intellectual achievement, confidence, engagement, cooperation, and character. Re-storying education is one way to activate this.

Stories help students think for themselves, respect themselves, and value each other. Humility and kindness are the core lessons of fairy tales, reminding students of what's most important in life. Many fables teach self-protection and healthy skepticism, and are excellent lead-ins to serious discussions on hard topics like drugs, violence, teen prostitution, and sexually transmitted disease. Myths open the door to the deeper questions: Why are we here? What is the meaning of human life? What is our place in the universe?

Story teaches us to aspire, not for instant gratification, but for the kind of nobility that comes from behaving wisely. Stories teach us that what a protagonist does or doesn't do is highly important to how things come out. Today when apathy, aggression, isolation, and fear pervade our schools, it's time for tales that remind us: What we do and how we interact make all the difference.

How do wisdom tales support the body's capacity to heal?

Health-care professionals from surgeons to nurses' aides are keen on the importance of state of mind to any healing process. Research shows that things that improve attitude—things such as touch, friendship, music, and meditation—strengthen people's ability to heal. Family physician Mary Hoagland-Scher says that losing oneself to a creative process has a trickle-down effect that contributes to overall health and well-being. As a young volunteer in a pediatrics ward, and later as a trainer for hospital staff, I saw storytelling facilitate immediate rapport between patients and their caregivers and healers. Well-chosen wisdom tales impart solace and encouragement to patients, and help to reduce their emotional stress. We know that stress reduction helps the body's immune response and promotes the growth of healthy tissue.

Eastern traditions have steadily drawn from the rejuvenating power of the mythic imagination. After accupressure treatments, my Chinese doctor tells me to relax and gaze at a picture of Kuan Yin, the gentle Bodhisattva of East Asian lore. My yoga teacher helps injured patients master strengthening postures by describing the mythic warriors embodied by those postures, and by narrating their mythic combat against oppressive foes. Today in the West, storytelling and other complementary health aids are being used in clinics and hospitals. Medical institutions are embracing the idea of treating the whole patient—mind, body, and soul. Awakening the imagination through story does just that.

How do wisdom tales console anxiety and depression, and call forth character?

Anxiety, depression, and character flaws have probably always been part of the human condition. Story has long served to elucidate this condition, to help broaden our philosophical perspective, and encourage personal integrity. Story reminds us that even the bleakest night can be followed by a golden dawn, and even the most outcast person can find his place in the world. Story has always been a source of solace and encouragement for suffering humans. It has always endorsed integrity of character, and taught the importance of behaving honorably. Today our increased need for anti-depressant and anxiety-reducing drugs may well correspond to a loss of myth and a drastic reduction in time spent, as native Hawaiians put it, "talking story."

At present, psychotherapy employs the anxiety-relieving power of the narrative process, but there comes a point when personal story requires mirroring through myth. As author and psychologist James Hillman points out, psychology gets mired in themes of infantile wounds and parental failings. Fairy tales astutely mirror these dynamics in their opening scenes, but later show the adventuresome way through and beyond. Without a richly storied perspective we're left with reductionistic views that often fail to account for the extraordinary strength and resilience of the human soul. We overemphasize the traumas which wounded us, and underemphasize our own resourcefulness in setting things right. We expend imaginative energy remembering early deprivation, and we sometimes forget to imagine the glimmer of a worthwhile future unfolding. Overemphasis on past trauma can easily lead to hinging one's personal story on the themes of regret, symptomology, victimization, and repetition. If personal story ends there, there has been no healing. We must also learn to get our hearts and minds around personal themes of grace, devotion, challenge, gratitude, transcendence, learning, adjusting, creating, reshaping, healing, and moving forward. As author and psychologist Ginette Paris says, "It's not simply what wounds you that constitutes your story, it's what you do about it."

Sometimes stories reach us when nothing else can. A woman named Diane grew withdrawn and depressed after losing the man she considered the love of her life. Self-help literature on loss and grieving did not reach her, but the myth of the Japanese sun goddess Amaterasu, moved her deeply. Like Diane, Amaterasu faced a difficult loss, and responded by withdrawing from life. In the myth Diane saw her own suffering and withdrawal, and also found a guide to healing. For many months, Diane carried the myth with her as a source of emotional restoration.

Learning to think metaphorically, thematically, and mythologically about one's own life, and to share this through *talking story* with others is a healing revelation for individuals and groups. In my view, traditional lore is still our best shot at activating and animating these creative processes in the psyche. It's still a great source of encouragement for change, and remains a most powerful reminder that, to borrow a metaphor from Carl Jung, we are all "in the soup" together. Storytelling helps reduce isolation. It strengthens compassion, mirrors self-worth, boosts resiliency, and encourages personal integrity. Ultimately story helps us toward loving participation in the human drama. We cannot escape or fully redeem this passion play, for life is dark and light, beautiful and cruel, and we humans are fallible. But a well-storied imagination beholds the richness of the world, cultivates a perspective that is at once sagely and humble, and opts to embrace life.

Is there a right time and place for telling wisdom tales?

Most storytelling traditions observed rules about when tales could be told and who could tell them. It was serious business, for telling the right tale at the right time ushered in the seasons and helped maintain the cosmic order. Such was the case with "The Dance of the Deer," a sacred drama enacted by descendants of the Maya in Central America. This ancient story was not to be told until the stars were right. Knowledgeable elders said when, and virtually every villager complied to do his or her part. In full costume, after several days fasting, villagers spent the better part of a day enacting the tale. The proceedings venerated the guardian spirit of the village, the animal powers in the surrounding forest, and the four directions. Villagers reached a shared state of devotion that reinforced their ties to the land and to each other. Enacting the story at the right time and in the right way brought renewal and strengthened the life force of the land and its people.

Today, anyone can go to the library and find a version of "The Dance of the Deer" in an anthology of folk tales. Anyone can read or tell it at whim to anyone, at anytime, and in any place. In the eyes of some Mayan elders, this is a sign of the crumbling of the world.

Our society views things quite differently. Here, universal access to literature is a hallmark of cultural advancement. Our love of free speech so shapes our thought, that it's hard for us to appreciate the wisdom of "right time, right place, and right people." Yet this is precisely the internal discretion a storyteller has to develop if he or she is to do justice to the stories, the listeners, and the ancestors to whom the stories belong.

I learned a wonderful version of "The Dance of the Deer" twenty-some years ago in Guatemala, and have never told it aloud, though I often go back to it for inspiration. An elder gave me permission to tell it, and I've kept an eye out for the right occasion. But whenever I've come close, there has arisen in me a distinct hesitation to handle this sacred story outside its rightful context. How could one teller, in the usual public forums, do it justice? At present this story-ritual is in a kind of limbo. Abbreviated take-offs of it are performed for tourists, while the real thing has been tossed aside as a quaint relic with no real purpose. Young Guatemalans trying to embrace what they see on television, shrug off the ritual as "old people's stuff." Many believe that spiritual devotion to earth, forest, village, and the spirits who guard them, is irrelevant and passé.

Some readers might cry out, "We need such stories now more than ever!" And I agree. But how and when the tale will reemerge remains to be seen. It may come in some surprising form. Perhaps it will come through contemporary theater in Chiapas, Guatemala City, or Pasadena. Perhaps it will surface through poetry, magical realism, science fiction, or creative nonfiction. Something tells me the myth will reincarnate with renewed vitality at some point in time.

Stories have an uncanny way of being reborn when we need them. Irish storytellers put it in mystical terms: Long ago, they say, the great tellers of Ireland gathered to reconstruct the famous Tain (pronounced *toyn*) of the Ulster Cycle. To their sorrow and dismay, they found many episodes had been forgotten entirely. A group of them journeyed east in hopes of retrieving lost episodes from an old sage. Along the way, they came to the grave of the greatest of all ancestral poets, Fergus. The elders went to seek lodgings, while a young apprentice stayed behind at the grave. He recited a poem to honor the memory of Fergus, and before he knew what was happening, a fog began swirling around him. For three days and nights, the apprentice could not be found. He was in the Otherworld with Fergus himself, who stood radiant and godlike before him. At the apprentice's request, Fergus recited the Tain from start to finish. When the telling was complete, the apprentice bid his ancestor good-bye and returned to his elders who anxiously awaited him at Fergus's grave. You can imagine their joy when the young apprentice restored to them all the lost episodes of the Tain. The journey east was not necessary after all, for the ancestral voice had come directly to them from the Otherworld.

More recently there are other examples of the return of lost myths. In this century the ancient Sumerian myth of the goddess Inanna has returned to strike a chord in the collective psyche. In recent decades Sumerologists have pieced together and deciphered fragmented cuneiform tablets comprising Inanna's horrific trials and marvelous exploits. Collaboration between translator Samuel Noah Kramer and storyteller Diane Wolkstein has made accessible these glorious works that were for centuries, lost. Inanna's theme of descent, death, and rebirth has been taken to heart by thousands.

Perhaps the stories have their own say about when to disappear and when to come back again. An East Indian folk tale says stories have minds of their own. They yearn to be told. When storytellers get lazy, the untold stories feel forsaken. They sit up at night fretting amongst themselves. If neglected too long, the stories become belligerent and plot retaliation. How dare the storytellers be so remiss? It is their job, after all, to give the stories life.

Storytelling today involves serving ancestral material in a modern context. Right place, right time, and right people are obviously open to interpretation. We have no hard and fast rules to guide us, but we can strive to respect the story, its culture of origin and the ancestral tellers who developed it.

Storytellers do expect each other to uphold some basic courtesies. Most wisdom tales found in books like this one are considered part of the public domain, but it's still appropriate to credit the culture from which the story came. The most straightforward way to do so is to say a few words of praise, gratitude, and recognition as you introduce the tale. This furthers our appreciation for the cultures of the world. If you're retelling someone's version of a tale, such as one of my versions herein, or one of Wolkstein's versions of the Descent of Inanna, remember these were often painstakingly worked out, and it's good to credit the person. It's also important to know that some Native tellers are the designated keepers of their tribal stories. If you are fortunate enough to hear one, you'll be expected to get permission before repeating it. Some traditions say tales belong to the ancestors at large, and anyone can tell them, as long as it's done with skill and respect. Others say, "That's our tale. You must ask permission to tell it." The best we storytellers can do is strive to be aware, considerate, respectful, and acknowledging of the sources.

It helps to know your motive for telling a tale at a given time and place. There's a bit of a show-off in most everyone, and rightfully so. Without it we'd be too shy for the art of storytelling to have evolved in the first place. But even a show-off like Coyote eventually learns it's important to consider others. It pays to stop and think: Will this tale be a gift to those present? Does it suit the particular time and place? When in doubt, discuss these questions with someone you trust. When two people put their heads together, it's usually possible to determine right time, right place, and right people. Doing so will improve your chances of doing justice to the listeners, the story, and those who have shaped it.

How do wisdom tales instill wonder and respect for the natural world?

From the prevailing Western point of view, the world is a storehouse of natural resources subject to human exploitation and mastery. This perspective has given rise to the commodification of nature and an excessive rate of consumption that our planet cannot sustain. Environmentalist and philosopher David Abram urges us to reintegrate the wisdom retained in the oral traditions of the world, which teach that humanity depends wholly upon "conviviality with what is not human." Old stories abound with such conviviality. They spring from the animistic turf of the ancestors and convey a mystical reverence for what Abram calls the "more-than-human world."

In the oral traditions of the Pacific Northwest, Mount Shasta is the home of Sky Spirit Chief. Raven frees the sun and brings light to the world. Coyote slays a monster and creates human beings. Bear and Badger, Eagle and Owl, River and Rock, Fire and Smoke all possess unique medicine powers and are revered as wise teachers. Even Slug has her place and her purpose.

In a place like Ireland, it's difficult to go for a stroll without bumping into a hill, a rock, a plain, a well, or a river with mythical import. A Gaelic-speaking storyteller walks past a rocky outcropping, and an age-old adventure of the place comes to mind—the tale of exiled lovers who took shelter there—or wanderers who unwittingly stepped into the Otherworld. In Celtic lore, no place is more sacred than the Otherworld, the land of immortals and ancestors. The stories remind us that the Otherworld is no remote celestial realm; it is right here within the earthly domain, and perceptible with the five bodily senses. Celtic heroines and heroes stumble into the Otherworld by getting lost in the fog, or by following the sound of faery music on a moonlit night. The Otherworld lies betwixt the dark and the dawn, between the bark and the tree, betwixt the mist and the rain, between the sod and the soil. Malidoma Somé, who is both Western scholar and Dagara tribal elder, says in the Dagara tradition of West Africa, there is no distinction between the natural and the supernatural. Where would the ancestral spirits reside, if not in the crane, the cloud, the cave, the buffalo, and the tree?

We Westerners fancy ourselves the masters of our destinies. The mythic perspective suggests that human destiny is a grand collaboration with the more-than-human world. The heroes and heroines of old coproduce their destinies in, (to borrow a phrase from physicist Mae-Wan Ho) a kind of "mutual entanglement" with a multitude of natural forces. A hero's destiny might be incubated by a sojourn in a hollow tree. A heroine's pilgrimage might be spurred on by her encounters with the wind. Local guardians and helpers such as a grandfather ape or a talking whale show up at pivotal moments to guide heroes and heroines down fateful pathways. The local rocks, herbs, and earthy substances such as nettles, salt, and soil play crucial roles in the adventure. Creatures such as the peacock and the tiger, and entities such as the melon and the feather help the heroine leap from oblivion to fulfillment, and lead the hero from isolation to love.

In old stories humans are not separate from the world, but of the world. The Earth's creatures and elements are not commodified; nor are they reduced to the mechanical or the symbolic. Smoke from a peace pipe does not merely *represent* prayer, it *is* prayer. Sunlight does not simply *symbolize* the life force, it *is* the life force. The mountain is not emblematic of First Mother's home, it *is* First Mother's home. From the ancestral point of view, tools made from natural materials, such as Maui's bone fishhook and Coyote's flint knife, emanate character and purpose. A carving tool might be so full of its own sort of personhood that the carver refers to it as "he" or "she." Even the round of the seasons has beingness. The year itself has ears and must be honored with stories that appease winter's fierceness, coax forth the reluctant spring, welcome the sumptuous summer, and celebrate the hallowed harvest.

Our contemporary world view has fostered many advancements but it has also set us apart from the world and to some degree, from each other. We have manufactured a false sense of independence, for in truth our dependence on the intricate web of life touches every aspect of our being. The old stories awaken and strengthen the sense that we are powerful and deep only inasmuch as we are in rapport with the *other*. Wisdom tales restore to us a sense of what poet Thich Nhat Hanh calls the "inter-beingness" of things. Stories humble us and remind us of our place in the incomprehensibly grand whorl of the cosmos. Everywhere I go with stories, whether to centers of learning and contemplation, to halls of healing and human service, to outdoor education programs, or to grassroots groups; I find people hungry to regain a playful sense of wonder and connection with the natural world.

When storytelling, we pay attention to the more-than-human world, we notice how the beings of a place will join in the telling. A tree will creak, a branch will fall, a crow will caw, a spider will descend, or a horse will neigh at key junctures in the tale. It's as if they know their importance in the story and want to chime in to drive home the point. Even when telling stories in a downtown conference center, don't be surprised if the oak floor squeaks when you mention acorns, the candles flicker when you speak of the wind, or a moth flits about the stage when you describe the moonlight.

How does one learn wisdom tales by heart, and is it okay to improvise?

To learn and tell stories by heart you need no new gear, talents, or skills. The art relies on dynamic forces already present within you and your listeners: curiosity, memory, and inspiration. Early Greek story-tellers believed that to activate these forces was no less than calling upon the goddesses themselves.

Let's start with *curiosity*. Remember Pandora's unquenchable urge to know what was inside the box? Remember Psyche's irresistible yearning to view her mystery lover in the lamplight? When a story grabs you, you hunger to see and to know all. This age-old hankering was voiced by Greek myth teller Hesiod, some twenty-seven hundred years ago in his hymn to the Muses. He entreated the Muses to tell the tale of creation in full, sparing not a single detail. The human psyche thrives on hearing the who, what, where, why, when, and how of things, whether it's taking in a profound myth, or an intriguing little yarn. This longing, this seemingly limitless yen to know, is key to listener-teller rapport. In telling stories, the more you trust the listener's curiosity, the more confidence you'll gain in the stories themselves, and in your ability to tell them.

In telling wisdom tales, no gimmicks are necessary to ignite the initial spark of listener curiosity. Wisdom tales are constructed to do so in the first few lines. "Long ago, the first man and woman roamed the earth, looking for food to assuage their hunger." Who wouldn't be curious to know what happened next? "Long ago a newborn babe was left alone in the forest to die." Who wouldn't stick around to hear how she fared? "There was once a young woman who turned down all the suitors who came her way, until one day..." Who wouldn't settle in to find out who seduced her? When a resonant tale is brought forth, its first lines strike a chord within the listeners. They lean into the story and give it their ears. If you pause they say, "Keep going." Distractions fall away. Your memory sharpens. Action and detail take on extraordinary realness. Your job is to tell the tale in full, like Hesiod's Muses, to satisfy the listeners' curiosity by revealing creation one detail at a time.

Masterful storytellers develop a knack for this, but virtually everyone has stumbled upon the dynamics of curiosity when common conversation rolls into narrative gear. Let's take an example: My father, generally a reserved fellow, happens to be a deft teller of jokes and anecdotes, with an intuitive grasp of curiosity. At gatherings he waits for a lull in the conversation. Then he indicates that he has something to say. People listen, at first mostly out of politeness. Then Dad phrases the setup simply, and whether it concerns a cowboy on a barstool, or a Scotsman on the golf course, you feel as if he really knows the guy. His every pause and facial expression implies he is taking listeners into his confidence. He proceeds steadily and deliberately, and soon everyone in the room is wondering, what the cowboy or the Scotsman is going to do next. That wondering has a momentum of its own. It acts as a sort of siphon, drawing the story out of the teller, or out of some deeper place in the collective psyche. This siphoning, and the shared focus it creates, energizes the whole gathering. The more we hear and tell stories, the more we develop an intuitive grasp of the power of curiosity and how to use it.

With the hearing of good jokes, our curiosity leads to laughter inspired by life's pithy ironies. With the telling of wisdom tales, our curiosity leads to something deeper and more complex. The first man and first woman find nourishment, but not without sacrifice. The abandoned infant is found and adopted, but grows up to face another loss. The fussy young woman gets married, and then the real trouble begins. As with Pandora and Psyche, our curiosity leads us away from innocence into an understanding of life's complications, challenges, and woes. But we must trust that these goddesses want consciousness, knowledge, and understanding, and that's what wisdom tales are about. As storytellers we must trust that a listener's curiosity will lead them to the understanding they need and desire.

🌺 🌺 🌺

The human *memory* is truly "infinite in faculty," and strengthening the memory is much easier and more enjoyable than you might expect. Ancestral tellers saw memory as a goddess, the undisputed mother of story. The Greeks called her Mnemosyne, and named mnemonics, the art of memory, after her. Like contemporary brain researchers, early storytellers understood the power of emotions and sensations to strengthen long-term memory, and they put this principle to work. I developed the following method using the ancient principles of mnemonics, keeping in mind Mnemosyne's fondness for emotion and sensation. Beginners and experienced storytellers who've tried this approach report with glee that leaning by heart is much faster and more enjoyable than rote memorization.

I heartily encourage you to give "learning by heart" a try. In storytelling seminars, students often say they have "a bad memory" and therefore will have to read aloud, rather than learn their chosen story by heart. I don't challenge this assumption. Instead I ask students to do the following exercise. The exercise takes less than an hour and nearly always results in them vastly out-performing their own expectations.

They begin by silently reading and then rereading their chosen tale. I then ask them to sit or lie down in a comfortable position. I guide them to relax, close their eyes, and make an imaginary picture of the story's first scene. I encourage them to bring the scene to life in their mind's eye, and to engage all five senses. Their faces grow vibrant as they get internally engrossed with the sounds, smells, sights, tastes, and textures of the first scene. I then guide them in studying the mood or emotional atmosphere of the scene. Fleshing out the sensate and emotional dimensions of the scene establishes a palpable imaginary "place" in their memories, a place they can return to each time they tell the story.

I then direct the students to proceed through what they remember of the story, scene by scene. I ask them to bring their full attention to the characters and action, even if recollection seems fuzzy. At each phase I remind them to flesh out the scene, bringing awareness to the sensate and emotional details. Students continue their internal reverie to the story's end. Then I ask them to open their eyes and recount the experience. Most students tell the whole story in detail with surprising accuracy, and few lapses, as if they'd just awakened from sleep with full recall of a vivid dream. Internalizing the tale in this way makes it theirs. It is not just a matter of summarizing something they have read, it is describing an experience they have internalized. The difference is palpable. Students practically fall over when I say, "You're already telling this story by heart." Repeating this deceptively simple exercise two or three times on consecutive days usually serves as ample preparation for telling the story by heart to others.

🌸   🌸   🌸

Before the written word, the storyteller's prodigious memory served as the local library. Tellers employed numerous mnemonic devices (memory prompters) that enabled them to retain vast mythologies, histories, cosmologies, genealogies, and laws. Greek orators, Hawaiian kahunas, and Celtic bards took the art of memory to astonishing heights. Preliterate mnemonic devices included strings of symbolic knots kept in the pocket, magic oghams carved on stones, elaborate star charts, drum rhythms, and dance sequences. Though present-day mnemonic tricks will never rival those of old, we can still put ancient principles to work. Some tellers find sketching each scene of the tale helps to secure the story's place in long-term memory. Others use a story wand with pictorial symbols to guide them through complicated twists and turns of plot. Melodies and rhythms provide a kind of mnemonic trellis for the story to grow on. Anchoring scenes with memorable sounds, images, or phrases increases their shelf-life in our long-term memory banks. Songs, prayers, and praise poems have long been used to please the goddess, to create in the storyteller a sense of devotion, thus awakening memory, and evoking a spirit of inspiration.

Hesiod's hymn to the Muses illustrates the link between memory and *inspiration*. He praised the mountain on which the Muses were born. He praised the mother who bore them, none other than Mnemosyne herself. I like to think of Mnemosyne and Muse, memory and inspiration, as the life streams of story. Mnemosyne, like an unfathomable cistern, is the boundless, eternal source. To serve her, is to embrace the discipline of mnemonics, to learn old tales by heart and to preserve them for generations to come. With this under the belt, a teller can court the daughter, the Muse, who is spontaneous and likes to improvise, reshaping the banks of the river as she flows. To serve her is to follow the inspiration of the moment. A storyteller can lean toward the mother or the daughter. A tale can be the same every time it's told, or it can vary with each audience, locale, occasion, or mood. Storytelling is most vital when the teller respects and is able to dance with both Mnemosyne and the Muse.

Such a dance has shaped the retellings in this book. When a story really grabs me, I begin absorbing it with a strong allegiance to Mnemosyne. I honor the form and nuance of a tale as received, whether from a person or from a book. As the tale takes up residence inside me, I prowl more books, seeking variations, so as to get a taste of the other ways it's been told. A bit of creative musing helps me select and combine details from the different variations. Then I begin telling the tale in various settings. I try out different versions to see how they sit in a room, and what expressions they bring to people's faces. Musing usually leads to pulling away a bit of clay here and exposing a bit of rock there, revealing the tale's essence. Innovative touches give the river sparkle and flow. But Hesiod's Muses boasted of the flow of their lies, as well as truths. Experienced storytellers know that when innovation goes too far it starts to erode the basic integrity of a tale. When I begin to forget the original version as received, it's usually a sign I need to go back to Mnemosyne and study the sources again. This mother-daughter mode seems to serve stories in the long run. It retains story essence, while heightening relevance and rejuvenating the art.

Mnemosyne and Muse, replication and innovation breathe life into old wisdom tales. If the telling grows boring or stagnant, you might be clinging to Mnemosyne, without serving her real cause, which is to preserve and pass on. Maybe it's time to take a risk, to converse with the daughter, who brings life and relevance to the telling. On the other hand, if the telling gets amorphous, out of control or contrived, it usually means freedom and invention are working against you. You may be trying to abandon the mother and run off with the daughter. Just remember, with wisdom tales, the Muse functions best in the proximity of her mother. When telling feels stuck or stilted it helps to ask: Who am I ignoring, here, the mother or the daughter? Is it time to go back to the source, or break free and improvise? A good teller serves a story by bringing forth its fundamental design, the way a good pruner brings out the essential grace of a tree. The secret is in the balance between improving and preserving.

Inspiration finds her way to the scene not only when telling by heart but also when reading aloud. The mood of the moment may inspire a different cadence or rhythm, a distinctive accent or tone. The reading never comes out the same way twice, and each reading lends a different interpretation to the story. I like to think of a well-woven story on the page as one of Mnemosyne's tapestries. Between the lines lies a mountain scene in which her beautiful daughter dances beside a sacred well.

The Stories

How Brigit Got Lands for the Poor

IRELAND | (603 words)

ABOUT BRIGIT: Preceding Saint Brigit of Ireland was the pre-Christian goddess Brigit, whose sacred shrines and holy wells still dot the countryside today. Brigit's fire shrine at Kildare is said to have burned long and bright, attended by priestesses until church fathers deemed it pagan and shut it down in 1220 AD. But living on in the hearts and minds of the Celts, Brigit found her way back into the spiritual life of the people, by being canonized a saint. The old Celtic rituals of Imbolc were celebrated in Brigit's honor each February first, now St. Brigit's day.

Long ago in Ireland, there were a few wealthy landholders who owned great tracts of fertile land, while the poor were forced up into the rocky hills to eke out a living from the sparse soil. One year the crops went bad and the poor could barely scrape together an onion or a carrot for their supper. Brigit went to one of the richest landholders and said, "The harvest is grim this year, and the peasants need your help."

The landholder replied, "Ah, Brigit, I'll think on it, but in truth, if the people would only work harder they surely could fend for themselves."

A few weeks passed and the situation grew worse. Brigit went again to the landholder and said, "The peasants have no food. They've taken to the hills to eat shamrocks and grass. What will you do for them?"

"Now, Brigit," said the landholder, "Don't get pushy. I'm a busy man. Why is it you're here talking to me, when you should be talking to the peasants about what they can do for themselves? I've no time for this, now be gone with you."

Another week passed, and the situation became grave. Brigit went again to the landholder and in a rage she cried, "You've done nothing to help and now the children are starving! I demand that you give land to the poor!"

"Well, Brigit," said the landholder, "It couldn't be that bad. You don't look to be starved yourself, nor lacking for warm clothes. 'Tis a fine wool cloak you wear on your back. Let it not be said I'm a stingy man. Here's what we'll do: You go out to the plain. Choose any spot. Spread your white cloak on the ground, and the plot that it covers, I'll donate to the poor."

"Tax free?" asked Brigit.

"All right, tax free," said the landholder, "but don't ask for anything more."

So that day Brigit and three of her sisters went out to the very center of the fertile plain. Each took hold of a corner of the white cloak. Brigit said, "All right now, girls, pull it taut." They did so, and then Brigit cried, "Now take a step backward." Each of them took a step back, one to the north, one to the south, one to the east, and one to the west, and as they did, the cloak expanded. Then Brigit cried, "All right, keep walking!" They did, and as they did so, the cloak continued to expand until it covered the whole expanse of the plain.

That afternoon as usual, the landholder went up into his tower to look out and survey his lands. At first glance it looked as if a snow had fallen. Then he saw that the rocks above were bare. "The cloak," he whispered, falling to his knees, now seeing providence at work in the matter. When he saw Brigit striding up the walkway, he leaned out the window and cried, "Mercy, Brigit, I'll keep to my word! The whole of the plain belongs to the poor, and I'll throw in a hundred bags of oat seed that they might prosper by it!"

"That's fine for tomorrow," said Brigit, "but what will you do for today?"

"For today?" said the landholder. "Why, a feast for today, a feast for all."

"What sort of a feast?" asked Brigit.

"Why, a feast of stews, and roasts, and compotes, and mashes, and stuffings, and jellies, and cakes," replied the landholder.

"And bags to take home?" asked Brigit.

"Why of course, bags to take home," assured the landholder.

"Very well, then," said Brigit, "I'll spread the word."

"Aye, Brigit, I'm sure you will, and I don't mind saying, that if you spread the word as efficiently as you spread the cloak, not a soul will miss this feast."

WOMEN'S ESTEEM AND EMPOWERMENT | SACRED FEMININE: The Celts once marched under Brigit's banners and honored her as their proud goddess. Her name meant "fiery arrow," and they believed she brought them invincibility. Even through times when women in Ireland were denied the right to own land or receive an education, Brigit remained a role model endowed with fierce courage, mystical powers, and boundless maternal love. She still serves as a source of healing and strength for men and women in the church and beyond.

ADVOCACY FOR CHILDREN | FIGHTING POVERTY AND HUNGER | GREED AND ACQUISITIVENESS | JUSTICE AND FAIRNESS | COURAGE, INTEGRITY, RESILIENCE | EMOTIONAL RESILIENCE | INNOVATION: Surrounding the issues of poverty and hunger in the world is the sense that there is nothing we can do, that these problems stem from economic, political, social, and climatic forces beyond our control. The landholder in this tale seems a greedy sort, and we'd like to think we're nothing at all like him, but the truth is, most of us at one time or another have been lulled by complacency. It is easy for the fortunate, absorbed in the business of increasing wealth, to be oblivious to poverty and hunger in their own communities.

Brigit on the other hand, stands for a less complacent side of humanity. Something keeps her fierce and focused—perhaps her faith, perhaps her love of children, perhaps her innate fiery nature, perhaps her vision of something better. Her story encourages us to step out of complacency, and to persist in what we know to be right. This will not make saints of us, nor will it end suffering overnight, but acting in accord with the fire in our hearts nourishes others in need, and that in turn, nourishes our integrity. Brigit's flame ignites the heart of the landholder. His smugness transfigures into awe, his self-certainty into faith, his arrogance into humility, and his stinginess into generosity.

GENEROSITY: The prosperity gap between rich and poor widens daily. In the global economy, as in the story, it appears that human greed and human need are both reaching epidemic proportions. Many wealthy individuals and families strive to lessen the gap. They work at finding innovative ways to reach out and share. Told in philanthropic gatherings, and nonprofit fund-raisers, this tale encourages generosity, and celebrates the magnanimous spirit of those who give.

Finn McCoul Learns to Run

IRELAND | (1,098 words)

ABOUT FINN MCCOUL: *Fionn macCumhaill and the fianna warriors are said to have thrived during the third century, though their earliest appearances in written literature do not begin until centuries later. Their extensive adventures comprise a part of Irish mythology known as the Finn, or the Oisin cycle. Manuscripts dating from the twelfth century and later give varying portrayals of our hero, now better known as Finn McCoul. Some groups of tales depict the fianna as a band of huntsmen, while others portray them as a royal militia. Still others portray them as the tireless slayers of menacing hags, dark magicians, and unsavory monsters. The Finn cycle is thought in many ways to be a lore of the people, reshaped by each successive generation. Twentieth-century scholars were astonished to find oral renditions of the tales still circulating among "illiterate" Gaelic-speaking peasants in Ireland and Scotland. Thanks to the hearthside telling of simple folk, the tales continued to metamorphose well into the twentieth century. Peig Sayers, one of Ireland's best loved tellers, who came from a tiny fishing village in the Blasket Islands, gave numerous tales to the Irish Folklore Commission before her death in 1958.*

In my retellings I am indebted to many tellers, scholars, editors, and retellers, including James Stephens, Lady Augusta Gregory, Richard Dorson, Sean O'Sullivan, Joanna Cole, and Proinsias MacCana.

About Faery: Finn McCoul marries a woman of the Faery race. I am often asked the difference between the Celtic word Faery, and the more common word fairy. Both refer to mysterious beings encountered by chance in green and forested places. But while fairies are generally viewed as sprightly, shy, diminutive, charming, and endearing, Faeries are daunting immortal beings resembling humans, but exceeding us in stature and beauty, and awing us with their enigmatic powers. Faeries dwell in magnificent palaces underground, and in the mystical land of Faery, a mysterious place difficult for humans to access. Some find their way there by accident or through the use of incantation. One may enter Faery by entering the fog, or a hillside cave. To enter Faery is to enter another dimension, betwixt and between everyday reality, and unfettered by the limitations of time and space.

Long ago in a castle in Ireland, on a dark night when there was not so much as a sliver of a moon to light up the sky, the old king paced about his chamber. His daughter had gone into labor. When a healthy son was born the king did not rejoice. He grew troubled, for a prophet whose vision never erred had once told him, "Your daughter will birth a white-haired son. He shall be called Finn. His skill, wisdom, leadership, and good deeds will far surpass your own." The king was a jealous man. He didn't wish to be surpassed in any way, not now, not ever, not even by his own flesh and blood. So in the wee hours of the morning when both new mother and new babe were fast asleep, he crept into the birthing chamber and snatched the infant from his mother's side. The old king hid Finn under his cloak and stole out into the dark night. When he was confident that there was no witness to his evil deed, he grabbed little Finn by the long white hair and hurled him into the lake to drown.

But our Finn had a destiny before him and it was not so easy to finish him off. His grandmother was herself a wise druid. She ran to the shore, and gazed across the dark water 'til she saw Finn's long white hair floating like a ribbon in the middle of the lake. She feared he might already be drowned. She threw her cloak to the ground and kicked off her sandals. Then she crooked her knees, spread her arms wide and sprang upward. The instant her feet left ground she changed into a long necked crane. On graceful wings she flew out over the water and swooped low to snatch up little Finn's long white hair in her bill. With strong wing strokes she flew him safely to shore. There she changed back into an old woman the instant her feet touched land. She wrapped little Finn in her apron and ran like a fox to hide in the woods before the king's men could catch them.

In the woods Grandmother found a large oak. She took an ax and hollowed it out so that she and Finn could live there safely out of sight. The thunder of hooves often shook the earth as the king's men searched the woods, but Granny and Finn stayed snug and safe. By the time Finn was five years old Granny had instructed him in the fine arts of speaking and writing, so that come adulthood, he could convey his thoughts with eloquence. She acquainted him with all the stories of the gods, sages, and heroes. But there was little room in the oak to move about, and as a result, Finn hadn't yet learned to walk. Grandmother lay sleepless at night thinking she'd failed him in the most basic lesson of all. How could he get along in the world and fulfill his destiny if he couldn't walk? She thought of a way to teach him. One pitch-dark night when not so much as a trace of a star could be seen twinkling in the sky, she took little Finn in her arms and carried him out to the hills. She stood him up on his own two feet and said, "Look, Finn, can you see what I've got in my hand?"

"'Tis dark, Granny," Finn replied, "But I'll guess by the look of it, 'tis a bundle of herbs."

"Good lad," said Granny, "'Tis a bundle of herbs. Nettles to be precise. Stinging nettles, to put a fine point on it."

"Granny," said Finn, "Do you mean to say there are wicked plants in the world, just as there are wicked men?"

"God made the world, Finn, and only God knows why, but what is wicked at one time is good the next. Enough talk. Now I'll teach you a little game."

"A game, Granny?"

"Aye, Finn, a grand game known and loved by five-year-olds the world over— 'tis called walking."

"Walking, Granny?"

"Aye, lad, and here's how we'll learn. I'll stand just behind you, and I'll start by giving your left heel a poke with the stinging nettle." Granny gave Finn's left heel a poke, and he let out a yelp and thrust his left foot forward. Then she quickly gave his right foot a poke and he thrust it forward. Soon it was one foot in front of the other, faster and faster 'til they'd reached the top of the hill.

"'Tis a grand game indeed, this walking," said young Finn. "Now Granny, 'tis only fair that you go first, and I take a turn poking at your heels." If there was one thing Granny had tried to teach Finn it was fairness, so she let him have his turn with the stinging nettles. Not liking it at all, Granny went faster and faster, and Finn kept up every inch of the way.

At last she stopped and whirled 'round. She picked the lad up and gave him a big hug. "Finn, you're a natural-born athlete! I set out to teach you to walk, and within an hour you've learned to run!"

"Like Cu Chulainn's hounds, Granny, like the kings horses!"

"Aye Finn, like the wind itself. And that's enough learning for one night. My legs are tired and my heels are sore."

They returned to the oak, and Granny lit a candle. Finn saw her heels were swollen with great red welts, while his own heels were fine. He felt pity for the old woman and placed his hands one over each heel. In a moments time he lifted his hands and Granny's heels were soothed and the red was gone entirely. Then he fell into bed and said, "A story please, Gran?"

"Aye," said Granny. "A story of things to come. You, Finn McCoul, have given me a glimpse of the future. I see you'll not only be a great athlete, but you'll be a healer as well. You'll be a slayer of monsters and a defender of the people. You'll have a fine wife who'll give you a fine son, called Oisin [oo-SHEEN]. He'll be the greatest poet of all Ireland. His poems will be about you Finn, you and your grand adventures." Then she kissed Finn's brow, for sleep was upon him, after all, it had been a big night. "Sweet dreams and blessing on you, Finn McCoul," said Granny.

"Bless you too, Gran," said Finn McCoul.

THE MORE-THAN-HUMAN WORLD | RESPECT FOR NATURE: As a druiddess, Granny has the capacity to shape-shift into animal forms. She is right at home living in a hollowed-out tree, and using herbs to teach crucial lessons. Her druidic knack for befriending the more-than-human world resembles the skills of shamans the world over. Knowledge and rapport with nature heightens Granny's abilities to nurture, to teach, to heal, and to resist evil and oppression. Stories of this kind are particularly poignant to us now as we become increasingly out of touch with nature and the restorative powers of nature.

ELDER WISDOM | YOUTH-ELDER ALLIANCE | WOMEN AND EDUCATION | WOMEN'S ESTEEM AND EMPOWERMENT: Finn exhibits unwavering respect for his dedicated matriarch, and rightfully so, his very survival depends on Granny's strength, wisdom, and care. Granny is an unusually potent and well-rounded elder female, making this tale a special tribute to elder women. When I tell it in mixed groups, the elder women beam. People old and young take it to heart and receive it as a much needed balm, in part because the image of the elder feminine is so ruefully invisible in our society. After hearing it, one elder gentleman told me he planned to go home and tell it to his wife straightaway, as she herself was a feisty granny who didn't receive nearly enough acknowledgment for the care she gave others.

HEALING FROM ABANDONMENT | CAST-OUTS AND RUNAWAYS | COOPERATION AND DEVOTION | LOVING KINDNESS | ADVOCACY FOR CHILDREN | EMOTIONAL RESILIENCE | EARLY CHILDHOOD BONDING | ADOPTION AND FOSTERING: This tale can be heartening to children who feel cast out. It shows them that the worthiest child can be rejected for no good reason, and it encourages them to accept help from loving surrogates. The tale demonstrates deep affection and regard for children. It exquisitely illustrates the beauty of the elder's bonding process with the infant, toddler, and young child. Granny's love brings out the eager learner in young Finn. Without strain, she knows just how to make the best of his innate need to please. This tale illustrates the unparalleled satisfaction which comes from helping a child grow and develop. For that reason it works well in family bonding and parenting groups. For adults who desire to heal early emotional wounds, this tale evokes the archetypal nurturing feminine in her most down-to-earth form. It is a great source of encouragement for adopted and foster children and their families.

HEALING TOUCH: When Finn sees Granny's sore heels his innate gift of healing is called forth. He spontaneously engages in the laying on of hands, directing what Asian healers call *reike* or *chi*, the universal life force which has the power to heal. Many healing practitioners are drawn to the stories of Finn McCoul because of Finn's gift of hands on healing.

Finn and the Salmon of Wisdom

IRELAND | (2,105 words)

(for background on Finn McCoul see page 25)

In the days of Finn McCoul, a huntsman had to run through the woods as swiftly as the arrow flies. He had to be able to bend below the lowest branches and leap above the highest, never slowing down for even an instant. It was unacceptable for a huntsman in flight or pursuit to get so much as a leaf or twig caught in his long braided hair. In those days it was known that the best trainers for young lads were seasoned old crones. Who but a grandmother watches each child with the eye of an eagle to see what their special moves might be? Who but an elder auntie remembers the ancestors well enough to recognize their particular agility manifesting yet again in the next generation? We know that none can surpass an old druiddess in either patience or firmness, and that is why it was lucky for Finn McCoul to be raised by his granny with the help of his aunties, who were fine druiddesses all. On his fifteenth birthday Finn said, "Beloved Crones, I thank you for teaching me everything I know, but the time has come for me to compete with those my own age. I'd like to go to the castle at the edge of the lake and join in the games at the fair."

"All right, Finn McCoul, go if you must," said the old aunt seated at the fireside.

"Show them what stuff you're made of," said the other aunt who was older still.

Said Granny, "You have my blessing, Finn. I'll make but one request. Show them your strong limbs and your muscular back, but wear this cap and keep your hair concealed at all times so none can see it. For if the jealous old king sees your long white hair, he'll know you on the spot. And as sure as I'm your old granny, he'll set out to kill you, just as he did when you were a wee babe. It was long ago foretold that you'll surpass him when you come of age. He's a jealous old sort who won't be surpassed if he can help it." So Finn tucked his hair under the cap and went to his grandfather's castle where he entered every match at the fair. Whether swimming, running, leaping, pulling, or throwing, Finn outdid the rest hands down. At the end when he held all the banners and they lifted him onto their shoulders and cheered his victories, a gust of wind came along and the cap fell to the ground. Everyone saw Finn's long white hair tumble to his waist. "I might have suspected as much," growled the old king, and he ordered his men to seize Finn McCoul and kill him on the spot.

But of course Granny and the druiddess aunts had taught Finn McCoul to run as swiftly as a hound, and that he did. Horseman after horseman came in chase, but none could catch him. After a long while, though, young Finn grew tired. That's when Grandmother appeared. She picked him up and put him across her back, placing one of his feet in each of her pockets. She gained a good lead, and Finn remarked admiringly, "Granny, you never said you could run this fast."

"Aye," said she. "Didn't I ever tell you, save your greatest feats for the direst moments?"

"Not before this," said Finn, "But I shan't forget it now." With Finn still on her back, Grandmother ran like a gale force wind. After a while she told Finn to look behind to see who chased them.

"A man on a brown horse," he said.

"No problem," Granny said, "I'll outrun him." And so she did. When she grew thirsty she said, "Put your hand out, Finn, and snatch us a dew drop from the heather. Finn placed a drop on her tongue and it refreshed her. Later she detected a change in hoof beats. She said, "Look behind, Finn, and see who follows."

"'Tis a man on a white horse," said Finn.

"Good," said Grandmother, "I can always outrun a white horse." When she grew hungry she said, "Put out your hand, Finn McCoul.

Pick a berry from the vine for your old granny." He put a juicy black-berry on Granny's tongue and she was nourished. Much later Grandmother grew tired, for she'd been outrunning horses for a day and a night, and all the while with Finn on her back. "Glance behind, Finn, and see who pursues us."

"A man on a black horse, Gran," said Finn.

"Pity," said Grandmother, "The old prophecy says I can never out-run a black horse. So you must now listen closely. Do exactly as I say. When I say *leap*, you must leap off my back and run like mad. You must keep left at the crossroads, and make your way toward the River Boyne. There you'll find a wise bard to give you instruction. For, as I've always said, a good man gets educated, Finn McCoul. No man should hurl a spear who cannot first hurl a poem."

"But what of you, Grandmother?" Finn asked.

"I got on all right before you were born, and I'll get on all right without you hereafter. Now *leap!*" Despite the reluctance in his heart, Finn leapt. He ran like he'd never run before and did not look back. As for Grandmother, she stood there and waited for the king's horse-man. He charged up to her and shouted, "Old woman, where is Finn McCoul?"

"Why should I tell you?" said Gran, "So you can slay the bravest lad in all Ireland? What good would that do you? You're no more than a lad yourself. Aren't you tired of taking orders from that evil old buz-zard of a king?"

At this the horseman twisted around in his boots and said nothing. "Let's do the world a favor," said Granny, undoing her long white hair. "Why don't you take my hair as a trophy for the old so-and-so? Tell him you chopped Finn McCoul into a thousand pieces and all that's left to show for it is his hair."

The horseman agreed. With one stroke of his sword, he cut Grandmother's hair. He tied it to his belt and remounted. Then he headed back down the road. Granny called after him, "Good lad. You'll join the ranks of Finn McCoul one day, and all Erin will be the better for it." Then she returned to her sister druids, for there were many more young champions to train.

And as for Finn, he journeyed on as Granny had instructed until he reached the River Boyne. He came upon a spot where the river widened into a little lake. There he met an old bard who was also called Finn. Young Finn did not wish to sound impudent so he held off telling the elder that he too was named Finn. The old sage said, "Here I sit, year in and year out, beside this lake, for wise ones have long foretold that one called Finn shall catch and eat the salmon of wisdom from this very lake. So whether I like it or not, I must fish. Now, tell me young one, what is your quest?"

Young Finn replied, "My elders have instructed me well. I possess a champion's skills, and have bested my opponents at the fair. But what good is skill alone? I seek wisdom, so I might put skill to wise use in the world."

The elder Finn said, "Young champion, remain here and serve me, and I shall teach you the secret knowing of bards, for a man without poetry is a man without soul. First, I'm in need of rest. While I rest, you search the lake for the salmon of wisdom."

So young Finn walked along the shore. Soon he spied the salmon of wisdom circling in the water. He stepped onto a flat rock where he could see her better, but the rock was slippery and Finn lost his footing. He fell deep into the icy water. What a shock! He got his bearings and swam clumsily to shore, his cloak and shoes full of water, weighing him down. He pulled himself out and what should be twined in his long white hair, but the very salmon the old bard was seeking. Finn climbed out of the water and carried the hefty fish back to Finn the old sage. The elder awoke and said, "Wonder of wonders, you've caught the salmon! Well, now we must cook it, so its wisdom can be brought into the world." The two Finns built a fire, and placed the salmon on a spit. Then Finn the elder desired another nap. "Watch the salmon. Make sure it cooks to perfection. Don't let the skin blister, and don't taste so much as a drop of its juice," he instructed.

Finn the younger obeyed. He turned the salmon carefully so it could cook evenly on both sides. After a while he noticed a bit of skin blistering up ever so slightly. Wanting it to remain smooth for the elder, Finn pressed it lightly with his thumb. Hot juices spurted out and burnt him sorely. On reflex he put his thumb to his mouth to soothe it. But the hot salmon juice kept on burning through the skin, through the pad of his thumb and down to the bone, all the way to the very marrow. Finn kept sucking his thumb to soothe the pain, and while so doing, he had what would today be called an enlightenment. He saw the whole design of the universe, and how all things vast and minute fit together as they should. His heart was momentarily filled with the compassion of an elder, and his eye penetrated the secrets of times past and present, so that for a fraction of a moment, he possessed the wisdom of a prophet—all this in the soothing of a burn.

Soon the elder awoke and asked, "Did you taste so much as a drop of the salmon's juice?" Young Finn explained about the blister that had formed on the skin of the fish, and how he'd set out to smooth it with the tip of his thumb. He explained there was nothing he could do but put thumb to mouth to soothe it. Finn the elder scratched his long beard. "This is strange," said he. "Young champion, tell me, how is it that I've spent years searching for the salmon, and you who've only just arrived, are the one to catch it? Who are you lad, what is your name?"

"If I may say so with no lack of respect to yourself, sir, my name is Finn, too."

"Finn-too? What sort of a name is that? 'Tisn't Irish."

"Excuse me, Sir, I mean my name is also Finn."

"Also-Finn? How many names did your mother bequeath to you?"

"Forgive me, Sir, I mean to say that my name is Finn, Finn McCoul."

"Your name is Finn, then," said the elder scratching his beard ever more fervently. The young one nodded.

"Well," said the elder, "Sit down young Finn, and eat this salmon, every last bite." The next day the old bard commenced to instruct young Finn in all the poetic wisdom he possessed. Finn worked hard day in and day out to absorb what the master could teach him.

Some years later the old sage looked at Finn and said, "Finn McCoul, manhood is upon you. It's time you went forth into the world to prove yourself through good deeds."

At this young Finn protested, "But the world is treacherous, Master. 'Tis full of trouble and sickness, and evil kings who find multitudes of men to do their bidding. How will I know what to do in such a world?"

Finn the sage replied, "Rely upon all that I and druiddesses have taught you. In your moments of greatest confusion and doubt, remember the salmon and bite your thumb. Taste the marrow. For true wisdom lies in the marrow bone." What could Finn do, but bid his dear elder farewell and go forth into the world? Good deeds won him notoriety far and wide. In time there formed around him a band of worthy champions with hearts as good as gold. Their adventures, loves, and good deeds were many. This is not to say, of course, that their follies were few, for every Irish hero gets in a muddle or two. But Finn, and Finn alone, is famous for getting out of scrapes by biting his thumb.

THE MORE-THAN-HUMAN WORLD | REVERENCE FOR NATURE | ANIMALS AS HELPERS AND TEACHERS: In Celtic lore the salmon of wisdom dwells in a sacred pool. The fish has attained its knowledge by eating a hazelnut which dropped into the pool from a branch of the tree of wisdom growing beside the pool. The champion who eats the salmon gains all-knowledge and takes it into the human realm. The sages of old wanted us to understand that nature is the source. We are the humble recipients of nature's gifts only inasmuch as we place ourselves in mindful rapport with the more-than-human world. This concept is invaluable to us now, as we teeter on the brink of either restoring or severing our rapport with the natural world. Many scientists say our very survival depends upon reestablishing our harmony with nature.

ELDER WISDOM | HELP FROM WISE ELDERS | WOMEN'S ESTEEM AND EMPOWERMENT | COOPERATION AND DEVOTION | YOUTH-ELDER ALLIANCE: Once again, our hero is protected and guided by his grandmother whose wily intuition and astonishing stamina see him through the impossible. It is Granny who knows what Finn must learn, and from whom he must learn it. I've told this tale at many gatherings spanning the generations. It enhances the esteem of elder women, delights young and old, and inspires people of all ages to share reminiscences about their own grannies.

ATHLETIC EXCELLENCE | INITIATION | MEN'S INITIATION | EMANCIPATION FROM HOME | UNSTABLE IDENTITY | MEN'S ESTEEM AND EMPOWERMENT | EMOTIONAL RESILIENCE: This coming of age tale is made up of initiatory trials. In the beginning Finn competes with youths his age as a healthy way of measuring and affirming his excellence. Later, the unexpected chase after the fair puts him to an even greater test of courage, stamina, and strength. In keeping with the Celtic warrior tradition, the old druiddess is again his sponsor. She sends him off to Finn the elder at the River Boyne, where he undergoes his next level of training. In the end, he emerges from his ascetic retreat to become a leader among men. This tale was thoroughly enjoyed by a youth named Jason who had spent his teens in the foster care of two elder aunts. For Jason the tale celebrated his going off to college. It honored his accomplishments and the loving aunts who had raised him. It also cast an optimistic light upon the journey ahead and the mentorships to come.

MENTORSHIP | PASSION FOR LEARNING | DROPOUT PREVENTION | JEALOUSY, ENVY, AND COMPETITION: Our Celtic ancestors held wisdom and erudition in the highest regard. Through young Finn's relationships with Finn the bard, we are reminded of the sacred pact between learner and mentor, and the importance of gratitude and respect on both sides. Unlike the jealous grandfather, Finn the elder is a true mentor in the highest sense, one who realizes that knowledge is not his private tenure, but a sustaining form of nourishment which must be passed on. This tale honors dedicated teachers and professors who act with true generosity. It is a striking tribute to the fruits of athletic and academic discipline, and for that reason it makes an excellent commemorative for graduations. When told to reluctant students, it also serves as a compelling dropout deterrent.

PASSING ON THE TORCH | RITES OF PASSAGE: Youths cannot fully shine without the blessings of their elders. Much is lost in family life as well as in politics and corporate culture when elders cannot gracefully pass on the torch. The contrast between young Finn's jealous grandfather and the more supportive elder Finn, holds a lesson for older people in roles of authority. We must at some point bestow the gifts of power, knowledge, and support to the coming generation. Part of the wisdom of elderhood is knowing when to pass on the torch.

INTUITION | MALE INTUITION | ATHLETIC EXCELLENCE | ECSTASY AND ELA-TION: Finn's enlightenment experience upon first biting his thumb activates and intensifies his intuition, so that he momentarily sees and knows all. His enlightenment is like a Tibetan mystic's experience of Nirvana, wherein the veil of illusion is lifted, and the whole of the cosmos is perceived in its exquisite entirety. Reality, including the suffering, is seen to hold such unfathomable beauty and integrity, that the mystic's only response is one of pure joy. Not unlike monks in the Tibetan tradition, Irish monks used to purify themselves through fasting, meditation, and solitude in the wilderness. Surely Finn the elder is part of this tradition. But in the case of Finn McCoul, I find it especially delightful and very Irish, that after a three-day fast he finds enlightenment in the form of a delicious spit-roasted salmon.

Finn and Saeva

IRELAND | (2,640 words)

(for background on Finn McCoul see p. 25)

*T*here was one great love in the life of Finn McCoul—Saeva, beautiful Saeva with the dark eyes and the flaming hair. Finn had been out in the world going from town to town proving himself to be an exemplary hunter and protector. He'd already gathered followers and had formed a band of skilled huntsmen called the fianna Finn. They roved the distant byways and the lonely shores, and occasionally returned to their main camp on the plain of Allen. With the people needing meat for their tables, and with fending off the invading Danes and such, the fianna Finn were never short on work and Finn McCoul was a busy man.

One evening after a day's vigorous hunt, all those men who'd been fierce for the chase now grew somber and silent trudging home. Their hounds walked quietly with their heads straight ahead as if they had no more zest for sniffing about. But then suddenly, a red doe darted across the path in front of them. The hounds sprang forward and commenced to yelp. Now the hunt was on, full force as if it were the first chase of the day. Such was the stamina of the fianna Finn and their hounds. Finn's two magical dogs, Bran and Sceolan [Skoh-lan] shot ahead swift as arrows, and their lean gray bodies soon became one lucid pucker and lash of speed.

Finn adored these two dogs above all else in the world. The chase progressed, but they couldn't catch up with the doe, and Finn could see plainly that the doe had not yet stretched to full speed. "Bran, my love, Sceolan, my heart," he cried, "let it not be said you were outrun by a doe."

Soon enough the doe led them into the flower-filled meadows at the outskirts of the town of Allen. There she lay down in the grass and rolled over. And what Finn next saw gave him a start, for it went against every instinct of the hunt. The dogs started wriggling like puppies and wagging their tails. They flopped down with the doe and began licking her ears as if she were a long-lost member of the pack. When Finn came upon them he left his knife in its sheath. His hands naturally went to scratching the ears of the dogs. But what surprised him was how easily his fingers found their way to the ears of the doe. And there they scratched with equal affection. And so the great hunter led the fianna Finn into Allen, with his two beloved dogs leaping about him in joy, and the frolicsome doe cavorting with the dogs like old pals, nuzzling Finn's elbow as if she'd loved him all her life.

The women of Allen came out to greet them. Once they got over their surprise, they began to laugh, and one of them said, "A strange day it is Finn McCoul when venison walks to town on the hoof, instead of hoisted on the huntsmen's shoulders." Soon enough they all agreed such a marvelous deer should not be killed. One woman said, "I'd sooner have oatcake in me belly, and enjoy the company of this deer, than have venison in me belly and enjoy the company of an oatcake." So that night the women of Allen served a supper of oatcakes and carrot stew. And all through the meal they admired the beautiful deer who'd come to them so miraculously. The elders recalled the day Finn's magic dog Bran had come to them from the land of Sidh [shee], the land of Faery, and they said this deer had the look of Faery on her too.

That night at bedtime Finn McCoul snuffed all the candles in his chamber, and climbed into bed. He dozed off to sleep with one eye open, so he could not be caught off guard. The open eye rolled in its socket this way and that, surveying the room while the rest of Finn was sleeping. Soon the eye caught a glimpse of someone in the doorway. Finn sat up opening the second eye and said, "Who's there?"

"You don't know me, Sir, but I know you," said the lovely voice of a lady. "I've often had occasion to watch you as you're roving the woods and hills."

"How could that be?" said Finn, lighting candles so he might set eyes on the figure that went with the voice. "I and the fianna Finn hunt in lonely places where no humans wander."

"Suffice it to say," said the lady, "that I too inhabit such places."

Finn raised a candle so its light would fall upon her face. Her astonishing beauty made his heart leap. Her forehead was high and white. A torrent of red hair fell down around her shoulders and back. Her lips shone like ripe apples. Her nose was fine and straight, as was the gaze from her dark and somber eyes. Her face had the shape of a jewel, and her skin was dusted with freckles that looked to be made of gold. She stood before him, embodying at once the graceful modesty of a doe and the high nobility of a queen. "I must be dreaming," he thought to himself. He bit his trusty thumb, for it was an oracle of truth. At once he knew this was no dream, but the love of his life come to meet him.

"Lady," said Finn, "I know every queen in Erin, yet I know you not. Your radiance is purer than a flame. How is it we have not yet met?"

"You know the queens of Erin, yes," said the lady, "but I am a woman of the Sidh. My name is Saeva."

"Well, good Lady Saeva, what do you require of me?"

"Protection," said she.

"That I'll give gladly," said Finn, "and what sort of protection is needed?"

"Protection from an evil Faery king, a magician who tries to imprison me with love spells. I refused his hand in marriage, and now no matter how far and fast I flee he's there watching me from every hill, from every rock, from every tree."

"I'll do all in my power to combat him."

"Good," said Saeva, "for I love him not. I love another."

Finn's heart now sank to the pit of his stomach, but being a brave and well-reared sort he said, "Lady Saeva, if your beloved is yet unmarried, I shall see to it that you and he are wed in a style befitting the queen that you are." Finn's heart shrank with each word until it was nothing but a lead pellet.

"I don't know that you are master in the matter," said Lady Saeva.

At this Finn frowned, "Save the high king and the other kings of Erin, there is no man not under my authority."

"Ah," said Saeva, "'tis a rare man, Finn McCoul, has authority over his own heart."

"Then, 'tis me you love!" cried Finn, with his heart swelling as it rose back to its proper place in his chest. "Lady, no finer news has ever touched these ears. The thought that you loved another nearly finished me."

Finn reached for her and she fell into his arms. Between them passed every endearment known to the Irish tongue, and every endearment known to the Faeries. And when these ran out they began inventing new endearments of their own. And they gave the same inventiveness to their kissing and caressing. They voiced all the vows, pledges, and promises of a royal wedding. Finn gave himself to Saeva, body and soul, and she gave herself to him. They promised to be true and never part.

From that day on, Finn McCoul was a changed man. A room or a landscape without Saeva in it was bleak and lifeless. He ceased to hunt. He ceased to lead the fianna Finn. He ceased to hear the songs and stories of poets and ceased to be amused by magicians, for all these and more were in his wife. And also in her was something beyond all this which he could not name. And this thing he loved more than all the world, more than life itself.

Now it happened that the men of Lochlann came warring against Ireland. Finn had no choice but to lead the fianna into battle. He was a fierce warrior when the need arose, but a wrathful edge now came to his warring because it separated him from his wife. After the invaders were defeated and driven out, Finn prepared to return swiftly to Allen. "Stay for the victory feast," his fellow warriors implored, but Finn would have none of it. He wouldn't rest until he'd reached Saeva's side. He knew she'd be waiting at the window, and she'd run out to meet him when he reached the wide plain of Allen. He strode swiftly and didn't stop for food nor drink 'til he reached the plain. Once there he began waving his spear so Saeva would see from the window that it was he, but she came not. He ran onward.

"Saeva must think I stayed at the feast," he told himself. Running faster, he thought, "Were I the one waiting, I'd have rushed out to greet her by now." He ran on thinking, "Oh, women are a proud breed. They don't like to appear over eager. She waits calmly at the window, but her heart is pounding for joy to see me coming." Soon he arrived at the gate.

Within the gates of Allen there was great disorder. When the women saw Finn, they put their aprons to their faces and wept. "Where is the Flower of Allen?" cried Finn, "Where is my wife?" No one would answer. Finn scowled at the women and they ran in every direction. At last Rough Buzzer came forward and said, "I don't know Chieftain, to confess it truly, I don't know."

"Then tell me what you do know," said Finn.

"When you had been gone but one day, we all kept watch at the top of the hill. The Flower of Allen was with us. She kept a close watch and cried out that the fianna chief was coming over the ridge. She ran out to meet you herself directly."

"It was not I," cried Finn. "I was in battle."

"It bore your shape and visage, sir, as well as your armor and sword, and it was accompanied by the dogs Bran and Sceolan. We men were distrustful. Never had we known you to return before the end of a battle, so we urged our lady to wait."

"This was well advised," said Finn.

"Aye," said Rough Buzzer, "But she would not be advised. She ran to the figure saying, 'Beloved husband, joyous news, joyous news, we're going to have a child.' She ran toward your appearance with arms outstretched. When she reached it, it extended a hazel wand, and where your own bride had stood, there in her place stood a beautiful red doe. She turned and ran toward us but the dogs caught her by the throat and dragged her back to the impostor. We rushed out to save her, but as we neared them they vanished. Forgive us, Dear Chieftain, that we could not save your wife." And now Rough Buzzer, who was a stalwart man with nerves of iron and a granite heart, broke down in tears and wept like a baby.

Finn went to the inner chamber, to the bed he had shared with his bride. He curled up and wept like an orphan. He beat his breast and tore out his hair. He cried 'til there was nothing left in him, and then he cried some more. He did not eat, speak, laugh, or pray for a very long time. For the next seven years when he wasn't hunting or fighting off Danes, he was searching the hills and forests for his lady Saeva. He forbade the killing of deer, and always at his side were his magic dogs Bran and Sccolan, for he knew they were wise dogs and would do his lady no harm. And all during the years of his grief Finn seemed to have lost his gift of healing, and he stopped biting his thumb. It was as if something had dried up inside. He could hunt like a lion and fight like a boar, but he could not coax his hands to heal the sick or restore the wounded, and he could not coax the wisdom out of his thumb.

One day Finn and the fianna were on a hunt deep in the forest. All their dogs circled round and made a huge commotion. Finn saw that Bran and Sceolan were at the heart of it protecting some small creature Finn could not see. He made his way through to see a small boy seated on the ground. He was a beautiful prince of a boy with long golden hair and sparkling brown eyes. He gazed at Finn without a trace of fear. Above the lad's brow was a vicious bruise. Without thinking or hesitating Finn placed his healing hands on the lad's brow, and held them there gently. The lad gazed up at Finn with a look of noble trust, and Finn's heart melted. When he removed his hand the lad's wound was healed and it was impossible to tell at all that he'd been bruised. Finn lifted him up and cradled him in his arms. He said, "My little prince, my darling dear, where are you from?

And how is it you've been left here all alone?" But of course the lad couldn't answer, for he knew not one word of Irish.

Then without thinking Finn bit his thumb, and images poured into his mind's eye and he had this vision: He saw the little lad living in a beautiful place, like Ireland but with an air of magic to it. "Faery," thought Finn, "the land of the Sidh." He saw the little lad living under the shelter of a great tree, and nestled beside him licking his cheek, was a lovely red doe. "Saeva," said Finn, with tears flooding to his eyes. Then the harmony of the scene was broken by a tall man dressed in black who entered and came between them. "The evil Faery king," moaned Finn. Next he saw the king raise a hazel wand to force the doe away. She wept and tried to resist, and the lad wept and tried to stay with her, but the man hit the lad with the hazel wand, striking his brow, knocking the lad unconscious. "My son," said Finn, burying his head in the lad's shirt. "Bran and Sceolan knew you from the start and now I know you, My Little Prince, son of my heart and the Flower of Allen. We shall call you Oisin [oo-SHEEN], Little Fawn, and you and I shall never part."

From that day on Finn McCoul was himself again, only finer. All the care he'd given to Saeva now found a place to light in the boy. Finn trained Oisin as carefully as Granny had trained Finn. When in doubt about raising a son on his own, Finn bit his thumb and father wisdom poured into his heart. When the lad broke the odd bone, suffered scrapes, scratches, bee stings, or stinging nettles, the healing power flowed from Finn's hands. As for Oisin, he grew up to be a splendid hunter and warrior, but his greatest fame came from being a poet, and telling tales like this one. He went back to Faery to see his mother once, and returned to tell of it. 'Tis Oisin himself we have to thank for the stories of his brave father, Finn McCoul.

LOVE AND ALCHEMICAL UNION | MEN'S INITIATION: The storytellers and philosophers of antiquity were absorbed with the idea of erotic chemistry and the attraction of opposites. Sun and moon, gold and silver, sulfur and salt, earth and sky come together to spawn the miraculous, to unite heaven and earth, to create a new world, or to conceive a magical child. In Celtic romance as in great myths the world over, there may erupt irresistible attractions between humans and immortals. They unite to produce extraordinary offspring: the finest poets, heroes, and queens.

Human lovers at the height of passion experience their own version of the alchemical union. It may be experienced as a diffusion of boundaries, a blessed confusion as to where one's own skin ends and the beloved's begins. Oftentimes, as with Finn and Saeva, the passion and devotion are disrupted, and the bliss does not last, but the experience is nonetheless transformational and initiatory, in that it brings about a surrender of will and opening to love. These tales are as important to us as tales of lasting love, for they remind us that all things must pass. Even the most committed couples fall in and out of love, and their sense of passion and purpose wax and wane. Short-lived unions can also evoke the alchemical spark. Following a divorce, a middle-aged man named Jacob fell in love with a woman named Talia. "Talia and I did not have the makings of a marriage," he said, "but there's no doubt she was my Saeva. The chemistry was undeniable. The sexual and spiritual awakening she brought me will be with me for the rest of my life. Like Finn McCoul, I learned to surrender, and I'm a better man for it."

DOMESTIC VIOLENCE | LOVING KINDNESS | COOPERATION AND DEVOTION | EMOTIONAL RESILIENCE: The evil enchanter resorts to violence when things don't go his way. In contrast, Finn McCoul is an intrepid fighter who nonetheless surrenders to the tender yearnings of his heart. As the previous tale tells us, Finn's knowledge of the spear and sword are tempered by the teachings of the sages. As this tale tells us, his warring spirit is tamed and balanced by devotion to his beloved wife. This was an important lesson the Celtic bards wished to convey through the medium of the Celtic romance. For though Celtic women are said to have enjoyed more privileges than other women in old Europe (inclusion in the druidic tradition, for example), Celtic law did not always protect women from the warring spirits of their husbands. Among some tribes it was legal for an outraged husband to kill the wife who displeased him. Through tales like this one, Celtic bards promoted chivalry by lauding the warrior who is mild and loving at home. Today we still need images of the gentle warrior and the nurturing husband, for domestic violence is pandemic. Crime statistics show staggering numbers of women who are beaten and killed by their husbands, and it is estimated that much spousal abuse goes unreported. This is a prime tale for men's groups, couple's groups, and for individual men and women wishing to replace rage with resilience, and striving to temper the warrior within.

MEN'S ESTEEM AND EMPOWERMENT | NURTURING FATHERS | ADVOCACY FOR CHILDREN: Finn feels profound affection for little Oisin and treats him with the utmost care and esteem, making this tale a potent one for parenting and fathers' groups. Finn's warrior energy is complemented by his fatherly intuition and paternal tenderness. His ongoing commitment to Oisin serves as a reminder of the importance of day-to-day paternal love. This tale encourages fathers to make time for positive relationships with their children. It supports those men who go against stereotypes and actively engage in child care. It also encourages mothers to support fathers who commit to active fathering.

INTUITION | MALE INTUITION | UNSTABLE IDENTITY: Finn accesses hidden truth by biting his thumb. When he first meets Saeva, the thumb affirms his hope that she is more than a mere apparition. Later the thumb enables him to see that the little prince who speaks no Irish is actually his son. This revelation comes to him in fragmentary dreamlike images. Suddenly the family story can be understood in its entirety. One man remarked, "My favorite insight in the story is about male intuition. I was brought up with the phrase *women's intuition*, but it's not strictly a women's thing. It's there for me, it's just a matter of using it."

ECSTASY AND ELATION | RESTORING BLOCKED GIFTS | INSPIRATION LOST AND REGAINED: Otherworldly Saeva awakened Finn's heart and suddenly every experience he shared with her was vivid beyond belief. He was the same man, but was newly filled with inspiration and purpose. Finn's falling in love with Saeva was not unlike the experience of Jody, a fledgling poetry student enamored with literary pursuits that filled her with inspiration and purpose. "My love affair with poetry lasted about as long as Finn and Saeva. By the middle of my second year, I crashed. I found out my poetry teacher wasn't perfect, the academic world is pretty mediocre, and the publishing industry is jaded. I felt like Finn McCoul after losing the love of his life: completely flat." As time went on, Jody came to understand it was normal for one's sense of inspiration to fluctuate. "When Finn meets Oisin, the intuition and healing come flooding back. That is helpful for me to think about when my creative juices run dry. It reminds me that if you respond to life with an open heart and take time for the small things, the inspiration comes back when you least expect it."

PROLONGED OR COMPLICATED GRIEF: A musician named Gunter suffered an especially prolonged bereavement following the death of Arianna, his wife and musical partner. After three unproductive years his friends and family feared he'd never work again. This tale offered Gunter great solace. He and Arianna had no children, but Oisin became a symbol for him of all they had created together. "It's up to me to nurture the legacy we started, our musical exploration. Arianna would want me to carry on and see it through."

THE WOUNDED HEALER | HEALING TOUCH: The motif of Finn's healing hands comes strongly into play in the reviving of young Oisin. This scenario is inspiring to anyone gifted with healing touch. A chiropractor said, "Hearing this tale I'm reminded of my own family wounds. I got into my field because both my parents had spinal injuries. Stories like this keep us in touch with our inner life. They keep us grateful and humble."

LONELINESS | THE INACCESSIBLE LOVER: Circumstances prevent Finn from sharing his life with his beloved Saeva. As you will see in "Diarmuid [DER-mud] and Grania," the fifth and final tale, Finn's longing for Saeva haunts his elder years. Longing for the unavailable lover gives a bittersweet cast to any life, but in the case of Finn McCoul, the longing turns toxic and the tragic results injure many lives. A man named Jack was forty-seven when he took the Finn tales to heart focusing on the theme of the inaccessible lover. Jack had never been married. Friends said he was "too picky" when it came to women, and that as a result he would wind up lonely and bitter. Jack felt destined to be alone because the woman he loved had married another, some twenty years before. Try as he might, he could not rekindle the magic with anyone else. These tales got him reflecting: "I'm what you call a true romantic. I was in love once, and I've been dwelling in reminiscences ever since. The story 'Finn and Saeva,' makes me cry, because it sums up my life. Everyone says I'm hooked on a rarefied notion of love that no real woman could live up to. If I want a real relationship I have to learn to value what's present and real, here and now."

REVERENCE FOR NATURE | ANIMALS AS HELPERS AND TEACHERS | THE MORE-THAN-HUMAN WORLD: There is otherworldly power in Finn McCoul's athletic skill, and his oneness with animals. When telling this tale to groups, I've noticed certain faces light up at the mention of the deer and the magic dogs. Given the chance to tell their own stories, dog lovers and hunters gravitate together to tell their own uncanny wilderness adventures. When this happens, throw a few logs on the fire, because it will go on all night!

How Diarmuid Got The Love Spot

IRELAND | (1,026 words)

(for background on Finn McCoul see p. 25)

Long ago Finn McCoul and a handful of his finest men found themselves lost one night. Mind you, the men of the fianna were heroes all—able hunters, fleet-footed runners, and powerful defenders of Ireland's shores. They knew the provinces of Ireland like the backs of their hands, but so thick was the fog that night, they lost sight of the noses on their faces. There was no choice but to stop where they stood until the fog lifted and they could see their way again. They knew that a man wandering in the fog might stumble into the Otherworld and not return.

"'Tis a pity," said Finn McCoul, "that we slew no game today, for by morning there will be great hunger upon us."

"There is great hunger upon us now," said Oisin.

Conan walked about in the fog until he saw a light. He followed the light until he reached a little house. Peering into the window he saw a cat and an old man seated by the fire. He knocked on the door and when the old man answered, Conan confessed to him the discomfort that had befallen the fianna. "We would never turn away the fianna Finn," said the old man. So Conan returned to the others and led them back to the little house. There the old man welcomed them. He called to a girl in the kitchen and asked her to prepare a meal. She set places at the table and served the food. Just as the men began to eat, a sheep broke free from his tether at the back of the house. This sheep charged into the room and leapt up on the table.

Goll stood up to grasp the sheep, but the creature lunged and butted his head against Goll's chest knocking him to the floor.

"I'll handle it," said Oisin. He stood up and when he did the sheep faced off and gave him a butt that knocked him to the wall. Finn himself sprang to his feet, for he didn't like to see his men shamed by a sheep. No sooner had he stood up than the sheep rammed him against the hearth. Conan gave it a try, as did Oscar, and soon each member of the fianna was winded and sore from his run-in with the sheep. Said the old man, "Cat, arise, and tether the sheep." Sure enough, the cat yawned, stretched, and got up from his spot at the hearth. He jumped to the tabletop and nudged the sheep into submission. He led the sheep to his tether at back of the house and the sheep troubled them no more.

You might think the men ate in peace, but they'd lost their hunger. Sorer than their bruised backsides were their hearts, for a heavy shame had befallen them. Far and wide they were known for slaying terrible monsters and menacing giants. Many were the times they'd saved Ireland from the invading Danes. And now, would it be said they were bested by a sheep? The old man saw their defeat and said, "You must eat. And when you have finished I will explain why you are the world's bravest men." So, they filled their bellies and sat back to hear the old man's counsel. "This is no common fog, nor is it a common night. You have met no mere creatures here, but the essential forces of the cosmos itself. You have wrestled with the world, for the strength of the world is in that sheep. But even the world submits to death, and this is death," he said pointing to the cat. The old man's words made them feel like talking, and they conversed at the table until he said their room was ready and they could go off to bed.

The five of them went to bed in a single room with a sixth bed that was empty. By and by the girl came into the room and when she did, she filled it with light as if she'd brought a candle, but all she brought was her beauty. Finn couldn't sleep with the glow of her filling the room, so he climbed out of his own bed and tiptoed toward hers. She sat up and whispered, "Go back to your bed, Finn McCoul. I was yours long ago, but never again." Finn had no idea what she meant, for he was sure he'd never laid eyes on her before this night. Befuddled, he returned to his bed.

Before long, Conan crept up from his bed to gaze upon the beauteous glow of her. "Go back to your bed, Conan," she said, "I was yours long ago, but never again." Conan returned to his pillow scratching his head.

Now Oscar arose and quietly approached her. "Where do you think you're going?" asked she.

"Going?" said Oscar, "to your side, if you'll allow it."

"I'll allow no such thing, now back to your bed."

Soon Oisin up and crept to her bedside and she sent him away like the others. Now there was only Finn's shy young cousin, Diarmuid [Der-mud]. After a time Diarmuid quietly made for her side. She told him she might never be his, but she told him to bend close to her. When he bent down, she put her hand to his forehead, and there she placed a love-spot. Ever after, no woman who set eyes on him could help but adore him body and soul. You might think this was a blessing, and indeed it was, but as a wise one once said, "what's good one day is evil the next." And in the years to come it would oft' be said that the love-spot brought more grief than joy, but that's another story. As for the radiant girl who bestowed the love-spot, she was youth itself.

In the morning the fianna awoke. They looked outside to see the fog was gone. Breakfast awaited them at the table, but the girl and the old man were nowhere to be found. Finn and his men walked down the mountainside in silence. There was sadness in them, but the shame had passed. This thought stayed with Finn

McCoul, *a man of years can acquire many things, but youth he can never recapture.*

THE MORE-THAN-HUMAN WORLD | THE INEVITABILITY OF OLD AGE AND DEATH | ELDER WISDOM | HUMILITY | EMOTIONAL RESILIENCE: The fianna are stopped by the fog, brought to their knees by the sheep, and humiliated by the cat. Only later does the old man explain that these beings are actually the cosmos, the world, and death, which naturally have mastery over humankind. Youth, the radiant girl, seems approachable in her bed, but alas, she too, has the upper hand. No man, not even an Irish hero, can recapture youth once it has passed. No human being can avoid yielding to these greater inevitabilities, and though this fact is widely known, it is not deeply understood. Like the sheep, it must be grappled with. Like the girl, it must be approached. This grappling and approaching becomes meaningful to those of us who have reached our middle years, begun to gray, to sag, and to slow down. Who but a wizened elder could explain these lessons to the fianna, and still impart encouragement? The old man praises their valor, and yet shows them their limits in relation to the cosmic forces. This tale reminds us that we are visitors in the house of the world, and yet, if we live our lives fully, embracing each adventure, as do the fianna, we may acquire the depth, character, and wisdom of the old man.

Diarmuid and Grania

IRELAND | (3,634 words)

(too complex for small children)
(for background on Finn McCoul see p. 25)

*F*inn McCoul was the leader of Ireland's finest band of huntsmen, the fianna Finn. One night he tossed and turned until sunrise. He got up and walked out to the plain of Allen. His son, Oisin, caught sight of him and went out to meet him on the green. "Why are you not sleeping, Father?" said Oisin.

Finn sighed, "Ah me, how can a man rest when he's lonely?" Oisin's heart went out to his father whose second wife had recently died. They stood near the spot where Finn had lost Oisin's mother many long years before. The morning fog sat motionless around them.

"You shouldn't be alone," said Oisin. "You should have a new wife."

"Difficult at my age," said Finn. "Who would have me?"

"Why, any woman you want. All you have to do is throw a glance her way and the fianna will fetch her for you, willing or not."

Just then, Finn's advisor, the old druid came toward them out of the fog. "I can get you a woman," said the druid. "Grania, daughter of Cormac, the High King. No woman surpasses her in form and figure, nor in manner and speech."

"There's one problem," said Finn. "The High King and I aren't on the best of terms."

"We'll go to him on your behalf," said Oisin. And so it was agreed. Oisin and the druid went to Cormac and told him they'd come to ask for Grania's hand for Finn McCoul.

The King replied, "Every champion, king, and prince of Ireland has asked for my daughter's hand and she's refused them all. McCoul and I are not on the friendliest of terms. If I say 'yes,' and she says 'no,' he'll hold it against me. Better if we go to her directly. Whatever she replies, you must be my witness. Remember the answer comes from her lips and not mine." So they went to Grania's house. The king sat at the head of the table and said, "Grania, meet the druid and advisor of Finn McCoul and his son, the champion Oisin. They've come on behalf of Finn to see if you'll consent to be his wife."

Grania replied, "If you find him to be a fitting son-in-law, Father, then I'll find him to be a fitting husband." It was smoother than anyone had expected. They made a feast to celebrate that night, and it was agreed that in two weeks' time, Finn and Grania would be wed.

When the wedding day came, Finn led the many bands of the fianna to the green where the High King awaited. Cormac had taken special care to pack the sky with banners and fill the air with the sound of whistles and drums. That way Finn would know there was no bad blood between them. As for Grania, her heart sank when she saw Finn was no man in his prime, but a man around whom old age had begun to settle. She said to the women, "I see now that he is as old as my father. It would have been more fitting if Finn had asked for my hand on behalf of his son, Oisin, rather than the other way 'round."

When Grania and Finn had been introduced and had a moment to themselves, he asked riddles to test whether she was truly as quick-witted as he'd been told. "What is purer than fresh snow?" Finn asked.

"The truth," replied Grania.

"What is best in a champion?" asked Finn.

"For his actions to be high and his pride to be low," Grania replied.

"What is sharper than a sword?" he probed.

"The wit of a woman between two men," answered she.

"What is quicker than the wind?" he inquired.

"A woman's unencumbered wit," she replied.

Finn was satisfied that her beauty was great and that her answers were all clever and swift. As for Grania, she found in her heart no affection toward Finn McCoul. It seemed he was a man shaped by battle, and for herself she wanted a lover.

The guests were brought to the feasting house and led to their places at the tables. Fires glowed in the hearths at both ends of the hall. Cormac the High King welcomed his guests. Flasks were opened and blessed. Mead was poured into silver goblets, and soon lively talk brightened the hall. Roasted goose, duck, salmon, and pig, were all carried in on silver platters. The minstrels and bards sang of Grania's beauty and of Finn's adventures. Grania happened to be seated beside Finn's druid, whom she'd already met when he'd first sought her hand on behalf of Finn. She asked him the names of the champions of the fianna. She heard their names and deeds one by one until at last she got to the one she'd been wondering about all along. "Who is that sweetly-spoken man with the dark hair and the cheeks like rowan berries who sits beside Oisin, son of Finn?"

"That," said the druid, "is Diarmuid, the world's best lover of women." After a while scraps from the table were gathered and taken to the door to feed the hounds. In the excitement the dogs began to fight. Their howls were heard over the music and conversation, so Diarmuid went out to quiet them. He always wore a cap to conceal the love-spot on his forehead, for any woman who so much as glanced at it could not be satisfied until she'd given him her love. In the commotion the cap fell from his head. Grania, who was watching, upon seeing the love-spot, could not resist the instantaneous adoration that overtook her. Amorous she was, for the hair on top of his head and the ground beneath his feet, and utterly devoted she was, to everything else in between. She felt her lips tingle for all the future kisses he would plant there. She felt her womb leap with joy for the future children she would bear him. She felt her breasts surge with the sweet milk of love. The joy of it filled her veins and warmed her body throughout.

Grania knew what her course of action must be, and she knew not to waste time. She told her serving maid to fetch the golden chalice that could hold enough drink for nine times nine men. When the serving maid returned Grania filled it with the wine of enchantment, and told the maid to serve it 'round to the whole party beginning with Finn McCoul. Everyone who drank from the cup soon fell into a deep slumber. Grania went out to the door, "Diarmuid," she said boldly, "will you take my love and take me away from this house tonight?"

Diarmuid replied, "Finn McCoul is my chief and master, and I'll not tangle with the woman who has promised herself to him."

"All right," said Grania, "have it your way, but I still place you under druid-bond to take me away from here tonight, before Finn and my father awake."

"You place me under harsh bonds, Grania," said Diarmuid. "Why have you chosen me, when there are dozens here tonight worthy of your love?"

"I watched while you quieted the dogs, Diarmuid, and the love in my heart leapt out to you. As long as I live my love will never leap toward another, and that's how it is. No truer words can be spoken."

"But you know, Grania, as well as I do, that Finn McCoul leads the fianna, and it is the fianna who guard the walls tonight. We'll not find passage from these walls." The lovers, for that is what they were destined to become, went 'round and 'round about the matter of their escape, and at last they settled on a route through Grania's back gate.

Oisin had not drunk the enchanted wine, and when Diarmuid asked him what to do he said, "You have no choice what with the bonds she's put on you. It's not your fault. Just stay clear of Finn, until we can make plain to him that Grania saw the love-spot. Finn knows how it came to you, and he knows there's no resisting its power."

Oscar had not drunk the wine either, so Diarmuid asked the same of him. "Go with Grania, for you know well that no man can go against druid-bonds." The other champions of the fianna who remained yet awake said the same. Grania was a prize and her love was worth fleeing for. There was no helping what had happened. And besides, Finn McCoul was a big-hearted man. Surely, given time, he would forgive.

Now if I were an Irish teller of old, we might settle in a fortnight. Each eve at sundown we'd sit by the fire and I'd tell a portion of the lengthy pursuit of Diarmuid and Grania. We'd grow so enmeshed in the tale, that our legs and backs would know stone by stone and step by step the weariness of their flight. We'd know heartbeat upon breath the fright of being hunted and the loneliness of being long departed from friends. But since we live today and we have only now, I'll glide over their arduous flight the way a great bird soars over the land.

Suffice it to say, the waters of forgiveness did not flow from Finn's cup. He stayed on the heels of the lovers the way a hound stays on a hind. Each of their sly evasions felt to him like a slap. He chased them across lonely bogs and wintry moors, into the deep woods and over the mountains. The longer the chase, the more he felt mocked. He sent giants after them, armies too, even an old druiddess to catch them up in her spells. But Finn was never able to catch them, for by the foresight of Grania and by the skill of Diarmuid, they made clever escapes. They never slept where they had eaten, nor did they eat where they had cooked. Their only constant shelter was the love-bond between them. With the help of Diarmuid's foster-father, the Faery chief Angus mac Oc, they slipped out of Finn's well-crafted traps. A loyal youth named Muadan [moo-awn] carried their burdens, made their beds of soft rushes, and caught and roasted to their liking many a fine salmon.

Diarmuid, being a noble sort, refused to take Grania to bed, though every pore and wink of her wished it fiercely. But neither loyalty nor resolve could stave off the pangs of love between them. At some rocky and desolate place along the way, or perhaps at some mossy wooded place, they came together as man and woman, husband and wife. Before the pursuit was over, Grania was heavy with child. By that time Finn and the fleeing lovers were all dragged down by the weight of shame and grief. Many a fine beast and many a worthy champion had been slain in the pursuit. But what turned Finn's heart toward reconciliation was this: The death of his druiddess aunt. He had sent her to kill Diarmuid through magic, and there she met her death. She flew through the air on a lily pad and aimed to shoot a deadly dart at Diarmuid. Diarmuid laid down on his back and cast upward his red javelin whereupon it pierced the druiddess's heart and killed her on the spot. This loss weakened Finn's taste for revenge. At last he agreed to make peace.

Angus mac Oc negotiated the peace, going from one camp to the other until agreement was won. Finn was forbidden to hunt in the woods belonging to Grania's father, and Grania and Diarmuid were to be left in peace at a distant retreat called Rath Grania. Grania's sister wed Finn McCoul as a gesture of peace between the two families. Diarmuid and Grania had four sons and a daughter in all, and they prospered and lived well.

There came a time, when all the struggle seemed long behind them. Grania said to Diarmuid, "Husband, we have here a great household, fine musicians and craftsmen, the best huntsmen and cooks, but my father, Cormac the High King, has never been a guest in this house. Do you not think it odd, Dear Husband, that my own father and my own sister have never eaten a meal under this roof? Is there some reason why we cannot honor them with a feast?"

"You know very well, the reason, My Love," replied Diarmuid. "We cannot invite your sister without inviting her husband, and Finn McCoul remains an enemy of mine."

"Has not the peace been kept, Diarmuid, these many long years? The old troubles are long forgotten."

Diarmuid agreed to a feast, but not at Rath Grania. "We shall feast at the home of our daughter," he said. "Neutral ground will be wiser." Grania held high hopes for the feast. There would be a joyous reunion with her father and sister. And more to the point, she could find a fitting husband for her daughter. If there existed a proper suitor, he would no doubt be found in the service of Cormac the High King, or among the fianna led by Finn McCoul. Grania and her daughter set about preparing the feast. They worked night and day for twelve months. At last the day came. The high chiefs of Erin began to arrive. Then came Grania's father, Cormac, and all his company. Then came Finn McCoul and the fianna Finn. This was no simple feast. All the guests stayed on, enjoying themselves for a year and a day. There were deer hunts and duck hunts, followed by feasting and dancing. There were gifts given, and praises sung. There were chess tournaments, and running matches, shooting matches, races, and stories told for weeks on end.

Then on the last night of the year, Diarmuid awoke with a start. Grania put her arms around him and asked what was the matter. "I heard a hound yelping," he replied. Grania felt sure it was a Faery hound and bid him lie down and go back to sleep. Three times his rest was disturbed by the hound and three times Grania gentled him back to sleep. At sunup Diarmuid resolved to go look for the hound. Grania told him to take with him the sword of Manannan as well as the red javelin. But instead Diarmuid chose another sword and took the yellow javelin. Off he went with his favorite hound at his side.

He walked until he came to the top of a hill and there he met Finn McCoul standing alone. "Is it you, Finn, who conducts this chase? For I've heard the hounds yelping all night."

"We never set out to hunt," replied Finn, "but last night one of the hounds got loose. He crossed the trail of a wild boar, and the chase has been on ever since. They've looped over this hill six times now and I can hear them coming this way again. The boar is the most ferocious in all Ireland, and we must leave the hill to him."

Diarmuid replied, "I've never fled in fright from any beast and do not intend to start now."

Finn said, "This, Cousin Diarmuid, is no ordinary boar, and you are under druid-bonds never to hunt a boar, so come away from here at once." Diarmuid knew nothing of such bonds, so Finn explained that long ago Diarmuid's father had killed a boy. In a rage the boy's father had cursed him to lose his only son to a violent death at the tusk of a wild boar. "To protect you," Finn said, "your foster father, Angus, placed a druid-bond over you that you should never hunt a boar."

"This is news to me," said Diarmuid, "but I can feel the pounding hooves grow ever stronger, so I'd better get off this hill at once. Please, Finn, for protection give me your magic hound, Bran. For I'll find safe passage with Bran on one side and my hound on the other."

"I won't agree to that," said Finn. "Bran stays with me at all times."

"Finn McCoul," said Diarmuid, "You've been civil this whole year, and said not an ill-word against me. Still, I fear you've designed this hunt to entice me to my death." Just then the wild boar charged up the hill to them. Diarmuid drew his yellow javelin and foisted it, but it didn't harm a bristle on the boar's head. Then Diarmuid drew his sword and the boar charged him again. With all his might Diarmuid brought the sword down on the boar's neck. No blood was shed, but the sword broke in two. Diarmuid flew up into the air and landed on the boar's back, facing its tail. The boar tore down the hill and Diarmuid held on for dear life. Then the boar tore back up the hill again. Once at the summit it leapt and threw Diarmuid to the ground, whereupon it gored his belly causing his guts to spill down his legs. As Diarmuid lay dying, Finn said, "Diarmuid, I wish the women of Ireland could see you now. The beauty is gone from you. You look nothing but monstrous."

Diarmuid said, "Your healing hands could save me, Finn."

Just then Oscar, Oisin, and Conan came over the rise. It was common knowledge that a drink of water from Finn's cupped hands could heal the deadliest of wounds. Oscar cried, "Get him a drink, Finn."

Finn replied, "There's no water on this hill."

"That's not true," said Diarmuid. His cloak grew dark with blood while his face grew ever paler. "There's a spring nearby. I can hear the water flowing." Oscar and Oisin bid Finn go. Finn made his way to the spring and filled his cupped hands with water. Then he walked slowly back to Diarmuid and the others.

"Hurry!" cried Conan.

"Don't rush me," said Finn. "If you rush me I'll spill." Before Finn reached Diarmuid's side, the water had run through his hands.

"You chose to spill it, Finn McCoul, for you planned my death today," moaned Diarmuid.

"You're still a jealous fool, Finn!" cried Conan. "Go back! Get Diarmuid some water!"

Finn hesitated. Then Oscar cried, "You, Finn, are closer kin to me than Diarmuid, but I swear, if you don't heal him, neither you nor I shall leave this hill." At that Finn returned to the spring for more water, for he couldn't lose Oscar's love. He kept his palms tightly joined all the way back to where Diarmuid lay, but at the last it spilled before reaching his lips. When Finn saw the life fast fading from Diarmuid's body his jealousy turned to pity. In earnest he ran to the spring. He cupped his big hands and scooped a generous handful of water. He walked swiftly and smoothly back to Diarmuid's side, but it was too late. By the time the healing waters reached Diarmuid's mouth, the life had gone from his body.

When Finn and the huntsmen returned to the house with Diarmuid's favorite hound, Grania understood at once that her husband was dead. She was pregnant at the time and on the spot gave still birth to three sons. Long and sorrowful wails echoed for miles around that night and many nights to follow.

In the months to come, Grania grieved and raged. She rallied her sons to avenge their father's death. Finn tried to enlist Oisin, Oscar, and Conan, but they refused to defend him. Then Finn hired a hundred warriors from abroad. The avenging sons were like their mother in foresight and like their father in skill. They slew every last one of Finn's hired troops. At last he saw the folly of fighting them. He went to Grania pleading for peace and forgiveness. Grania would have none of it. She turned her sharp tongue on Finn and lashed him for his stubborn foolishness, for his smallness as a man, for his stinginess in holding a grudge, and for his murderous jealousy. Finn wept. He said Diarmuid always had been the better man, purer in heart, gentler in manner, and greater in skill. After a while, there was no telling who had loved him more, Grania or Finn. Grief had purged Grania's soul. She had no fight left in her. She asked her sons to keep peace.

Grania went to live with her daughter, for being home made her miss Diarmuid all the more. When her sister took ill, she went to her side at the plain of Allen. Harboring no more hate in her heart, she felt sorry for Finn McCoul, who was shaken and frail, and often given to tears. Over the years they became friends. When her sister died, Grania made good on her old promise to become Finn's wife.

When Grania's sons heard of it they came warring after Finn. He pleaded with Grania to keep the peace, for he was no warrior. Grania's sons taunted her for befriending the enemy. They were headstrong like their mother, but had Diarmuid's soft heart. They had families of their own, and better things to strive for than revenge. Finn bid them no ill. Looking at their faces he was reminded of his own youth and old times with Diarmuid. He gave to them lands and respected stations. He had become an ancient man, and Grania, too, had grown old. It is said they lived together in peace to the end of their days. The old troubles arose no more. In Finn, Grania had found a friend, someone who loved Diarmuid and missed him as much as she. In Grania, Finn had found a match, a willful woman, who knew sorrow as much as he.

AGE APPROPRIATENESS: *The tellers of old generally reserved the more sophisticated episodes of the Finn cycle for adults. The same notion still applies today. What details a teller puts forth, how chaste or lusty the love scenes, how morally complex the hero or heroine, depend upon the age and sophistication of the listeners. This tale is sexy, and deeply tragic, and is best shared among thoughtful adults. Finn's homicidal jealousy is a fascinating subject for adult discussion, but it is disheartening for the young who simply want to love and admire their hero. For that reason, I do not tell this tale to children.*

UNHEALTHY COMPETITION | THE FUTILITY OF VIOLENCE | ONGOING QUARRELS | LOYALTY | MISUSE OF POWER | MISGUIDED LEADERSHIP | JEALOUSY, ENVY, AND COMPETITION: Tragic myths like "Diarmuid and Grania" call for an examination of human complexity. They challenge us to temper our ideals with an understanding of the frailties beneath the skin. This tale reminds us of regrettable moments in our own lives—moments when our less-than-noble emotions get the better of us. When less-than-noble emotions lead to regrettable actions, we teeter on the brink of tragedy, for such actions may cause irreversible harm. This tale inspires endless discussion on the tragic elements of character and destiny and is no less pertinent now, than it was centuries ago. No human being is exempt from self-importance, bitterness, and pent-up rage. When these give way to violence and relentless competition, great loss ensues, and no good is won. In the end we wind up loving Finn McCoul, not because we admire him as a hero, but because we see him as a man, and we understand the source of his weakness.

PROLONGED OR COMPLICATED GRIEF | FORGIVENESS: Who would expect that after her children were grown Grania would wind up with Finn after all? When they first met she disliked him because he was a man "shaped by war." Yet warring was not his deepest nature, it was what he turned to after his beloved Saeva had been taken from him. Perhaps he was truly a man shaped by sudden, irrevocable loss—the loss of his mother, the loss of his grandmother, the loss of Saeva, his second wife, his druidess aunt, and of Diarmuid himself. In the end, Grania sees Finn as a man shaped by loss. And ironically, what they share in common outweighs their differences.

REVERENCE FOR NATURE | THE MORE-THAN-HUMAN WORLD | HEALING TOUCH | WOUNDED HEALER: Finn McCoul has the gift of hands-on healing, and the shamanic gift of being in rapport with the element water, so much so that a sip from Finn's cupped hand will restore even the most wounded champion. In this tale Finn misuses the gift by allowing his jealousy to interfere with the healing art. The tragic turn of events reminds healers of all kinds to remember our oaths and obligations to serve. During the course of our careers, all health-care providers experience the obligation to set aside our own needs and desires in order to offer the best possible care to those being served.

Maureen the Red

IRELAND | (2,340 words)

*L*ong ago in a peaceful glen there lived a prosperous pair, a farmer and a weaver who were married and shared great joy in living together. As nature would have it, they were expecting their first child. One morning an old tinker woman came to the door begging for a bite to eat. The weaver got up from her loom, bade the guest welcome, and laid the table with bread, cheese, butter, tea, and cream. The tinker woman ate her fill and then offered this blessing, "May your firstborn child be a beautiful daughter."

The days, and weeks, and months passed by, and sure enough, the firstborn was a lovely girl. Not long after, the couple was expecting their second child. Again the old tinker woman came to the door, and the lady of the house got up from her weaving, and bade the old woman come in. She warmed herself by the fire and ate 'til she was satisfied. Before leaving she offered the blessing, "May your second child be a lovely girl." And in due time the second girl was born, as lovely as the first, if that were possible.

As the years passed by, the little girls grew more and more darling so that even a hard-hearted person would go soft at the sight of them. The old tinker woman happened by once again, and wouldn't you know, the lady of the house was again with child, but on this day she was tired and cross. Instead of inviting the old woman in she stood in the doorway and said she had no lunch to offer. The tinker woman turned away into the rain, but before reaching the gate she called back, "May your third child be an ugly little goat." But with the howl of the wind and the rain pouring down in sheets, the lady of the house did not hear it.

And wouldn't you know, as fate would have it, the third and last daughter was born with bristly red hair on her head, and on her pointed chin, little goat whiskers to match it. And everyone said, "There's a tinker's curse upon that child," but her mother and father saw past the strange face into the heart of the girl. They named her Maureen Rua, meaning *Maureen the Red*, and they loved her as dearly they loved the first two, and that was that.

As the first two daughters grew older they made trips to the town to buy thread and needles for their mother. Everyone said, "Good day to you, darling colleens. All the best to your mother the weaver, and to your father the good farmer, and didn't God bless them with beauty when he made you." But when their mother bade them take Maureen, it was different. The townspeople didn't know what to say. The worst of them of them smirked, while others turned away, and the best of them could only spit out a quick "Good day." This was so hurtful to the two eldest that when the three went to town, they took to walking ahead of Maureen, and pretended not to know her. They took extra care to put on ribbons, and check their faces in the glass, to always make sure their pleasing beauty was the first thing people would notice.

Now the pleasure of a good home might last forever, and then again it might not. One day, out of the blue, the farmer took sick and died. Try as she might, the weaver could not run the farm and keep up the house, even with the help of the three girls. At last the eldest said, "Mother, there's naught to do, except that we three girls should go off to seek our fortunes in the world."

The mother took the last of her oats and made cakes for them. All she had was enough for three cakes. She longed to give one to each of her daughters, but if she did so, she herself would starve. She said to the first, "Daughter, will you take half a cake and a mother's blessing, or will you take a whole cake without it." The first daughter was a practical girl. "Mother, I'll take the whole cake, for your blessing will not stave off the hunger on my journey." The mother put the same question to her second daughter. She knew the world could be hard, for she had watched her father die. "I'll grow hungry soon enough, Mother, and what good will a blessing do me?" But when the question was put to Maureen, she said half a cake would do just fine as long as she had her mother's blessing.

No sooner had they gotten out of their mother's sight, than the two eldest tried everything they could think of to get rid of Maureen. They tied her to a tree and ran, but when they got to the next crossroads, she was there waiting for them. They pushed her into the bog and clamped dirt on top, but it was the same story. Then they tied a big rock onto her ankle and threw her into the lake, but a mile down the road, she was there waiting. So they got tired and decided to put up with her.

Nightfall was nearly upon them. Out ahead they saw a great castle all lit up, so they went to the door and asked for shelter. The lady of the house and her three daughters invited them to spend the night. They soon found that the lord of the house was a giant. That night, Maureen and her sisters were put to bed in the same room with the giant's three daughters. The giant's three lay in one bed, and our three in the other. Maureen dreaded sleep, for she knew the giant was up to no good. She woke her sisters and bade them help her push the bed to the corner of the room. Then she quietly went over and snatched the nightcaps off the heads of the three sleeping sisters. Our three put them on, got back into bed and pretended to sleep. Soon they heard the footsteps of the giant and his wife coming down the hall. "Mind you," said the Giant's wife, "find the right bed. Those three are nearest the door with no caps on." The clumsy old giant went into the dark room feeling his way around until he found the three with no caps on. He took out a great knife and ran them through. He scooped them up, put them in a bag and mumbled, "We'll have a fine supper tomorrow when one of them is baked, one of them fried, and one is boiled." As soon as he was out of the room Maureen and her sisters climbed out the window and down the wall. They ran as fast as their legs would go and didn't stop until morning.

In the morning they came to a town where a great king ruled with his three fine sons. As Maureen and her sisters entered the gates of the town, the king's eldest son looked down from his window and spied Maureen's eldest sister. It was love at first sight, and he wanted to marry her. When the second son saw the second sister, same thing. But when the king's youngest son set eyes on Maureen Rua, with her stiff red brush top and her whiskered chin, marriage did not cross his mind.

The two eldest sons set to pestering their father until he invited the girls to dine. While dining that night, the two eldest sisters talked of nothing but how Maureen had saved them from the evil giant and how lucky they were to have a sister so clever and brave. "That giant is an old enemy of mine," said the king, "with special powers which give him advantage over me and my men. He's got a cloak of invisibility which enables him to sneak in and steal from my royal coffers. If you, Maureen, could seize the cloak, and bring it to me, then I'll put on a fine wedding for your eldest sister and my eldest son."

So that very night Maureen returned to the giant's castle. She crept into the chamber where the giant and his wife slept. The cloak of invisibility was draped over the foot of the bed. Maureen snatched it up and wrapped herself in it, and back she went to the king's castle. That night it was the king himself who spent the evening talking about the skill of Maureen Rua and how cleverly she bested the giant. "That giant has a sword of light, Maureen, that shines like a beacon in the night. If you could take possession of it and bring it to me, I'll put on a fine wedding for your second sister and my second son."

As you might guess, Maureen set right to the task. She took a great sack of salt and returned to the giant's castle. She climbed up on top of the kitchen roof, and stood above the chimney where the giant's wife was boiling a big kettle of bones for stew. For each pinch of salt that the lady of the house put in, Maureen threw fistfuls down the chimney. Later on that night the giant lay sleepless, moaning for water. "You've drunk every drop in the house," said the wife. "You'll have to go to the well."

" 'Tis you should go to the well," said the giant, " 'Twas you who oversalted the stew."

" 'Twas you, foolish husband, who slew our own daughters."

"We'll not speak of that," said the giant. "Now go for the water or *you'll* wind up in a stew."

" 'Tis dark outside," said the wife.

"Take the sword of light," said the giant. At that the lady of the house got up and took the sword of light out to the well. Who should be there tucked out of sight, but our Maureen? No sooner did the lady set the sword down, than Maureen was there to snatch it up. Off she ran like the wind, back to the king's palace.

The next night at supper the king naturally led the discussion to the topic of Maureen's wit and bravery in besting the giant. "That troublesome giant owns a pair of seven-league boots. If you could bring those to me, Maureen, you yourself shall marry my youngest son." By this time the king's youngest son looked at Maureen with eyes of admiration, and he gave her a bright nod.

So that night she again crept into the giant's chamber. She found the seven-league boots and slipped her feet into them. Just then the giant awoke and leapt up. Maureen ran for the door and the giant ran after. "At last I have you, my fine colleen!" cried the giant. He grabbed

Maureen by the hair, plucked the boots off her, and stuffed her into a sack. He hung her to the kitchen rafter, and went out to the woods to cut the biggest club he could find. "A good thrashing will tenderize you nicely before roasting," said he.

The lady of the house slept through all the racket, but what woke her soon after was the sound of singing coming from the kitchen. She got up and saw the sack swaying gently back and forth. The sound of singing sweetened the room and reminded her of her own three girls. "Why are you singing in that bag?" asked the lady.

"I'm thrilled to be going to Heaven," said Maureen.

"If I get in the bag with you, might I go to Heaven, too?" asked the lady, "for I'm getting tired of staying here with the old so-and-so."

"Sorry," said Maureen, "only one can go."

"Perhaps you'd have the kindness in your heart to let it be me," said the giant's wife, wearily.

"Perhaps," said Maureen, "for a price."

"What price?"

"All the gold and silver your husband has ever stolen," said Maureen.

"Fine," said the wife, and she went 'round the place gathering up all the tea sets and candlesticks the giant had robbed from the people of the land. Then she cut Maureen down and they traded places. Maureen leapt back into the seven-league boots and was gone.

When the giant returned to the kitchen he was puzzled by the singing that came from the bag, so he gave it a wallop. The yelling that followed had a familiar ring to it, so he opened the bag to have a peek. When his wife told him the whole tale of going to Heaven and the gold and silver, he surged with fury. He went after Maureen and gained on her steadily, hollering out all the way, "I'll get you my fine colleen, my clever one. I'll have your hide, and you'll make a fine supper." As they reached the river, his great fist was nearly in reach of her bristly waft of hair. She leapt the river, and he followed, but you know which of them had on the seven-league boots. Maureen sailed clear to the other bank, while the giant fell short. He got swept into the current and drowned. At supper that night, Maureen took a seat of honor at the table. She presented the seven-league boots and all the gold and silver to be returned to its rightful owners.

The next day a triple wedding was held. Up front sat the weaver woman beaming with pride. When the youngest prince turned to Maureen he saw clean into her, past the peculiarities of her face, to the radiant essence at the heart of her. So strong did it burn, her whole life through, with courage and love, that it ignited others, and brought out the best in them. The name, Maureen Rua, became a proud name bearing great honor for queens and the daughters of queens, long after our Maureen was dead and gone.

WOMEN'S ESTEEM AND EMPOWERMENT | EMOTIONAL RESILIENCE | COURAGE, INTEGRITY, RESILIENCE | EXCLUSION | COPING WITH REJECTION | THE ALCHEMY OF SELFHOOD: Like other Celtic heroines, Maureen Rua is a strong, proactive female, not easily discouraged by rejection. Her resilient spirit is a marvelous inspiration to anyone facing hardships or feeling shunned. This tale gives us a visceral sense of what it means to operate from a place of inner strength. Despite exclusion and sudden loss, Maureen does not collapse, become despondent, or lose her ability to perceive and to achieve. From the archetypal point of view, the gold and silver she reclaims from the giant might be said to parallel her own finest mettle, the balance of masculine and feminine in her character.

INTUITION | MISUSE OF POWER | JUSTICE AND FAIRNESS | CRAVINGS AND TROUBLESOME DESIRES | GREED AND ACQUISITIVENESS | SCARCITY | SUSTAINABILITY: Maureen's gut intuition about the giant, and her will to act on it, saved her and her sisters from being devoured. Let's muse for a moment on the sorts of giants we need to outwit today, for the sake of our well-being, even our very survival: The giant may show up in the form of greed, oppressive ideas, tyrannical standards, or mere sluggishness. The giant may manifest in the form of blind consumerism, cruelty to children, or poor leadership. Maureen's wit awakens ours, and reminds us to be keen and creative in how we protect life and the precious resources which enrich and sustain us. The giant's stealing and hoarding had plagued the land and people for a long time. Maureen sought to redistribute the wealth where it belonged. Such themes of justice and sustainability have long been important to the Irish whose limited land and resources have been exploited by others.

CREATIVE COURAGE | ADVENTURESOME SPIRIT | ATHLETIC EXCELLENCE | SELF-RELIANCE | SELF DETERMINATION | WOMEN'S INITIATION | RITES OF PASSAGE | INNOVATION | COOPERATION AND DEVOTION | RESPONSIBLE USE OF TECHNOLOGY | THE JOY OF LIFE-AFFIRMING WORK: In stories like this one, we can think of the good king as a visionary, an embodiment of inspired leadership, coming from within oneself or one's community. Right off, our good king sees

Maureen as what today might be called a "cultural creative," someone capable of breaking through, where others have fallen short. Seizing the cloak, the sword, and the boots, and returning the stolen gold and silver, are initiatory tasks for Maureen—tests of stamina, wit, and skill—but they are also healing tasks for the culture. A group of young environmentalists mused on the significance of the cloak of invisibility: "To be effective earth stewards we sometimes need to do clandestine research to observe what's kept hidden." They likened the sword of light to "a beacon of intelligence enabling us to see newly revealed truths, and to bring light to difficult problems in the community." They felt the boots suggest "the human capacity to transcend, to leap vast chasms, to get beyond what the greedy giant demands." Brought to bear on personal and social difficulties as well as environmental, the cloak, the sword, and the boots, yield a bigness of heart, and unexpected rewards.

EXPANDING NARROW DEFINITIONS OF BEAUTY | HONORING TRUE ESSENCE | INNER BEAUTY | SISTERLY SOLIDARITY | LOVING KINDNESS | MATE SELECTION: The poems of Jalaludin Rumi tell us to embrace our flaws, and to be grateful for our grief, for they are what get us in touch with our deepest wellsprings of love and compassion. Looked at this way, we see Maureen's peculiar face, which is such a curse and causes her such pain, as a crucial and ennobling part of her. Without that face, she would not be Maureen Rua, and she might not have had to reach so deeply inside herself to find her extraordinary confidence and courage. The soul often expresses itself through pain and peculiarities, rarely through perfection. The sisters' obsession with their appearance is short-lived, because in Maureen they soon see beyond superficialities to her radiant essence. The youngest prince marries Maureen for herself, and not for her looks. In our looks-obsessed society appearances constantly sway and seduce us. Political candidates change their image moment to moment based on opinion polls. People in show business go under the needle and knife to be surgically sculpted to starlike perfection. If we take this tale to heart, it serves as a powerful antidote to superficial image-making, reminding us that essence is greater than image, and peculiarities house the soul.

The Key Flower

WALES | (596 words)

Long ago atop a green hill in Wales, a shepherd watched his flocks peacefully grazing. In the grass at his feet he noticed an unusual flower. Its blossom bore the shape of a key. He picked it and put it in his buttonhole. All morning he enjoyed its sweet scent. That afternoon he led the sheep to another hill. There on the hillside he came upon a stone door that he had never seen before. He wondered if somehow he'd got lost, but no, looking around he saw this was indeed the old familiar valley where the sheep had always grazed.

The shepherd tried opening the stone door but it wouldn't budge. Then he noticed it had a little keyhole. Chancing that the key flower might fit, he tried it in the hole. To his surprise it fit perfectly. When he turned the key flower the stone door opened.

You might expect it to be dark and chilly inside that hill, but it wasn't. From the center of the hill there shone a light that glistened like sunrise on a lake. The shepherd stepped inside and walked toward it. There he found all manner of treasures: mounds of shimmering gold and shining silver, heaps of bright emeralds, rubies, sapphires and pearls. The poor astonished shepherd could barely catch his breath, for such riches were beyond imagining. He thought of his loved ones waiting back at the cottage, and began stuffing his pockets to the brim. He took off his socks and used them as pouches. He used his wool cap as a sack.

Hurriedly he set out for home. The weight of the riches was great upon him, but his gait was light nonetheless, for he imagined the joy on his loved ones' faces when he shared with them the dazzling gems.

The further he got from the hill, the lighter the load seemed to grow. Soon he could no longer feel the weight of it. He stopped to check his pockets and pouches. To his great dismay they were filled, not with jewels, nor riches, but with leaves—crumbly dry leaves—the likes of which he would rake up and toss on the compost heap. The shepherd turned his pockets inside out. The bits of dry leaves blew away on the wind. The shepherd trudged home, puzzling over the day, trying to make sense of what had happened.

When he got home, he wanted to tell the story of the key flower, the stone door, and the riches inside the hill. But when he tried to speak of it, his throat grew dry and his thoughts scattered. He knew whatever he said would sound foolish, so he kept still.

In the days and weeks to come, he often searched for the stone door, but he never found it. He often scanned the grassy hills for another key flower, though none was ever to be found.

It wasn't until much later, sitting at the fireside one night, that he decided to tell his tale. In his mind's eye he saw it all with great clarity as if it had been yesterday. The thoughts formed freely in his mind and flowed from his lips like a bright river. Afterwards, his loved ones remarked what a fine story it was, and that he was a good teller of tales. He told them it was all true, every last detail, and they scoffed, "What a rascal you are."

As the years passed by, the memory of that afternoon stayed bright within him. Even as a very old man thinking about it brought a smile to his lips.

SOURCE: *Three years ago I phoned Maxine Thompson, one of the beloved storytellers of my youth. Back in the fifties she was a white-haired elder with a milky soft voice. Now her voice is even softer, but her love and wisdom hold firm. Maxine said, "Have I ever told you the tale of the key flower?" I said, "No," and she proceeded to tell this tale that her mother told when she was young. (Neither of us has ever seen the tale in print.)*

INTANGIBLE TREASURES: Maxine said the tale was about "life's rare moments of illumination and grace . . . things that can't be grasped, measured, or held onto." She said that thinking of the tale she was reminded "the best things in life are not things."

With that in mind I later shared the tale with a woman who'd lost all her "things" in a house fire. "Life's not about holding onto your stuff," she said, "and I'm just now learning it's not about finding another key flower, either. It's about remembering the past, and looking to the future, while living in the present, here and now. This moment, that is the one thing that is truly ours."

THE MORE-THAN-HUMAN WORLD | ECSTASY AND ELATION | PEAK EXPERI-ENCE: Naturalist philosopher David Abram told me this tale is about those amazing unexpected moments when we stumble upon a natural wonder, such as a double rainbow or a pod of leaping whales. Suddenly the world reveals in full its true exuberance and we are struck through with the wonder of it. The naturalist's peak experience is not unlike that of the surfer who's just had the ride of a lifetime, the monk who experiences a flash of enlightenment, or the love-struck newlyweds on their honeymoon. We can evoke the memory of such experiences, we can partially relive them through the imagination, we can strive to capture them through art, music, and poetry, but like the key flower, they are by nature ephemeral. Try as we might, we cannot stuff our pockets with the exuberance of peak moments and tote it home with us. A bittersweetness befalls us when our rare mood dissipates, and, as Yeats's poem on ecstasy says, "the common round of day resumes." Like the shepherd, our best hope is to internalize the moment of illumination, to keep it alive as he does, in the heart and in the mind's eye. Recently a meditation student reflecting on this tale said, "Nirvana can't be captured, and expecting to possess it is a definite setup for failure. Meditation is about daily practice, like tending your sheep. If a transcendent moment comes, it comes unexpectedly. There is no hope of ever finding the key flower without doing daily practice. In the mystic traditions, illumination strikes, maybe only once. The true mystic makes it the beacon of a lifetime, guiding each step thereafter."

The Love of Powel and Rhiannon

WALES | (2,639 words)

ABOUT POWEL AND RHIANNON: *Descendants of the Celts of old Europe, the Welsh have long been great lovers of literature and romance. The following two tales are adapted from the Mabinogion [mab-i-NOH-gion], a collection of eleven stories derived from centuries of oral storytelling. Welsh bards learned by heart the "bones," or the outline of the stories, and extemporized to fill in the details. The tales of the Mabinogion are thought to have been shaped over the centuries through the combining of myth, popular folklore, and pseudo-history. The earliest known written version of the collection dates from 1325, though earlier texts are presumed to have existed. In translating from written texts, poets and scholars must contend with omissions and inconsistencies, yet in these tales the humor, magic, intrigue, pathos, and vitality of the Celts comes through without fail.*

Powel is a nobleman of great heart, who in his lifetime faces numerous moral dilemmas, yet nearly always finds a way to behave honorably. He does this not for public appearances, but in keeping with the dictates of his heart. Rhiannon is a noblewoman of great courage, wit, self-possession, and uncanny powers which awe and mystify.

Long ago in old Wales, back in the times when feasts lasted for days and weeks, Lord Powel feasted with his friends at the finest of his seven palaces. When all at the table were satisfied, Lord Powel arose and asked his dearest companions to join him in taking the air.

They soon found themselves atop Gorseth Arberth, an old Faery mound known for its powers of enchantment. From its height they could see the vast lay of the plains and green hills. "Is it true, Lord Powel," asked one of the men, "that standing atop this Faery hill during the feasting days, one can expect to receive a blow, or see a wonder?"

"Yes," said Powel, " 'Tis true, but surrounded by my friends I fear no blows, so let us all take a seat and await the wonder."

They had not waited long when they spied a lady coming toward them on horseback. The horse was of extraordinary size, and as pure white as new fallen snow. The lady was draped in a garment of gold and shone like sunlight itself. She passed below the hill walking the horse slowly at an even pace. Try as they might the men could not tear their gazes from her. "Men," said Powel, "who knows this lady, for I would like to call her by name." But among all of Powel's friends, there was not one who knew her. "Quickly," Powel said to the swiftest of runners, "go out and greet her, and find out her name."

The runner shot out to meet her, and though the lady's horse proceeded slowly as before, the runner could not catch up. When he saw that his best sprint put him farther and farther behind, he returned saying, "Lord Powel, there is no runner among us who can overtake her."

"Then mount up, one of you, and go after her." Now the lady was past the hill and making her way slowly across the open plain. One of Powel's horsemen charged down the hill with clods of dirt flying up behind him. He dug his spurs into the horse's sides, but to no avail, for though he charged ahead full speed, and the lady's horse was only walking, the distance between them grew greater and greater.

The horseman returned saying it would take a winged horse to catch her. "So," said Lord Powel, "this is the wonder: a lady whose horse walks faster than my best horses can run. Let us go back to the palace and ponder it."

They spent the evening feasting, and slept it off that night. The following day, after the first meal had filled them, Lord Powel arose. "Come, my friends, the same group as before. We shall sit atop Gorseth Arberth, to behold whatever wonder we might see." And then to a young rider Powel quietly said, "Bring the swiftest horse and be ready to ride." They had not waited long atop the hill when the same golden-cloaked lady came along upon the same great white horse. "Quickly, Lad," said Powel, "go out to meet her." The lad wasted no time, but as his backside touched the saddle and his hands gripped the reins, the lady had already passed by them, even though the eye could plainly see the horse's steady walk was no swifter than it was on the day before. "Make haste, Lad!" shouted Powel. The lad and his horse bounded down the hill, and tore after the lady. His cape flapped wildly in the wind, while her cape lay gently over her shoulders and down her back, completely unruffled. He ran the horse to near exhaustion, and still could not shorten the growing space between himself and the radiant lady.

The rider gave up and returned. "Clearly it avails none to pursue her," said Powel. "But I would surely like to know whose errand she attends to, for it must be someone of great importance. Let us go back to the palace and ponder." They spent the remains of the day with feasting and amusement, and rested until it was time to get up and feast again, for that's how it was in the times of old. After the first feast of the day, they felt strong and Lord Powel asked, "Where are those men who were with me yesterday and the day before on the Faery mound of Gorseth Arberth?"

"Here," the men chimed, "we are all here, Lord, never far from your call."

"Good, then," said Powel, "we shall return to the hill."

This time Powel mounted his horse and sat atop the hill, ready to ride. At first sight of the lady he charged down. Well ahead of her, he thought to be there on the plain waiting when she passed by. But somehow the stretch of land between himself and the plain seemed ever longer the faster he galloped. As for the lady, her gently plodding horse had already passed by the hill, and was leaving an ever-increasing space between herself and Powel. "Lady," called Powel in desperation. "For the sake of whomever you most love in this world and the next, please stop and have a word."

"I'll gladly linger," the lady replied, turning her horse around. "It might have been far better for your horses, Lord Powel, had you asked me to stop three days sooner."

"Lady," said Powel, now able to look into her eyes which were fixed right on him, "where are you off to, and for whom do you journey?"

She replied, "I go on my own errand, and it is for myself that I journey."

"Greetings to you then," said Powel, "and a thousand welcomes." Powel thought that of all the women he had ever laid eyes on there was none so beautiful as she. "Lady," said Powel, "could you not reveal something of your purpose?"

"Happily," said she. "My chief quest is to see and to speak with yourself."

"I am greatly pleased," said Powel, "and might I ask your name, and what service I can offer?"

"My name is Rhiannon. My father, Hevyth Hen, sought to give me to a husband not of my choosing, but I refused, out of love for you. And I won't take any husband, other than yourself."

"Lady," said Powel, "more swiftly than your horse can walk, I say yes to this!"

"Very well," said Rhiannon. "Meet me this day one year from now at the palace of Hevyth Hen, and be prepared to wed."

"Gladly," said Powel.

"Remain in good health," said Lady Rhiannon, "and don't forget this promise."

So Powel and Rhiannon parted, and he returned to his guests. Question upon question was put to him regarding the lady on horseback, but Powel managed to turn the discourse to other matters. The twelve months passed, and Powel made ready one hundred horsemen to accompany him to the palace of Hevyth Hen. As he neared the palace gates he was greeted by a great fanfare of whistles, pipes, and drums. Boughs and flowers adorned the palace gates, and Powel was received as warmly as a son or brother. Powel was led to the feasting table and given the seat of honor between Rhiannon and her father. Inspired conversation flowed between them as they feasted on rare delights.

Just as the after-dinner carousal began, there entered into the center of the hall a tall auburn-haired youth of princely stature, clothed in garments of satin. "Greeting of the Heavens, be on you, my soul," said Powel. "Welcome, and take a seat."

The youth stood squarely before them, "I won't take a seat just yet, Lord Powel, for I come with a singular purpose."

"Very well," said Powel, "I welcome you to stand and state your purpose, for we celebrate a precious union this night and my heart brims over with good will."

"I come," said the man in satin, "to make a special request of you, Lord Powel."

"By all means," said Powel, "On my wedding night I'll refuse no man his heart's desire."

"Of all the earthly replies," whispered Rhiannon, "why did you say that?"

"Speak up, my soul, come forth with it," said Powel to the young noble.

"Lord Powel has promised," said the visitor, "to grant my request, and the whole court is my witness."

"What do you so crave of me?" asked Powel.

"The lady by your side, Lord Powel, and your seat of honor at this table."

Powel sat dumbfounded.

Rhiannon pressed her elbow into his ribs and whispered, "Never has a man made worse use of his wits, than you have just now." Rhiannon and Powel turned their heads away from the others, and Rhiannon went on, "This is Lord Gwawl, the man Father nearly forced me to marry. You must uphold your word, or lose the people's trust."

"How can I uphold my word?" whispered Powel.

"You're a nobleman, you must," whispered Rhiannon.

"The words I spoke were born of a light heart," said Powel.

"Light then and heavy now, my beloved, for a noble who loses the court's trust is himself lost. Here is what we must do. It is in your power to bestow me upon Gwawl, and you must do so, in accord with your promise. But the feast is in my charge, and I have say over the seats at my table. Gwawl shall not take a seat this night. I will engage to marry him twelve months hence. In the meantime I will give you a small bag. You must come to the pre-wedding feast a year from now, dressed as a beggar, begging for your little bag to be filled with food. The bag shall be enchanted, and no amount of food or drink will fill it. Gwawl will grow impatient, for his heart is not as light as yours. He'll ask when the bag shall ever be full. You shall reply, 'It can only be full when a great prince arises and presses down the contents with both feet.' I will urge him to tread down the food, and when his two feet are in the bag, you shall pull it over his head and tie it shut. Have a good bugle-horn under your rags, and when the bag is secure, call your knights and let them come down upon the palace. Then we shall make our requests."

Rhiannon and Powel turned back toward the others. Lord Gwawl said, "Powel has had ample time to answer my request."

"Indeed," said Powel. "As for who sits at this table it is for my Lady to say."

"Dear friend," said Rhiannon, "I have made welcome Powel's hosts, and given this banquet in their honor. I cannot refuse them this moment for another. However, come to this house one year from now. I shall make a feast in your honor, as you and I shall be wed."

So Gwawl departed, and after the feast Powel returned to one of his seven palaces. It is said that all that year Gwawl was as cocky as a man could be and Powel was just as lonely.

After the twelve months had passed, one hundred of Powel's best men went to the palace of Hevyth Hen and hid themselves beyond the orchard. Powel himself was shoeless and clad in greasy old rags, and beneath his tattered cloak was the little enchanted bag and the bugle. Inside the palace the feast had begun and Gwawl sat between Rhiannon and her father Hevyth Hen.

During the carousal after the feast, there came into the hall a poor beggar, clad in rags, hunched over and limping. He asked that he might pose a request to Lord Gwawl. Lord Gwawl who was wise to his own wily ways, and therefore cautious with others replied, "If the request be just and good, then I shall grant it." The beggar carried in his hand a small bag and asked only for the right to fill it with scraps from the table, so he could take it home to his poor sick mother who was deaf and blind. Now Gwawl was an impatient man, but he did not want to appear heartless to the plight of a poor beggar, so he bade the beggar welcome to fill the bag. Now the beggar, who was really Lord Powel, began filling the bag with bread and potatoes, with meat and fowl, with fine stuffings made of hazelnuts, and those made of berries and chestnuts, and as the bag was enchanted, so it would never be full.

At last Lord Gwawl could wait no longer and cried out, "Beggar man, pray tell, when will the bag be full?"

"The bag will be full," said the beggar, "when a wise noble, who is good and kind, comes forth and stomps down the contents with both feet."

Rhiannon urged Gwawl forward, and he arose from his seat, striding to the center of the hall where the beggar stood holding the bag. In his mind Gwawl thought it fortunate this night to be seen by the court as a both good and kind. First he put one foot into the bag, and then the other, and then suddenly all was darkness for poor Gwawl, for the bag was up over his head, and Powel was tying it shut. Then Powel blew his horn loudly and shrilly until the hundred men came down upon the palace. When the best of his men came into the hall Rhiannon stood up and said, "Welcome gentlemen, you're just in time for a game of fox in the bag, for it is a fox indeed who tricks a man in his most gentle and least guarded moment."

The whole court marked the truth of Rhiannon's words, for they recalled how Powel had been tricked the year before. Rhiannon looked at her father for courage and stepped forth standing squarely in front of the beggar man. "Lord Powel," she said to the beggar who now stood upright and strong. "You come here this night, in the middle of a feast, quite unannounced. Perhaps you should show your good will by offering a boon to my poets and minstrels who will play for us tonight. And perhaps the fox in the bag who has caused you much anguish, should make a gift to my minstrels on your account."

From inside the bag Gwawl called out, "Very well," for he was the sort to go mad when kept in a tight space.

"Indeed," said Rhiannon, "and perhaps it would also be good and just if Lord Gwawl would promise to release me to marry Powel, and agree that on both sides offenses have been equal, trick for trick, tit for tat. Therefore in addition he should swear never to take revenge on us for the shame caused him this night."

"Agreed," said Gwawl. "Now release me this instant!"

And so Gwawl was released to the poets and minstrels who asked of him all manner of gifts, gold, satin garments, and sweet wines. And not wanting to appear the fox, or the fool, Gwawl agreed to every last request, and retired to his own domain, less cocky, they say, than before.

The very next day, the rightful couple, Powel and Rhiannon were wed. There was no finer feast day ever or since. Their tribulations and loneliness ceased and gave way to a time of joy that lasted four years until hardship again came their way. But that is another tale for another time. For now, may we remember the bards and poets of old

Wales. Without their truth in telling, we might never know that through his great heart Lord Powel won and lost Lady Rhiannon, and Lady Rhiannon, through her great wit, won him back again.

MORE-THAN-HUMAN WORLD | WOMEN'S ESTEEM AND EMPOWERMENT | SELF RELIANCE: This tale brings to life the mysterious power of the Celtic goddess, for in Rhiannon's self-possessed, time-bending composure, we are reminded of the power of nature itself. No manner of speedy, athletic, vigorous inquiry and pursuit will unlock her mystery. She must be approached with supplication like the great wandering mare, Epona, mother goddess of the free-roaming Celts. Men and women alike take great delight in Rhiannon's abilities and how they carry the tale. Like all heroine tales, this one lifts the esteem of women everywhere.

MAN OF HEART | OPPORTUNISM | CUNNING AND CONNING | TRICKS AND TRICKING | SCAMMING | WORTHY USE OF DECEPTION: Rhiannon's father chooses for her Gwawl, a handsome, self-referential, opportunistic prince, whom Rhiannon does not love. For herself, Rhiannon chooses Powel, a man of heart, one who loves his friends, and who gives his heart wholly to joy and generosity on his wedding night. The consequence of his naive generosity, his unguarded heart, is one lonely, humble year, a year that is inconsequential in the grand scheme of his love for Rhiannon. If anything, the lonely year Rhiannon spends engaged to Gwawl serves to cement her love, trust, and working together with Powel. All of this is further tested when even more complex difficulties arise for them in the following tale. Rhiannon bests Gwawl the con artist with an even more clever con of her own.

LOVE AND ALCHEMICAL UNION | COOPERATION AND DEVOTION | RITES OF PASSAGE | INITIATION: No matter what people's gender or gender preference, nearly everyone hungers for a passionate connection with a beloved. In the romances of the Celts we see couples such as Finn and Saeva, Diarmuid and Grania, Rhiannon and Powel, coming together under a fated star. For these lovers no other mate will do. They are destined to be together and when they come together things happen. A fountain of tenderness overflows, an explosion of sexual energy occurs, a warring man grows peaceful, a magical child is born, a nation is inspired, prosperity befalls the land, a grown man becomes childlike and foolish, a woman's strength changes history. Like the Lovers in the Tarot, like a "good match" in the Vedic Astrological tradition, when complementary forces attract, a certain chemistry is ignited, and the couple accomplish things they could not have done alone. In alchemy it is said that the silver lunar essence of the queen and the golden solar essence of the king come together to create a conjunctio, a mystical union of a third and higher character than either gold or silver alone. This is why the Celtic chalice (grail) is either gold with silver ornamentation or silver with gold ornamentation. The combination is greater than either on its own. When in falling in love, the conjunctio strikes and transforms our hearts, it is a great blessing. The soul is touched by something unfathomable and unquestionably sacred. Love is indeed a teacher and an initiator. It creates an unexpected bigness of heart and the capacity for great sexual pleasure. This tale stirs hearts at weddings, bridal showers, and in any event that aims to honor love.

The Vindication of Lady Rhiannon

WALES | (957 words)

(for more information on Welsh myth see p. 67)

Lord Powel and Lady Rhiannon had been married four years when a beautiful son was born to them. After the birth nursemaids were left to watch over the babe while Rhiannon slept. During the night the nursemaids dozed off, and when they awoke the babe was gone. They scurried around the palace and found no trace of him anywhere. Surely they'd be imprisoned for their neglect, and what would become of their own daughters and sons? The terrified women decided they had no choice but to blame Lady Rhiannon herself, for they reasoned the court would be lenient with the noblewoman. They killed a puppy and smeared its blood on the lady's gown, and said that she had killed her own son in a fit of post-partum madness.

"For pity's sake," cried Rhiannon, "What's happened to my son? Charge me not falsely. No harm will come to you by telling the truth." But the frightened nursemaids told their tale so many times they began to believe it themselves. Half mad with grief, Rhiannon feared she might have done the unthinkable. The court demanded Powel imprison her, but Powel said, "Of a truth, no manner of testimony could make me lock up my beloved wife." The court then set a penance for Rhiannon. So heart-sick was she at the loss of her child, that the penance came as a comfort to her.

Each day she went out to the palace gates. Whosoever should enter, be it a wandering bard, a peasant, or a nobleman, Rhiannon was obliged to bear them upon her back, and carry them over the bridge and through the gate. All the while she would tell them this was her penance for murdering her own child.

Now it happened that in a nearby land, there was a Lord called Teirnyon who kept a famous mare. She was the finest in any kingdom. Every year on the first of May she foaled, and every year the foal was gone missing on the second of May. One year Teirnyon said to his wife, "I shall keep watch all night in the stable, and may the vengeance of hell be on me if I cannot learn what becomes of the missing foals."

So Teirnyon took sword in hand and hid himself in the hay. Soon he heard a loud thrashing in the hedge outside. Then a great hairy arm came in through the window and its huge claw snatched up the foal by the mane. Teirnyon raised up his sword and struck off the arm at the elbow. The claw fell to the floor and a tumultuous wailing commenced outside the window. Teirnyon charged out into the night after the monster, but it entered the thicket where it was too dark to see. The Lord returned to the stable and saw the claw was open and twitching. What should lie in it but a baby boy, wrapped in clothes of royal satin. Teirnyon took the baby to his wife where she slept. "Lady, I shant disturb you if you're sleeping," said he.

"The sound of your voice could never disturb me," said the wife dreamily.

"Then here is a babe for you," said Teirnyon, "since you've long desired one."

"Husband," she cried taking the babe into her arms, "by the gods, what have you been up to?"

Teirnyon told her the whole story. They knew by the babe's garment that he was born of gentle lineage. They baptized him and nursed him in the court until he was one year old. He walked stoutly about and sized up equally to a child of three. After a second year he was as a child of six, and at the age of four, he bribed the stablemen to let him take the horses to water. The foal that was born the same night was reared with care so the boy could have him when he was ready to ride.

One day they heard of the tidings of the Lady Rhiannon and the penance she was doing for murdering her child. Teirnyon inquired into the matter and found there was much reason to doubt the accusations against her. He pondered the sad event, and how it coincided with the appearance of his foster son. Teirnyon asked a nobleman who knew Lord Powel to look upon the boy. Upon seeing the boy, the nobleman was struck by his great resemblance to Lord Powel. Teirnyon's heart grew heavy. In his mind there was no doubt that his foster son was indeed Powel's child, and he told his wife it was wrong of them to keep him. The Lady agreed they should take the boy and relieve poor Rhiannon of her suffering.

They equipped themselves to travel, and it was not long before they arrived at the palace gate. Rhiannon called out, "Chieftain, go no farther. I shall carry you and all your company across the bridge and through the gate, for this is my penance for murdering my own son."

"Fair Lady," said Teirnyon, "think not that you will bear me or any of my company upon your back! For with me is your own dear son who was robbed from you the day he was born."

"If this be true," cried Rhiannon, "then it's an end to my trouble, and the onset of great joy." Thus the boy was named *Pryderi*, which means, *an end to trouble*. The matter was looked into by the court, and Rhiannon's innocence was soon proved, and made known throughout the land. As for Pryderi, he grew to be the most comely and skilled lad in the kingdom, for he was reared with the love and wisdom of his parents and his foster parents too. This tale came from the lips of Welsh bards who loved Rhiannon and never once believed the indictment against her. All the while she was doing penance, they said not a dubious word, spoke only of her goodness, and prayed for a swift end to her trouble.

UNSTABLE IDENTITY | DISENFRANCHISEMENT | MISPLACED BLAME | FALSE WORDS AND INSTIGATING TROUBLE: Most of us at one time or another have been blamed for something we did not do. This tale gives us courage when we feel misunderstood or wrongfully blamed. For a woman named Janelle, this tale cut close to the bone, and she took it to heart. In the course of an adversarial divorce she was falsely accused of child abuse. Suddenly what was most essential to her identity, her sense of herself as a good mother, was called into question. False allegations were made and all sorts of experts began probing into her home life. Every sign of stress exhibited by her children became "evidence" of her abuse and neglect. Janelle already felt anxious and guilty about having to take a second job, and having less time with her kids when they needed her most. "To be accused, like that, when I was already on shaky ground, I found myself thinking, 'If I were really a good mother, this wouldn't be happening to me.'" Rhiannon's story drove home the point that good people do get wrongly accused. Janelle took comfort in the notion that the truth would come out eventually, and it did. "I thought the accusation would permanently cloud people's opinion of me, but it didn't work that way. People actually reached out more." In the months following resolution, I noted Janelle's whole stance in life shifted from one of tentativeness to one of confidence. She and I talked this over and concluded that her ordeal had been a kind of initiation. "It was a trial by fire," she said. "I came away from it with a greater sense of my own strength, and more trust in myself. I won't be so easily pushed around in the future."

HARDSHIP AS AN OPPORTUNITY | PROLONGED OR COMPLICATED GRIEF |LOVING KINDNESS | COOPERATION AND DEVOTION | FOSTERING AND ADOPTION | ADVOCACY FOR CHILDREN | HUMILITY | EMOTIONAL RESILIENCE | LOSS, COURAGE, AND TRANSFORMATION | COURAGE, INTEGRITY, RESILIENCE: The Celtic Romance tells us that wherever there is big love, there is also failure, tragedy, or loss. This need not be seen as maudlin, or pessimistic, but "of a truth," as Lord Powel says. No heart stays aloft forever, and no love goes untested. If our own shortcomings do not betray us, circumstances will. In this tale, Rhiannon, Powel, Pryderi, Terinyon, and his wife, all endure great loss and sacrifice, yet the resilience, humility, and goodness of each of their characters prevails. Love subjected to such tests can become great. All four parents transcend their need to lay sole claim to the child. They find an inclusive, expansive way to coparent Pryderi. This tale sets a fine example of gracious and cooperative coparenting. It serves as an inspiration for foster parents, stepparents, and divorced parents striving to act as allies in blended families.

The Stolen Child

SCOTLAND | (1,869 words)

Long ago on a gray day, a young mother walked along the edge of a high sea cliff, carrying her young babe in her arms. Now if you or I had seen her, we would have thought she was a girl carrying her baby brother. But no, the child was hers and he was all she had in the world. It had been a long while since they'd had anything to eat or drink. The young mother heard the sound of trickling water coming from the cliff's edge. She lay her babe in the heather and climbed down to a rocky ledge to get a drink. She drank deeply of the sweet spring water, and turned to climb back up. She must have placed her foot on a slippery spot, for she lost her footing, hit her head, and was knocked out cold.

It happened that two women of the Faery race came walking by. They spied the babe lying in the heather. There is nothing more highly prized among Faeries than a human babe. The first Faery said to the second, "What a fine wee babe."

"Aye, fine indeed," said the other. "I see neither mother nor father about. 'Twould be our part to take the child and care for him ourselves."

"'Twould," said the first. "This is no place for a lone wee babe, for if the wind and the cold don't kill him, the hunger will." And so they picked him up and went on their way.

You might think the young mother died there on the ledge, but no. It happened that on the sea below two fishermen came along in their dory. The elder glanced up and spied her on the ledge. "Look there on that high ledge, and tell me what you see."

"A heap of old rags," said the younger.

"'Tis a body, to be sure," said the elder, and they brought the dory in to have a closer look. They tied the boat to a rock, hoisted a fishnet and some rope over their shoulders, and climbed up the cliff. "'Tis a bonny wee lass!" said the elder. They placed the young woman in the net and carefully lowered her down to the boat. The fishermen took her home to their village and gave her into the care of an old midwife. The midwife had the knowledge of healing herbs and she knew just how to care for the young woman. Soon enough the midwife noticed milk seeping from her patient's breasts and she sent the villagers out to look for an infant. The villagers searched high and low, but found no trace.

In a few days' time, the young woman came 'round. She sat bolt upright in the bed, and cried, "Where is my son? Where is my dearest wee babe?" The young woman tried to get up but her broken bones would not let her. "Be still, Lass," said the old midwife. "We've searched far and wide, and seen no trace of your child."

The young mother wept a flood of tears but she knew in her heart her child was not dead. She knew it would be up to her to find him. "I'll not rest til I find my son," she told the old midwife.

"I've no doubt you'll find him," said the old woman, but first we must heal these broken bones. Such a search as you're in for requires strong legs and a strong back."

Weeks went by. The milk stopped flowing from the young mother's breasts, but she didn't lose hope. The day finally came when our heroine was able to get up from her bed. Soon she was strong enough to set out on her journey. The old midwife packed her a blanket and a bundle of food and said, "You're always welcome here. Don't forget to come back and pay me a visit. There is one thing I want you to remember, and that is this: you have gifts in you that are yet to be discovered." With that the young woman said good-bye to the villagers and set out on her journey.

She searched every village and croft, every hill, glen and crag. She inquired of all she met, but found no trace of her son. Then one night she made her bed under an oak tree near a green hill. When the moon rose and cast its light upon the hill, she was astonished to see the hill open up, and a procession of Faeries emerge. There were Faeries on horseback, Faeries on foot, Faeries singing and dancing, Faeries wearing velvet caps and cloaks of fur, Faeries with golden slippers with bells on the toes. That night she fell asleep and dreamt she was talking to the old midwife.

In this dream the old midwife handed her a warm mug of tea and said, "There is nothing Faeries love more than a human child."

This aroused great hope in the young mother. She believed her child might indeed be alive and well, living with the Faeries underground. "How does one gain entrance into a Faery hill?" she asked.

The midwife replied, "It takes one splendid gift to gain entrance, and one splendid gift to get out again." At that the young woman awoke. She heard faint singing and the sound of bells growing ever louder. She sat up to see the Faeries proceeding back into their hill again. When the sun rose, she nibbled some bread and studied the Faery hill. It looked lovely and green like any other, and there was no trace of an opening to be seen.

In her bones she knew that her son was inside that hill, among the Faeries, but how she would retrieve him she knew not. She wondered how she might acquire a splendid gift to gain entrance and a splendid gift to exit again. She rolled up her blanket and walked to the sea. There she sat gazing out at the water, listening to the sound of the waves rolling in. She had not a penny with which to buy a fine gift, and she had no skills to make one. She felt ill-equipped for any such task and she despised herself for it. A great weariness came upon her. She put her head in her hands and wept until she fell asleep.

She awoke to a pleasing and mysterious sound. She looked around and saw a curved whalebone beside her. The wind rushing through it produced a melodic hum. The curve of it reminded her of a harp. She got up and without thinking she took it in her arms and held it as she had seen harpists do. In the sand nearby were strands of gut from an old fishnet. She took a strand and began fretting it through the bone in imitation of a harp. When she had finished, she was amazed at how much it resembled a real harp. She plucked the strings, and though she didn't know how to play, the sound was lovely, and she knew she had a gift to please even the most particular Faery.

The wind began to blow, and without thinking she picked up the remains of the net. She went to the bluff and grabbed a handful of the eider down that had collected there in the grass. Everyone knows there is no down more pearly and light, more full of sheen than down from the eider ducks who make their nests on the bluff. She went from one clump of grass to the next until her apron was full of eider down. Carefully she placed the down into the knots of the net until she'd produced a fine eider cloak. The wind lifted the cloak and she found it light as a feather and bright as a sun-drenched cloud. She knew she now had two gifts to delight even the most particular Faery.

That evening she returned to the Faery hill, and made her bed in the nearby trees out of sight. As the moon rose, the Faery hill opened. One by one and two by two the faeries emerged from the hill. They proceeded, singing and laughing through the glen. She tried to sleep, but sleep would not come. Just before dawn she heard the Faeries returning. She stood up and readied herself with the two fine gifts, the cloak and the harp in hand. All but two Faery women had reentered the hill. The young mother ran up to them and held the white cloak for them to see. The eider feathers glistened in the first rosy rays of the morning sun. "I must have that cloak," said one Faery woman. "I saw it first," said the other. She let go of the cloak and let the two of them argue as she strode into the Faery hill, harp in hand.

Inside the Faery hill was nothing short of a grand palace. It had a marble floor, carved stone pillars and tapestries of gold and silver. The Faery guards rushed forward to seize her, but before they could she held up the harp and struck a chord. So sweet and irresistible was the sound, all the Faeries fell silent. Whatever weakness humans have for fine music, Faeries have a hundredfold. "Come forward with that harp," said a deep, resonant voice. The crowd parted and she saw the Faery king himself seated on a high golden throne. She plucked the chord again, and all the Faeries went into a kind of trance.

As the young woman neared the throne she saw a golden crib right beside the king, and in it she could hear her own wee babe cooing. At once she felt great excitement and great terror. It took all her courage to stride smoothly and boldly toward the king. "I must have that harp," said the king.

"I must have that child," said the young woman.

"I'll give you the babe's weight in gold," said the king. The young woman plucked the strings a third time and this time the king himself weakened. "The harp first," he said.

"The child first," she countered. The king nodded to one of his servants, and the babe was scooped up and handed into its mother's arms. The king took the harp and began to play. So sweet and plaintive was the sound that the Faeries went into a trance. They seemed not to notice the young woman as she turned and ran out into the light of day. Babe in arms, she ran like the wind and didn't look back. She left behind the blanket and her bundle of bread. She had nothing to feed the wee babe, but as she held him, a small miracle occurred. The milk came back to her breasts and she was quite able to feed him.

She took her son back to the fishing village and they received a great welcome. She moved into a little cottage and took odd jobs here and there. Her son grew to be a strong little boy whom everyone loved. As for the young woman, she made a habit of going to the shore and gathering up whatever remnants had washed in on the tide. She became known far and wide as one who makes fine things of cast-off remnants and shards.

ADVOCACY FOR CHILDREN | GOOD MOTHERS | WOMEN'S ESTEEM AND EMPOWERMENT | SELF-RELIANCE: This tale is encouraging to all parents, for parenting under the best of circumstances requires stamina, creativity, and resourcefulness. The tale is especially heartening to single mothers. The will to survive and create healthy lives for their children seems to give some single mothers extraordinary stamina and gumption. This tale salutes those like Karla who considered this her touchstone story. "I used to take a lot of drugs," she said, "but now I have my son to think about. I have to be strong and make a decent life for him. Now I have a reason to make something of myself."

CREATIVE COURAGE | THE JOY OF LIFE-AFFIRMING WORK | HUMILITY | MORE-THAN-HUMAN WORLD: This tale speaks to those times when we feel ourselves to be utterly lacking in inner resources. The young mother feels she has no abilities and nothing to offer. She hits rock bottom and stays there for a spell. This tale reminds us that by following our dreams and by humbly engaging with the raw materials of the world (i.e., found feathers and bone), we too can create something of beauty, integrity, and purpose. If we are lucky, these creations lead us, as they lead the young mother, to life-affirming work.

WOMEN'S INITIATION | HARDSHIP AS AN OPPORTUNITY | EMOTIONAL RESILIENCE | CHANGE AS AN OPPORTUNITY TO CREATE ANEW | INSPIRATION LOST AND REGAINED: Mircea Eliade, in his book *Rites and Symbols of Initiation*, wrote that the ordeals depicted in folk and fairy tales parallel the initiatory rites once practiced by ancestral groups. This story is a particularly good example. Like an initiate, the young mother descends into the darkness of oblivion and experiences the exhaustion of her will. She surrenders her ego, and in so doing, receives guidance and inspiration from mysterious sources. With renewed vision, she consciously enters the Otherworld, bargains with the king, reclaims her child, and is welcomed back into the village. There she begins anew. These age-old metaphors still hold meaning for women on the precipice of change. Wendy, a woman recovering from breast cancer, took this story to heart as mirroring the ordeals she had gone through: "When you're that close to death, you feel stripped of everything. You begin to feel the interplay between relying on your own power, and having to surrender to a greater power, knowing when to hold on, and when to let go."

HELP FROM WISE ELDERS | ELDER WISDOM | LOVING KINDNESS | HEALING TOUCH | DREAM AS GUIDE: Without the perception and persistence of the old fisherman who found her, the young mother would surely have died. Without the love and healing skills of the midwife, she might never have regained her strength and courage. The secret to entering the hill came from the old midwife through a dream. Here there is an almost mystical quality to the way guidance and strength are imparted from elder to youth. Some would simply say the midwife spoke to our heroine through her dream. Others would say our heroine had internalized the old woman's kindness, and that internalization showed itself in the dream. Still others would say that the old midwife had awakened the wise old woman within our heroine, and that the inner wise woman spoke through the dream. We may never know for sure which of these ways of seeing is most apt, but one thing is clear: during times of distress and transition, wise elders are crucial. Their guidance and blessings inspire and soothe us as nothing else can. They help us to transcend our small egos and find our greater self.

Gold Tree and Silver Tree

SCOTLAND | (1,910 words)

(too frightening for small children)

Long ago there lived a young princess by the name of Gold Tree. She was as lovely a child as had ever walked the green hills of Scotland. Her mother had died, and Gold Tree was very sad, but she did not lose heart, for her father was a kind man. He loved Gold Tree dearly, and did everything in his power to comfort her. As time passed he found a new wife, and this is when Gold Tree's troubles began.

The new wife was called Silver Tree. She was a beautiful woman who thought a great deal of herself and little of others. Her greatest worry was that some day she would meet someone lovelier than herself. The instant Silver Tree set eyes upon young Gold Tree, she despised her, for she feared the girl's beauty would someday surpass her own.

The years went by and Gold Tree became a beautiful young woman. One day she and Silver Tree took a walk together in the forest. Silver Tree liked to go to a certain pond where she could sit on a rock and look down at her reflection in the still, dark water. On that particular day there happened to be a trout swimming near the surface of the water. "Little Trout," said the queen, "won't you tell me, am I not the loveliest woman in all the world?"

"No indeed," answered the trout.

The shock of his reply nearly took her breath away. "Who is it then?" asked the queen.

"Why it is the princess, Gold Tree."

Silver Tree was so taken aback she was speechless. Without a word of explanation she whirled around and stormed back to the palace. Gold Tree followed and each time she asked what was wrong, Silver Tree huffed at her in disgust and walked faster. When they reached the palace the queen took to her bed and grew violently ill. She refused to eat or drink until she had worked herself into quite a desperate state. The king feared his beautiful wife might die. He begged her to eat and said he would do everything in his power to help her. She pulled him close and said, "There is but one thing that would save me from my death, but I do not think you would obtain it for me."

"These words do not do me justice, Dear Wife," said the king, "for there is nothing in my power I wouldn't do for you."

"Very well then," said Silver Tree, "I shall recover only when Gold Tree's heart is torn from her breast and served to me for my supper."

The king thought his wife to be deliriously ill, for nothing else would cause such mad rantings. He sent a servant out to kill an old he-goat. "Give the meat to the country folk, all but the heart," said the king. "The heart must be dressed and cooked and served to the queen for her supper." The servant went out and did as he was told.

It happened on that very day that a prince came calling from far away. He was courteous and good, handsome and gentle, and he sought Gold Tree's hand in marriage. Gold Tree talked it over with her father. They did not mention Silver Tree, but in their hearts they both knew it would be best if Gold Tree never saw her again. She packed her things and set sail at once. When the ship disappeared into the distance, the king announced that his dear daughter had suddenly died. People throughout the land wept and grieved, all except Silver Tree. She lay in bed and when the goat's heart was served to her on a silver plate, she believed it to be the heart of Gold Tree. She tasted it, and was satisfied. Immediately she got up from her sickbed and was in her right mind once again. She dressed in somber black like the other mourners, but she skipped lightly about the palace as if it were a holiday.

The months passed by and Silver Tree was content. As for the princess Gold Tree, she found great joy, for her prince loved her as truly as the day was long. Each day was happier than the last. Then one day Silver Tree went walking through the woods to view her reflection in the still pond. When she arrived there and gazed at her image in the water, she saw the little trout swimming back and forth.

"There you are, little trout," she said. "Tell me, am I not the most beautiful woman in all the world?"

"No indeed," replied the little trout who knew all things and could not help but speak the truth.

"What do you mean?" asked the queen. "If I am not the most beautiful, then who is?"

"Why the princess, Gold Tree."

"But that's impossible," cried the queen. "I ate her heart myself, and gave her a grand funeral."

"Not so," replied the trout. "She married a rich prince and lives happily with him in a faraway land."

Silver Tree went home fuming. She couldn't bear the thought of Gold Tree's beauty pleasing admiring eyes, even in a faraway land. She ordered a ship ready to set sail immediately, and off she went, across the sea to put a stop to it once and for all. She carried with her a small vial of poison and a briar wand with sharp thorns.

It happened that Gold Tree's husband was off on a hunt the day Silver Tree's ship sailed into port. Gold Tree looked out her window and saw her father's flag flying high upon the mast. She knew at once that it was Silver Tree, come to destroy her happiness. She locked herself in the tower and refused to come out. The servants came and knocked at the door, saying, "Your mother misses you, and she's made the long journey just to see that you're all right." Gold Tree still would not come out. Silver Tree herself came to the door and said, "I've come all this way to see you, Dear Daughter. Would you not so much as put your finger out the keyhole so I can give it a kiss?"

Gold Tree did not wish to be unkind. She put her finger through the keyhole. Silver Tree told the servants to go so they could talk over family matters in private. When the servants were gone, Silver Tree stuck Gold Tree's finger with a poison thorn. Gold Tree fell down dead. Silver Tree went back to her ship and sailed away, pleased that she had seen to the deed herself this time. "If you want something done right," she thought, "you have to do it yourself."

When the prince returned, he was brokenhearted to find his dear wife dead. He couldn't bear to have her buried, so he kept her body there in the tower on a velvet blanket on a lovely little hand-carved bed. There she lay for weeks and then months. Death did not change her. She lay as one sleeping, so when her husband was lonely he went to her. Sometimes he talked and sometimes he wept.

As the years passed, the prince's advisors told him to remarry. "The people need a princess to rule beside the prince," they said. At last he conceded and they selected for him a woman who was noble and wise. The prince respected his new wife, but she could never replace Gold Tree. The couple ruled the land together, but Gold Tree still dwelled in his heart. The new princess understood this for she was wise and had a kind heart.

One day she went to the tower and gazed at the body of Gold Tree. "How lovely she is," thought the second wife. She looked closely at the hands and noticed something. "What's this?" she said aloud and plucked the thorn from Gold Tree's finger. When she did so, the color came back to Gold Tree's cheeks and she began breathing. Then she sat upright and looked around. The two women began talking and it didn't take long before each had told the other every detail of her story.

That evening the second wife said to the husband, "Dearest, I have a surprise for you. Your beloved Gold Tree is not dead after all. She has come back to you." When Gold Tree came into the room the prince nearly fainted. When he realized the truth of his good fortune his heart leapt for joy. Gold Tree and the prince embraced. The second wife said, "I will leave you two, for your sorrow has been great and you should be together as you were meant to be."

"No," said Gold Tree, "you saved my life. If not for you I'd have remained in that tower forever. You must stay with us. You and I will be as sisters." Gold Tree took her husband's hand and said, "She shall be our advisor," and the prince agreed. The second wife stayed on, as their advisor, and was as dear to them as a sister.

You might think they lived forever in peace, but no. For once again Silver Tree went to the still pond. She put the same old question to the trout and the trout gave the same old answer. Silver Tree wasted no time in obtaining a vial of poison. She ordered ready her finest long ship and set sail at once.

The prince was away attending to matters of state. Gold Tree looked out the window and saw her father's ship coming to shore. "It's Silver Tree!" she cried. "She'll never leave me in peace. She won't be happy until I'm dead." Her advisor said, "Don't be afraid. We'll go to the harbor and greet Silver Tree. That will surprise her."

They donned their fine cloaks and went to the harbor. When Silver Tree stepped off the ship they were there on the ramp to greet her. "Welcome, Queen Silver Tree," said the advisor. "My, but you have come a long way. You must love Gold Tree very much."

"Indeed I do," replied Silver Tree, "so much so that I have brought her a taste of the finest wine in all the world." She held out a beautiful silver goblet with poisoned wine in it. "Please, Dear Daughter, accept this loving cup."

The advisor said, "Queen Silver Tree, it is customary in our land for those offering a loving cup to take the first sip."

"I'll not deny the customs of the land," said Silver Tree raising the cup to her lips. She planned to keep her lips closed and merely make the appearance of swallowing, but when the goblet touched her lips, a large wave rolled beneath them, causing the ramp to sway. The wine flowed into Silver Tree's mouth and down her throat. She gasped and fell dead. They gave her a burial at sea, and no one mourned, for they knew she had taken a fatal dose of her own medicine.

After that when Gold Tree saw her father's long ship coming into port, her heart filled with gladness instead of fear. She lived to a ripe old age, long enough to see her daughters and granddaughters grow lovelier with each passing day. It pleased Gold Tree to gaze at their faces and behold therein the beauty of her own mother's face.

AGE APPROPRIATENESS: *Some stories are too troubling for young children, and this is one of them. There is little actual violence here, but no theme is more disturbing than that of a presumed nurturer who plots the demise of a child. Teens mature at different rates, but I find most teens, fourteen and up are capable of learning from this story without being traumatized by it.*

ANIMALS AS HELPERS AND TEACHERS | THE MORE-THAN-HUMAN WORLD | FOREST AS A PLACE OF TRUTH AND TRANSFORMATION: As is the case with fish in many Celtic tales, the little trout in this one is a wisdom figure, an oracle of truth. Among our ancestors it was believed that sacred places and creatures possessed all knowledge, and that we could expand our understanding by learning to tune in. If the wisdom of the more-than-human world were widely acknowledged today, we might be more eager to protect old-growth forests and pristine streams. Telling this tale in intimate seminars, I often ask what listeners identified with in the story. After some thought, a burly wilderness hiker said, "At first I thought I could only identify with the innocence of Gold Tree, and then I remembered doing my AA work. I went camping alone many times, to come to terms with my more difficult truths. I can't relate to Silver Tree's superficial question to the trout, but I can relate to going into the woods with your most probing questions, and being startled by the answers you get."

HEALING MOTHER WOUNDS: "Mother-love" is as crucial as food. Whether it comes from a parent, grandparent, sibling, or other surrogate, care from a consistent nurturer is the foundation for a child's well-being in the world. Stories like this one shake us at the core, because we sense how devastating it is for a growing child to receive poisonous emotions in place of love. It is especially insidious that Silver Tree's malicious narcissism is disguised as affection.

"It's crazy-making," said Sondra, a thirty-two-year-old who took this story to heart. "My mother phones me every day with supposed concern, but her real intent is to destroy my confidence." Sondra typically allowed her mother to undermine her before important events. "I keep hoping Mom will support me in a loving way, and meanwhile, I keep swallowing the poison. When the phone rings, I panic like Gold Tree when she sees the ship, but I don't do anything to protect myself. I just pick up the phone and take what Mom dishes out." Sondra's "rebellious" sister and her "independent" brother managed to keep their mother's emotional toxicity at bay. Sondra learned from their examples and from the story to be her own protective friend.

FAMILIAL HOMICIDE | THE FUTILITY OF VIOLENCE | MISUSE OF POWER | DENIAL AND DECEPTION | DOMESTIC VIOLENCE: Silver Tree's actions put us in touch with a dark tragedy in the human story. I worked with a thirty-three year old woman named Caitlin whose mentally ill mother had tried to kill her several times in childhood. "I can't tell you how much this story means to me. My mother is like Silver Tree, by all appearances, she's fine. You can't tell by looking at her that she put rat poison in my brother's and my food. People say stuff like, 'Your mother is so charming and thoughtful,' and I just want to scream. Every shred of sanity and self-respect I have I've earned through hard work. This is the only story that really hits the nail on the head. My brother loves it too."

ENVY AND SELF-IMAGE | JEALOUSY, ENVY, AND COMPETITION | UNHEALTHY COMPETITION | EXPANDING NARROW DEFINITIONS OF BEAUTY | SISTERLY SOLIDARITY: If you work closely with a group of women, or teenage girls, sooner or later the themes of beauty, vanity, and envy are bound to arise. This tale illustrates how extreme vanity and envy can poison lives and destroy relationships. Most females over the age of fourteen benefit from hearing this tale as an invitation to discuss these and other interpersonal issues such as competition between sisters and friends, and between mothers and daughters. This tale usually gives rise to a wide array of responses, for it touches upon many wounds and woes for women, including the fear of not being pretty enough, and anger about the narrow definition of beauty imposed by the cosmetic and entertainment industries. Women value the healing bonds of sisterhood portrayed in the tale, and find it encouraging that goodness, fairness, and cooperation win out. The tale encourages teenage girls to support each other rather than try to outdo each other. It models flexibility, innovation, inclusiveness, and the importance of appreciation between trusting friends.

A NOTE ON WICKED STEPMOTHERS: *People sometimes resent the "bum rap" given to stepmothers in fairy tales. It is important to honor stepmothering, since it turns out to be a meaningful role touching many lives. I have a personal stake in this, since I am a stepmother who mothered four stepchildren full-time during their growing-up years. When they were young, I feared that stories with evil step-mothers would make them distrust me, so I avoided such tales.*

When they got older my grandmother said, "Your kids are bright enough not to buy into stereotypes." Trusting she was right, I told this tale to Oona, the eldest who was then fourteen.

"I love that fish," Oona said, "and the way Silver Tree gets what she deserves in the end."

I asked, "Do you think the story suggests all stepmoms are mean?"

Oona replied, "No. It totally depends on the person." Then she added, "When we first came to live with you, I was afraid you would be mean, but you turned out to be nice instead, and I'm glad you're our stepmom." We went on to talk about what it had been like for her to let a second mother-figure into her life, and the blessings and challenges of bonds between women. We both felt grateful that the story had opened the door for this talk.

Teens who hear lots of stories and who are old enough to grasp metaphor, understand that the "good mother" can be found in the heart of any caring loved one, an older sibling, a father, or a surrogate parent of either gender. Wise teens also perceive that the "wicked stepmother" represents a self-centered, begrudging approach to life. Most teens are capable of identifying that anyone can harbor such an attitude. When handled intelligently, wicked stepmother tales evoke discussion rather than promote stereotypes.

Old Sultan

GERMAN | (677 words)

ABOUT THE BROTHERS GRIMM: *Early in the nineteenth century, brothers Jakob and Wilhelm Grimm collected tales from elder tellers in the towns and villages of Germany. In 1819 they published 210 stories in the now world famous GRIMMS' TALES FOR YOUNG AND OLD. This and the following five tales are from that collection. Like other fairy tales, they elevate nobility of character above all else. They inspire resilience, and teach us the importance of observation and discernment. They encourage us to find love, and to do all in our power to co-create our unique destinies with aid from wise ones including animals, angels, and elders.*

Long ago there was a loyal old dog called Sultan. After giving many years service to a farmer, Sultan grew old. One by one his teeth fell out so that when he bit down it was only gum meeting gum. His eyes had gone milky with age, and his eyesight was no longer sharp. One day the farmer said to his wife, "Sultan no longer pulls his weight around here. Tomorrow I shall have to shoot him."

The wife felt sorry for the old dog, "Sultan has served us long and well. Shall we not care for him in his old age?"

"How impractical," said the farmer. "Do I look rich? If thieves broke into the barn, Sultan would sleep right through it. We have cared for him as long as he has served us, but those days are over."

Old Sultan lay snoozing not far off. Those of you who love dogs won't be surprised to know he understood every word. That evening Sultan slipped off to the woods to commiserate with his friend the wolf. "Don't worry, my friend," said the wolf. "Tomorrow when your master and mistress go to cut hay, they will bring along the child as they always do. They think me far more blood-thirsty than I really am, and we shall make use of their fear. I shall creep up and carry the child off by the collar. You, my friend, shall charge after me, as you did when you were a young guard dog. I shall drop the child and run, and you shall look the hero."

Sultan loved the strategy, and the next day he and the wolf carried it off exactly as planned. The master and mistress shrieked desperately as the wolf ran off with their child, and when Sultan brought the child back to them, they fell upon both child and dog with kisses and tears of joy. "We shall feed and protect you as long as your old heart keeps beating!" exclaimed the farmer. "Dear Wife," he said, "let's take pause to warm some broth for old Sultan. And while we're at it, let's give him my pillow that he might rest his old bones in comfort."

In the days to come, Sultan was given all the amenities an old dog could wish for. One evening his friend the wolf paid him a visit. They spoke of how well their strategy had worked. "We are good friends," said the wolf. "I scratch your back and you scratch mine. Surely if I go after one of the farmer's plump sheep, you will look the other way."

"Don't count on it," replied Sultan. "I cannot scratch your back by betraying my master."

"You'll be sorry for this," said the wolf storming off in a huff. The wolf stewed over the matter all night. The next day he sent the boar to challenge Sultan to come into the forest and settle it after sundown. Poor Sultan had no one to stand beside him except the old barn cat, who was missing one leg. As the cat limped along beside Sultan in the moonlight, its silver tail stood straight up with fear. From a distance the cat's tail resembled a sword. "Just how harsh was your challenge?" the wolf asked the boar.

"Not that harsh," said the boar, hiding under the brush in fear. The wolf suddenly felt foolish and jumped up a tree to hide.

When Sultan and the cat arrived at the designated place, all they saw of the wolf and the boar was the boar's ear sticking out from under the leaves. The cat mistook it for a mouse, and pounced upon the boar's head and bit it forcefully. The boar cried out, "I don't have any quarrel with you! It's the one up the tree who is looking for trouble."

Sultan and the cat looked up to see the wolf in the tree. The wolf felt foolish, and climbed down. "Sultan," he said, "we are old friends. Let's not allow this problem to divide us." Old Sultan agreed, and they remained friends 'til the end of their days.

ANIMALS AS HELPERS AND TEACHERS | THE MORE-THAN-HUMAN WORLD | INTANGIBLE TREASURES | GENEROSITY | GRATITUDE | LOVING KINDNESS: Old Sultan is more than a watchdog. He is as sensitive as any human. He is full of feeling and loyalty; he has friendships and an inner life. No one who has spent time paying attention to dogs, cats, birds, or other creatures would deny this level of their reality. The tale reminds us to regard the non-human creatures of the world as full beings in their own right, and thus perhaps to extend to them the gratitude, generosity, and loving kindness they deserve.

LOYALTY: Today we often wonder if life-long loyalty is a thing of the past. The very concept of loyalty comes into question as we change jobs, careers, residences, spouses, and football teams. This tale reminds us that we cannot be practical and mercenary about everything. Some bonds need to be honored for life. Relationships that no longer serve a practical purpose might still be crucial to the heart and soul.

RECIPROCITY | SCARCITY | MISGUIDED LEADERSHIP | JUSTICE AND FAIRNESS | WORTHY USE OF DECEPTION: This tale inspires intelligent discussion on the moral dilemmas surrounding such topics as reciprocity, deception, and scarcity. Useful questions to illicit discussion include: When is it foolish to provide for someone who does not give in return? When is it appropriate to do so? Another question people love to discuss is: Did the life-and-death circumstances justify deceiving the farmer? Was it fair of the wolf to expect Sultan to repay him by betraying his master? Discerning right action from wrong is a matter of nuance, open to endless interpretation. The story provides no definitive answers, but helps us to give voice to our own moral codes.

LETTING GO | ONGOING QUARRELS | FORGIVENESS | DISPUTE RESOLUTION: This tale can be heartening to people stuck in a power struggle. It illustrates how powerful another can seem when we are in conflict, and reminds us that their sword might not be as menacing as it seems. The tale also points to embarrassing positions we can all wind up in. It illustrates how to back down after having made excessive demands, how to let go, how to extend forgiveness, and how to make up after a quarrel.

The Goose Girl at the Spring

GERMANY | (2,281 words)

(for background on Grimms' fairy tales see p. 91)

*L*ong ago, in a lonely spot high in the mountains, there lived an old woman. Her cottage was nestled in a small clearing amid a vast forest. There she kept a fine flock of geese—the sort whose feathers are used for pillows and quilts. Each day the old woman took her basket through the woods to an abandoned orchard where little apples and pears grew wild from the scraggly old trees. Once the basket was filled with fruit, she stuffed the edges with handfuls of sweet grass and clover for her geese. Farmers in the region gossiped amongst themselves that she was older than the hills—unnaturally old—and must be a witch to have lived so long. Such folk frowned and hurried past when they met her in the woods. She smiled and greeted them cheerfully, nonetheless.

One day a handsome young man ventured down the path. Birds chirped and the breeze lifted the boughs of the trees making the sun's light dance here and there upon the forest floor. He came upon the old woman packing grass and clover between the apples and pears in her basket. She was a slight little thing, and he felt sorry to think of her carrying such a load. "Good morning, Grandmother!" he called in the customary way.

"Good morning, Lad," she merrily replied.

"Is there no one to carry your load?" he asked.

"Only my granddaughter, but she's busy minding the geese."

"With all due respect," he ventured, " it looks too heavy for the likes of you."

"Well," said the old woman, "the rich turn away from such chores, but we peasants have a saying, 'Don't turn around, you'll only see how bent your back is.'" She laughed and winked at the lad, who took the joke well considering he was the son of a wealthy count.

"May I help you with your load, then?" he asked.

"About time you offered!" she said, jabbing him in the ribs. She hoisted the basket to her shoulder and then onto his and he sank with the weight it.

"You must have rocks in here," he exclaimed.

"Don't publicize your coddled upbringing," said the old woman.

"How far is your place?" asked the lad, trying to buck up.

"No more than an hour's walk," she replied, smiling at him with gleaming eyes and long yellow teeth. She skipped lightly up the trail. The young count had never labored so hard in all his life. He could barely keep up. Half-way to the cottage the woman took a running leap and landed on top of the basket. It was all the lad could do to keep his footing and stay upright. She was a tiny wisp of a woman, and yet weighed on him as heavily as a boulder.

The lad was panting by now, and his coat was soggy with sweat. "If you insist on riding up there," he said, "I must stop and rest."

"Nonsense!" said the old woman. "Rest when you get to my place, unless, of course, you're a pampered little gentleman who can't carry a measly bushel of pears." The young count was furious, and tried to throw off the load, but no amount of wriggling would loosen it from his shoulders. At last the old woman jumped down. "Dear Young Sir," she chided, "don't make matters worse by losing your temper. Why look at you. You're as red as an old tom turkey, and twice as flustered!"

The lad rallied strength and forced himself onward. The old woman went behind and each time he slowed down, she laughed and lashed him with a switch. His legs trembled as if made of water. Just when he thought he could go no further, they arrived at the cottage.

"Daughter!" called, the old woman. "Bring a cool drink for the good gentleman who helped me." When the goose girl came round the corner, her looks so shocked the young count that he had to turn away. From the neck down she was a girl, right enough, but her face was gray and creased like the skin on the foot of a goose. She handed him a dipper of water. Then the old woman said, "Go inside, Daughter. This young fellow has earned a rest. Besides, I wouldn't want to leave you alone with him. You two might fall in love." Then she smirked at the count and said, "Find a nice spot to rest. I'll be back with a small reward for your trouble." He lay down in the clearing amid the primroses and wild thyme and fell asleep.

When the old woman returned she nudged him and said, "Get up, now. You can't lollygag all day." Then more gently she said, "I've given you a rough time, haven't I?" Before he could answer she went on, "Well, you're young and you'll survive it." Then she handed him a small box carved from an emerald. "Take it, you've earned it," she said. "It will bring you good luck." He thanked the old woman, said good-bye, and went on his way.

Traveling onward, he felt refreshed for a time, but as he progressed the forest grew darker and thicker until no light came through the branches above. It was hard to tell if it was night, day, or twilight. Each turn looked the same as the last and he wondered if he were walking in circles. Finally, he sat down, gave over to fatigue, and fell into a deep sleep.

When he awoke, he couldn't tell how long he'd been sleeping. He got up, walked down the road, and soon came to a clearing. The sun shone down on a sparkling brook in the middle of a sloping green meadow. Fragrant wild flowers danced on the breeze.

Across the valley stood a formidable castle surrounded by a moat. Its drawbridge was lowered and out came six men in red coats, riding sleek horses with braided tails. The horsemen rode in twos and came out to greet the young count. They escorted him to the palace and brought him before the king and queen.

The young count knelt and drew the emerald box from his pocket. He set it at the queen's feet. She gestured, and he rose and handed her the box. No sooner had she lifted its lid and looked inside, then she fell to the floor in a dead faint. The guards feared the worst. They grabbed the lad by the collar and tied his hands. But before they could take him away, the queen awakened and cried out, "Free him." She waved for the guards to leave, and when she was alone with the young count, she took him into her confidence. "I must tell you my story," she began, "Only then will you understand why your gift gave me such a shock. My husband is getting on in years. Some time ago, he decided to divide the kingdom among our three daughters. He said the one who loved him best, would win the largest share.

"In front of all the courtiers, each said she loved him dearly. Our oldest two tried to outdo each other. The first said she loved her father as dearly as she loved cakes and pies. Our second daughter said she loved her father as dearly as she loved money. Our third daughter was an especially good lass, but she was not one for flattery. She simply said, 'Father, I love you dearly.'

"'Yes, but how dearly?' the king persisted. He stood close and whispered, 'Daughter, don't stand silent and make me look a fool.'

"At last she said, 'Life would be joyless without Father, just as good food is tasteless without salt.'

"The king flew into a rage, 'What? You love me as you love common salt? Then salt you shall have!' He gave the kingdom to our eldest two and sent the youngest away with nothing but a bag of salt strapped to her back.

"He soon lamented his foolishness, but it was too late. We sent troops out to search for her. We searched the land for many years, but found no trace, until today. For you see, when my youngest daughter wept, pearls, not tears, fell from her eyes. Pearls exactly like these," she said rattling the contents of the emerald box. Now young man, you must lead us to our daughter!"

"I will tell you all I know, Your Highness, but I fear it will not help. The pearls were given to me by an old woman. Believe me, I saw nothing of the princess."

"All the same," said the queen, "you must take us to the old woman."

That very night the young count, the king, and the queen set out. They went alone, on foot, so they might see and hear all. The old king's legs were stiff with arthritis. He ambled along slowly, but even so, the lad marveled at their headway. For it seemed to him they were approaching the old woman's cottage in no time at all. He decided to go ahead to see what he could see. "The old witch is difficult," he thought, "but maybe I can get something out of the goose girl."

Now at that very moment the old woman heard an owl hoot just outside her window. She got up and began sweeping the floor and shaking out the rugs as if she expected guests. "Grandmother," said the goose girl, "it's late. Save the chores for morning when we're rested."

"This is not just any night," said the old woman. "Mark my words, it will change your life. Go to the spring now and wash. Put on the dress you wore when you first came to me —the night I found you hiding from the king's men. This is our last night together."

"Grandmother, please, don't send me away. Haven't I served you well?"

"I'm the one who'll be leaving, and I insist on a proper good-bye. Now do as I say, Dear, and trust me, a new life is about to begin."

The girl went to the pond. The moon shone brightly on the water. The geese slept along the shore with their heads tucked under their wings. They were so used to her, they slept undisturbed. She sat at the edge of the water. "What will become of me?" she wondered.

It happened that the lad saw the full moon's light shining on the water. He mistook it for the old woman's lamplight. Then, peering between the trees he saw the goose girl at the water's edge.

"How can I approach without frightening her?" he thought silently to himself. He watched her kneel to wash, and then he saw an extraordinary thing. She took hold of the skin on her face and gave it a tug. The scaly goose flesh peeled off in one piece. Beneath it, her skin was smooth and radiant. She was no goose girl at all, but a lovely young woman. She looked so sad, his heart ached for her. Then she burst into tears, and wouldn't you know—her tears were not made of water, but of glistening white pearls. The lad hurried back to tell the queen and king.

When he told what he had seen their hopes soared, and their feet moved quickly. The three of them soon arrived at the cottage door. The old woman called, "Daughter! Come see our visitors!" Just then the lovely girl came in, and as soon as she saw her parents, she burst into tears once more. Pearls fell from her eyes and bounced on the floor in every direction. Both her parents embraced her and all three wept and wept.

When the king was finally able to speak he said, "My Daughter, I have wronged you so! You have lived in loneliness and misery these many years, all because of my foolishness!"

The princess replied, "Father, it is you who have lived in loneliness and misery. You have paid for your wrongs through your own sorrow. As for me, I have been safe, and in good company."

"Your forgiveness is the sweetest of gifts," said the king, who began weeping all over again. When he was able speak he said, "I foolishly gave all to your sisters, and have nothing left to offer you."

"Father, I will stay here in the forest, with my kind old grand-mother."

At that moment they turned to thank the old woman, but she was gone. They went outside and called for her, but she did not reply. Then they heard a rumbling and felt the earth shaking. They looked around and where the house had been, there stood a huge mansion in its place. The commotion awakened the geese and the whole flock came running and squawking to see what had happened.

"The old woman told me to bid her good-bye," said the princess. "She must be gone for good."

The king turned to the young count. "We have you to thank, too," he said. "You've brought us to our daughter. How can we repay you?"

"Perhaps by allowing me to be of service," he said.

"You can have a post in my kingdom: a knighthood, or anything else you wish."

"Well, I'd like to stay here and be of service to the princess, if she'll have me."

The princess smiled. The two fell in love, and in time they were married. Did they remain happy in the forest until the end of their days? Perhaps they did. But one thing is sure, they never forgot the kindness of the wise old woman.

INITIATION | MEN'S INITIATION | THE MORE-THAN-HUMAN WORLD | MAN OF HEART | LONELINESS | UNSTABLE IDENTITY | FOREST AS A PLACE OF TRANSFORMATION | EMANCIPATION FROM HOME | EMOTIONAL RESILIENCE: As Mircea Eliade, eminent scholar of myth and religion, points out, the trials endured by fairy tale heroes echo the coming-of-age ordeals practiced by ancestral groups the world over. In this tale, the young count leaves behind the comforts of home and travels alone in the forest. This begins an initiatory quest. Despite his high station in life, he offers his service to an old peasant woman and submits to her teasing and taunting. He comes to terms with repulsive and attractive aspects of the feminine. He endures disorientation, solves a family riddle, performs a heroic task, and finds love.

One young husband, Sirus, especially liked the way the count resolves his repulsion/attraction to the Goose Girl. "My view of women," Sirus confided, "was pretty much shaped by Hollywood movies and the *Sports Illustrated* swimsuit issue. My wife, Molly, is attractive, but when we first got close, I was taken aback by the scar she had from surgery, and by her being chubby. How she looked was different from what I thought I needed. I reacted like the count when he sees the goose-face. But I kept coming back, because of the deeper connection Molly and I have. Like a lot of guys, I've had to come to terms with those expectations. Now we have two daughters, and I'm a lot more real with what it's all about."

WOMEN'S INITIATION | HUMILITY | UNSTABLE IDENTITY | INNER BEAUTY | EXPANDING NARROW DEFINITIONS OF BEAUTY: Our heroine submits to a humbling loss of beauty, wealth, and identity, and endures a period of anonymity and seclusion. As with all rites of passage, the Goose Girl's ordeals culminate in a new definition of self, celebration with loved ones, and the start of a new life. In groups for women and girls, this tale provides a mirror through which we can view our own initiatory trials. The story encourages women to take heart and embrace life-affirming changes, even when it means saying good-bye to familiar old comforts, and facing the unknown. Rising to these challenges with integrity, the heroine's inner beauty emerges.

RITES OF PASSAGE: Today there is much interest in devising meaningful rituals to mark life passages. The following initiatory themes from this story can serve as stepping stones to ritual: (1) guidance from a special elder; (2) solitude in a natural setting; (3) a humble, meditative task; (4) closure of an old conflict;

(5) resolve to go forward; (6) celebration of wholeness and looking to the future. These themes are pertinent to those on the brink of adulthood, as well as older adults at meaningful crossroads in life. The themes proved useful to Daria, a fifty-four-year-old whose husband left her the same year her youngest child went off to college. Daria could not get over feeling "cast off." She wanted to incorporate initiatory themes from "The Goose Girl" into her own healing ritual. She asked her women's group to help her, and this is what they came up with. (The numbers correspond with the six themes above.)

(1) She asked her aunt and godmother to share with her their experiences of loss and change.

(2) Each morning she set aside time for self-reflection, journal-writing, and a "solitude walk" on the beach. Through these activities she focused on her grief over the loss of her "old self," and her "old life."

(3) Following a long-standing dream, she took on the task of restoring an old kayak.

(4) She met with her ex-husband and expressed accountability for her part in their breakup.

(5) She began to explore possibilities as to where she would live and what she might do with the rest of her life.

(6) On her fifty-fifth birthday she and her friends camped out near a natural hot-spring. She told the story of the difficulties she had faced and how she'd gotten through them. Her friends acknowledged her passage through a life-changing ordeal. They sang to her, presented her with symbolic gifts, and toasted her future and her wholeness as an elder woman.

Daria's six-part ritual took about five weeks in all. Using the themes in this tale as a basis for ritual has many possibilities. In weekend intensives I have found ways to incorporate all six initiatory themes into a group ritual. Mircea Eliade reminds us that among traditional cultures, life-passage rituals can take a few days to a few years, depending upon the culture. When the spirit of initiation is awakened in someone's life, creative possibilities abound, and rituals can be custom-fit to suit the situation.

THE ALCHEMY OF SELFHOOD: The presence of gems and minerals in a story can be a sign of selfhood. In the Vedic tradition, emeralds call in the energy of Mercury, the messenger and communicator. With the emerald box, the count and the old woman activate communication between the princess and her family. I like to think of the pearls within the emerald box as the luminous feminine shining within. The sight of the pearls gives everyone hope that the princess is alive! One husband took this as an empowering talisman for his wife and bought her earrings of emerald and pearl.

MISUSE OF POWER | MISGUIDED LEADERSHIP | TRUTHFULNESS | SIBLING RIVALRY | UNHEALTHY COMPETITION: This tale reminds us how easily power can be misused, and how much damage can be done through misguided leadership. Like Shakespeare's King Lear, the king in our story is haunted by self-doubt. To assuage it he sets up a competition between his daughters, and whoever makes the greatest show of flattery will receive the greatest reward. The eldest two pander to the king's weakness, but the third cannot barter false emotion. Her response reminds us of those times in life when anything less than frankness will damage the soul, when one must have the courage to be truthful, come what may. These themes are pertinent to people of all ages. Teens love to discuss the temptation to "suck-up" to someone in hopes of a payoff. The tale elicits fruitful discussions on the social, familial, and soulful complexities of truth-telling. It also serves as a reminder to parents to avoid instigating unhealthy competition between siblings.

HEALING FATHER WOUNDS | CAST-OUTS AND RUNAWAYS | DISENFRANCHISE-MENT | EXCLUSION | DEPRIVATION | LOVING KINDNESS | LOSS, COURAGE, TRANS-FORMATION | FORGIVENESS | HUMILITY: Traditionally, children look to father figures not only for affection, but also for protection, and for assistance in gaining independence and autonomy. It is particularly damaging then, when a father prematurely casts out a child without means or protection. Many homeless teens who are labeled "runaways" have actually been cast out. Oftentimes the child assumes he or she is worthless, and acts out self-defeating behaviors, but the king's youngest daughter models a better way. She accepts the help of a protective grandmother who offers her affection and shelter and gives her humble but useful tasks. While sequestered in the forest, the princess holds onto the one thing which is truly hers, her salt-of-the-earth integrity. Not having lost that, she is later able to forgive her father. He, in turn, humbly faces what he has done, and laments his foolishness and cruelty. The liberating love that showers the family at that point reminds us what all children know in their bones: acknowledgment is healing. (Survivors of holocaust and apartheid atrocities, as well as domestic violence, say acknowledgment is far more important to them than restitution.) Reaching a place of truth and humility, the king celebrates his daughter's wholeness. She does not focus on what the king might owe her, but on proceeding with the life she has found for herself.

COPING WITH REJECTION | HEALING FROM ABANDONMENT | COURAGE, INTEGRITY, RESILIENCE: The heroine models positive coping with the pain of rejection, and courage in the face of hardship. The story shows how a person rejected and cast out can find alternative sources of support, and learn to be a resource for him or herself. This is why the tale is an excellent source of encouragement for anyone striving to overcome hurt, hardship, or loss. "The Goose Girl at the Spring" celebrates what's best in us and demonstrates that in the end, integrity is its own reward. Both hero and heroine act in accord with the higher values of respect for self and other. For people of all ages the tale resonates with our inner nobility and affirms our desires to act in difficult times from the strength of our character.

ELDER WISDOM | HELP FROM WISE ELDERS | YOUTH-ELDER ALLIANCE | ADOPTION AND FOSTERING | GENEROSITY | ISOLATION: Storytelling is one way to shine the light of esteem onto those whom society neglects. Elders never tire of stories like this one, in which an old man or woman holds a key role. They delight in the old woman's earthy wiles, audacious wit, and whole-hearted generosity. As the story opens, we learn that the neighboring farmers shun her. Many elders upon hearing this tale say they too feel shunned by society at large. In the end, the old woman's goodness, her intuitive powers, and conjure skills are all plain to see. Often after hearing this tale, gray-haired listeners who had previously been silent, begin to speak. Some of them feel encouraged to form new alliances with young people and to strengthen ties with the young people they already know and love. "I started feeling isolated after I retired," said one woman. "Volunteering for a local youth organization has been a godsend to me."

One foster father told me this is an excellent tale for foster parents. "We feel overextended and under recognized," he said. "One bad foster parent gets reported in the news, and suddenly we're all thought to be rotten. The old woman is just the kind of foster parent people need to hear about."

Snow White and Rose Red

GERMANY | (1,862 words)

(for background on Grimms' fairy tales see p. 91)

There was once a woman living in a cottage with her two daughters. The girls' father had long since died, and they made ends meet as best they could. In the garden out front grew two rosebushes, one with white roses and the other red. Bearing resemblance to the rosebushes, the girls were called Snow White and Rose Red. In all the world there were never two children more kind and good, nor so willing and cheerful. Snow White liked to stay home helping their mother or reading aloud to her when the work was done. Rose Red liked to run in the fields chasing butterflies. The girls loved each other so dearly, they held hands wherever they went. They vowed never to be parted and their mother reminded them always to share between them whatever good things came their way.

The two sisters roamed the forest together, picking berries and making friends with the animals. The hare ate lettuce right out of their hands, while the doe browsed peacefully beside them. When the girls were near, the birds sang sweetly, and even the wary stag came out of his hiding place in the thicket to greet them. If by chance the girls should linger in the forest until overtaken by the night, they did not fear. They simply lay down side by side on the moss and slept until morning. Their mother knew they were safe and didn't fret.

One moonless night they slept in the woods, and awoke at dawn to see a beautiful child dressed in shining white robes. The child smiled upon them and quietly disappeared through the trees. Only then did they see they had slept near a cliff, and could easily have gone over the edge in the darkness. Later their mother said the child in white must have been the angel of the forest who watched over them, keeping them from harm.

Snow White and Rose Red cleaned their mother's cottage 'til it was a joy to behold. Rose Red kept house in the summer. Every morning, she brought a rose from each bush to her mother's bedside. In winter Snow White tended the fire and polished the brass kettle 'til it shone like gold. In the evening, when snowflakes whirled around outside, their mother would say, "Bolt the door, Snow White." The girls would draw near the hearth and spin wool into yarn while their mother read aloud.

One winter evening there came a knock at the door. The mother said, "It must be a traveler seeking shelter. Rose Red, let him in." Rose Red drew back the bolt, and who should poke his head in, but a big black bear, covered with snow. Rose Red shrieked and leapt back. Snow White hid beneath the table.

The bear said, "Don't be afraid. I won't harm you. All I ask is to sit by the fire." Pitying the half-frozen creature, the mother invited him to lie down at the hearth. She told her daughters the bear meant no harm, and gradually their fears faded. He asked the girls to brush the snow from his fur, so they swept his coat with a broom. Then he stretched out before the fire, sighing contentedly. Soon the girls got used to him and began to play. They put their feet on him and rolled him this way and that. They snatched at his fur and whipped him with a switch, and laughed when he growled playfully.

The good-natured bear put up with much mischief, but when it got out of hand he cried, "Children, children, let me live! Snow White and Rose Red, you'll thrash your suitor til he's dead!" At bedtime the mother invited the bear to rest beside the hearth until morning. At daybreak the girls let him out and he lumbered across the snow and into the forest.

From then on he came each evening to enjoy their company and the warmth of the fire. He always let the girls rough-house and tease him as much as they liked. They grew so fond of the bear, they looked forward to his visits each night, and never latched the door until he arrived.

One morning they saw the snow had melted. The birds flitted about making new nests, and the forest and meadow were bursting with spring flowers and green buds. The bear said, "Snow White, I must leave and won't see you again until the winter returns and the ground freezes over."

She asked, "Where will you go, Dear Bear?"

The bear said he must go to the forest to guard his treasures from covetous, thieving dwarves. "In winter, they stay in their caves," he said, "but in summer, they ferret about, stealing whatever buried treasures they can find." Snow White bid him a sad farewell and opened the door for him to go. As he passed through, his fur caught on the latch, and tore just slightly. Snow White thought she saw gold glimmer through the tiny hole, but it might have been the morning sunlight glinting in her eyes. Soon the big bear disappeared through the trees.

Some time later, the mother sent the girls to the forest to gather kindling. They found a fallen tree from which to gather twigs. On the other side of the trunk they heard rustling in the grass. As they drew near, they saw it was a dwarf with a shriveled face and a long snow-white beard. The tip of his beard was caught in a cleft in the trunk, and the little man jumped furiously about trying to free himself. He glared with fiery eyes at the girls and shouted, "Don't just stand there like fools! DO something!"

Rose Red asked, "How did your beard get snagged in the tree?"

The dwarf snapped, "You nosy goose, if you must know, we dwarves use only small bits of firewood to cook our modest meals—not like you greedy humans! I was trying to split the log, and when I drove the wedge in, my beard got caught. But you spoiled brats don't seem to care."

Each girl took a turn, but it was no use; they couldn't free the dwarf's whiskers. "I'll go fetch help," said Rose Red.

"Help indeed!" scoffed the dwarf. "There are two of you and that's too many."

Snow White said, "Don't be so impatient, Mr. Dwarf. I have an idea." She took a pair of sewing scissors from her pocket and snipped the tip of the beard.

The moment the dwarf was free, he reached under the tree and grasped a sack of gold that had been hidden beneath the roots. "The devil take you!" he growled. "How dare you snip my whiskers!" With that, the ungrateful fellow hoisted the sack to his shoulder and stomped away.

Some days later Snow White and Rose Red decided to catch some fish for supper. As they neared the stream, they saw something bounce toward the water like a large grasshopper. Coming closer they saw it was the dwarf. "Careful not to fall in, Sir," said Rose Red.

"You idiot!" scolded the dwarf. "Can't you see the damned fish has me by the beard?" He'd been fishing, when along came a breeze that tangled his long white beard in the line. To make matters worse, a big fish had chomped on the bait and began a tug of war with the dwarf. He clutched at saplings on the bank, but the fish was stronger. Without help, the dwarf could easily drown. The girls grasped him tightly, and tried to unwind his beard, but it was badly tangled. What could they do but resort to the scissors? With all their strength and a bit of handiwork, they managed to cut through the matted mess and free the dwarf. "You wicked toads!" he cried. "It wasn't enough for you to snip off the tip of my beautiful beard. You had to go and chop the best of it. You've disfigured me!" Then he picked up a bag of pearls that was hidden in the rushes. He slung it over his shoulder and stormed off without offering a word of thanks.

One day the mother sent the girls to buy needles, thread, lace, and ribbons at a nearby town. To get there, they walked across a rocky heath. A large bird of prey flew high overhead, slowly spiraling closer and closer to the earth. All of a sudden, it extended its talons and swooped down near a rock in front of them. They heard a bloodcurdling cry. They rushed forth to see the eagle had pounced on their old friend, Mr. Dwarf, and was about to fly off with him. The kindly girls held onto the dwarf with all their might, until at last the bird let go and flew away. The ungrateful dwarf shrieked, "You clumsy clods! Did you have to pull so hard? Look how you've wrinkled my jacket." Then he picked up a bag of jewels, and disappeared into his cave beneath the rock. By then the girls were quite used to his cross tone and though it hadn't bothered them much before, it bothered them even less now.

They completed their errands in town, and headed back across the heath toward home. The dwarf hadn't expected anyone to pass by his cave so late in the day. When the girls walked past he had the jewels spread on the ground for counting. The dwarf looked up, quite startled to see them. The evening sun glistened brightly upon the many colored gems. The girls gazed in amazement. "Don't stand there gawking like ninnies!" he shouted, his face going crimson with rage. But before he could hurl more harsh words, they heard a growl, and a black bear came loping out of the forest. The dwarf leapt to his feet and tried to make for his cave, but instantly the bear was upon him. "Please spare me, Mr. Bear. These two girls are as plump as spring quail. They'd make a much tastier meal than my scrawny limbs. Eat them! Eat them!" The bear raised his great paw and smote the dwarf with one blow.

The sisters ran for cover. The bear called, "Snow White and Rose Red, wait, don't run away." They recognized the voice of their dear friend. When he caught up with them, his furry coat fell to the ground, and before them stood a handsome young man all dressed in gold. "I am a prince," he explained. "That dwarf stole all my treasures, and placed a curse on me, changing me to a bear. But now his death has restored my human form."

The prince reclaimed all his treasures from the cave. Snow White married the prince, and Rose Red married his brother. The sisters brought their mother to the palace. She left her old life behind, except for the two rosebushes, which she transplanted outside her new window. Every year the most beautiful roses bloomed, white from one bush, and red from the other. She lived there contentedly to the end of her days.

THE MORE-THAN-HUMAN WORLD | FOREST AS A PLACE OF TRANSFORMATION | ANIMALS AS HELPERS AND TEACHERS | REVERENCE FOR NATURE: This charming tale is like the magic bag of food that storyteller Gioia Timpanelli talks about. It gives and gives and cannot be used up. Among the tale's many beneficial messages is the all-pervasive message that nature is alive, and eager to befriend us if we will only avail ourselves of it. The girls are not without fear, for they tremble when they meet a strange bear, but they are also able to discern to what degree they can safely interrelate with other forest beings. This makes them integral forest dwellers, friendly with many species. Such story motifs have often been dismissed as "romantic" and "sentimental" idealizations of nature, but at a time when countless species are going extinct, and nature's realm grows ever smaller, we need tales which amplify the pleasures of forest dwelling, which honor the diversity of species, and the magic of the more-than-human world. This tale helps young and old to value the forest as a sacred and mystical place.

LOVING KINDNESS | SISTERLY SOLIDARITY | FAMILIAL COOPERATION | TEACHING THROUGH EXAMPLE | GOOD MOTHERS: The harmony and affection between the two sisters could also be dismissed as "sentimental." I might dismiss it too, if I had not seen time and again that children who are taught through example to be kind and loving, generally behave that way, even toward their siblings. Siblings who remain life-long friends share a unique legacy of family history and blood ties, commonalties that enable an extraordinary intimacy to thrive.

LOVE AND THE ALCHEMICAL UNION | MAN OF HEART | THE ALCHEMY OF SELF-HOOD: For adults this tale gives insight into the abilities to love despite difficulties and to see the golden prince beneath the skin. Sharon felt the need to learn about love, and took this tale to heart to help her do so. She had grown up completely sheltered from contact with boys. "I knew nothing about men, really, except they scared me. When I graduated from college and started dating, I didn't have a clue whether a guy cared for me, or was just out to use me." From age 25 to 35 Sharon deemed herself "a magnet for guys who weren't that nice." After a few years' celibacy, she met Alan, a man whom she found to be intelligent, warm, funny, and kind. "Finally, a decent guy in my life, but I was still terrified and on guard all the time. Alan sensed it, and didn't try to seduce me. He was just like the bear, a big, warm, playful friend. Just sitting beside him at the movies was sexy and reassuring at the same time. Not jumping into anything physical, I was able to perceive the gold in him, before we ever touched. His kindness and patience helped me to see the gold in myself, too. When we actually started being sexual, it opened up a whole new world for me, and was really exciting."

MISPLACED BLAME: Alan could also relate to the tale. "My dad was usually out of town," he said, "but when he was around, he was about as snarly as the dwarf. No matter how good my intentions were, he always put a dark spin on whatever I tried to do, and blamed me for whatever went wrong." Whenever the dwarfish attitude came up between Alan and Sharon in the form of fear, mistrust, impatience, or blame, they tried to be extra patient with each other. Alan said, "If we start getting harsh and persnickety, that's a sign that we're letting the dwarf get all the riches."

"That's when we try to step back," Sharon said. "If we can be patient like the bear, and in good humor like the girls, we can usually get back on a better footing with each other."

Choosing a Bride

GERMANY | (157 words)

(for background on Grimms' fairy tales see p. 91)

*T*here was once a young shepherd who had reached a marrying age. He knew of three sisters in a nearby village, all of them pretty, and all of them available. "How shall I choose?" he asked his mother. "Ask them to lunch. Set some cheese before them, and watch how they eat it."

The young shepherd did just that. One of the sisters sliced the cheese and gobbled it down, rind and all. The second sliced the rind off, but she did so leaving behind a thick margin of cheese that went to waste. The third took care to peel off the rind and set it aside, leaving behind no wasted cheese.

The shepherd watched carefully, and after the sisters had gone, he reported all to his mother. "Ah," said the mother, "that third one, she's the one to marry." The shepherd proposed, and she accepted, and they lived together happily until the end of their days.

DECISIONS | MATE SELECTION | LOVING KINDNESS: This deceptively simple tale may draw criticism from skeptics. I once told it in a therapy group for older teen boys, and their initial responses were: "How come the guy can't choose for himself?" and "Who cares how somebody eats?"

Telling it in a divorce recovery group for men, I met with similar first responses: "Shouldn't love be about chemistry, not manners?" "If the guy has to ask his mother every time he makes a decision, the marriage will never work out," and "A woman shouldn't have to audition to be my girlfriend." These comments are all valid if we view the story superficially. But a key suggestion in both groups brought the discussion to a deeper level. I suggested to the men, that within them was the capacity to *mother themselves,* to care for themselves with loving kindness. When it came to decision making, they could consult the "experienced, attuned, caring," part of themselves. Most of them agreed that inner mothering exists, but that listening to it is a challenge.

As the men spoke of their "disastrous histories" of choosing the wrong women, they started having fun with the metaphors. "It's not that I don't see the indicators," said one. "With most women the *inappropriate cheese cutting,* is usually pretty obvious on the first date. It's just that I ignore it until I'm in too deep." The men listed the kinds of indicators they would want to steer clear of in future. It included everything from lying, extreme credit card debt, and child neglect, to sexual misconduct, eating disorders, and substance abuse. All agreed that if their "seeking shepherd" were a bit more observant and attuned, and their decision-making process included a bit more self-mothering, their future choices would be much more positive.

SUSTAINABILITY | ELDER WISDOM | WISDOM OF COMMON PEOPLE: Looked at from another angle, this little tale uses romance to make a point about sustainability and respecting resources. For the farmers of old Europe, cows were the measure of wealth, and quality cheeses were not only a matter of pride, they were life-sustaining nourishment. The desirable sweetheart in the tale is the one whose actions reveal her understanding and respect. She does not mindlessly consume that which is non-nutritive (the rind), and she is not wasteful of the nourishment offered. If we take this as a metaphor for present-day sustainability, we can say the beloved is neither a mindless consumer, nor is she wasteful. She understands the value of life and she participates in life in a balanced and responsible way. Embracing such balance creates the possibility for true happiness on this earth.

Rapunzel

GERMANY | (1124 words)

(for background on Grimms' fairy tales see p. 91)

*T*here was once a couple who had everything they could wish for—except the one thing they desired most—a child. Behind their home was a garden wall, and beyond it, lay an enchanting garden belonging to a formidable old woman. The wife gazed down upon the garden from her window and there she spied a bed of savory green rapunzel. This choice lettuce looked so fresh and delicious that her mouth began to water. By the next day she could think of nothing else. Her craving grew until she began to pine. Her husband saw her suffering and asked, "Dear Wife, what's wrong?"

"Oh," she replied, "I shall waste away unless I get some of that rapunzel that grows in the neighbor's garden." This put the husband on the spot, for everyone feared the old woman and no one dared approach her or trespass in her garden. But with his wife so full of longing, what could he do? That night he surreptitiously ventured over the garden wall and picked a handful of rapunzel. The instant he returned his wife made herself a salad and gobbled it down. The rapunzel pleased her greatly, but the next day her craving grew three-fold.

That night her husband trespassed once again. But this time, just as he climbed down the far side of the garden wall, he heard the old woman shout, "How dare you sneak about my place like a thief! You've been stealing my rapunzel and you'll pay for it!"

The husband pleaded, "Old Woman, be merciful. My poor wife suffers so, and only your rapunzel will cheer her."

"Is that right?" said the old woman, "Very well, then, Rapunzel she shall have. From this day forward you may help yourselves to as much rapunzel as you wish. But in exchange, you must swear to give me your first child when it is born. I shall care for it like a mother and give it a good life." What could the poor man do, but agree? Some months later, when his wife birthed a daughter, the old woman came for the infant, named her Rapunzel, and took her away.

Rapunzel grew more lovely each day until there was no lovelier child on the face of the earth. When she turned twelve years of age, the old woman took her deep into the forest and shut her into a tower, to keep her unspoiled by the world. This tower had no door and no stairway, only a single window at the top. When the old woman wanted to visit the girl, she stood below and called, "Rapunzel, Rapunzel, let down your hair." Rapunzel had very long hair which she wore in braids and wrapped around her head like a golden crown. When the old woman called, she unwound them, and hooked them over the window latch, allowing them to fall all the way to the ground. The old woman climbed the braids as if they were a ladder. The days, months, and years passed by. Rapunzel did not grow lonely or bored, because she knew no better.

One day a king's son happened to be passing through the forest on horseback. He heard sweet singing and followed the sound to the tower, for Rapunzel often sang to pass the time. He lingered a while to enjoy her lilting song, and then looked for a door, that he might compliment the singer. He was perplexed at the lack of a door, but the voice moved him so, that he returned each day to listen. Once, as he stood behind a tree, he saw the old woman come to the foot of the tower. He heard her call, "Rapunzel, Rapunzel, let down your hair." Rapunzel lowered her braids, and the old woman climbed up. This was a lesson the king's son would not forget.

The following day, he returned to the tower at dusk and called, "Rapunzel, Rapunzel, let down your hair." Her hair fell to the ground and the prince climbed up just as the old woman had done. Upon seeing him, Rapunzel leapt back, for never before had she seen a man. But the prince spoke softly and kindly, explaining how much he'd enjoyed her singing. Before long she forgot her fears. He told her of the wide world, and declared his love.

He asked Rapunzel to marry him, and once he explained marriage to her satisfaction, she agreed saying, "The old woman visits by day, and so you must come to me by night. Each time you come, bring a skein of silk thread, and I shall weave myself a ladder."

The old woman suspected nothing until one day Rapunzel asked, "Tell me Godmother, why you take so long to climb my hair when the prince climbs up in seconds?"

The old woman shouted, "You wicked girl! I tried to keep you shut away from the world!" In a rage she grabbed Rapunzel by the hair, snatched up a pair of scissors and lopped the braids off just below her ears. Then she fixed them to the latch, and dragged Rapunzel out the window with her. She took Rapunzel to a bleak and deserted place, and left her alone to fend for herself.

That evening the old woman carefully secured the severed braids to the window latch. When the prince called "Rapunzel, Rapunzel, let down your hair," she lowered the braids to the ground where he stood. The prince climbed up the tower and into the window only to find Rapunzel gone and the old woman ready to assail him. "You've come for your little love bird, no doubt. There'll be no more snuggling in this nest! The cat has caught her, and will now scratch your eyes out!" She lunged upon him, but the prince managed to fling himself from the tower. He fell to the brambles below, and as fate would have it, sharp thorns punctured his eyes and blinded him.

After that the poor prince wandered through the woods for a very long time, subsisting on berries and roots, mourning over the loss of his beloved. He wandered aimlessly until at last he came to the place where Rapunzel was living. In the distance he heard sorrowful singing, and the voice seemed familiar, so he moved toward it. As he neared, Rapunzel recognized her dear husband. She fell upon him, weeping profusely. Her tears spilled into his eyes, restoring his sight. Not only did he rejoice to see his beloved, but also to see their twin babies, a girl and a boy. They all four went to his kingdom and received a royal welcome. There they lived contentedly 'til the end of their days.

ISOLATION | MAN OF HEART | HEALING MOTHER WOUNDS: Most of us know what it's like to feel isolated, either by choice or by circumstance, and longing for something missing is part of what it means to be human. This tale is born of longing and the complications of longing, beginning with the wife's longing for a child, her craving the rapunzel, and the unthinkable sacrifice which follows. A woman named Kendra strongly identified with Rapunzel's legacy of "isolation and longing that you don't even recognize because you have nothing else to compare it to." As the prince happened into Rapunzel's life, so Corey, a man from another city, happened into Kendra's. He took to her and wanted to carry on an e-mail correspondence as a way of seeing what might develop. "Other people carry on cyber relationships quite easily," said Kendra, "but for me, getting and answering e-mails is like being invaded. Having a man in my life, even on these limited terms, is difficult. I know Corey's a good man, but I'd almost rather be left alone in my tower, except that's difficult too. Corey keeps sending me skeins of yarn to make the ladder, but I haven't started weaving."

Kendra looked at the familial roots of her isolation. She described her mother as "so overprotective she smothered me." One day Kendra revealed, "I've always told myself Mom sheltered me out of love, but if I'm honest, I have to admit she did it for selfish reasons, too, like not wanting me to have a life, because she felt empty herself." As with Rapunzel, Kendra's struggle with isolation did not heal overnight. "It's difficult to give myself permission for a relationship, let alone to make something of my life. My mother's perspective is that I really don't need anyone else, not even myself, because I'll always have her. My progress on this is painfully slow, so it comforts me to remember how long Rapunzel suffered. Yet she eventually got a life, and that gives me hope that I will too."

CRAVINGS AND TROUBLESOME DESIRES: People who struggle with the tendency toward addiction appreciate the wife's urgent craving at the beginning of this tale. Speaking of the marijuana addiction he and his wife shared, one husband said, "We've lost a lot due to being hooked on herb. We never literally lost our firstborn, but we lost many precious times with him because we were too zoned out to be present."

The wife said, "It's been a long, grueling route to living drug free, and sometimes we feel like the craving is interminable. But it's like the story: If we ever get to where we both see clearly and function day to day, it will be because we got through our grief and pulled together as a family. That's the only thing strong enough to get us through." For this couple, as for many, Rapunzel provided sustaining images for long-term recovery.

Rumpelstiltskin

GERMANY | (1,085 words)

(for background on Grimms' fairy tales see p. 91)

Long ago there was a poor miller who had little to brag about except, perhaps, the beauty and goodness of his daughter. By chance one day he happened to speak with the king, and striving to impress him, the miller boasted, "My daughter can perform the wondrous feat of spinning straw into gold."

The king replied, "That sort of skill greatly intrigues me. Bring your daughter to the palace tomorrow, and I'll see for myself." The next day she arrived and the king led her to a room full of straw. He showed her the spinning wheel and ordered her to work. "I expect a room full of gold, when I return tomorrow morning," he said. "If you disappoint me, you'll die." Then he locked the door and left her alone in the room.

The miller's daughter had no idea what to do. She could no sooner spin straw into gold, than she could sprout wings and fly, or make the sun shine at night. The king had left her no leeway at all, and the thought of losing her life over it terrified her. There was nothing to do but weep, and so she wept. Suddenly the door popped open and a little man stepped in. "Good evening, Miss Miller," he said, "Why do you weep as if the world were coming to an end?"

"I'm supposed to spin straw into gold and I don't know how," she said.

The little fellow asked, "If I spin it for you, what will you give me?"

The girl put her hand to her throat, "My necklace," she replied.

At that the little man took the necklace, and sat down to spin. He turned the wheel three times, whir, whir, whir, and the spool was full of shimmering gold. Again he turned it three times, and a second spool was full of gold. All night he worked magic, until by morning each and every bit of straw was spun into gold.

Soon the king arrived. He was overjoyed to see spools of gold from wall to wall. The sight made him hungry for more, such was the greed in his heart. He whisked the miller's daughter to a larger room full of straw and said, "If you value your life, you'll spin all this into gold for my coffers."

Again she found herself locked into a room facing an impossible task. Overcome with fatigue, she wept. Then the little man popped in as before. "Miss Miller, if I spin the straw into gold, what will you give me?"

She touched her hand and said, "The ring off my finger."

The sprightly fellow took the ring and sat down to spin. All night he worked tirelessly, and by sunrise the room was full of shimmering gold. The king was delighted. Greedier than ever, he took the miller's daughter to a room with still larger heaps of straw and said, "If you manage to spin all this into gold, you shall live, and I shall make you my bride." To himself he thought that though her origins were modest, in all the world there was no woman who could fill his coffers so swiftly.

When she found herself alone once again, the little man showed up for the third time and asked, "If I spin the gold, what will you give me?" The miller's daughter replied that she had nothing left to give. "Well then," said the little man, "promise me this: If you become queen, you'll give me your first born child."

Now the girl was in a bind. There was no telling what the future might bring, but unless she agreed, she'd have no future at all. "Very well," she said. Again the little man set nimbly and swiftly to work.

By morning the king had his third room full of gold. He married the miller's beautiful daughter and she became queen.

In a year's time she gave birth to a lovely child. She'd nearly forgotten the little man, but one day he appeared in her room and said, "I've come for the child." The queen begged the him to take jewels, gold, riches of all kinds, anything but her child. But he insisted, "I prefer a living thing to all the wealth in the world." Then the queen wept and protested so bitterly that the little man felt sorry for her. He proposed that if she could guess his name within three days' time, she could keep the child.

The queen stayed up all night, frantically racking her brain, going over all the names she'd ever heard. The next day she sent a messenger to inquire throughout the countryside about other names she might have missed. The next day when the little man came, she rattled off the whole list from Algernon and Balthazar to Wagner and Zachary, but after each, the little man said no. The second day she sent servants to all the remote regions, to collect the rarest of names. She tried Ribcage, Shortribs, Muttonchops, Lambchops, but none of these were correct, either.

On the third day the messenger returned from his rounds and said, "At the end of the day I walked along the forest's edge, and rounding a bend I found myself at the foot of a hill. It was just the sort of spot where a fox and a hare might bid each other good evening. There was a rustic hut with a fire burning outside, and a silly little man dancing around the fire. And guess what he sang: 'Today I brew, tomorrow I bake, the next day the queen's child I'll take. My name is Rumpelstiltskin, but guess it, no one can.'"

This news thrilled the queen. Soon the little man appeared to hear her final guesses. She said, "Perhaps your name is Tom." The little man shook his head no. "Well, maybe you're called Dick." No again. "Is your name, by chance, Harry?" asked the queen. "No, your Majesty," said the little man growing more cocky by the moment. "Hmmm," said the queen looking at her list, "Maybe you go by the name, Rumpelstiltskin."

"Fie!" said the little man flailing his arms, "How did you know? The devil told you!" he yelled and stamped his right foot with such fury he drove it into the ground up to his thigh. Raging fiendishly, he yanked so hard on his left foot that he split himself in two. After that nothing came between the queen and her child.

GREED AND ACQUISITIVENESS | PERFECTIONISM | OPPORTUNISM | SUSTAIN-ABILITY: This tale offers metaphors for our cultural epidemic of greed, drivenness, and the obsession with productivity. To get this in perspective, let's first consider the myths of old which portray our world as animated by four interdependent seasons, one of dormancy, one of germination, one of growth, and one of harvest. Ancestral storytellers knew that spiritual and psychological wellness require all four, and only the complete cycle brings renewal and sustainability. Without wisdom tales to uphold this truth, it is easy for the human psyche to get caught in the mentality of the opportunistic king, demanding more gold. Our prevailing myths depict continual expansion, and characterize wellness as synonymous with nonstop growth and production. The earth, thousands of living species, and our own psyches are paying a huge toll. Prosperity alone does not quell our anxiety, for down deep, we know what Rumpelstiltskin knows, that wealth cannot hold a candle to life.

A young investor named Isaac suffered from high stress and anxiety. He came to me for counseling, and among other things, we turned to this tale for illumination. "I can relate to every character," he said, "but especially the king and the daughter. Like the king, I just stumbled into some good luck and it filled my coffers overnight. But like the girl, I've felt tremendous pressure to keep the growth going at exponentially higher levels. Now it feels like the price for all this is just too high. I don't have a firstborn to give up, but at the rate I'm going, my health is about shot, and I can't seem to sustain a relationship long enough to have a firstborn." The tale illustrated Isaac's problem, and also offered a solution. He found a less stressful approach in the rapport between the queen and her messenger. "The messenger brings in a more mellow paradigm for how to run your work-day," he noted. "Staying up all night wracking your brain like the queen freaking out over her kid, that's typical in the stock market. But it doesn't help in the long run. An even-keeled approach is more effective. But what the story says to me, is that the greed, the adrenaline, the big gains, all that is temporal. You have to look at the bigger picture and ask yourself, 'What does all this sustain?' If it supports your family and your community, then it's great. If it destroys the earth and ruins your health, then you're living ass-backwards, and you may as well just break yourself in two and be done with it, like the little man."

GOOD MOTHERS: The tale's metaphors apply not only to Wall-Street whiz kids, but to people of many walks of life. When I told it in a women's group, a mother named Judy said, "I'm as insecure as the miller, and I'm always trying to win favor by making unrealistic promises to others. My husband says I volunteer for every committee in sight, and he's right. I'd really rather be more like the queen and focus on my kids."

A younger mother said she identified with the way the miller's daughter changed after having a child, "I grew up almost overnight once I had a baby. I became much stronger doing things for her than I was doing things for myself and even for my husband."

Yet another woman added, "Until I became a mother, I was only partially committed to things. Whether or not I read anything worthwhile, or exercised, or ate right didn't really matter. When I became a mom I suddenly felt, "All my actions count. I'm a caregiver and role model for the next generation. I can't just wait around to see what's gonna happen. I have to do my part.'"

The Farmer's Hidden Treasure

AN AESOP'S FABLE FROM GREECE | (383 words)

ABOUT AESOP: *The following four tales are attributed to Aesop. Greek Historian Herodotus called Aesop "the maker of stories." He tells us Aesop was a Greek slave alive in the sixth century. Scholars are not altogether convinced that Aesop actually existed, and they doubt that a single man created all two thousand tales known today as Aesop's Fables. That Aesop himself is a legend should not surprise us, for storytelling is an art in which great fictions are called upon to bring forth essential truths. It only follows that the quintessential storyteller himself would be the stuff of fiction.*

An old man had spent his lifetime farming a fertile valley. On his dying day, his sons and daughters gathered at his bedside waiting for him to speak. At last he opened his eyes. He labored to take a deep breath and said, "Tend the land well, and you will prosper." Then he closed his eyes and nodded off to sleep. The siblings began whispering about how rich they'd be after selling the land. Again the old man opened his eyes. He gathered his strength and said, "I must tell you a secret. A treasure lies within the valley, no deeper than a foot beneath the ground." These words were the farmer's last.

After he died, his daughters and sons surmised he must have buried gold someplace in the valley. They decided not to sell the land right away. That fall they carefully plowed around each tree and loosened the soil around every vine. They painstakingly pulled weeds, searching all the while for buried gold. Try as they might, they found none. But since the land was so nicely turned, they decided to till in some rich compost, just as their father would have done.

Come spring, they plowed again, searching beneath every clod of soil for buried treasure, but all they found was rich earth. The farm was in top shape, and they could have sold it for an ample sum. But after going to so much trouble, they decided to plant crops instead. All summer they tended the crops and when fall came along, they celebrated a grand harvest. Then they plowed extra deep, determined to find the gold. This time they loosened every clump of dirt by hand. Still, the only satisfaction they gained was that of working the soil.

Over the years their satisfaction grew until they couldn't imagine selling the farm. Where else could they so readily enjoy the turn of the seasons and the bounty of the land? Where else could they so fully partake in the abundant fruits of the earth? How else could they so plainly see the results of their own efforts? They came to understand that their father's last words had not been about gold at all, but something finer.

Moral: *Fertile earth is the finest of treasures,* or, *Fulfillment comes from meaningful work.*

ELDERS WISDOM | HELP FROM WISE ELDERS | WORTHY USE OF DECEPTION | COOPERATION AND DEVOTION | DEVOTION | LOYALTY | FAMILIAL COOPERATION | LOSS, COURAGE, TRANSFORMATION | TEACHING THROUGH EXAMPLE | WALKING ONE'S TALK | POSTERITY | GRATITUDE: Countless tales from wisdom traditions the world over depict soft-spoken elders imparting wisdom to the next generation. In our youth-crazed culture, older adults often feel undervalued and pushed aside. They wonder whether or not their advice is deeply considered, or merely humored and quietly dismissed. In this tale, the old man knows human nature, and misleads his offspring into learning a most valuable lesson, that of loyalty and devotion to the land. The tale gently pokes fun at young people's tendency to dismiss elders, but it shows that in time, we may come to see the wisdom of their words. This tale is pleasing to anyone interested in honoring elders, bridging youth-elder gaps, and appreciating the value of intergenerational cooperation. A grieving son told this fable at his father's memorial service as a way of honoring his father and his father's gentle but persistent ways. Old friends in the congregation chuckled knowingly when he said, "Dad walked his talk, and eventually we kids did too."

SUSTAINABILITY | REVERENCE FOR NATURE | THE MORE-THAN-HUMAN WORLD | EARTH AS SACRED | HONORING THE EARTH | INTANGIBLE TREASURES | AGRICULTURE: This tale hits home with impassioned horticulturists of all kinds, especially those who want to preserve and promote sustainable small farms. It goes over brilliantly at county fairs and harvest feasts, at farmer's markets and in cooperative gardeners' groups. The tale reminds us that there is no turning back when farms give way to shopping malls, golf courses, and race tracks. The short-term gain from such ventures is rarely worth the loss of fresh local produce and the agrarian way of life. The agricultural cycle, the sun and rain, and the soil itself are alive, and affirm our vitality and ties to the earth. To be in sync with these is a gift beyond compare.

THE JOY OF LIFE-AFFIRMING WORK | GRATITUDE: Every human desires his/her life's labors to go toward some viable end, and yet it is easy, as storyteller Jim Harrison said through one of his protagonists, "to piss your life away on nonsense." Like the soil in a fertile valley, a human life abounds with potential, and one would hope that with well-directed effort, one's natural gifts would blossom and come to fruition. In many respects, this is the key to genuine selfhood and a meaningful life. I return to this tale when I need reminding what a privilege it is simply to spend oneself on life-affirming work.

The Horse and the Lion

AN AESOP'S FABLE FROM GREECE | (291 words)

(for background on Aesop see p. 117)

Lion was the biggest predator on the plains. You might think his main activity was hunting, but truly, his favorite pastime was to lie around in the sunshine. He didn't care to work hard to run down prey. He waited for other animals to catch their prey. Then he would roar ferociously until they slunk to the side and let him have his fill.

The fleet-footed herd animals had the most delectable flesh. Lion watched the horses come to the watering hole. One young horse in particular had a nice plump rear-end. "Oh, how I would like to get my teeth into that," the lion thought, licking his chops. Soon Lion formed a plan. He told all the animals he'd studied medicine and could cure any pain that might ail them. Playing doctor he would win their trust, and draw them close to him. Once in his clutches, they would be easy prey.

The horse was no fool. He saw what Lion was up to. He stepped forward and played along. "My hind hoof hurts. I think it has a thorn in it." Lion put on airs of great concern. He positioned himself at the horse's rear and pretended to examine the hoof. He studied it with great care, all the while calculating just how to pounce upon the young horse's rump. Lion twitched in anticipation. The split second he crouched to leap, the other animals gasped, but Horse stood ready. He swiftly kicked Lion's chest and sent him reeling. The animals had seen enough. In future they kept their distance from the "doctor."

MORAL: *Don't believe everything you hear,* or, *Two can practice the art of deception.*

ANIMALS AS HELPERS AND TEACHERS | AUTHORITY AND HEALTHY SKEPTICISM | UNHEALTHY ENTITLEMENT | MISUSE OF POWER | DENIAL AND DECEPTION: In stories the world over animals grapple with problems, they observe, they think and talk, and are the carriers of lessons we humans need to learn. In Aesop's fables the animals are mirrors in which we can plainly see some of our own traits. It is human nature to want to place all trust in those whom we lionize, and for that reason it is especially disturbing to be conned by authority figures who pretend to have our interest at heart. This meaty little fable speaks to those times when we need instinctive "horse-sense" to sniff out the real motive behind false promises.

SCAMMING | SEXUAL ABUSE PREVENTION | CUNNING AND CONNING | TRICKS AND TRICKING: Con-artists typically prey upon youths and elders in need of attention and care. Vulnerable youths find this tale compelling, memorable, and to the point. It illustrates the typical pretenses of child molesters and drug pushers who get close to youngsters by posing as friends. In prevention education with elders, this tale encourages them to be wary of present-day scam artists such as falsely credentialed doctors and bogus repairmen. The idea is not to discourage trust or to engender suspicion, but to help vulnerable folks to be discerning so they are more able to look out for themselves.

WORTHY USE OF DECEPTION: In the end the horse out-smarts the lion, not by confronting him face-to-face, but by pretending to be fooled. The second moral, *Two can practice the art of deception,* is about out-conning the con. Like a good undercover cop, the horse plays along, and beats the lion at his own game. This story was one of the favorites of a battered wife who heroically sneaked her kids out of a violent home. In menacing situations the art of deception can be a life-saving ploy.

The Horse, the Stag, and the Man

AN AESOP'S FABLE FROM GREECE | (244 words)

(for background on Aesop see p. 117)

*L*ong ago a horse roamed freely on the plain. Since no other creature grazed there, the horse had all the tender green grass to himself. Then one day a stag appeared. He too, wandered freely about the plain, helping himself to the sweet new shoots of grass. The horse took offense. The grass was his, and he should not have to share it. Oh, he might share it with a little rabbit or a mouse, but certainly he should not have to share it with one who ate so much as the stag.

One day a man came along. The horse told the man all his troubles. Here's how the man proposed to help: "If you put this bit in your mouth," he said, "and let me ride on your back, then I will make spears to hunt the stag and all his kin."

The thought of getting even with the stag so pleased the horse, he did not consider what he was getting into. The man kept his word. He made spears and hunted the stag. Ever after, the stag and his family became wary and shy. They retreated into the forest where they ate mostly leaves, and were seldom seen on the plain. But the horse never again roamed freely. The man kept him in a corral where he had nothing to eat but dry hay. Never again did the horse enjoy the sweet green shoots of grass.

> MORAL: *Revenge is not always sweet*, or, *Beware those who profit from the disputes of others.*

SUSTAINABILITY: This tale is as pertinent now as ever, as open lands diminish and land use is hotly debated in many communities. Those who would protect salmon streams feel impinged upon by farmers and visa versa. Today the wild creatures of the world struggle to survive under ever more crowded conditions. This tale reminds us to mindfully consider all sides in confronting the problems of land use, for if we do not, we may create lose-lose situations for all species.

SCARCITY | SACRIFICE | SIBLING RIVALRY | GREED AND ACQUISITIVENESS | REVENGE AND RETRIBUTION | UNHEALTHY ENTITLEMENT | UNHEALTHY COMPETITION | LOSE-LOSE SITUATIONS | ONGOING QUARRELS | DISPUTE RESOLUTION | JUSTICE AND FAIRNESS: The dynamic between the horse and the stag shows itself in nearly every setting imaginable, for it is human nature to fret over whether or not one will get one's due. This tale is excellent for most situations where dispute resolution is called for. It parallels many of the sorts of competitive squabbles that arise between siblings, spouses, neighbors, and nations. It illustrates what happens when the fear of scarcity clouds our ability to think and see clearly. The fable warns us that disputing parties who seek revenge leave themselves all the more vulnerable to an exploitive third party.

Every child knows what it's like to worry that another child might get all the goodies. Trouble begins when, like the horse, the child jumps to the conclusion that his fair share is sure to be denied. If he then takes the path of retribution, he is likely to hurt others and bring punishment upon himself. A classic example is that of a child who fears he won't get a big enough slice of cake. He becomes grabby, and the whole cake tumbles to the floor, where the dog chomps it down in seconds flat.

In similarly childish disputes between adults, the stakes are higher. Many couples caught in power struggles learn the hard way that it's impossible to punish one's spouse, without hurting oneself in the bargain. Vengeful divorce almost always results in a lose-lose situation. One divorcing couple took this story to heart. They realized that if they did not stop trying to sabotage each other, the only ones to profit would be the divorce lawyers.

The Mother Crab and Her Child

AN AESOP'S FABLE FROM GREECE | (121 words)

(for background on Aesop see p. 117)

A mother crab and her small child were making their way along the shore. The crab watched her child and noticed that wherever she was going, she always skittered sideways to get there. "My Dear," she said, "you walk sideways, but it would be so much more graceful if you would walk straight ahead."

"Mother, show me how to walk straight ahead, and I will do my best to follow." The mother had never paid attention to her own way of walking. She tried to move straight ahead, but her legs would not cooperate. After many fruitless tries, she admitted, she too, walked sideways. "I'm sorry, Dearest," said the mother crab, "I shall not expect you to walk that way, since I cannot do so myself."

Moral: *Example is the strongest teacher,* or, *Wise parents take stock of the child's true nature.*

TEACHING THROUGH EXAMPLE | WALKING ONE'S TALK | HUMILITY: This tale is important for parents, teachers, coaches, and mentors. Roman was upset when his seven-year-old son, Marc, got reprimanded for using foul language on the playground. Roman was especially embarrassed to find out that Marc, when asked where he learned such language, replied, "my dad." The teacher and Roman were basketball buddies. The teacher said, "Roman, can I tell you a fable about this problem?"

Roman said, "I can guess where this is going, but shoot."

The teacher paraphrased the above, changing it from a mother-daughter tale to a father son tale. He added, "Roman, Marc worships the ground you walk on. He'd do anything to emulate you."

Roman replied, "Okay, I get it. I can't just tell him. I have to walk the talk."

HONORING TRUE ESSENCE | GOOD MOTHERS: All of us are born with distinct gifts and limitations. Part of the job of elders is to observe children with open minds and hearts, and honor their essential nature. Oftentimes, misplaced parental expectations say more about the parent's aborted dreams than the child's true abilities. This was true of Rachel, a ballet dancer who had to retire due to stress-related illness. Unable to let go, Rachel became obsessed with her daughter Kelly's dance training. This was so stressful to Kelly that she developed ulcers, just as Rachel had, and their doctor sent them to family therapy. Rachel was irritated when I first told her this tale, but the more we explored the problem, the more honest she became. Eventually she admitted that neither she nor Kelly were temperamentally suited for competitive dance careers. Like the mother crab, Rachel realized it was unkind to deny Kelly's essential nature. Rachel later lamented that she had been a bad mother. I reminded her of the story and said, "The difference between a bad mother and a good one is not that one makes mistakes and the other doesn't. It's that one corrects her mistakes and the other doesn't."

Kore, Queen of Darkness, Maiden of Light

GREECE | (939 words)

(may be too morally complex for young children)

ABOUT THE MYTH: *In this classic Greek myth the gods and goddesses struggle in a family drama of love and longing, lust and violation, lies and truth, stubbornness and compromise that comes to define the cycle of the seasons on the Earth.*

Long ago, before the passing seasons ever showed their faces on the earth, there was one long season of summer. The dark hours of night passed quickly, while the daylight hours lingered. Bees made perpetual rounds to trees forever laden with blossoms and fruit. Kore, the lovely maiden, retained the freshness of a new blossom, while her mother, Demeter, the goddess of golden grains, remained forever in full bloom. They spent endless days roaming the hills and groves of old Greece, bestowing their blessings upon fields of corn, leaving behind them a wake of laughter and song.

One day they parted briefly, while Demeter went to the seashore to see her lover. Kore stayed behind, picking flowers in a green valley. She had gathered a handful of fragrant narcissus when she noticed the ground trembling beneath her feet. Suddenly the earth split open before her and up from the chasm there roared the sound of thundering hooves. A blinding whorl of dust engulfed her, powerful arms seized her, and no amount of struggle could prevent her from being taking down into the gaping darkness of the world below. Her abductor was none other than Hades, king of the Underworld. After having his way with her, he entreated her to stay with him and be queen of the Underworld. Kore wept floods of tears and cried out for her mother. For many days Hades persisted with soft entreaties. He spoke gently to her and brought her enticing plates of food, but she denied him and refused to eat a single bite of food from the Underworld.

Demeter searched without rest, without food or drink, enlisting the help of everyone she met. The voices of searchers rang from hill to hill, "Kore! Kore!" But no trace of her was found. On the ninth day of the search, old Hecate, guardian of crossroads, came forth and told Demeter she had heard a scream for help and the voice of a distressed girl crying, "Rape! Rape!" But when Hecate ran to the rescue, there was no one in sight. On the tenth day of the search Demeter met a herdsman who'd witnessed a frightful scene the very day Kore had vanished. The earth began to quake, startling the herdsman and his companion. A great chasm opened, and the two herdsmen could but watch as their whole herd of pigs tumbled into darkness. Suddenly out of nowhere, a charging black chariot drawn by black horses surged forth and nearly trampled them. Through the clouds of dust and the deafening clamor, they dimly perceived the driver clasping to his side a shrieking girl. The chariot plunged into the chasm, and the Earth closed up behind them. Once the dust had settled only the faint smell of narcissus remained.

Upon hearing this Demeter's blood boiled. Wretched to think of some unknown scoundrel abducting Kore, but the thought of Hades, Demeter's own brother, violating her—this took the goddess to the brink of madness.

To verify the account, Demeter and Hecate went to the sun, Helios, who witnesses all. Their suspicions were confirmed. Further, they learned that Zeus, chief of the gods, brother of Demeter and Hades, had given Hades his covert blessing. Utterly betrayed, convulsed by inconsolable grief, seized by unquenchable hate toward her brothers, Demeter wandered the earth, revoking her blessings of bounty and fruition from all living things. Plants and trees withered, livestock went barren, the hulls of dead bees and butterflies littered the Earth. The human race languished and people began to starve. High on Mt. Olympus, Zeus himself grew care-worn, for life on Earth depended upon Demeter's bounty. In her hands rested the fate of all living things. He sent gifts and conciliatory messages, but Demeter swore the land would remain barren until Kore returned.

Zeus knew he had to act fast. He sent word to Demeter that Kore could only return if she had not eaten the food of the Underworld. He ordered Hades to bring Kore to meet with her mother at Eleusis. Having no choice but to accept, Hades told Kore to prepare for the journey. Kore was ecstatic at the hope of returning to her mother. Hades' gardener, however, complicated things by announcing he had seen Kore pick a pomegranate from Hades' orchard. He reported having seen her taste a few morsels of the fruit. He was taken to Eleusis to bear witness.

At Eleusis, the mother-daughter reunion produced a moment's elation, but joys were dashed when the gardener spoke. Stubborn to the last, Demeter refused to restore Earth's bounty. Rhea, mother of the gods, came forth to craft a compromise. She suggested that since Kore had eaten only a few bites of the Underworld fruit, it would be unfair to doom her to the underworld forever. Rhea proposed that Kore spend part of the year ruling alongside Hades as underworld queen. During these months the land would be barren and her title would be Persephone, Queen of the Dead. The rest of the year she would return to her mother and together they would restore Earth's bounty and preside over the growing season. All parties agreed and old Hecate saw to it that the agreement was kept.

Demeter restored prosperity to the land and rewarded those who had helped her. As keeper of the crossroads, Hecate vowed to watch over Kore during the seasonal shifts: in autumn when *Kore the Maiden* becomes *Persephone Queen of the Dead*, and in spring, when she rises up from darkness to bless the fields anew. Ever since that day, all living things have endured the round of changing seasons on this earth.

MISUSE OF POWER | JUSTICE AND FAIRNESS | ADVOCACY FOR CHILDREN | DENIAL AND DECEPTION | ISOLATION: Those who have experienced incest or rape know the complicated dynamics which tear families apart when taboos are broken and boundaries are violated. I've worked with families who've had no words to express the fear, grief, shame, indignation, and powerlessness they feel. This story seems to break the ice and open the door for communication. Youngsters who have been violated almost invariably feel at fault and alone in all the world, and it helps them enormously to hear that such things also happened to Kore. Outraged and grief-stricken non-offending parents connect strongly with Demeter, and appreciate her fierce tenacity. There is much in the story people wish to emulate, such as parents advocating for kids, the seeking of sound help and careful investigation. People also find within the tale things which they question and abhor, such as Zeus and Hades secretly being in cahoots, and feeling entitled to abduct, violate, and deceive. The story has a way of getting people to articulate their own sense of justice.

LONGING FOR LIGHT | WINTER BLUES | DEPRIVATION | SACRED FEMININE | RESTORING BLOCKED GIFTS | INSPIRATION LOST AND REGAINED: In addition to the social and familial implications of the tale we can also ask what the story holds as a metaphor for the inner life.

An artist named Nancy likened Kore's disappearance to her on-again, off-again connection with the muse: "There is an incredible loss, a sense of barren deadness. I get depressed, no creative urges come, and everything seems bleak. Every October I used to think I'd never paint again. Then I began to realize my creative work and my moods run in cycles. Just like Kore, what goes down, eventually comes back up, ready to create anew."

Franklin, a writer experiencing writer's block, examined Zeus and Hades as the interior "power-brokers" who "capture and control" his "fresh impulses and uncensored ideas," which he associated with Kore. Franklin wanted Kore to prevail, yet was mature enough to know that as a professional writer who needed to pay the bills, he would always have to contend with some element of compromise. "It's hard to strike a balance," he said, "between Kore's innocent freedom of expression, and the powers that be in the publishing world. There have been a few times when I got well paid under contract, and at the same time was able to stay connected with a fresh, spontaneous voice. That's the best case scenario. When the right compromise is struck, it's as if Rhea showed up and balanced the forces. I'd like to put the goddesses in charge of my creative work."

MISUSE OF POWER | DISPUTE RESOLUTION | JUSTICE AND FAIRNESS: April and her husband Saul used this as a teaching tale in their dispute resolution course as a way to open discussion on the challenges their trainees would face. Saul said, "Our line of work attracts idealistic folks who want to see justice enforced in its purest form. But disputes always occur in the real world, and people have to learn to work with the given power structure, the given mores, etc."

April added, "It's a tough revelation, but we want people to balance their idealism with a little pragmatism."

Pythagoras and the White Beans

GREECE | (525 words)

ABOUT PYTHAGORAS: *This legend is generously peppered with fact. But as is the case with many legends, facts and fiction blend into a compelling yarn that carries more than a kernel of truth.*

An old legend says the Oracle at Delphi foretold the birth of Pythagoras, a mathematician who would be blessed with divine intelligence. He was born in the year 580 BC. In addition to being a mathematician, he was a gifted philosopher, an important astronomer, a prominent mystic, and a brilliant musical theorist. He studied fervently under esteemed teachers from China, India, Egypt, and Persia. *All is number*, was his motto and he taught his students that numbers were endowed with vibrant qualities, and were related with specific virtues, genders, deities, colors, and ideals. Pythagoras was ahead of his time in understanding that the earth was round and that the planets, sun, and moon each had their own courses of motion. His Eastern training led him to believe the human soul transmigrates after death to inhabit another living being, such as an animal.

Pythagoras rejected the flowing robes favored by his fellow Greeks and dressed instead in Persian trousers. He let his hair and beard grow long, which added to his mystique. His famous talks combined mathematical demonstrations with compelling parables. Musicians played, curtains were drawn, and Pythagoras would appear before his followers in golden sandals with a golden wreath encircling his head. His attendants bore bowls of brightly colored sand so that he could pour out lines and digits to demonstrate his theorems. His wit was so piercing, listeners thought him to be the son of the god Apollo. Legends say Pythagoras conversed with daemons and listened to the music of the stars.

In his elder years he founded a mystic school, progressive in many ways, including opening its doors to women. Students took a five-year vow of silence. They abstained from eating meat and fish and used neither wood nor leather. The school attracted wealthy aristocrats, and to study with Pythagoras they had to renounce all property and possessions. Mathematics was divine knowledge and students had to purify their bodies and minds to render themselves worthy. Through understanding the secrets of numbers they would know the key to life itself.

Geometric shapes, especially the pentagram, were endowed with sacred powers. Fire was not only a symbol of truth, it embodied truth and had to be handled with reverence. Elements, animals, metals, musical scales, even vegetables were associated with divine forces, and had to be treated as such. The white bean, a near-perfect source of nutrition, was the essence of perfection itself.

Legend has it that Pythagoras once banned a disrespectful student from the school. The ex-student grew ever more bitter. He spread vicious rumors about Pythagoras and poisoned the townspeople's minds against him. Eventually the troublemaker led an angry mob to kill him. It is said that his followers formed a human bridge with their bodies, enabling Pythagoras to escape. But when in flight he came upon a field of white beans, he gave himself up rather than see the sacred plants trampled by an angry mob. Thus was his devotion to the divine essence of ordinary things. Even those who would dismiss his mysticism as "superstitious" have to marvel at his comprehending Earth's spherical shape 1800 years before the concept was once again asserted by Copernicus.

INSPIRING INTEREST IN MATH | NUMBERS AND THE SACRED: High school math teacher Catherine Goetsche gave me a version of this tale, along with others she uses to spark the imaginations of her geometry students. "Pythagoras is a favorite among my students," she said. "The whole idea of numbers as mystical entities with divine powers, really intrigues students, especially the gifted ones with an intuitive grasp of math. The fact that Pythagoras founded his school nearly 2500 years ago gives students some historical perspective. The fascination with numbers has been with us a long time."

REVERENCE FOR NATURE | THE MORE-THAN-HUMAN WORLD | TEACHING THROUGH EXAMPLE | SACRIFICE | MISPLACED BLAME | PASSION FOR LEARNING | MENTORSHIP: Pythagoras experienced the natural world as imbued with the divine essence and pregnant with its mystery. This tale shows a teacher willing to make the ultimate sacrifice for what he holds true. He does not place himself and his teachings above the natural perfection of the white bean. In the end his affection for all life is greater than his need to protect his own individual life. Carl Jung, toward the end of his life, was asked about his belief in God. He replied, "I do not *believe*, I *know*." Pythagoras must have experienced a similar *knowing* of the divine in all things. Perhaps the daemons had shown him his soul would transmigrate and live on through some other natural form.

The Moon in the Well

TURKEY | (582 words)

Who is Nasruddin? Tales of the infamous Turkish fool, Nasruddin Hodja, go back at least five centuries. It is said that when Nasruddin was a schoolboy, he witnessed a mischievious prank which delighted the students and annoyed the schoolmaster. Afterward the schoolmaster attempted to punish each student in a suitable way. When he got to Nasruddin he asked, "What was your part in this?"

Nasruddin replied, "I watched and I laughed."

"You watched and you laughed?" said the master.

"Yes," said young Nasruddin, "I watched and I laughed."

"Very well then," said the master, "from this day forth, when people deal with you, they will watch and they will laugh."

Ever since that day people have watched and laughed at the antics of Nasruddin. Later, to pass the time, people recounted his capers and laughed some more. Today there are hundreds of tales about Nasruddin who, later in life, like so many folkloric tricksters, became a wise teacher-priest, and earned the title Hodja.

One quiet evening, Nasruddin Hodja sat reading sacred texts by the lamplight. After a few pages his eyes grew heavy. He thought how nice it would be if his dear wife would bring him a cool drink of water. "Fatima," he called, craning his neck toward the kitchen, but the kitchen was dark and Fatima did not reply. "She must have gone off to bed," said the Hodja. He hoisted himself to his feet and shuffled into the kitchen where Fatima kept the water jug. "It's empty," said Nasruddin. "I shall have to go to the well and fill it."

As he stepped out into the night air, the sweet fragrance of jasmine surrounded him. "What a pleasant evening," said Nasruddin to himself. He went to the well at the center of the courtyard. He lifted the bucket and peered into the dark water. "Fatima, come quickly!" he called. "The moon has fallen into the well!" Fatima must have been sleeping soundly, for she did not come, and Nasruddin had to face the grave situation all alone. "Keep calm," he told himself. "Be brave. If you do not act quickly and wisely, the moon shall drown in the well!"

How could one man alone salvage the situation? Only by being a true hero. Nasruddin trembled at the thought of it: The fate of the moon lay in his hands. Here was his chance to be remembered as a hero for all time. He looked this way and that for a pole, a stick, anything to get hold of the moon. Frantically he whirled about until his baggy pantaloon caught on something that held him fast. Then Nasruddin looked down and saw he was caught on the metal hook used for lowering the bucket into the well. He seized the hook and freed himself. Then he grasped the rope in one hand and the hook in the other. "Hold on, Moon. I will save you," he cried.

He lowered the hook and trolled back and forth across the surface of the water. "Dear Moon, do not lose heart," said the Hodja. "Just grab the hook and I'll pull you out." The hook snagged one of the jutting stones that lined the edge of the well. As soon as the Hodja felt it tug he cried, "Good Moon, hold tight! On the count of three, jump as high as you can!" Then Nasruddin cried, "One," and pulled with all his might. Then he called, "Two," and pulled twice as hard. Then he yelled, "Three!" and yanked with a force greater than the strongest ox. At that moment the rock came loose. It flew up into the air while the Hodja fell backwards onto the ground.

For a moment he lay there dazed, but soon he opened his eyes, and what did he see? Why, the moon in all her splendor shining down from the sky. His plan had worked. With sheer determination and brute strength, he had catapulted the moon to her rightful place.

The back of his head was sore, but what did it matter? The bump would be a reminder of his heroism. He went back into the house and put himself to bed. There he lay smiling. Even after closing his eyes he could still see the brilliant light of the moon shining down through the window. With every pore of his being he drank in that light, and basked in the glory of his great deed.

THE MORE-THAN-HUMAN WORLD | HUMOR | TAKING OURSELVES LESS SERI-OUSLY: The famous Hodja may well be the prototype for the near-sighted cartoon elder, Mr. Magoo, for both bumble about in their own little world. Nasruddin reminds us that we all view reality through our own idiosyncratic lens. What we perceive as objective truth, is merely one limited view. A woman named Lauren saw herself in this tale and had the self-awareness to admit, "I like to think I'm doing favors for people, but it's often pointed out that I'm just trying to play the savior."

A fellow named Aaron said, "'The Moon in the Well' is the perfect example of what's meant by the phrase, 'He's a legend in his own mind.' My wife says I get like that sometimes, and I guess she's right." Chuckling at the lovable Hodja invites us chuckle at ourselves, and learn to take ourselves less seriously.

The Last Feast

TURKEY | (583 words)

(for background on Nasruddin see p. 129)

The Hodja had but one sheep. During the day he took it to graze in a grassy field. There it mingled with other sheep. Even though Nasruddin's eyesight was poor, he gazed at the flock and remarked that his sheep was the best. "See how mine is plumper and whiter than the rest? See how his wool is the best among them?" The shepherds chuckled behind the Hodja's back, for indeed there was nothing remarkable about his mangy old sheep.

One day one of the shepherds began pulling Nasruddin's leg. He said, "What a shame that your fine sheep shall go to waste."

"What do you mean?" asked the Hodja.

"Well, everyone knows the world is coming to an end tomorrow. What a shame that we shall never feast upon the flesh of your prized sheep."

"The world is coming to an end?" asked the Hodja.

All the shepherds nodded emphatically. One of them said, "Yes, everyone is talking about it."

Another chimed in, "Why this is common knowledge, surely you must have known."

"Yes," said Nasruddin, not wanting to appear ignorant, "I've known about it for a while."

"We just think it's sad that no one will ever enjoy the exquisite taste of this fine sheep of yours."

Nasruddin did not want to slaughter his only sheep, but what was the good of sparing its life when it would only die tomorrow anyway, along with everyone else? He decided to make a grand gesture. "Very well," he said. "Join me at the river's edge tomorrow for our final meal. I shall roast you the best mutton you've ever tasted." The shepherds had to make great efforts to stifle their laughter until the Hodja was out of hearing range.

The following morning Nasruddin set about making a grand feast of figs, couscous, pistachios, and of course, mutton roasted on a spit. He kept the fire going, and each time smoke got in his eyes he rubbed the tears away. Soon all the tears made him sadder and sadder. "What a pity the world will end! We shall never again feast together, nor swim in the lovely river during the heat of the day."

"A swim sounds good," said one of the shepherds, and soon all of them were peeling off their shoes and clothes and diving into the river. Nasruddin wanted to swim, too, but then he thought better of it. After all, he was hosting the last feast in the world, and he wanted to make everything right. The shepherds splashed and swam about, refreshing themselves, working up an appetite. Nasruddin's blubbering made his friends feel uneasy. They enjoyed fooling him, but they hadn't intended to make him so sad. They tried to cheer him by calling out "Umm, that mutton smells good," and indeed this was true, for the mutton sizzled to perfection over the hot coals.

At a certain point the smells began to change. The fire grew extra smoky and smelled, not of meat, but of things sour and rank. The shepherds climbed up on the bank to see what was the matter. "What are you burning?" they asked Nasruddin.

"Oh, my friends, I wanted to tidy up. Your clothes were strewn about. I thought about folding them, but they were smelly and unwashed. I thought about washing them, but with the end so near, why bother? I simply burned them instead. You came into the world naked and naked you shall leave it! Come now, let's eat!"

HUMOR | CUNNING AND CONNING | TRICKS AND TRICKING | RECIPROCITY | FALSE WORDS INSTIGATING TROUBLE | LOSE-LOSE SITUATIONS: Learning to play a trick is a developmental accomplishment for a small child. When a child wants to fool someone, he has to be clever, stealthy, patient, and imaginative. He has to anticipate how the other will react. In order that the trick come off as fun and not mean, it has to be done in a spirit of generosity. It's surprising how often children have an instinctive ken for this. Most children find a way to pull off stunts that amuse and poke fun without injury. However, the art of good trickery eludes some, and especially in group settings as in college and the military, a predatory meanness can prevail. In this story when Nasruddin falls for the trick hook, line, and sinker, his friends learn that tricks can have unexpected consequences. In telling this tale to children and teens I often ask whether the tricks played strikes them as mostly mean or mostly fun, and whether the friends deserved to have their clothes burned. Young people love to hash this over and discuss the etiquette of trickery. They also relish recounting personal stories of tricks that worked and tricks that went too far.

Fair Pay

TURKEY | (472 words)

(for background on Nasruddin see p. 129)

The Hodja was riding his donkey along a trail through the woods when he came upon a woodcutter and his companion. The wood-cutter was dripping with sweat, and it was no wonder, for he worked quickly, swinging his big muscular arms powerfully and rhythmically. All around him were neat stacks of wood ready to load onto the wagon and carry into town. The woodcutter's companion sat perched on a woodpile, and didn't trouble himself with loading the wagon. He hadn't a drop of sweat on his brow and his hands were unsoiled. He called out, "Keep cutting, my robust friend, my hale and hearty part-ner! Just one more tree and the task will be done." Each time the woodcutter brought the ax down hard upon the green wood, the companion let out a grunt, "Ughhhh."

This struck Nasruddin as very peculiar. He asked, "Why do you grunt with each blow, when it is your friend who does the work?"

The companion replied, "Oh, that's how I help him. I cheer him on and do all the grunting and groaning, so he can be free to chop the wood. Imagine how discouraging his task would be without me!" The Hodja shook his head, gave his donkey a nudge, and continued on down the road.

Later that day he encountered the two men again in the market place, near the center of town. The woodcutter had struck a deal and had received a good price for his wood. The companion protested loudly that he should be granted his fair share. When he saw the Hodja he called out, "Wise one, you were there! You saw how I did my part. Tell my friend to pay up!"

The Hodja scratched his beard. "Hmmm," he said. "Tell me again how the work was divided."

The companion whose hands were still not soiled by work said, "My friend cut the wood, and I did all the grunting, groaning, and cheering."

"Oh yes," said the Hodja. "Well then, Mr. Woodcutter, hand over the money and I'll count out your companion's fair share."

The woodcutter did not want to hand over the money. But out of respect for the wise one, he reached into his vest pocket, withdrew his newly earned bag of gold coins, and handed it over. From a nearby merchant the Hodja borrowed a silver coin tray for counting out the coins. He took three gold coins from the pouch and dropped them onto the silver tray. They resounded as they struck it. "Did you hear that?" asked the Hodja.

"Yes," replied the companion smiling.

"Good," said the Hodja. "You gave noise, and now you've received noise in return." Then the wise one put the three coins back into the bag with the others, and gave it back to the woodcutter, for such is the wisdom of Nasruddin.

HUMOR | JUSTICE AND FAIRNESS | CUNNING AND CONNING | WALKING ONE'S TALK | RECIPROCITY | OPPORTUNISM: Charlotte was on a gymnastics team with twelve other girls. She was exceedingly bright, and continually succeeded in conning her friends. She would suggest an activity, such as movies or shopping, and later in the ticket line or at the cash register she'd ask to borrow, saying she'd "forgotten" her wallet. The next day, when her friends would tell her to pay up, she'd bamboozle them with deft evasions. When it came to putting away mats after practice, Charlotte often disappeared, and on the bus she connived to get the best seat. Each time she was questioned on these matters, she came up with quick justifications, got upset, and made others feel they were in the wrong for questioning. The coach asked me for a relevant story, and I suggested this one. She told it at practice, saying she wanted to talk about fairness. Charlotte's teammates discussed the tale at length, saying they knew what it was like to be duped by a "woodcutter's companion." Without naming names, they threw poignant glances in Charlotte's direction. "Charlotte was a little miffed," the coach told me later, "but that week she quietly paid back the debts. She knew we had her number, and she didn't want to be pegged a 'wood-cutter's companion.'"

SCAMMING | UNHEALTHY ENTITLEMENT | GREED AND ACQUISITIVENESS | DISPUTE RESOLUTION: Some people think of themselves as unworthy, and others, like the woodcutter's companion, think of themselves as especially worthy, entitled to receive without giving in return. When this tendency becomes habitual, the person has to continually make new acquaintances, as the old ones begin to feel used. It is often easiest with such people to avoid confrontation and quietly write them off. It takes a courageous friend to hold them accountable and insist on fairness.

Unhealthy entitlement usually stems from an unhealthy self-concept. A person may undervalue her own resourcefulness and think, "Others are capable of producing. I am not, therefore, they should provide for me." Or, the person may exaggerate their own worth and devalue others, thinking, "I'm special, let others pay my way." People caught in either of these modes don't want attention brought to the problem, and often find ways to blame others. When disputes arise over who is entitled to what, resolution may require the help of a respected third party like the Hodja.

Hypatia's Gifts

EGYPT | (456 words)

ABOUT HYPATIA: *Female mathematician Hypatia was born around the middle of the fourth century in Alexandria, Egypt. Much of what is known of her life comes to us through the writings of Synesius, her most devoted pupil. Six of his letters to Hypatia have survived. The following tale is more factual than fictitious, for though the life story of this living "oracle" is the stuff of legend, it also happens to be historically accurate.*

*T*heon, the learned mathematician, adored his clever young daughter, Hypatia, more than he loved learning itself. Hypatia's mother had died when she was a baby and for solace she often climbed into her father's lap as he calculated figures. As she grew so did her father's pride, for she daily proved herself to be bright beyond measure.

The scholarly institutions of the day did not welcome girls, but this did not deter Theon. He trained Hypatia in the arts, literature, science, philosophy, and the religions of the world. He taught her to be inquisitive, and to see the heart of truth in all faiths. He taught her the art of persuasive speech, and saw that she underwent vigorous athletic training.

Hypatia absorbed the teachings of the wise ones whose lectures she attended. Soon she began writing, teaching, and touring around the Mediterranean giving lectures of her own. Even those who scoffed at the idea of a woman scholar admitted she was one of the most formidable thinkers of her time. Most famous were her compelling lectures on the subjects of algebra, astronomy, religion, and philosophy. Her intelligence, poise, and erudition so stunned the intellects of the time, they deemed her an oracle, a mouthpiece of the gods.

Tensions mounted in Alexandria between rivaling religious sects. Church fathers sought to secure dominance by casting out other religions. They leveled the Egyptian temple of Serapis, killing those who tried to defend it. Some say they destroyed the great library of Alexandria. One thing is certain: They saw Hypatia as a threat because she openly condoned religious freedom and urged people to think for themselves. Church officials defamed all mathematicians as charlatans. They called Hypatia a satanic enchantress, accusing her of loving music and befriending musicians, a sure sign of evil.

It was Hypatia's custom to travel through Alexandria in an open chariot. One day along her usual route, a frenzied mob, spurred by a zealous archbishop, set upon her. They dragged her into a nearby church, stripped her naked, and beat her to death with roofing tiles. Then they tore her to bits, took her remains into the street, and burnt them. You can imagine the terror this struck in the hearts of young women hoping to follow in Hypatia's footsteps by studying religion and math.

Hypatia's enemies took her life but not her teachings. She was the first woman to go down in history as a renowned and influential thinker, and her works were not forgotten. Scholars today recognize her as the greatest mathematician and astronomer of her time. She lives on as an icon of courage and erudition. Perhaps her spirit comes to life each time a devoted student perseveres against difficult odds.

MISUSE OF POWER | MISGUIDED LEADERSHIP | MISPLACED BLAME | EXCLUSION | DISENFRANCHISEMENT | WOMEN AND EDUCATION | DROPOUT PREVENTION | INSPIRING INTEREST IN MATH | NURTURING FATHERS | MENTORSHIP | THE FUTILITY OF VIOLENCE | PASSION FOR LEARNING | CREATIVE COURAGE | COURAGE, INTEGRITY, RESILIENCE: This tale is an inspiration to anyone who has felt marginalized, or excluded. One teacher told me his gay and lesbian students saw Hypatia as a role model. Women trying to get beyond societally imposed gender roles also feel encouraged by this tale. It is a boost to all math students, but especially to girls. The story also stresses the supreme privilege of obtaining an education. This tale can be used for dropout prevention, or to celebrate women's excellence in any field. One father who wanted to impart academic encouragement to his two daughters, felt moved to tears when he told them this tale. Whenever they lost heart and became discouraged about school, he retold the tale to encourage them and to rekindle their commitment to excellence.

The Sesame Seed

EGYPT | (974 words)

*T*here was once a king who often sailed up and down the Nile. One day while returning to port, he saw a fisherwoman knee deep in the water, casting out her nets. She was not the most beautiful woman he had ever seen, but something about her struck him. Later the king could not get the woman out of his mind. He sent his advisor to find out whether she was single, married, or widowed.

The advisor returned saying, "The woman is married to a fisherman, and though he is poor, he is thought well of by his neighbors."

"What a shame," said the king.

The advisor said, "Don't be discouraged. You are the king, and can have whatever, or whomever you want. If your conscience allows, there are ways to get rid of the husband." The two put their heads together and devised a plan.

The next day the king sent for the husband. "Fisherman," he said, "I shall ask something of you, and if you don't succeed, I'll have your head chopped off. You must come before me tomorrow riding and walking."

"At the same time?" asked the fisherman.

"Yes, at the same time!" snapped the king.

The fisherman went home and told his wife the whole puzzling story. "It's truly a paradox," said the husband. "How can I ride and walk at the same time?"

"Don't worry," said the wife. She went off to take counsel with her sister.

"Borrow my she-goat," said the sister. "Tell your husband to go to the palace with his back-side planted on the she-goat's back, and his feet dragging on the ground."

When the king saw the man coming to court both walking and riding he knew he'd been outsmarted. "Well, fisherman," he said, "I'm going to require another task. Tomorrow you must appear before me dressed naked."

The distraught fisherman went home and told his wife that being dressed naked was a great paradox, truly impossible. "Don't worry," said the wife, and she went to take counsel from her sister.

The sister said, "Tell your husband in the morning instead of putting on clothes, he must drape a fishing net over his shoulders." This is exactly what the fisherman did.

When the king saw the fisherman dressed naked, he realized the fisherman understood paradox, and that the third and final task must be truly impossible. "Fisherman," he said, "I want you to bring to the court, an infant who tells riddles and tall tales. If you fail, I'll have your head."

The fisherman went home and in great distress said to his wife, "Now I'm done for. Where on earth is there an infant who can tell riddles and tall tales?"

"I don't know," said the wife, "but I shall ask my sister."

After hearing the third task, the sister said, "There is but one class of infant who can tell tall tales and riddles, and that is one who is half jinn and half human. There just happens to be such an infant in a nearby town."

So the next morning the fisherman went before the king holding the seven-day-old infant in his arms. "You expect this one to tell riddles and tall tales?" bellowed the king.

The fisherman said nothing, but the infant called out, "Peace be on you, Oh Great King." The king was taken aback, and the infant began his tall tale. "I'm a well-to-do fellow and here's how I got my wealth. Fifty years ago I was poor and hungry. I stood beneath a date palm heavily laden with fruit. I tossed clods of dried earth trying to knock the dates down. But the dates held fast. Those dates were sticky as dates will be, and the dirt held fast to the dates, until there was nearly an acre of land up there in the tree."

There was nothing the king loved more than a tall tale, "That's very reasonable," he said. "Go on with the tale, little teller."

"So," said the infant, "I got a plow and an ox and a handful of sesame seeds. I climbed the tree, and plowed, and planted, and the rains came, and the crops grew, and made me a wealthy man. I bought lands and have prospered ever since. Only there is one thing bothering me."

"What's that?" asked the king.

"Since that first harvest there's been one sesame seed stuck in the bark of that date palm tree. I've been obsessed with it for fifty years. No matter how hard I poke and prod I can't get hold of it. So, Great King, here's the riddle: Should I forget about it and move on?"

The king was so delighted by the infant teller of riddles and tall tales, that he cried, "Of, course, clever one! You're a rich man. You'll never want for sesame seeds. Forget about it!"

The infant replied, "You seem to be a wise king, so why not follow your own advice?"

"My own advice?" puzzled the king.

"Yes," cried the infant. "Your life is full of ease and pleasure. You have dozens of women showering you with affection. So forget about the one you cannot have. Let it go."

This was a king who had planned that morning to behead someone. But the infant's words went into his ears, down through his heart, and into his belly. All the way through him these words rang true. A smile came to his lips, and he said, "So be it. Go forth good fisherman and may God bless you and your wife."

And that is the tale of the king and the fisherwoman, and the husband, and the sister, and the goat, and the net, and the half-jinn infant, and the sesame seed. So let us remember, my friends, when we think we cannot contend with paradox, perhaps we can. And before we go lusting after things beyond our reach, we must first take stock of the good things we already have.

UNHEALTHY ENTITLEMENT | MISGUIDED LEADERSHIP | MISUSE OF POWER | JUSTICE AND FAIRNESS | THE INACCESSIBLE LOVER | LETTING GO | HUMILITY | TAKING OURSELVES LESS SERIOUSLY | GRATITUDE: All of us at one time or another become fixated on someone or something that would be best let go. Like the king we may try all sorts of power maneuvers, but true joy will only come to us in accepting that in the bigger scheme of things we probably have plenty to be grateful for, and the sought-after object of desire might not be what we actually need. When put forth by the clever young half jinni, this truth is so resonant that the king's grace and humility are restored. The half-jinni acts as a marvelous arbitrator, befriending and delighting the king, priming him to see his own foibles, guiding him to enjoy the luxury of being able to laugh at himself, and let go.

GREED AND ACQUISITIVENESS | SUSTAINABILITY | GRATITUDE | INTANGIBLE TREASURES: This tale is especially relevant in our materialistic society, where we take much for granted, and where we often obsess over what we next hope to acquire. The simplicity movement encourages us to take stock of what we have, and regarding those things we crave, to ask, "Do I really need that?" and, "Will I own it, or will it own me?" Sweeter than acquisition, and more elusive, is the sense of pleasure and gratitude in what we already have.

COOPERATION AND DEVOTION | ELDER WISDOM | HELP FROM WISE ELDERS: As in so many wisdom tales, counsel is sought from a wise elder—in this case, the sister. She is not intimidated by paradox. She is wise enough to know that two contradictory things can both be true at the same time. If the fisherman had been either walking or riding, either clothed or naked, he would have been enacting the either/or mentality which supports dualistic thought. This tale can serve as a marvelous introduction to the subject of paradox. It reminds us of times in our lives when the milk is both separate from and joined to the cream. For lovers, parents, friends, and employers it may suggest those moments when we must be both fierce and forgiving, both loving and strict, both demanding and kind. "That's how we had to be when our teenage daughter got herpes," said parents, Dave and Patricia. "We had to show her how much we love her, and we had to lay down the law."

The wise elder comes to life whenever we transcend either-or thinking to embrace a greater whole. A CEO named Daphne said her greatest paradox was that at work she liked to be in charge of things, but that deep down she felt fragile and hated making decisions: "I guess the wise elder would ask me not to reject either part of myself, but to try to be conscious of and responsible for both."

THE MORE-THAN-HUMAN WORLD | SUSTAINABILITY | INTANGIBLE TREASURES: In Middle Eastern countries the date palm is seen as the tree of life. In the story within our story the date palm stands as a compelling central image. Rooted, enduring, and abundant, it stands in contrast with the themes of scarcity, obsession, and greed. The image itself is nourishing, calming, and healing. It speaks of things which outlast all acquisitions, and reminds us that the cycle of life itself is the one lasting treasure.

Why Death is Like the Banana Tree

MADAGASCAR | (237 words)

God wanted the first man and woman to be able to choose the kind of death they would have. One day he asked, "Would you prefer to die like the moon, or like the banana tree?" The couple did not know what it meant to die like the moon or the banana tree, so God explained, "Each month the moon dies and fades away, but it revives bit by bit to live again. When the banana tree dies, it does not come back, but it leaves behind green shoots so that its offspring can carry on in its place. You may have offspring to take your place, or you may revive each month like the moon. You choose."

The couple considered the options for some time. If they chose to be childless, they would always be restored to life, like the moon. It would be lonely, however, and they would have no one to help them with their work, no one to teach, to love, or to strive for. They told God they preferred to be fruitful like the banana tree. God granted their wish. They had many fine children and a happy life and then they died. Since then there has been much love and new life on this earth, replenishing generation after generation. But since the first couple chose, each individual's life is brief, and in the end the body withers like a banana tree.

DEATH | SACRIFICE | ACCEPTING MORTALITY: This gem from Madagascar offers the tree of life as a symbol of the everlasting. It suggests that much of the richness of the human experience is tied to our mortality. We would not endeavor to love and to create, if it weren't for our role as mortal creatures with finite lives in which we eventually grow old and die.

POSTERITY | LIFE-DEATH-REBIRTH CYCLE | THE INEVITABILITY OF OLD AGE AND DEATH | GRIEF AND LOSS: A seventy-seven-year-old woman named Iris considered herself to be an agnostic. She was diagnosed with cancer and her doctor said she had between three and six months to live. Iris found herself reviewing her life. Had she lived it well? Had she done enough for her loved ones? Would any part of her live on, or would she simply become "food for the worms"? Iris was assigned a hospice counselor, and somewhere in the course of their dialogue, the counselor introduced this tale. Iris found it resonated with her sensibilities about death. She couldn't picture herself sitting on a cloud among harp-playing angels, but she could picture her progeny, thriving like a fruitful orchard in her wake. "That's enough for me," she told the counselor, "that they carry on, living full lives when I'm gone." The story affirmed her view of posterity and satisfied her sense of life and death as complementary parts of a greater continuity.

REVERENCE FOR NATURE | THE MORE-THAN-HUMAN WORLD: Like so many of the tales of old, the reference points for understanding are great things in the natural world. In this case God calls upon the restorative powers of the moon and the banana tree to illustrate the options for human immortality.

How Death Came to Humankind

A LUBA STORY FROM AFRICA | (320 words)

Long ago in the days of the ancestors, people had not yet been visited by Death. Not being acquainted with Death, they knew nothing of grief and mourning. One day it came to the attention of Kalumba, the Creator, that Life and Death were journeying along the roadway. It would not be long before they would reach the village, and have contact with people for the first time. Kalumba wanted Life to be welcomed into the village, but he wanted Death to be kept away. The Creator told Dog and Goat to keep watch at the roadside. "When Life comes along," Kalumba instructed, "you must greet him and let him pass, but whatever happens, do not let Death into the village."

Dog and Goat took their assigned place at the roadside. Goat turned to Dog and said, "You are always falling asleep. I don't know why Kalumba entrusted this job to you."

Dog argued, "I will stay wide awake until Life has passed and we have captured Death."

After much dispute about Dog's sleeping habits, Goat wandered off to nibble some grass. Dog built a fire, and tried hard to stay awake, yet as time passed, he could not help but fall asleep. Dog had been snoozing a short while, when Death came along and passed unnoticed. Later, Goat returned to take his turn as sentinel on the roadway. He watched carefully, and when Life happened along, Goat seized him. "Oh," said Goat, when he realize his mistake, "I meant to capture that other one. Is he coming?" "No," replied Life, "he has already gone ahead, to the village."

Ever since that day, humankind has been acquainted with Death, and thus they have come to know grief. Would it have been different if Goat had kept watch throughout? The people in that village say, "yes," but in the end, how can we know? Life and Death travel the same roadways. Even Kalumba could not change this.

DEATH | ACCEPTING MORTALITY | GRIEF AND LOSS | THE INEVITABILITY OF OLD AGE AND DEATH: This tale can be consoling in the months following the death of a loved one. It's also meaningful in preparation for one's own death. It gives an interesting reply to the questions so often asked in grief, "What did I do to deserve this?" or, "How could God allow my loved one to die?" The tale offers assurance that death is not a punishment meted out by a judgmental God. Conversely, the creator wanted to spare people from death, but even stronger than Kalumba's wishes is the natural law: Life and death travel the same roadways.

The Twisted Message

AN AKAMBA STORY FROM AFRICA | (383 words)

God created men and women. Their life was short and difficult. God felt mercy toward them, and he did not want their deaths to be forever. "When they die they will be born anew," he decided. "I shall create the afterlife."

He placed them in their own region, while he stayed at home. At that time some animals could travel between God's realm and the realm of the humans. Two such travelers were Weaverbird and Chameleon. God watched how they behaved. Weaverbird did everything rapidly. When he spoke, out of his mouth came many lies. Chameleon took a long time to do anything. When he spoke, out of his mouth came the truth.

God chose Chameleon to take a message to the people. He said, "Chameleon, go to the region where I have placed the people. Tell them to take solace. When they die, it will not be for good. Their spirit shall live on." Chameleon set out. Weaverbird stayed with God.

Of course, Chameleon traveled slowly and took a very long time. At last he arrived in the region where the people lived. Everyone gathered around to hear the message. Chameleon began to speak. "Ah- umm God says... God says... God says I should tell you . . ." It was taking Chameleon a very long time to relay the message.

Weaverbird grew restless. He told God, "I am going to step out for a moment." He flew to the region where the humans lived. Because he was so quick, he arrived there in no time at all. He listened for a moment while Chameleon stammered on, "God says. . . . God says . . . God told me to tell you . . . "

Weaverbird butted in and blurted out, "God says when a person's life ends, they will shrivel up like an old root and die off for good."

Finally Chameleon said, "God says when humans die their spirit shall live on."

The poor humans did not know whom to believe. They feared the Weaverbird was right, but they hoped what Chameleon said was true. Suddenly Magpie swooped down from a nearby tree, "The first words are the wisest," he said. Having heard this, the humans feared Magpie was right. Perhaps death was the end for their kind. Because of the twisted message, people live with doubt to this very day.

DEATH: Most of the world's people believe the soul possesses some manner of eternal life, but rarely is our faith iron-clad. Most of us, facing our own death, or the death of a loved one, find ourselves visited by doubt. "The Twisted Message" is especially meaningful in addressing such doubt. A woman named Marcy took this story to heart while caring for her dying father. When Marcy's mother had died years before, her father had offered heart-felt assurances that they would someday rejoin in "a better place." Now that he lay dying, he questioned the existence of any such place. "I told Dad the story," Marcy said, "and it helped him feel less ashamed about losing faith. Now when he gets scared, I tell him, 'Don't believe the weaverbird.' He likes that a lot."

IMPRESSIONABILITY | FALSE WORDS AND INSTIGATING TROUBLE | POSTERITY: A young mother dying of cancer told me she wanted nothing more than to watch over her young son once she had passed. Prior to becoming ill she had worked in a science lab, where several of her most respected colleagues were staunch empiricists. They so articulately conveyed their disbelief in the afterlife, that her underlying faith was shaken. Her brother and husband supported her spiritual inclinations, and encouraged her to "believe the chameleon." A few days before her death she grew peaceful and said, "Just because my colleagues are articulate doesn't mean they're right. I don't want to be foolishly impressionable like those people in the story. My heart says the chameleon is right."

Queen Hyena's Funeral

A YORUBA TALE FROM AFRICA | (316 words)

Today all the wild animals fear each other and keep apart. Long ago it was different. The various animals worked together in a large council. They held gatherings and lived as one kingdom.

Hyena was a prominent leader. Much of his strength came from his mother who guided him all the years of his life. She was his faithful supporter until one day, her time on earth came to an end. When Queen Hyena died, Hyena fell into a great despair. Who would support and protect him?

Hyena planned his mother's funeral. Everything had to be perfect. "All the animals must show their respects," he commanded. The council invited everyone. They took great pains to arrange a funeral and feast to honor the queen. But no matter how much effort they put into it, Hyena could not be satisfied. First he was cross and irritable. Then he became tyrannical. When the dancing came to a close, he ordered the dancers to keep going until they dropped.

Hyena was afraid the guests might leave. He wanted more food to insure they would stay. The council told him they had prepared plenty of food for the next several days, but Hyena would not be convinced. He sought out Leopard and Lion, two guests who were fond of hunting. He persuaded them to supply more meat by killing a few lesser-known guests, Pig, Sheep, and Goat. It took little effort to kill these trusting guests. Lion and Leopard so enjoyed the killing, they began going after other guests. Soon mayhem broke out. Terrified guests ran for their lives. Hyena was left alone to bury his mother. Even an orphan's funeral would have been better attended.

That was the last time all the animals came together in one place. Now they keep to themselves, especially the hyenas whom no one trusts. They keep a wary distance from everyone.

PROLONGED OR COMPLICATED GRIEF | SCARCITY | ACCEPTING MORTALITY: The death of one's parent nearly always holds some sorrow or requires some reckoning, no matter what the circumstances. If there was too little love, the lack of it comes to the fore when one is faced with the finality of death. If there were strong ties, as in this tale, then the parent's death leaves a gaping hole. We all know that when a loved ones dies, it is healthy for the bereaved to come together to support each other in their grief. Hyena is unable to accept the support offered by others. He loses touch with what is important, and his grief becomes toxic and destructive.

A man named Adam feared something similar might happen when his father passed away after much suffering. Adam felt tempted to attack his siblings who had been less devoted during their father's illness. Adam took this tale to heart as an example of what *not* to do. Instead of blaming and bickering, or simply distancing himself, he resolved to accept the support offered by his siblings, despite their differences.

Not All at Once

PERSIA | (191 words)

Long ago there was a mullah who went to a house of learning to offer his teachings. He had hoped for a full house of eager listeners, but only one man, a humble stable attendant, had shown up to listen. The mullah wondered whether it would be worthwhile to speak at all. At last he turned to the man and asked, "Shall I go ahead and speak, even though you are an audience of one?"

"Master, I am not a learned man, but if I entered the stable, and found it empty except for one horse, I would feed that one horse, nonetheless."

The mullah heeded these words and began to speak as planned. He became wholly engrossed with the subject matter and spoke on at great length. The humble stable attendant listened respectfully. After two hours the mullah paused, "I could go on all night," he said to his listener. "Shall I continue?"

"Master," replied the attendant, "I am not a learned man, but if I came into the stable, and found there but one horse, I would surely feed it, but I would not feed it all the grain in the stable."

KNOWLEDGE TEMPERED BY WISDOM | LESS IS MORE | HUMILITY | HUMOR | TAKING OURSELVES LESS SERIOUSLY | THE WISDOM OF COMMON PEOPLE: The stablehand's two pieces of advice resonate on many levels. In the book *Oriental Stories as Tools in Psychotherapy*, author Nossrat Peseschkian uses a version of this tale to illustrate a common pitfall in the healing and teaching arts: the problem of quantity vs. quality. Today, large classes and heavy patient loads are set up to serve a high volume of people. This tale reminds us of the importance of one-on-one encounters. In wise tales the world over we see sages, druids, shamans, and elders offering their services to one seeker at a time. When I ask people to recall their most memorable learning or healing experiences, they often tell of a private moment with a teacher or healer when they felt seen or understood as an individual, and when the knowledge offered was custom-fit, rather than designed for the masses.

Less is more applies to the number of people served, and also to the amount of guidance offered. The stable hand's second bit of advice illustrates the importance of offering only as much as can be absorbed by the recipient in a single sitting. Teachers and therapists delight in the opportunity to share knowledge, yet there is great wisdom in knowing when one has offered enough.

Two Wives Are Less Than One

PERSIA | (330 words)

Two friends met in the marketplace and struck up a chat. "Having two wives, my friend," said the first, "that is a pleasure every man should know."

"Two wives?" exclaimed the other, "I can hardly imagine."

"I tell you it is truly marvelous! If you tire of one, you can go straight to the other. Life never grows monotonous. It is like an endless buffet of gourmet delights, a garden in which there is always something blooming."

The man with only one wife couldn't stop thinking about his friend's good fortune. His wife was a fine woman, and quite attractive as well, but one grows tired of the same old thing. Why shouldn't he have multiple pleasures like his friend? Not long after that, he took a second wife. On their wedding night he went to her bed and tried to snuggle close to her. She said, "I saw you kiss your first wife goodnight. It's obvious you love her. Go lie with her, and leave me alone. I am not just some new toy to spice up your marriage."

Dismayed, he went to the bed of his first wife. He tried to snuggle close to her, but she snapped, "Go lie with your new wife, since I am no longer enough for you." The poor man had nowhere to go. It was the same, night after night. Finally he took refuge in the mosque. When he got inside he saw there was one other person there. "A homeless person seeking shelter," thought the man to himself. To his astonishment he saw it was his friend, the one who had boasted of the pleasures of two wives. "What are you doing here?" he asked.

"I've no place to sleep at home, my two wives won't have a thing to do with me."

"Why on earth did you tell me it was a blessing having two wives?"

"Because," the friend replied sheepishly, "it has been so lonely here at the mosque."

LESS IS MORE | GREED AND ACQUISITIVENESS | UNHEALTHY ENTITLEMENT | ISOLATION | HUMOR | LOVE TRIANGLES: Dr. Peseschkian uses this Persian tale in couples counseling to underscore the difficulties of love triangles. In many cases, when the initial heat cools down, no one is fulfilled, and much damage is done. Some people say it reveals the problem of greed and excessive entitlement.

FALSE WORDS AND INSTIGATING TROUBLE | IMPRESSIONABILITY: I like to use the tale to illustrate the human foible of being overly impressionable, gullible, or too easily persuaded. The tale suggests that just because something *sounds* great, doesn't mean it *is* great. In the case of the two friends, what is touted as sheer Heaven turns out to be pure Hell.

Three Scholars and a Lion

INDIA | (500 words)

*F*our friends had grown up together in a small village. Three of them had the benefit of book learning, while the fourth merely had common sense. One day the four friends conversed over tea. One of them said, "Our village is small, and opportunities are scarce. With learned minds like ours, we should travel the world, and make our fortunes. There is no limit to what we can accomplish." They decided to take to the road and visit grand cities where their scholarly minds would be appreciated. As they were planning, one of them took pause. "I'm thinking," he said, stroking his whiskers. "We three scholars have stayed up many a night, poring over textbooks, so that we might distinguish ourselves with knowledge. Our friend here is a fine fellow, but why should he be permitted to accompany us, when by comparison he has so little to offer?"

The scholars mulled over the question until it was agreed that the unschooled friend should indeed be permitted to come along. After all, he had been dear to them since childhood.

The next day they packed a few belongings and set out on their journey. They had not gone far when they came upon a heap of bones lying on the ground. One scholar specialized in bones. He said, "My friends, these are the bones of a lion. I can reassemble them in no time. We have here before us a grand opportunity to put our scholarship to work."

"Indeed," said the second scholar. "There is nothing I would like more than a chance to prove I can regenerate flesh and blood upon these bones."

"Brilliant!" said the third scholar, "and I have the technology to restore the creature to life."

So the scholars set to work, using all their specialized know-how to reassemble the lion and bring it back to life. The fourth fellow, the one lacking in book-learning said, "My friends, forgive me, for I am not as learned as you, but would it not be unwise to bring this dead lion to life? Will he not be hungry and ferocious? And won't he look upon us as easy prey?"

One scholar said, "Dear friend, how can you question the validity of our great endeavor?"

The second said, "What good is our hard-earned knowledge if it can't be put to use?"

The third said, "Think how rich and famous we shall be once we have mastered life and defied death! Finally our wealth will equal our knowledge."

"Well said!" cried the other two scholars. It was decided.

The nonscholar cried, "Well if you must proceed, at least give me time to get out of harm's way." He climbed up a tree just as the lion breathed its first breath. The creature opened its eyes, rose to its feet, twitched its tail, and without delay pounced upon the three scholars, and gobbled them down.

Their unschooled friend stayed in the tree until the lion had gone. Then he returned home alone, and told his fellow villagers the whole story. To this day the people of that village have great respect for the wonders of knowledge, and even more respect for common sense.

RESPONSIBLE USE OF TECHNOLOGY: The scholars' technical know-how gives them great power, but such power proves disastrous when unwisely utilized. Like "The Sorcerer's Apprentice," this tale reminds us that the human temptation to use technology without precaution, and for the wrong reasons, is an age-old problem. Today, this lesson is as meaningful as ever. Scientist Mae Wan Ho warns of the dark side of wonder technologies such as genetic engineering. Like the methods of the three scholars, genetic engineering alters the essential structures of life, and even attempts to defy death, but at what cost? This is an excellent tale to spark discussion on ethics in science and technology.

THE WISDOM OF COMMON PEOPLE | CRAVINGS AND TROUBLESOME DESIRES | GREED AND ACQUISITIVENESS | MISGUIDED LEADERSHIP | AUTHORITY AND HEALTHY SKEPTICISM | REVERENCE FOR NATURE: In India environmental activist Vandana Shiva warns the common people that experts, authorities, and corporate officials are not always to be trusted. Sometimes those in power will endanger the public and the environment in order to generate wealth. Shiva encourages common folk with common sense to join together to demand clean drinking water and safe labor conditions. Because of her work, and that of others like her, Indian environmentalists, farmers, and laborers have gained a stronger voice. Tales like this one encourage them to emulate the man with common sense: to use their powers of observation, to practice free speech, and to act on self-protective instincts. This tale encourages people around the world to be informed, and to be appropriately watchful of those with the power to shape our lives.

KNOWLEDGE TEMPERED BY WISDOM | MISGUIDED LEADERSHIP | MISUSE OF POWER | CRAVINGS AND TROUBLESOME DESIRES | PEAK EXPERIENCE | HUMILITY | SACRIFICE | RESPONSIBLE USE OF TECHNOLOGY: This tale illustrates the trouble that can result when powerful knowledge is not guided by wisdom and concern for the greater good. Any time the urge to exert one's power and mastery wins out over the urge to be genuinely helpful, there is room for trouble. This tale reminds us that with knowledge, technology, and know-how comes responsibility. The humbling challenge is to contain knowledge in the greater vessel of wisdom. Sometimes the wisest thing is to practice restraint. For the excited scholars their peak experience was their last. If our world is to survive we must mindfully anticipate the full impact of our technologies, and not be blinded by enticing short-term gains.

How Death Came to be Feared

NEPAL | (501 words)

Long ago, in times of old, people did not fear Death. Death walked the earth with a tangible body, and when it was time for someone to die, Death walked right up to them. They willingly went with him to Yama Loka, the place of the dead. Death was understood by all to be a joyous passage, and so people did not make a fuss when Death showed up at their doors.

Death was very orderly and kept a tidy account book. He was always clear about whom to take and whom to leave alone. One day he studied the columns in his book and came to the name of a highly skilled, industrious young blacksmith whose time had come. Death knocked upon his door. Upon seeing Death, the blacksmith was not afraid, but he could not believe Death really planned to take him. "It couldn't be my time," he thought to himself. "I have not yet come close to fulfilling my many ambitions. Surely Death knows I have a great deal more to do before I depart this earth."

Out of respect the blacksmith invited Death into the sitting room. He served him food and drink, all the while thinking Death had just stopped by on his way to call upon someone else. After a while the blacksmith realized that Death intended to take him. That's when he thought of a plan to outwit Death. Some time before he had built an iron structure with many chambers. He told Death that before they went to Yama Loka, he would like Death to see his finest work.

He led Death into the building, from one chamber to the next until they reached the innermost chamber. "My how hard you've been working," said Death, quite impressed with the blacksmith's work.

The blacksmith replied, "If anyone knows about hard work it's you, Master Death. You must have a seat here and rest. Enjoy the coolness of the chamber. I will be right back with some refreshments for you." Death sat down and awaited the blacksmith's return. The blacksmith went back outside, each time locking and double locking all the iron gates to the inner chambers. He felt quite secure that Death would be unable to escape.

The blacksmith told no one, and if it had not been for Shiva and Parvati, Death might be trapped there still. Shiva, the great creator-destroyer, keeper of the universal law, detected an imbalance in the land of mortals on Earth. He entrusted his wife Parvati to set things right.

Beautiful Parvati went to the blacksmith's town in the guise of a voluptuous bar maid. She took a job in the blacksmith's favorite tavern. One evening she enticed him to drink more than usual, and soon he was telling her all his secrets. It wasn't long before the blacksmith passed out and Parvati took the keys to the iron chamber. She rescued

Death and he soon resumed his part in maintaining the great order. Ever since Death's distressing confinement he has been wary of mortals and refuses to risk walking in tangible form. As for mortals, they now fear Death, and have forgotten that dying is a joyous passage.

DEATH | THE INEVITABILITY OF OLD AGE AND DEATH | LIFE-DEATH-REBIRTH CYCLE: This delicious little tale offers an age-old Eastern outlook on death. Here death is not a pointless and tragic demise, but a joyous passage that helps maintain the greater cosmic order of living and dying. In our culture we tend to ignore death, and thoughts of death, until it approaches us or a loved one, and the tangible signs of death enter the house. In many Eastern traditions, however, people are taught to envision a peaceful death, and to cultivate a positive attitude toward death, so as to hold a broader view, and to die without anguish. Because death is the inevitable outcome of life, this tale holds meaning for all, and one need not be next on Death's list to appreciate it. It is meant not only to open the minds of the dying and their loved ones, but also to inform the living, to lighten our sense of life, as well as our sense of death.

WORTHY USE OF DECEPTION | CREATION AND DESTRUCTION: In the study of lies and truth telling, it is well known that most people, even the most upstanding, will stoop to deception to save their skin. Here the blacksmith's trick on Death is entirely forgivable, and in many ways admirable. He loves himself, he loves life, and wants to further develop his many potentials. He is powerless to resist Death directly, but he can trick and entrap him. This is a pleasing example of man's resourcefulness in bending the cosmic law to his favor. The tale takes us beyond the ethical realm of truth vs. lies, to the bigger sphere of Shiva and Parvati. Here, restoration of the great order is tantamount, and Parvati uses the most expeditious means to accomplish it: deception. Truth, deceit, victory, defeat: these are fleeting. Only the great cosmic order prevails.

The Potter's Wish

NEPAL | (482 words)

There once was a skilled potter who aimed for perfection in all undertakings. Before making pots he chanted sweet devotions to Lord Shiva. One day while he was praying a brilliant beam of light appeared before him. In the center of the light stood Lord Shiva himself. He smiled down upon the potter and said, "Your devotion touches my heart. I shall reward you by fulfilling your greatest desire."

Some would wish for wealth, power, or immortality, but the devout potter wanted only to make perfect clay pots which would never chip, crack, or break, and thus would remain untouched by the passage of time. The potter kept his head down while voicing his wish and then looked up at the god's radiant face. "Very well," said Shiva, with a half-smile that was neither joyous, nor mocking, nor pitying.

When the god vanished, the potter quickly set about making a large clay pot. When it was finished, he dropped it to the floor to see if it would break, yet the pot remained in perfect condition. The potter rushed out to the courtyard where he dashed the pot against a rock. No matter how hard he tried, he could not so much as scratch its perfect surface.

Word spread far and wide that the potter was selling unbreakable pots. Customers thronged from the neighboring towns to buy them. People were willing to pay extra for such extraordinary pots, but the humble potter kept to his old price. Never had he been so successful, and it brought him great joy. Then he learned the other potters in the district had been driven out of business. All they had to offer were breakable pots, and no one wanted to buy them. Soon the potter's own business began to dwindle. There were no more customers left, for everyone's kitchen was stocked with pots that would last forever. Now the potter himself was out of business and could no longer feed his family. All the potters were doomed to poverty and suffering.

One day while praying to Lord Shiva the potter wept, "Oh, Lord, how could one simple wish have created such misery?"

Lord Shiva took pity on him and appeared before him once again. "Devoted One, are you not happy with the results of your wish?"

"I made a great mistake, oh Lord!" said the potter. "Please take back the wish, for I never again want to make pots which will not break. I see now that no human creation is meant to be perfect, nor is it meant to outlast time. Pots are meant to break and be replaced."

Lord Shiva, who is known as the great Creator and Destroyer, replied, "I am pleased to see you now understand the essence of your craft." From that day on, clay pots resumed their true nature. Like all things made of clay, they once again began to crack, chip, and break.

Soon enough the potters were all back to work again and life went on. Ever after the devout potter felt a near-ecstatic gratitude each time he made a pot.

POTTERY | CHANGE AS AN OPPORTUNITY TO CREATE ANEW | CRAVINGS AND TROUBLESOME DESIRES | LIFE-DEATH-REBIRTH CYCLE | SUSTAINABILITY: Lord Shiva grants the potter's dearest wish, to create pots that are perfect and everlasting. Perhaps the potter's wish stems from the desire to make a lasting contribution, or perhaps it stems from the longing to transcend the earthly forces of destruction and decline. The story suggests that the craving for perfection can have troublesome consequences. The potter's seemingly innocent wish leads to great trouble. The story reminds us that at some levels the very essence of life is in the breaking and remaking of things. Lord Shiva, the creator, is also the great destroyer, a notion that seems paradoxical until we observe the forces of time and nature. The everlasting pots bring about a miserable stagnation, ruining the lively commerce of village life. The tale reminds us to participate in the flow, to appreciate that life consists of the crumbling of the old and the creation of the new. When things break, a new opportunity arises to contribute and to be creatively engaged.

DEVOTION | PERFECTIONISM | HUMILITY | TAKING OURSELVES LESS SERIOUSLY | LETTING GO | CREATION AND DESTRUCTION: "The Potter's Wish" sheds light not only on devotion, but also on perfectionism and the urge to control. I came across this urge in myself many times in the crafting of this book. I wanted each idea, each image, to be perfectly shaped and enduring. Again and again I had to accept that stories, themes, and ideas, like clay pots, are organic vessels. In writing as in other crafts, the work is never finished, nor does it reach perfection. One must humbly hope that the pots are serviceable, that they hold water, and let it go at that. I once told this tale in a group of self-avowed "perfectionists." A master gardener said, "I try to control every aspect of my landscapes, from drainage to the fragrance of the blooms. Last year a freak wind came along and downed several trees. I had a hard time accepting Lord Shiva's destruction, but what could I do? Then this year I began to appreciate the view and the light that comes through where the trees used to be." This tale suggests life is about doing one's best and accepting the outcome, rather than achieving perfection or maintaining control. Shiva might visit the world as a disastrous flood that wipes out an entire village. In the wake of the flood, however, Shiva might leave a wash of fertile topsoil allowing future villages to prosper. The story tells us there is something sacred in the forces of destruction and creation. In the face of these forces, human perfectionism is a kind of hubris. As W. B. Yeats said through the voice of Crazy Jane, "Nothing can be sole or whole that has not been rent." And so it is with life in the potter's village. Life's essential flow depends upon the making, breaking, and remaking of things.

The Monkeys Rescue the Moon

TIBET | (403 words)

Long ago, there was a band of monkeys living deep in the forest. They went to a watering hole each day where they drank and took their baths. One moonlit night the leader of the monkeys could not sleep. He got up to stretch his legs and get a drink of water. When he looked upon the dark surface of the water, what do you think he saw there? He saw the moon's bright reflection shining back at him. He thought the moon had fallen into the water.

"Wake up! Wake up!" he cried to his fellow monkeys. They climbed down from the trees where they were sleeping and gathered around the pool. "Look," said the leader. "The moon has fallen into the water. If we do not rescue it immediately, the night sky will be doomed forever to darkness. Get a branch so we can climb out over the water and rescue the moon." The monkeys scurried to find a long branch. "Hurry! Hurry!" said the leader. "The moon might sink at any moment!"

A feeble, old grandfather monkey looked up to the sky and saw the moon. He scratched himself and mumbled, "The moon is where it always is," but no one heard him. They were too busy dragging the long branch out from under the trees.

Some of the monkeys held the branch over the deep water while others climbed upon it and inched their way toward its tip. As more and more monkeys climbed onto the branch, it began to droop from the weight. It wasn't long before the branch gave out. Suddenly all the monkeys were pulled with it into the depths of the pool. Only the old one remained on shore. He looked sadly into the water. The moon was still reflected there, but his fellow monkeys were gone without a trace.

MISGUIDED LEADERSHIP | AUTHORITY AND HEALTHY SKEPTICISM: This Tibetan tale paints a sad picture of misguided leadership. Like the Turkish tale "The Moon in the Well," it involves a humorous brand of foolishness, but while the Turkish tale turns out joyously, the Tibetan tale takes a turn for the worse. Here, the monkey leader resembles a commander-in-chief who, without taking time for reflection or advice, hastily sends troops on an unnecessary mission that ends in disaster. This old tale reminds us of the importance of healthy skepticism and how dangerous it can be to blindly follow the leader.

The Boy and the Tiger

AN ULCHI TALE FROM SIBERIA | (914 words)

In the time of the ancestors, it was customary for a father and son to go hunting together. The father's part would be to trap and hunt game. The son's part would be to cut firewood and to make tea.

One night a father and son were asleep at their hunting camp, and the father had this dream: A great tiger came to him and said, "Return to the village alone. Leave your son to me." The man begged the tiger to let them both go. The tiger said, "Do as I say, or neither of you will return home alive."

The man awoke. He lay there in the middle of the night as his son slept peacefully beside him. The man thought, "A tiger is a powerful being not to be trifled with. If I do not obey, what will become of my wife and daughters?" The hunter knew he had no choice. He got up quietly, and trudged home, leaving his son alone in the woods. "I shall return in a few days," he said to himself with a heavy heart. "If I find my son's bones, I shall carry them home and give them a proper burial."

The boy awoke before dawn. "Father has gone hunting," he thought. He peered into the woods and there he saw two huge yellow eyes peering back at him. In terror the boy jumped from his bed and ran. The tiger came after him. The boy leapt onto the branch of a tall tree, and scurried up the trunk. The tiger followed at his heels so closely the boy felt the beast's hot breath on his feet. Just before the tiger could catch him, the boy sprang to the neighboring tree and climbed down its trunk to the ground. The tiger lunged after him, but the great creature got caught between two limbs and could not budge. Now the boy went back to the campfire. He made tea and awaited his father's return.

All day the boy kept the fire going. Evening fell and still his father had not returned. At last the boy grew tired and fell asleep. He dreamt of the great tiger, caught between the branches, growing thirsty and hungry. "Help me," said the tiger, "and I promise, plentiful rewards shall come your way." The boy awoke, and lay in the dark. "According to the ancestors," recalled the boy, "the tiger is an admirable being."

At dawn the boy took his ax and returned to the tree where the tiger was pinned. The boy hacked at its trunk until it cracked and fell. The tiger freed himself, gave a roar of gratitude and disappeared into the woods. That night the boy had another dream. The tiger told him where to set his traps and instructed him to draw a circle around them with his sleeve. When dawn came, the boy got up and did as the tiger had instructed. The next day he was overjoyed when in each and every trap he found a sable. What worked that day worked the next and the next, until the boy had amassed a great wealth of sable furs.

All this time, the hunter stayed in the village, thinking about his son and hoping beyond hope that he might return. At last with a sorrowful heart, the hunter set out to collect the bones of his only son.

As he neared camp, he was astonished to smell smoke and to see the glow of the fire. The hunter's heart leapt with joy. His knees went soft, and his gait grew clumsy. He rushed toward camp stepping on dry twigs that snapped loudly. The son called out, "Father! What took you so long?" Father and son were elated to be together again. Weeping the father said, "My Son, forgive me!"

The son said, "You're here, Father. That's all I care about." They loaded the luxuriant furs onto their sled and returned home. Imagine the joyous reception! After that, the family remained blessed by the luck the great tiger had bestowed upon the boy.

ANIMALS AS HELPERS AND TEACHERS | FOREST AS A PLACE OF TRANSFORMATION | THE MORE-THAN-HUMAN WORLD | REVERENCE FOR NATURE: Like so many wisdom tales, this one features a transformative encounter with a wondrous wild creature. Our ancestors regarded the creatures of the forest and the forest itself as alive with the power to awaken and draw forth our own greatest gifts. If this level of reverence moved us today, imagine how much more motivated we would be to protect forests and vulnerable species.

HARDSHIP AND UNFORESEEN BLESSINGS: One of the most paradoxical twists of human fate occurs when unforeseen blessings emerge from great hardship, loss, and pain. No contemporary example comes to mind more readily than the life of Nelson Mandela. We would expect twenty-seven years in prison to destroy a man, end his career, devastate his family, and dishearten his nation. Yet, over time, Mandela's imprisonment served, as Reverend Desmond Tutu said, "to bring out the gold of his spiritual self." He learned to see with the eyes of a tiger. His strength and resilience heartened millions living in the imprisonment of apartheid.

Sometimes hardship is the only thing that will force us to draw upon and to hone our deepest hidden strengths. This was true of a writer who came to writing late in life, after losing his job, and coming down with a debilitating illness. "I'm grateful to all the hardship," he said. "Without it I would have coasted through life, and never discovered my talent for writing." The "tiger" which threatened to end his life, blessed it instead, with unexpected gifts, just as it did for the boy.

DREAM AS GUIDE: Like "Wild Pony and Smoke," this tale exemplifies an approach to dreams common to our ancestors the world over. From the ancestral perspective a dream can carry immediate, applicable guidance. It can instruct us as to the interplay between our fate and the forces alive in the wider world. To ignore an instructive dream, or to ponder it without action, can be to ignore the tiger-brightness of a creative opportunity.

INITIATION | MALE INITIATION | MALE INTUITION | MEN'S ESTEEM AND EMPOWERMENT | CREATIVE COURAGE | EMOTIONAL RESILIENCE | SELF-RELIANCE | SELF-DETERMINATION | UNSTABLE IDENTITY | RITES OF PASSAGE | ISOLATION | HEALING FROM ABANDONMENT | LONELINESS | DISENFRANCHISEMENT | DEPRIVATION | COURAGE INTEGRITY RESILIENCE | FAMILIAL COOPERATION | FORGIVENESS | GENEROSITY | GRATITUDE: Coming of age is a frightful transition, no matter how you slice it. Every teenage boy whether he's deemed "promising," "average," or "underachieving," struggles at some level with the questions, "How will I survive?" "How will I measure up?" and "Will my striving have purpose?" Today when our sons come of age, we focus on the practical concerns—getting an education, a car, a job. These are important, but they only comprise half the story. The other half is the mystery that cannot be grasped in a concrete way. It can, however, be expressed through art, rites of passage, and stories like this one. These speak to the wonder, the awe, the terror, and the isolation in the heart of the soon-to-be-manly teen. Youths and teens whole-heartedly identify with the hunter's son. More often than not they appreciate the opportunity to identify the "tigers" in their own lives, and to voice their hopes for their yet untested gifts. When youths are given ample time and support with these questions, they ultimately take on a spiritual timbre. This tale resonates with something deep in the soul. It affirms boys' natural tendency toward cooperation and courage. It honors their instincts, intuition, and creative impulses, and models respect for elders, ancestors, and the ways of the natural world.

This story inspires people of all ages who are moving into uncharted territories, risking, learning, and aspiring toward new things. The youthful initiate within the heart of an elder takes encouragement from this tale. The tale teaches that life is neither easy nor safe, yet drawing upon one's deepest strengths one can make good. Whether told to girls, boys, men, women, youths, or elders, this tale is a love gift, for it affirms the yellow-eyed tiger in the human soul, and honors its admirable counterpart who dwells deep in the forest.

Why Hares Have Long Ears

A MANSI TALE FROM SIBERIA | (328 words)

Long ago when the creatures of the forest first appeared, Great Elk was the most awesome of animals. With his tremendous size and striking antlers he could be seen from far, far away. No other creature dared cross him.

One day Great Elk and his wife were out walking. Along the way they passed the little hare quietly nibbling a bit of grass. The elks gave him no notice. Great Elk said to his wife, "I have two old sets of antlers, and I hate for them to go to waste. We should give them to someone."

The she-elk replied, "Why don't we give one set to Reindeer, since he is our closest kin?"

"Good idea," said Elk, "but who should have the other?"

Before She-Elk could reply Little Hare overcame his shyness and spoke up, "Please, Great Elk, give it to me!"

Great Elk was taken aback, "You?" he said, looking down at Hare. "Little Brother, what use could you possibly make of my antlers?"

"I would strut them about and be noticed," said Hare. "All animals would be impressed, and my enemies would flee in fright."

"Very well then," said Great Elk, "they are yours."

Little Hare was delighted. He fastened the antlers to his head, and practiced strutting about. It went pretty well until a little cone dropped from a nearby cedar and bounced on Hare's head. Poor Hare was terrified. He scooted under the bushes to hide, and his new antlers got entangled in the brush. Now Hare was stuck and unable to free himself.

The elks had a good chuckle. Then Great Elk said, "Little Brother, this will never do. My antlers will only cause you trouble. You are timid by nature, and we must accept that. From now on, you will have long ears to let the world know how alert and inquisitive you are."

Ever since that day, Hare has been noticed for his long ears.

ENVY AND SELF-IMAGE | UNSTABLE IDENTITY | HONORING TRUE ESSENCE: Young children delight in fables telling how animals got their special traits. We all know what it's like to wish we had the special traits we admire in others. It seems to be human nature to want what others have, and to wish, as Hare wishes, for traits that draw recognition, awe, and respect. Like Hare, a quiet artist named Moss found recognition is not all it's cracked up to be. Moss envied his friend Marcus, an extroverted artist who always made a stir and commanded people's attention. One day Moss won a long-desired award, and a dinner was being given in his honor. "This was my chance to soak up the kind of attention Marcus usually gets," he said, "but afterward, I felt drained instead of pumped. It was nice to get all the kudos, but it takes a lot of energy to schmooze, and you'd be surprised how many people expect favors. The next day I unplugged the phone so I could just hunker down in the studio. My wife says my work's about attunement, and subtlety, not a big showy rack. Besides," he added with a grin, "the hare means fertility, prosperity, and good luck, and he moves a lot faster than the elk."

A woman named Jana took the ears metaphor to heart. Painfully shy by nature, Jana made a concerted effort to meet new friends. She went to interesting community events and forced herself to mill around and converse with people. Her fantasy was that in order to meet people, she should approach them with "big antlers" confidence. "I tried striding up to people with bold openers, but they came off as awkward and pre-rehearsed." This story helped Jana see her inquisitiveness as an asset. "At the town meeting I was all ears. I listened closely and asked a couple of good questions. Afterward, people approached me and thanked me for my questions. It was a better way to get noticed."

Whale Boy

A CHUKCHI TALE FROM SIBERIA | (553 words)

(too morally complex for young children)

Long ago, way up north, it was not uncommon for two or more women to share a single husband. One young woman married a hunter who already had a wife. He and his wife lived contentedly with their many children and spent all their time together. The new wife felt lonely, and comforted herself by taking long walks at the edge of the sea.

One morning as the sun came up, she saw something far out at sea. As she watched, it came toward her, faster and faster. Soon she saw it was the waterspout of a Greenland whale. As the whale neared the shore, a man emerged from its body. The young woman was pleased at the sight of him, and even more pleased to have his company. They talked all day until the sun went down.

After that the young wife sneaked away each evening with a pouch full of food. She would take it to the shore and pass the night with the whale man. One night the hunter suspected something and stealthily followed her. When the whale man came to the young woman, she embraced him and offered him food. But instead of eating it, he looked warily this way and that. He knew they were being watched, and without a word he ran back to the sea and hastened into his whale skin. Before he could swim away, the hunter charged forth and harpooned his side. The whale swam off with blood spurting from his wound.

Never again did the young wife see the whale man. She was with child, however, and in due time gave birth to a tiny whale. She nursed him and kept him in a leather water-pouch until he outgrew it. Then he lived in a water barrel until he outgrew that. Then they dug him a pool at the edge of the village. When he outgrew that, they had to drag him to the sea. The villagers feared the young wife would stay at the shore forever, watching for her child's waterspout. To prevent this, they sewed a squirrel-skin flap over his blowhole.

At first he was afraid to swim away, and he stayed at the shore with his mother. He often swam onto the beach, where she would nurse him, but gradually he learned to eat like other whales out at sea. One autumn day he swam off with another whale, and was not seen again until spring.

That spring and each spring that followed, he returned to his mother's village with large groups of whales. This made it easy for his mother's people to hunt. Some villagers began to brag about their constant feasting. Their lamps, well fueled with whale oil, burned brightly through the dark winters. Their prosperity abounded, all due to the special favor they received from Whale Boy.

A neighboring tribe grew envious. One day they sneaked up on Whale Boy and harpooned him to death. His mother's people soon found out. They set about taking revenge. Revenge did not end the trouble, but kept it going. The two tribes fought for a long time. Even today when people cannot end a quarrel, they bring up the names of those two tribes. The pond where Whale Boy once lived can still be seen.

ISOLATION | LONELINESS | UNSTABLE IDENTITY | CAST-OUTS AND RUNAWAYS | DISENFRANCHISEMENT | EXCLUSION | DEPRIVATION: This seemingly simple tale conveys many salient truths for our times. Let's begin at the beginning. Feeling left out, deprived, and lonely, as our heroine does at the start, is part of the human experience and few escape it. It is a necessary lesson, for we do not always fit in, and we cannot always partake of what others enjoy. In this seemingly simple tale, these themes play out in familial, spiritual, social, and economic arenas, just as they do in real life. In the beginning, the young wife's place in the family is not secure, nor is her identity as a wife. These could be the preconditions for a breakdown, but our heroine does not come undone. Instead she copes with loneliness by taking soothing walks at the seaside.

LOSS, COURAGE, AND TRANSFORMATION | HEALING FROM ABANDONMENT | ANIMALS AS HELPERS AND TEACHERS | THE MORE-THAN-HUMAN WORLD | REVERENCE FOR NATURE | INITIATION | DEVOTION | EMOTIONAL RESILIENCE | FAMILIAL COOPERATION: The adverse conditions, (isolation, deprivation, and suspension of identity) now become the ground for a transformational experience, a kind of initiation. Initiation almost invariably involves some level of deprivation, followed by a visitation from an animal or nature spirit. In this case, the whale who metamorphoses into human form becomes the young woman's beloved. Actual sustained rapport with a more-than-human companion brings to mind contemporary heroines like Jane Goodall and Dian Fossey. Such women enter intimate and transforming liaisons with the more-than-human world, and like our heroine, return to the village "pregnant" with wisdom to sustain others.

When the hunter harpoons the whale, he is never seen again, but part of his essence continues on within the young woman. Among indigenous people the natural world and the creatures in it are animated with the life force of the great spirit. Our heroine's encounter with Whale Man might parallel a saint's encounter with the dove of the holy spirit. When she returns to the village, she is not ostracized as an adulteress or pervert, but accepted and supported as the carrier of something sacred. When her whale child outgrows his bucket, the villagers build for him a sizable pond. Later when he outgrows the pond, they take him to sea. They are in many ways a healthy community responsive to "special needs." The whale boy blesses his mother and her people with ample game and ease in hunting. No longer disenfranchised, the young woman has a special role, her unique liaison has blessed the village.

LOSE-LOSE SITUATIONS | REVENGE AND RETRIBUTION | JEALOUSY, ENVY, AND COMPETITION | DEPRIVATION | ONGOING QUARRELS | HARDSHIP AS AN OPPORTUNITY | COURAGE, INTEGRITY, RESILIENCE | SCARCITY | SUSTAINABILITY | THE FUTILITY OF VIOLENCE: The original problem, that of being left out, less fortunate, and deprived, has been healed and transformed within the family and village, only to fester now between the two villages.

One tribe enjoys prosperity while their neighbors struggle. This discrepancy, and the clumsiness that surrounds it, is a precursor for trouble. The well-off do not realize they have enough. They acquire to excess and flaunt it. One act of aggression leads to another, and as with many war-torn regions in the world today, the troubles seem never-ending.

Deprivation profoundly affects the human soul. When the conditions are right, and the human heart is resilient, as with the young wife, deprivation can lead to spiritual awakening and transformation, a deep attachment to something greater than oneself, and a sense of enduring dignity and purpose. If conditions are adverse, and deprivation is foisted upon those already starved, it can give rise to deep and lasting hatred, an unquenchable thirst for revenge, and a justification for the unthinkable. We see this played out, not only in tribal wars, but recently in public schools where disenfranchised youth have sought the ultimate revenge upon teachers and peers.

This story reminds us of both ends of the spectrum: the blessings and the devastation that can come from going without. The tale brings home several simple and nonetheless important lessons:

(1) There is no gift greater than a resilient heart, one that can heal and transform.

(2) Our neighbors' well-being, or lack of well-being, affects us, maybe not immediately and obviously, but eventually and certainly. From the perspective of the Chukchi, that includes neighbors of all species. When one species is endangered, the entire web of life is affected.

(3) There is no underestimating the importance of behaviors like acceptance, inclusion, welcoming, and sharing.

(4) The best way to solve a war is to prevent it.

Because of these poignant lessons, this tale has broad application for the troubles of our times. Teens find it sparks insight regarding the loneliness and interpersonal problems they face. They find it heartening as to how they might cope and heal. The tale affirms young people's innate desire for peace, and encourages them to reach out to others and get along. The tale appeals to teens' interest in whales and their appreciation for indigenous peoples. For adults it speaks to the themes of initiation and spiritual transformation, as well as addressing important emotional, social, and cultural themes. Like so many tribal stories, this one reminds us of the importance of sustaining a healthy rapport with each other and with the more-than-human world.

Undecided

WEST SUMATRA, INDONESIA | (664 words)

Lebai Malang lived at the edge of a river in Central Sumatra. When he was not home praying, he was boating up and down the river, visiting people's homes to teach them to read and discuss the holy book.

One morning he received two invitations. A family from a village upstream was giving a feast, while a family from a village downstream was doing the same. "Two invitations," thought Lebai, "how shall I decide which feast to attend?" He dressed himself for a special occasion, but could not make up his mind whether to go upstream or down. He sipped tea and thought about the family upstream. They lived nearby, so he wouldn't have to paddle very far. But they were poor. They would slaughter just one water buffalo for the occasion. It was the custom to give the water buffalo's head to the most respected guest. "They don't know me that well," thought Lebai. "They might give the head to some other teacher, and then I would feel unlucky."

He thought about the family who lived downstream. They knew him well, and would show him respect. They were rich and would slaughter two buffaloes. "Surely one of the buffalo heads will be presented to me," thought Lebai, "and I will feel very lucky." But the rich family lived far downstream and it was a long way to paddle. Lebai was already hungry, so he decided to go upstream first, for a quick morning snack, then he would drift downstream with the current, and enjoy the afternoon feast at the home of the rich people.

As he paddled he passed boatload upon boatload of jubilant people dressed in bright holiday clothes. They were all headed downstream to the home of the rich family. Their boats were laden with gifts and covered dishes of savory-smelling food that made Lebai's mouth water. He recalled how the rich family had given away money at their last party. Surely he was headed in the wrong direction and should turn around and follow the others. He dipped his paddle deep in the water and turned his boat around.

After a while he saw he was passing by his very own house. Hunger gnawed at his belly, so he decided to stop briefly for a bite of cooked rice. Once inside the house Lebai was dismayed to see the rice pot had been knocked over, and the dog had eaten every last bite. Lebai threw up his hands and hurried back to his boat. He was tired and hungry now, but paddled as quickly as he could toward the village where the rich family lived. He thought about what he would say when presented with the buffalo head. He thought about how lovely it would be to enjoy a heaping plate of delicious food. By and by he neared the place. Then he saw an acquaintance who called out, "Lebai, this party has been going on since early morning. The gifts are all gone and the best foods have already been eaten. Let's go upstream to the other feast."

Lebai's head swam with confusion. He didn't want to miss out, so he turned his boat around and followed his friend. The sun had already reached its height and the day was winding down. Lebai grew weary with fatigue and hunger. His arms ached from so much paddling. It was quiet when he finally arrived at the home of the poor family. Tired guests were already making their way back to their boats. Empty platters of food lay about. Dogs sniffed around under the tables for scraps. Lebai was so disappointed he sat down by his boat, put his head in his hands, and began to sob.

The next day people talked about what good food they had eaten at the two feasts. They all commented that they had seen Lebai on the river, all dressed up for a party, going north and then going south. They asked one another, "Did you see Lebai at either feast?" No one had. Everyone had missed out on his company. It seemed he had spent the day paddling in indecision. One little boy pretended to be the learned Lebai, first paddling upstream, and then down, north, and then south.

Ever after, when the river people want to tease someone who cannot make up his mind, they make paddling gestures, this way and that, or simply call him, Lebai Malang, meaning *unlucky teacher*. Lebai was so busy changing directions, luck could not find him, and passed him by.

DECISIONS | CRAVINGS AND TROUBLESOME DESIRES | ISOLATION | LESS IS MORE | GREED AND ACQUISITIVENESS | LOSE-LOSE SITUATIONS | HUMILITY | TAKING OURSELVES LESS SERIOUSLY | HUMOR: One wants always to choose the right road, and to feel assured that things will turn out well. The torment of indecision can make one long for the simplicity of feeling whole-hearted and single-minded. In this Indonesian tale, all of Lebai's energy is used up second-guessing which of two invitations will be the most gratifying. In the end he misses out on both. This story doesn't give us an answer to the problem of indecision, but it gets people thinking. I told it at a community gathering for people of all ages. A ten-year-old boy said, "Lebai should have flipped a coin. That way at least he coulda had lunch."

A young mother said, "If Lebai would have followed his instinct, instead of trying to rationalize every detail, he could have gone to both feasts."

An elder gentleman said, "Less is more. Lebai tried to get it all, and got nothing instead." Even a simple tale like this one holds myriad meanings. Such is the magic of story.

The Frog

INDONESIA | (2,072 words)

The youngest of seven brothers was called by the name *Katak*, meaning *frog*. He got that name because he was more frog than human. He had greenish skin, thin lips and a mouth that spread from ear to ear. His arms were thin and his knees bent out to the sides. Instead of walking with one foot in front of the other, he hopped along and had trouble keeping up.

Katak lived with his parents and six brothers on an island in the Kai archipelago. The water surrounding this beautiful chain of islands teemed with fish and colorful coral. To make their living, the Kai people fished or worked as traders sailing from island to island. When the six elder brothers became men, they built a boat so they could seek their fortunes as traders. They cut a large tree and from its trunk, they carved a sturdy vessel. Katak watched in wonder, wishing he too could seek his fortune. At last he said, "Mother, can I sail away with my brothers?"

She replied, "My son, you are too frail. You'll only get in the way."

"Please, Mother," Katak pleaded. "I'll stay out of the way, I'll be brave. Tell me I can go. All I ask is that you give me one fine melon for the journey."

Katak's mother loved her youngest son. She gave him a small melon. The six brothers scoffed. One of them said, "Katak will be a nuisance at sea," but in the end they let him come along.

Katak did everything he could to prove himself worthy. When the sail came loose in a storm, none of the six brothers had the courage to climb the mast. Katak took the chance to prove he was willing and brave. He climbed the mast and fastened the sail. His effort saved the day, but his brothers did not give him credit.

They made their first stop on a desolate island. "Why are we stopping here?" asked Katak.

"To put you ashore," the brothers replied.

"By myself?" asked Katak.

"Yes," they said. "Don't worry. We'll stop for you on our way home."

Katak hopped around the island. He saw no sign of people anywhere. He had only one melon and no idea how long it would be before his brothers returned. He cut the melon open and scattered the seeds on a patch of fertile ground at the edge of the forest. Then he built himself a little hut. When his melon was gone he became very hungry, but it wasn't long before vines grew where he had scattered the seeds. Soon, little melons hung on the vines. One by one they grew larger and ripened. Now Katak had all the food he needed.

Before going to bed one night he admired his melon patch. One large melon was especially fine. If only his mother could see what a good gardener he was!

In the morning he went to admire the melon again and found it gone. "Who could be stealing my fruit?" he wondered aloud. That night he hid under a large leaf at the edge of the garden. After an hour or so he dozed off to sleep. In the middle of the night Katak awoke to the sound of heavy feet coming toward him from the forest. He peered out from under the leaf and saw a huge figure bending down to pick a melon. It was a giant who lived in the forest beneath the roots of a large tree. He was a shy fellow who only came out at night, so as not to be seen. Katak shouted, "You thief! I've caught you red-handed!" The giant recoiled in shame, for he was afraid of anything loud and boisterous, even if it was only a small frog.

"Please let me go without scolding," begged the giant in a trembling voice. "I will give you anything you ask for." Katak saw the giant wore a small ax at his belt.

"The ax looks most useful," said Katak.

The giant was not pleased to give up his prized possession, but he kept his word. "It is a magic ax," he told Katak. "If you strike the handle against something hard like a rock, a wall, or a tree, whatever you wish for shall come to you."

"Anything?" asked Katak.

"Yes, anything," replied the giant, "gold, riches, jewels, or fine clothing, but you must let me go without reproach."

"Very well," said Katak, "and if what you say proves to be true, you may have my garden and all its fruit."

By now you might be wondering what had become of Katak's six brothers. They went from port to port in the islands buying and selling fruit and fine cloth. On the way home, they did not stop to fetch Katak. They had other things on their minds and forgot him entirely. But Katak was not easily discouraged. When he saw their dugout sailing right past the island, leaving him behind, he quickly grabbed his magic ax. He tapped its handle against a rock. Suddenly the wind stopped and the boat stood still. The brothers grew more and more impatient. Then it occurred to one of them that they should row ashore and pick up Katak. No sooner did he voice this thought than the wind resumed and carried them smoothly ashore to Katak's island. Reunited, the seven brothers sailed home.

Katak's mother gave them a jubilant welcome. She was thrilled when six of her sons presented her with gifts. When Katak offered her nothing she frowned and said, "Katak, you sought your fortune and found none."

Katak said nothing. The next morning while his mother was taking her bath, he put his magic ax to work. After her bath she went to her room and found dresses and shoes in every style and color. There was Katak beaming at her. "I'm sorry for what I said, Dear Son," she cried. "These gifts are wondrous. You did find your fortune!" She wept, and wept, and thanked Katak for bringing her such finery.

"Mother," said Katak, "I've been thinking, wouldn't this be a good time for you to go to the king on my behalf and ask for his daughter's hand?"

"Why Katak, the king is a busy man. We mustn't waste his time on foolishness."

"This is not foolishness, Mother. You said yourself, I found my fortune."

Katak's mother had little hope, but she loved her son and so she went to the king and said, "My son wishes to marry one of your lovely daughters."

"Which son?" asked the king.

"Have you met my youngest, Katak?" the mother asked meekly.

"Katak!" shouted the king. "That frog!? Why should I want a frog for a son-in-law? My daughters know better than to choose him. Ask them yourself."

The mother was led to the part of the palace where the princesses whiled away the afternoon. She told them one of her sons sought a wife. They listened at first, but when they heard she was there for Katak, they made frog sounds and laughed hysterically. Katak's mother went home vowing never again to show her face near the palace. But Katak wouldn't take no for an answer. He pestered her every day until she returned to the princesses with the same question. Again the girls replied with laughter and rude croaks, and the poor woman went away greatly humiliated. Still, Katak badgered her to return. "Perhaps you're wearing them down, Mother. Perhaps one of them is thinking it over."

The youngest princess was indeed thinking it over. She thought to herself, "If his mother loves him so, then perhaps he is a lovable fellow."

When the king heard his daughter consent to marry Katak he could hardly believe his ears. "My youngest is willing to marry a frog?" he said. "How very odd." He turned to Katak's mother and said, "I will give my blessing only if the frog is able to prove himself. In the morning I expect to see a row of guards standing along the entire path between my door and the door to Katak's hut. I also expect loads of ornaments as a bridal gift. Not the sort made of shells or coral, but the sort made of gold and precious gems, as befits a king."

When the mother returned to Katak with the news he took it in stride and said, "Mother, do not be afraid tonight if you are awakened by thunder and lightning." That night no one could sleep. Thunder clamored and lightning flashed the whole night through. At dawn the sky cleared and the sun rose to cast a glorious light upon the countryside. People were astonished to see a long row of guards standing watch over the path between Katak's hut and the palace door. The king awoke to find his courtyard heaped full of priceless ornaments.

Good to his word, the king prepared a celebration the likes of which no one had ever seen. There was music and dancing, feasting, and singing and gifts given to all the guests. The other princesses did not think so much fuss should be made over their youngest sister. They made fun of Katak by putting him in a serving bowl. They took him to his wife and said, "Dear sister, here is your frog of a husband. No doubt he will embarrass our family for evermore." The young princess took Katak to her room where no one could mock him.

She prepared some food for her new husband and they comforted each other. Later when bridal customs required them to give gifts to her sister and the guests, Katak used his magic ax to conjure exquisite treasures. Despite all his generosity toward them, his wife's sisters did not accept him.

One day, not long after the wedding, Katak was alone in his room. He looked at himself in the mirror and wondered what it would be like to have the body of an ordinary man. He closed his eyes and struck his ax to the floor. When he opened his eyes there was a handsome man in the mirror looking back at him. The frog skin lay on the floor beside him. He hung it in the closet and conjured fine clothes for himself. Then he went outside and conjured a fine horse. He rode to the front door of the palace. When the sisters caught sight of him they presumed him to be a prince. Each of them hoped he was there as a suitor to ask for her hand in marriage. They tripped over each other trying to serve him delicious food and drink, but the only sister he would accept food from was the youngest.

Day after day Katak the frog would excuse himself to take a nap. Shortly thereafter he would visit the court in his princely form. The sisters were jealous at they way he showed favor to the youngest. Katak's wife herself wondered why the prince warmed up only to her. She also noticed that whenever the prince came to lunch, Katak always happened to be napping. One day before lunch she hid behind the curtain in Katak's room. To her astonishment he took off his frog attire and hung it in the closet. Her own dear husband, whom she loved even though he was a frog, was also a handsome prince.

She could have burst with joy, but instead, she kept still. When Katak left the room she went to the closet, grasped the frog skin and threw it into the fire.

Later when he returned to his room he saw the remains of charred frog skin in the ashes. "Dear Wife!" he shouted, "this will be the death of me!"

The young wife was terrified. "What can I do?" she cried. Then she heard a voice say, "Bathe him in coconut milk." She rushed to the kitchen for a jug of coconut milk. Meanwhile Katak was growing weaker and weaker. His wife helped him to the tub and poured coconut milk over every inch of him. It worked marvelously. Soon Katak grew strong again. After that he remained always in his princely form. He and his wife lived happily throughout their years despite those who tried to humiliate them. Katak kept his name, because he was not ashamed that he had once been a frog.

HEALING FROM ABANDONMENT | DISENFRANCHISEMENT | EXCLUSION | ISOLATION | COURAGE, INTEGRITY, AND RESILIENCE | COPING WITH REJECTION | ADVENTURESOME SPIRIT | EMANCIPATION FROM HOME | THE ALCHEMY OF SELF-HOOD | SIBLING RIVALRY: This Indonesian tale from the Isles of Kai resembles tales from around the world in which the youngest of several brothers is scoffed at and left behind. While the older brothers are seen as brimming with promise, the young one is thought to be too foolish, weak, and ineffective to amount to much. However, through ingenuity, resilience, courage, and luck, and by befriending magical beings, the youngest surges like a dark horse to unexpected success. Such tales speak of the quiet power of hidden potential, and the strength of the resilient heart. They remind us of great contributors who come from humble roots, and of implausible ideas which turn out to be ground-breaking discoveries. This tale honors the courageous soul who, even when shunned, refuses to give up. It encourages all who've been excluded and insists that just because one's gifts aren't recognized, doesn't mean they aren't meaningful. Just because one's dreams are far-fetched, doesn't mean they won't come true.

Katak's adventure portrays a familial/cultural drama which unfolds between dynamic characters. Such characters may resemble the cast of characters of the inner drama. Looking within we might find an aspect of self resembling Katak, a frail little misfit with big dreams. We might also find an inner big brother who is strong and practical with mainstream ambitions. We might also find an interior family who expect much from the big brother and little from the frog. The tale of Katak reminds us that it's sometimes worth giving the frog a chance, in fact, not to do so is to deny one's hidden potential.

A thirty-one-year-old man named Carl took this tale to heart. He was a gifted engineer, respected for making innovations in aerospace, but he felt inept at conversation. Carl took a storytelling seminar in hopes of improving and confided to others, "Professionally, I'm quite the 'big brother,' but I've been an untested frog when it comes to relationships." He was interested in a woman named Gayle, but did not approach her because he feared "bungling beyond repair." Voices predicting failure played over and over in his head, like the voices of Katak's mother and brothers. "I know I have to value myself for who I am and worry less about how I might appear to others," Carl said. "When it comes to women, I'm just afraid of getting emotionally ripped off."

An outspoken man in the seminar said, "Carl, if Katak hadn't gotten ripped off, he would never have gotten the magic ax!" Everyone in the workshop was after Carl to risk his skin.

Later that day Carl said, "I want to ask Gayle out, I'm just afraid I'll get burned."

Others in the seminar would not let Carl off the hook. Sheila, a soft-spoken woman, said, "Carl, getting burned is not the worst thing in the world, as long as you have coconut milk on hand." That sat well with Carl, and Katak's resilient courage became his touchstone. He dated Gayle a few times, and told us later it went well, but Sheila is the one he wound up with.

INNER BEAUTY | MATE SELECTION | LOVING KINDNESS | MAN OF HEART | LOYALTY | YOUTH-ELDER ALLIANCE: What qualities Katak seeks in a wife, we do not know. It would seem he was willing to take any of the sisters. However, his mother's many visits to the king's daughters serve as a kind of screening process through which the most sensitive and empathic of the sisters eventually makes herself known. Given time, the true character emerges and the choice becomes obvious. In this seemingly passive way, Katak weeds out the vain and superficial brides, and gets the one with inner beauty. The king's youngest daughter in turn is touched by Katak's mother's devotion, and posits that Katak might be worthy of this devotion. I'm reminded of what a wise old therapist once said about selecting a husband: "If his mother is a good solid woman, chances are he is a good, solid man." Even when he is a frog, the princess senses Katak's inner beauty and rightfully perceives him to be a man of heart.

MORE THAN HUMAN WORLD | FOREST AS A PLACE OF TRANSFORMATION | REVERENCE FOR NATURE | INITIATION | MEN'S INITIATION | MEN'S ESTEEM AND EMPOWERMENT | RITES OF PASSAGE | LOVING KINDNESS | MAN OF HEART | LOYALTY | THE ALCHEMY OF SELFHOOD | SACRED MASCULINE | SACRED FEMININE: As in cultures around the world, Katak's initiatory, coming of age experience involves withstanding solitude and the rough elements of nature. He braves the sea, climbs the mast in the windstorm, endures hunger and solitude on a desert island, resourcefully utilizes the melon for survival, and confronts the mysterious tree-giant. Succeeding at all these trials, he gets the magic ax: a wand, a phallus, a talisman, an instrument of empowerment, precision, and desire which he uses to reunite with his brothers, reward his mother, and win himself the right bride. Even having done all that, his slimy animal skin remains essential to his life force. When his wife burns it, it must be replaced immediately with another slimy covering, the coconut milk. Here we return to the phallus, for in some tropical cultures semen and coconut milk are said to be of the same essence. With the coconut milk, we also return to the forest and the tree, for as other South Pacific tales reveal, the coconut palm is the sustenance of the people. It seems the sacred masculine and feminine come together sweetly and tenderly at the end of this Indonesian tale. I return to this tale when I need a sense of what true love and loyalty are about.

Grandfather Ape

INDONESIA | (1,326 words)

*H*er father frowned the instant she was born. "You have a healthy baby girl," said the midwife. But this was the worst news possible, for all the while his wife had been pregnant, his only pleasure was to anticipate a son.

He wasted no time. As soon as the house grew quiet and his wife fell into a deep sleep, he packed the newborn in a bundle of rags and took her into the forest. He set her on the ground beside a rotting stump and left her to her fate. After a while she grew thirsty. She cried out for her mother, but of course her mother was not there. She cried and cried. The ants crawling nearby went about their work. What could they do? The birds watched helplessly, for they had no milk to feed her.

Then another creature came near. Perhaps he was attracted to her cries. "Little one," he said softly, "Have you been left to die? You must be frightened and hungry. I will see what I can do." Then Grandfather Ape, for that is who he was, lifted the infant into his arms. He took her to his home in a nearby tree. He knew which fruit juices she could drink, and which leaves made the softest bed. He constructed a little roof so when it rained she would stay warm and dry.

Time passed. When she grew bigger he built a hut for her and taught her to make food from the roots and fruits of the forest. He taught her to respect the insects and the birds. She learned how to use bark, branches, and leaves to make the mats and things she needed, but always respected the forest and never harmed the trees by stripping them bare.

When she became a young woman the old ape went searching for her parents. He followed the edge of the clearing and walked from village to village, but had no luck. Then he went to the blacksmith's forge where he liked to watch the men at work. First they built a fire. The hotter it grew the louder it roared. Then they melted lumps of ore and useless scraps of metal, so they could make them into useful pots and kettles. Grandfather climbed to the roof and called, "If you knew my granddaughter, you would be most pleased," but with all the hammering, no one could hear him. Disappointed, he returned home.

The next day he tried again, calling from the rooftop to the people below, but no one paid attention. Time after time he returned to the forge. Finally, one day, the youngest apprentice remarked to his friend, "Do you see that old ape sitting on the roof? He keeps speaking of his granddaughter as if he'd like us to meet her." That day the apprentice worked swiftly and kept an eye on Grandfather. When the old ape climbed down from the roof and returned to the forest the apprentice followed behind just out of sight. He made his way quietly so the ape would not hear him. The thick undergrowth made passage difficult. Sometimes the ape traveled along the ground and sometimes through the treetops, but the curious young apprentice kept pace and did not lose sight of him.

At last Grandfather Ape arrived at his hut. When the apprentice approached, Grandfather called out, "Who's there?"

"It is I, the blacksmith's apprentice. I've heard what you say about your granddaughter and I would like to meet her."

"Granddaughter," said the ape, "We have a guest. Fetch a ladder so he can come up."

"No," she whispered, "I've never seen a man before and I don't wish to see one now."

Grandfather said, "This apprentice is a good man."

"How do you know?" she asked.

"Because I have watched him work," said Grandfather. "He's come a long way to meet you. Now, let's be kind and fetch him a ladder."

So she fetched a ladder woven of rattan and lowered it down for the young apprentice. He climbed up and stood in the hut before her. Grandfather turned to her and said, "Let's offer our visitor some food."

"No," she whispered.

"Why not?" Grandfather asked.

"Because I am frightened," she replied.

Grandfather persisted, "This traveler is hungry and we must give him some food."

Finally the granddaughter conceded. She got out some bowls and filled them with delicious fruits. Soon the three sat together, eating and talking. After that the apprentice stayed with them. He was more than a passing visitor. He helped the old ape and was a companion to the young woman. He told her all about life in the village.

Back in the village his friends, the blacksmith, and especially his mother wondered where he had disappeared to. His mother prayed for his return. After a long time people lost hope of ever seeing him again.

Eventually the young woman and the apprentice were married. Grandfather Ape led the ceremony, for among other things, he was a priest. The newlyweds were happy for a time, but the apprentice grew more and more homesick for his friends and family. One day he said he wished to return home. Grandfather Ape did not answer, he merely whistled. When he whistled a brilliant rainbow appeared, its zenith arching high over the forest and its end touching the ground at their feet. Now the apprentice understood Grandfather Ape was not only a priest, but also a powerful magician.

Come," said Grandfather, and he stepped upon the rainbow just as you would step upon a footbridge. The young couple followed. They felt like gods traveling above the forest. They trembled whenever they looked down and saw treetops swaying below. They looked to the sides and saw clouds floating beside them. The wonder of it took their breath away.

When the apprentice's mother looked out and saw a rainbow conveying sky beings to the village, she gasped. When these beings walked right up to her door she gathered her courage and stepped out to meet them. Soon enough she recognized her dear son, "We thought you were dead!" she cried. She welcomed her new daughter-in-law and of course Grandfather Ape. She set about preparing a great feast to celebrate her son's marriage and his return to the village. After the meal, the apprentice announced they would not stay long. In the morning they would return to their forest home. That night they slept on rattan mats near the window. Grandfather slept in a tree just outside.

The next day they returned to the forest, for they had learned to live well there. After four days had passed, the ape said, "I will be leaving. Go about your usual tasks and do not wait for me." Then he left without saying where he was going. A few days later, the young woman went out to look for him. Under a big tree she found his dead body. When she knelt down to touch him his legs changed to iron shields, and his head to an iron helmet. His bones turned to pure gold. His arms and torso turned to earthenware bowls and iron utensils for mixing and cooking. His fingers and toes turned to pearls. He had thought of everything the young woman and her husband would need for their life together. She carried all these treasures home, and put each one in its place. The couple lived a peaceful life in the forest, going to the village often to share good times.

Even into old age the wife remembered her beloved grandfather. She respected the trees and the creatures of the forest as he had taught her. Even in hard times her heart was full of gratitude for all he had given, for without him she would have died as an infant. Now, she had all she needed to live a long and happy life. And that is what she did.

HEALING FROM ABANDONMENT | HEALING FATHER WOUNDS | ISOLATION | LOSS, COURAGE, TRANSFORMATION | LOVING KINDNESS | DISENFRANCHISEMENT | EXCLUSION | CAST-OUTS AND RUNAWAYS | EARLY CHILDHOOD BONDING | ADOPTION AND FOSTERING | NURTURING FATHERS | GENEROSITY | MAN OF HEART | MENTORSHIP | ELDER WISDOM | HELP FROM WISE ELDERS | YOUTH-ELDER ALLIANCE: Like other mammals, human infants are born to be held close and cared for. If a healthy infant is left alone too long its natural response is to wail until someone comes. Our ability to stand on our own develops as we mature, but the need to belong remains strong throughout our lives. All humans are vulnerable to feeling left out, lonesome, or neglected. This story imparts to people of all ages a bit of sweetness and solace at such times.

Grandfather Ape is the quintessential father-figure and spiritual elder. Like a good parent, teacher, or therapist, he instinctively tunes in to his foster daughter's developmental needs as she grows. His attunement to those needs is a healing force unto itself. Foster parents, foster fathers in particular, appreciate finding a male role model who is keenly nurturing and attentive. Grandfather Ape is an inspiration for all adults learning to slow down and tune in to the needs of kids. His example deepens the meaning of foster and stepparent roles and affirms the efforts of all dedicated healers and care-givers.

For those who've been orphaned, neglected, cast out, abandoned, or left alone too much, this tale can be a source of solace and self-worth, as well as a lesson in developing trust. A girl named Jenny drew enormous comfort from taking this story to heart. She was five when we met, and up until then, had lived with one temporary guardian after another. Jenny was capable of speaking, yet highly reluctant to speak. A loving couple wanted to adopt her. I asked her to make me a picture of what it would be like to have a home with them. She drew her adoptive parents holding hands beside the hearth. Near the door she drew a small indistinct blotch which looked as if it could roll out the door and not be missed. "What's this?" I asked, to which she replied, "Me."

After that I made a point to tell Jenny an encouraging story each week. "Grandfather Ape" was her favorite and she asked to hear it often. Grandfather Ape became a familiar figure, alive in her imagination, and there is no doubt in my mind that he was one of her healers. Gradually Jenny's self-portraits acquired limbs, hands, feet, and a face, and she came to understand the tangibility of being wanted and cared for. She's now seventeen and well adjusted to family life.

ANIMALS AS HELPERS AND TEACHERS | REVERENCE FOR NATURE | HONORING THE EARTH | EARTH AS SACRED | THE MORE-THAN-HUMAN WORLD | SUSTAINABILITY: The indigenous peoples of Indonesia make no distinction between the natural world and the spirit world. Animals, trees, rivers, and rainbows are conscious beings to be honored and respected. Stories like this one encourage us Westerners to regard the natural world as a holy creation full of wise guides and potential allies. If our society could absorb Grandfather Ape's life-affirming approach to living in the forest, we might begin to live more sustainably on this earth.

FOREST AS A PLACE OF TRANSFORMATION | SACRED MASCULINE | THE ALCHEMY OF SELFHOOD | INITIATION | RITES OF PASSAGE | LIFE-DEATH-REBIRTH CYCLE | WOMEN'S ESTEEM AND EMPOWERMENT | MEN'S ESTEEM AND EMPOWERMENT | LOVE AND THE ALCHEMICAL UNION | POSTERITY | GRATITUDE: Myths and stories hold meaning on many levels. In addition to its environmental and social implications, this tale is an allegory of the soul. It takes place deep in the uncharted forest, a mysterious, diverse habitat, not unlike the unconscious psyche. Our heroine would be doomed there if not for the old ape who appears to protect and guide her. Grandfather Ape embodies many archetypal powers that nurture and activate the girl's selfhood. These include the father and grandfather, the magician, and the wise elder. As father and grandfather he is the guardian of the girl's physical and emotional well-being. As magician and wise elder he guides her toward selfhood and her higher destiny.

Grandfather Ape also engages the young blacksmith who brings another kind of magic onto the scene, that of the element iron. Mircea Eliade, scholar of culture and religion, wrote that among many ancestral groups iron was seen to possess a resilient warrior spirit. Iron spears, shields, and swords gave warriors extraordinary strength and invincibility. Our heroine starts out timid in her seclusion, but meeting the blacksmith, she gains a pinch of the warrior's boldness. Iron was also a metal of the hearth, used in durable kettles and pots. When Grandfather Ape dies his body transforms into warrior's tools for strength and resilience, and cooking pots to insure our heroine's sustenance and a long and happy domestic life.

Smithcraft is credited with having inspired *alchemy*, a mystical art developed in Greece and Egypt some two thousand years ago. Scholar and psychologist Marie-Louise von Franz, interpreted alchemists' recipes as formulas for psychological transformation. Viewed this way, smithcraft is an apt metaphor for our heroine's soul-making. Smithcraft begins with seemingly useless lumps of ore. Through heating, pouring, molding, and tempering, the ore is transformed into valuable vessels of remarkable durability and strength. The act of transforming minerals parallels the task of forging one's character. The alchemy of this story says that the child once deemed useless by her father, can, with love and proper tempering, thrive. With help from Grandfather Ape, our heroine's true mettle emerges. She becomes whole and strong, and her life reflects it.

Kuan Yin's Vows

EAST ASIA | (1,569 words)

ABOUT KUAN YIN: *Surveying Kuan Yin's many incarnations in the Taoist and Buddhist traditions we encounter a goddess, a noblewoman, a wise Bodhisattva, and a peasant. She transcends national and religious boundaries and is many things to many people. Sometimes a folk-heroine, sometimes a contemplative muse, Kuan Yin is always a radiant angel of mercy.*

Long ago their was a bright young woman of noble birth named Kuan Yin. She wanted to study calligraphy, poetry, philosophy, and music, but her father had other plans.

He arranged for her to be married to an old nobleman who was rich, powerful, and much feared throughout the land. He owned vast farms, mines overflowing with gems, and ships to disperse his goods to all the towns along the river. The people grew poorer while his power and wealth increased with each passing day. Kuan Yin's father had been living on borrowed money. He couldn't go on that way forever, so to turn things around, he set his sights on the huge dowry he could get for marrying off Kuan Yin.

She went to her mother's chamber. "Please, Mother, I do not wish to marry."

"A daughter's place," replied the mother, "is to wish nothing more, nor less than what her father arranges."

"Mother, the man father has chosen is not only greedy, he is older than you and father put together. What virtue would be served by this marriage?"

"The virtue of obedience which befits a daughter and wife."

"Mother, I want to take vows of obedience—not as a wife—but as a Taoist nun. Please ask father to send me to the Temple of the White Bird where I may learn and live in peace."

"It is out of my hands," said her mother.

Kuan Yin threw herself to the floor and wept, but the matter was closed.

That night Kuan Yin packed a small bundle of food. She dressed herself like a servant, crept out the window, inched her way along the roof top, and climbed down the flowering vine until her feet touched ground. Then she ran like a rabbit without looking back. She found her way into the forest. There she met kind woodcutters and hunters who gave her food and shelter and pointed the way, until at last she arrived at the Temple of the White Bird.

Kuan Yin soon proved her devotion whole-heartedly immersing herself in every task that was required of her.

You can imagine how truly undone her father was the morning he found her gone. Everyone was dragged before him and questioned. One servant reported glimpsing someone on the roof that night, a graceful female shape dressed in servant's clothes. "Why didn't you call the guards?" shouted Kuan Yin's father.

"Forgive me, Oh Master," said the terrified servant. "Such a graceful figure on the roof, why, I thought I was dreaming." Kuan Yin's father ordered him beaten and he was promptly hauled away and thrashed.

The noble interrogated his wife. For days he thundered about intimidating her, but she said nothing. Then at last, he calmed down. One day he gently sighed, "Dear Wife, wouldn't it be lovely to see our beautiful Kuan Yin?"

She replied, "If you'll promise to treat Kuan Yin kindly, and gently entreat her to come home, I'll tell you where to find her." He promised, and she told him about the Temple of the White Bird.

Immediately the noble set out toward the forest in an armored coach flanked by six horsemen with swords clanking at their sides. The roads through the forest were narrow and muddy and each crossroads looked the same as the last. Whenever they met a woodcutter or huntsmen the noble demanded directions to the Temple of the White Bird. The woodcutters and huntsmen did not think it right to send such a brash group to the most serene of temples. So they nodded and gestured this way and that sending the noble and his men everywhere but the Temple. This went on for days. Kuan Yin's father hollered and raged until he lost his voice. Then he snorted and scowled. At last the coach wheels broke to bits, and the party returned home.

Night after night Kuan Yin's father stayed up late, pacing the floor. "I know what people say behind my back. They say a noble who can't control his daughter is nothing but a fool."

"Go to sleep, Husband," his wife would say. But he would fuss the whole night through, and fall exhausted to his bed at sunrise. His lands and enterprises, which had been on shaky ground before, now fell into complete neglect.

The fearsome old noble threatened to withdraw his offer of a grand dowry. At this Kuan Yin's father grew more desperate than ever. He ordered a Taoist priest to go to the Temple of the White Bird and bring Kuan Yin home by force. He threatened to behead him if he failed. The priest went to the Temple and spoke with the elder nun. She was so compassionate and wise he could not deceive her. He told her he feared for his life and for the life of Kuan Yin. She bade him fetch Kuan Yin's father and bring him to the temple unarmed.

Kuan Yin's father packed some of his wife's jewels, and set out with the priest for the temple. When at last they arrived, the elder nun came out to meet them. Kuan Yin's father tried to bribe her with jewels, but she took no interest. "Your daughter is our finest scholar," she said. "She studies with passion and learns well. We will not betray her."

The noble's blood simmered. He wanted to behead the nun and take Kuan Yin by force, but being unarmed, he had to use cunning instead. "My daughter disobeyed me," he said. "You must send her home to receive her punishment."

"Disobedience must be punished," said the nun who was cunning herself. "Let us punish Kuan Yin here at the temple by burdening her with extra work."

"What extra work?" asked the noble.

"Extra studies, extra meditations, extra lessons," said the nun.

"For Kuan Yin this is a reward!" scoffed the noble. "No, you must require her to do all the menial labor: the cooking, cleaning, sweeping, scrubbing, washing, mending, weaving, plowing, planting, hoeing, and weeding. That will teach her."

"But that's impossible," said the nun. "We share the menial work and it takes fifty of us to do it."

The noble smiled, "When she collapses, send her home to me. Just make sure it's in time for her wedding next month, or her fiancee will destroy this place." The nun knew of the old noble's ruthlessness. To protect the temple and those in it, she had to agree. All menial tasks fell to Kuan Yin, and none of the nuns were allowed to assist her.

The next day she set to work. From morning until night, from night until morning, she labored. By the third night she'd fallen so far behind the Temple of the White Bird was in complete disarray and Kuan Yin collapsed while sweeping the courtyard. In the morning when she awoke, she thought she was dreaming, for the courtyard looked neatly swept. She sat up and rubbed her eyes. Who should be finishing the last of the job, but the peacock who swept quite efficiently with his long luxuriant tail. She heartily thanked the peacock and ran to the kitchen to make breakfast, but the monkey was stirring the pot. She kissed the monkey and ran out to take the wash from the line. In the laundry yard the storks worked together with their long beaks folding the linen into perfect smooth squares. Beyond the wall, tiger tended the garden, loosening the soil with his great claws, and indoors fox scrubbed the stone floors with his bushy tail. Kuan Yin jumped for joy and gave thanks to all. No human hands assisted her, and yet with the help of the animals She resumed her studies.

Needless to say, Kuan Yin stayed at the Temple of the White Bird. And, as you might expect, the wealthy old noble found himself another young bride. A rage simmered in Kuan Yin's father's heart. With his fortune lost and his plans for recovery dashed, he lost his mind. Some say he set fire to the Temple of the White Bird, burning it to the ground. Others say he sent a swordsman to behead Kuan Yin, but the sword shattered before it met her throat. Eventually, he killed her with his own hands, such was his madness.

As for Kuan Yin, she went the way of all departed, and journeyed to the land of the dead. There she met many suffering souls and her heart brimmed with compassion. She sang for them to ease their loneliness and soften their sorrows. So sweet was the sound of her voice, that all took solace. Their grief was lightened, and their hearts were filled with affection for Kuan Yin. The Lord of the Dead, ruler of that place, did not like Kuan Yin. He thrived on sorrow and pain, loved the sound of his own voice above all things, and despised her singing. "Kuan Yin," he commanded, "Silence!" but each time he got out of hearing range she resumed singing again. At last he ran out of patience and banished her. Where do you think she got banished to? Why back to the land of the living, of course. She has returned many times, always with a heart full of compassion and a love of higher learning. To this very day her gentle presence eases troubled hearts, and her wisdom inspires.

DROPOUT PREVENTION | PASSION FOR LEARNING | WOMEN'S ESTEEM | WOMEN IN EDUCATION | SACRED FEMININE | DEVOTION: This and the following tale, "Mero's Bride," show Kuan Yin's passion for higher learning, for herself and for others. The tales can be told together or separately. "Kuan Yin's Vows," tells of times when education was off limits to women, and reminds us what a precious, hard-won privilege education is, especially to those who were formerly denied it. Through "Kuan Yin's Vows" and "Mero's Bride" we come to understand erudition as an aspect of spiritual devotion.

GREED AND ACQUISITIVENESS | MISUSE OF POWER | MISGUIDED LEADERSHIP | LOSE-LOSE SITUATIONS | REVENGE AND RETRIBUTION | THE FUTILITY OF VIOLENCE | FAMILIAL HOMICIDE | LOSS, COURAGE, AND TRANSFORMATION |

COURAGE, INTEGRITY, RESILIENCE | SELF DETERMINATION | WORTHY USE OF DECEPTION | YOUTH-ELDER ALLIANCE | WOUNDED HEALER | LIFE-DEATH-REBIRTH CYCLE | SACRED FEMININE: This is a quintessential tale of the survival of goodness and true nobility despite overwhelming oppression and corruption. Kuan Yin's father tries to force her to wed a dubious mate solely so he can collect a large dowry. Money is placed above true calling, true love, and the heart's deepest yearning. He feels betrayed when Kuan Yin won't cooperate, and yet he fails to see how his plan betrays her innermost soul. His heart is so consumed with revenge he plots retribution and eventually takes his daughter's life. The tale then takes us to the realm of the immortal soul to show that corruption and oppression have not "won." Kuan Yin burns brightly in the afterlife, bringing solace to troubled souls. If this tale is encouraging to you, imagine how encouraging it is to a refugee or a political prisoner. Kuan Yin is at once healer and healed, and the true winner is the immortal soul. Whether dwelling in the land of the living or the land of the dead, Kuan Yin's sacred values of beauty, compassion, erudition, and strength prevail.

FOREST AS A PLACE OF TRANSFORMATION | ANIMALS AS HELPERS AND TEACHERS | THE MORE-THAN-HUMAN WORLD: The forest itself takes on a protective quality, making Kuan Yin's passage safe and smooth and obstructing her father's intrusion. In Kuan Yin's dark hour she collapses and the animals of the forest come to her aid. Each has a skill to offer and performs a useful task with tireless devotion. From the perspective of archetypal psychology we might say the animal helpers represent inner resources, hidden aspects of self, not often relied upon, but coming to the fore in times of great need. From a more animistic, indigenous point of view, the animals of the forest are spirit allies, who pick up the slack when we are down, and even aid us in honing a more whole and conscious self.

Mero's Bride

EAST ASIA | (882 words)

(for background on Kuan Yin, see p. 179)

Kuan Yin's influence spans the centuries and enriches traditions from Taoism to Buddhism. She's come back in many forms to teach humankind, and to bring out the best in humanity. Once she took the form of a fisherman's daughter. She lived at the edge of the river in a little cottage with her parents. Each day she brought her basket of fresh fish to the market. She was such a lovable child, she won the hearts of many customers. When womanhood began to dawn across her flesh and countenance, she became so beautiful people went weak at the sight of her. They lined up to buy fish, just to get a closer look. All they could do was point to a fish and hand her a few coins, for the fisher maiden's beauty left everyone speechless.

One day a young man wishing to woo her gathered all his courage. He went to the market early and watched for her to come. Soon he could see her approaching, strolling as gracefully as a lily swaying on the breeze. He waited until she reached the very center of the crowded market. Then he stepped before her and in a clear voice announced, "With all my heart, Fishermaiden, I wish to be your devoted husband." The fishermaiden stood before him, smiling most compassionately. She did not reply, but she did not turn away either. Everyone waited in silence to hear how she would respond. Then suddenly, another young man rushed forward and cried, "But I too wish to be your devoted husband!" Then another rushed forward with the same pronouncement, and another, and another, until dozens clamored for her hand.

The fishermaiden bowed her head, and the crowd drew silent. Then she said, "So many fine suitors, how can I possibly choose? Can any of you by chance recite the Sutras of the Compassionate Kuan Yin?" The young men stood silently, for none had studied the sutras, let alone learned them by heart. "Ahh," replied the fishermaiden. "Whosoever shall learn to recite the sutras in one month's time, he shall be my husband."

You can imagine how fervently the young men set to reading, studying, and reciting. They worked like true scholars seized by a frenzy of academic passion. One month later they gathered in the market. Each took his turn before the crowd, reciting as clearly and sweetly as possible. Never had the young men of this village been so learned. It was a miracle. Mothers wept at their eloquence, fathers beamed with pride and grandparents fainted in shock. "Such excellent recitations," said the fishermaiden when it was finished. "But surely I cannot marry all of you! What would I do with so many husbands? Can any of you suitors explicate the meaning of the sutras?" All the suitors stood silent. They had recited well, but none had thought to consider what the sutras might mean. "Let us meet again in one month's time," said the fishermaiden. "If at that time one of you can explain the meaning of the Sutras of the Venerable Kuan Yin, he shall be my husband."

All month the young men pondered what the sutras might mean, but they couldn't make much headway. One young fellow named Mero, traveled far down the river and into the hills to meet a wise old sage. The wise sage held discourses each day. Gradually Miro began to understand. At the end of the month, Miro grasped the meaning of the sutras. When everyone gathered again at the market, Miro was the only one who could explain the sutras and he explained them magnificently. The fishermaiden smiled and said, "It takes a wise and compassionate heart to grasp the Sutras of Kuan Yin. I will be pleased to marry a man with such heart." She told Miro to come for her the next day at the little hut on the river's edge.

The next day Miro went as instructed. He knocked at the door and the fishermaiden's parents greeted him kindly. "We have been waiting for you," they said. "Come this way." They led him to a small room at the back of the house and told him to enter. He went inside to find his bride, but all he found was an open window. Outside the window he saw her footprints in the sand. He climbed through the window and followed the prints. They led all the way to the river's edge. There Miro found a pair of glistening golden sandals. Instantly he knew that the fishermaiden was none other than the beloved Bodhisattva herself, the Venerable Kuan Yin. His heart swelled with humility and gratitude for the sacred teachings which now burned in him. For without the mysterious interventions of Kuan Yin, he never would have discovered nor nurtured his higher gifts. Miro went on to become a great teacher, consulted by many far and wide for his wisdom and compassion. He started each and every day with this prayer. "Sainted Lady, thank you. Mystical Wife, Bodhisattva, Fragrant Lotus, Eternal Flame, Guiding Hand, Shining Pearl, thank you, thank you, for guiding me to my self, and the greater truth." And that is the story of Mero's bride. May it inspire us all to find and embrace our beloved disciplines with devotion, so that we may go forth into the world and offer our greater gifts.

THE INACCESSIBLE LOVER | LOVE AND ALCHEMICAL UNION | MAN OF HEART | PASSION FOR LEARNING | DEVOTION | MENTORSHIP | WORTHY USE OF DECEP-

TION | DROPOUT PREVENTION: Mero, like mythic heroes the world over, falls in love with an immortal in the guise of a beautiful women. The passion quickening inside him sets off an alchemical reaction, an activation of self, and he is catapulted from spiritual dormancy to a level of high spiritual animation. The mind alone could not achieve the vibrant erudition brought on by loving Kuan Yin, and neither could an available flesh-and-blood sweetheart, for spiritual activation of this kind is heighten by hunger. This was well understood by mystic poets down through the ages such as Rumi of Persia, Mira Bai of India, and Sor Juana of Mexico, all of whom cried out in their poems to invisible immortal beloved. This tale, and "Kuan Yin's Vows" both convey the sense of devotion which occurs when we fall in love with a subject, an alma mater, a muse, or an eminent figure in our field. My philosophy teacher in college understood the connection between devotion and learning. She awed us students by quoting the great philosophers at length without notes. I asked, "How do you retain all that?"

She replied, "I've fallen in love with every philosopher I've ever read. Love expands the mind." There's no doubt that the best teachers never tire of their subjects because of a quality of Eros which is sparked for them, a renewable passion which keeps them ever enamored of their work. If we're lucky, the love of learning is contagious and strikes the student as well. "Kuan Yin's Vows" and "Mero's Bride" work well in dropout prevention efforts with youth, to celebrate graduations, and to instill academic passion in students of all ages.

Amaterasu's Light

JAPAN | (683 words)

AMATERASU, BACKGROUND AND SOURCES: *The Japanese sun goddess is the principal deity in the Shinto tradition. She banishes darkness, weaves splendid clothing for the gods, and enables all life to flourish. Amaterasu's tales were written down in the two great sources of Japanese mythology, the KOJIKI, the Record of Ancient Matters and the NIHON SHOKI, the Chronicles of Japan. Amaterasu is the favorite daughter of the original parents who created Earth and eventually placed her in charge. Her brooding counterpart, Susanowo had first been given highest rank, but after causing much disturbance on Earth, was sent to rule the netherworld below.*

*A*materasu is the goddess of the sun. Each morning the first hint of her dawning inspires the birds to sing. Plants strive toward her and produce blossoms and fruits to please her. When her golden rays stream down to warm the earth, cats stretch contentedly and bees go to work. When she shines upon the waterfall it glistens like a shower of meteors.

Long ago there came a frightful day when Amaterasu abandoned her place in the sky and for a time left the world in total darkness. It all began when Susanowo, the god below, visited Amaterasu's realm. Some say he was her brother, for indeed he taunted her like a jealous sibling. Others say he was her husband. If so, he was a belligerent spouse, not given to love or kindness. On the next point everyone agrees: He brooded jealously, for Amaterasu's realm was bounteous and lovely while his was colorless and grim. When his jealousy turned to wrath he stormed violently across the land, leaving a wake of destruction.

Amaterasu made ready to defend the land. She flashed her brilliant swords of light, swords which could instantly burn away Susanowo's storm clouds. When Susanowo saw them flash, he knew he was done for. He gathered his storm clouds and shrank toward the horizon. Amaterasu put away her swords and went back to tending her fields of rice and beans.

Susanowo kept still by day, but at night wrecked havoc. He blustered and fumed until Amaterasu's aqueducts were demolished. This caused her bean fields to flood and her rice fields to whither. She suspected Susanowo, but didn't want to accuse. Instead she calmly set about repairing the aqueducts. Each day she restored the fields and each night he destroyed them again. In the end Amaterasu's persistent care won out. When harvest time came there was plenty of food. The people joyously prepared her temple for celebration and thanksgiving.

When Susanowo saw the people's devotion, his jealousy got roiled once more. He huffed and snorted, and spewed harsh winds. He churned up the sea and sent great waves thundering through the village. The streets became turbulent rivers, ripping homes off their foundations, including Amaterasu's temple. The people were washed out to sea. It happened so fast Amaterasu was powerless to save them.

All the joy drained from her heart. She did not set about restoring the land. Instead she retreated to a cave and shut herself in. She placed a great rock at the opening and refused to come out. Without

Amaterasu, darkness fell over the Earth. Plants shriveled and the moon got so chilly it nearly froze. It seemed Earth was doomed without Amaterasu's light.

The other gods called a meeting to decide what to do. Together they came up with a plan. They set about making a shrine outside Amaterasu's cave. From the trees they hung banners of fine silk. They lit candles and placed rich jewels in the tree branches. Opposite the mouth of the cave, they placed a large mirror. Beautiful goddesses gathered to dance and to sing. The sweet sound of their voices was most enticing and Amaterasu wondered how and why they were celebrating without her. She moved the rock ever so slightly to have a peek.

This is exactly what the gods had hoped for. They gave the rock a good push and Amaterasu's light shone forth. The first thing she saw was her own reflection in the mirror. All else paled by comparison. Not realizing it was her own image, she stepped forward to admire it. All the gods gathered around her to welcome her back. It did not take them long to convinced Amaterasu to rejoin them. They joyously escorted her back to her heavenly home. With Amaterasu's light shining down upon them the plants came back to life, the water regained its sparkle, and the moon began to glow again. Ever since that time Amaterasu's patience has not failed. Despite Susanowo's ongoing pranks, she rises each morning and sheds her warmth upon the Earth.

REVERENCE FOR NATURE | EARTH AS SACRED | THE MORE-THAN-HUMAN WORLD | WOMEN'S ESTEEM AND EMPOWERMENT | SACRED FEMININE | GRATITUDE: In the Shinto philosophy the natural world is not merely a collection of resources for the taking. All aspects of nature are imbued with spirit and must be honored accordingly. This tale reminds us not to take for granted Earth's bounty nor to forget our utter dependence upon the life-giving rays of the sun. The tale is also heartening to those who seek to draw nourishment from the sacred feminine. A woman named Karen said, "My whole life I've had spiritual inclinations, and I've looked to Christ and Buddha as the ultimate role models, but it's nice to discover this story, and to learn that the Shinto faith reveres nature and the goddess. It's nice to have a female among the spiritual models I look up to."

WINTER BLUES | LONGING FOR LIGHT | DEPRIVATION | EMOTIONAL RESILIENCE | HARDSHIP AS AN OPPORTUNITY: This tale can console sufferers of seasonal depression. Like "Kore, Queen of Darkness, Maiden of Light," "Maui Snares the Sun," and "Raven Brings Light," it reminds us that longing for sunshine during the darker months has always been part of the human experience. We can't dispense with winter blues, but we can influence how we think about them and how we choose to cope.

James, a school administrator felt embarrassed when his doctor diagnosed SAD, (Seasonal Affective Disorder). The doctor gave him several tools for coping, but James valued self reliance and was repelled by the idea of "leaning on crutches." This tale served to expand his thinking. Seeing the goddess brought to a standstill gave James permission to admit that every December something similar happened to him. Amaterasu's withdrawal and return was a compassion-inducing metaphor for his own bouts with depression. James came "out of the closet" as a sufferer of SAD. His school developed innovative ways to reach out to students and teachers coping with depression. James was amazed how many other silent sufferers came "out of their caves" to give and receive support.

GRIEF AND LOSS | PROLONGED OR COMPLICATED GRIEF | ISOLATION | RESTORING BLOCKED GIFTS | INSPIRATION LOST AND REGAINED | THE MORE-THAN-HUMAN WORLD: A grieving couple, Rita and Larry, took "Amaterasu's Light," to heart in a different way. In the months after their only child had taken his own life, Rita shut herself in, plagued with a nagging wish that she, too, could cease to live. She did not appreciate condolence or advice, but she did accept this story as a useful metaphor. Amaterasu's loss and withdrawal characterized what Rita was experiencing: the loss of what she held most dear, and the overwhelming urge to withdraw from life.

Rita refused to come out of her room, but in a few months time she became interested in the part of the story where Amaterasu chooses to "rejoin the living." Rita wrote in her journal, "When Amaterasu peeks out and sees her mirror image, she finds it pleasing. My trouble is, I can't get a pleasing image of myself if I'm not Sean's mother."

During this phase of grieving Larry was also heart-broken, but his sense of self remained intact. He acted as Rita's mirror, reflecting back to her the wonderful things she had done to make their life rich. He did this through notes and gentle conversation. In time, Rita began asking how the family garden was faring. Gradually her interest in life reawakened and she chose to rejoin the living. When it came time to disperse Sean's ashes, Rita and Larry "just knew" that the family garden was the place. Larry said, "Sean was a gentle soul. To him the world was pretty confusing, but the garden always made sense." For Rita and Larry, as for adherents to the Shinto tradition, nature's beneficent cycle of regeneration and renewal was a great source of solace. It gave them reason to live.

JEALOUSY, ENVY, AND COMPETITION | GENEROSITY | GRATITUDE | UNHEALTHY COMPETITION | SIBLING RIVALRY | REVENGE AND RETRIBUTION |

LOSE-LOSE SITUATIONS: While Amaterasu mirrors the magnanimous, nurturing, generous aspects of the human personality, her counterpart Susanowo reflects the less generous, more resentful, begrudging side. Susanowo has never gotten over being assigned to the lower realm, and is consumed with jealousy. This tale serves as a powerful reminder how miserable life is when revenge becomes the goal. The story suggests that in the face of opposition and strife one can choose to nurture and rebuild, or one can plot revenge. The first opens the door for the possibility of beauty, gratitude, and joy, the second brings only misery.

Maui Snares the Sun

POLYNESIA | (833 words)

MAUI, BACKGROUND AND SOURCES: *The hero-trickster, Maui is loved throughout Polynesia from New Zealand to Hawaii. His divine lineage and bold deeds vary from tale to tale and village to village. The youngest of several brothers, he's famous for prankster antics and useful inventions such as the spearhead, the fishhook, and the calabash of the winds, an important navigational device. As with North American tricksters Coyote and Raven, Maui's exploits better the world for humankind. They include fishing up the islands from the floor of the Pacific, obtaining fire, and expanding the daylight hours by lassoing the sun. My retellings of the Maui tales draw together snips, snatches, translations and re-tellings from Hawaiian and Maori sources. Notable nineteenth century elders who pre-served and passed down tales include King David Kalakaua, who wrote LEGENDS AND MYTHS OF HAWAII, and Katharine Luomala whose trick-ster cycle entitled "Maui of a Thousand Tricks" was printed in the Hawaiian newspaper, Kuokoa and can be found in Dorson's FOLKTALES.*

NOTE: *Hina* means woman. Maui's mother, sister, and wife share variations of the name.

Long ago, Maui watched his mother Hina-of-the-Fire as she worked. She had invented bark cloth called *tapa*. From it she made sleeping mats and clothes for her family. Maui watched her at work. She peeled a section of bark from a tree. She soaked and pounded the bark to make it soft, then she placed it in the sunshine to dry. You might think the tapa dried quickly, but no. At that time the days were short. The sun did not linger above warming the earth with golden rays. Instead the sun raced quickly across the sky. Maui saw that under these conditions it took several days for Hina's tapa to dry. He went to his older brothers. "Brothers," he said, "why don't you get a long rope and help me snare the sun?"

"Maui, is this another of your pranks?" they asked.

"If we catch the sun we can slow him down, and reel him in," said Maui. "Let's make him stay above long enough to dry Mother's tapa in a single day." So the brothers grabbed an old rope that was lying around. They made a lasso and waited at the very spot where the sun rose each morning. The moment the sun was up, the brothers swung the lasso up into the sky and snared him, but the sun is not easily stopped. The rope burst into flames and disappeared in a puff of smoke. Then the sun went speedily on his way as before.

Maui returned to the place where Hina-of-the-Fire was working. He sat down but did not rest. He kept wondering how to catch the sun. At last Hina said, "Maui, My Son, what are you thinking about?"

"I am wondering what sort of rope can withstand fire," Maui replied.

"Why do you puzzle over this?"

"Oh, no reason, Mother, just to amuse myself."

"You must ask your grandmother," Hina advised, "for she is a great maker of ropes." Hina told Maui where to find his grandmother's cooking place under a large wiliwili tree. When he arrived there he heard singing, and saw an old blind woman cooking bananas.

She heard his footstep and called out, "Who's there?"

Maui replied, "Greetings Grandmother, it is I, your grandson."

"Everyone is my grandchild when they smell bananas cooking," grumbled the old woman.

"Surely you remember me, Granny. I'm the youngest of Hina's sons," Maui spoke sweetly as he stealthily approached the steaming bananas.

"My grandsons are adventurers," replied the old woman. "They don't come around here, and I wouldn't know them if they did." She went on peeling bananas and singing to herself.

"I need your help, Grandmother," said Maui. He slowly reached over and stole the bananas from the fire. "I need a rope to capture the sun."

"What for?" asked the old woman.

"Why, to slow the sun down, Granny," he said, "to warm your old bones, and to make Mother's work more efficient."

Grandmother's blind eyes rolled suspiciously about their sockets. "What kind of a rascal tries to snare the sun?" she asked, reaching for the bananas and finding them gone.

"The same rascal who steals your bananas," Maui replied, leaping into Grandmother's lap. He gave her a big kiss, as when he was small. Now it all came back to her and she was satisfied that this was truly Hina's youngest, for no one else was sly enough to steal bananas from under her nose.

"There is but one substance to withstand the sun," she told him. "That would be the hair from your own sister's head. If your sister, Hina-of-the-Sea, agrees to give you her hair, then I shall help you braid it into a rope." Maui went to the sea to find his sister. Some say he sneaked up on her and stole her hair while she was sleeping. Others say she gave it freely and happily. But everyone agrees that Maui returned to the wiliwili tree with a good supply of his sister's hair. Grandmother set about teaching him to make a sturdy rope.

When the rope was complete they went to the spot where the sun rises. There they waited. At the right moment Maui threw his lasso into the air and cinched it 'round the belly of the sun. The sun struggled and hollered, but so strong was the rope, Sun could not get away. Maui cried, "Sun, your warmth is powerful and good. You must slow down, and linger above so those on Earth can benefit." The sun was an adventurer who loved to roam freely, but what could he do? His force was great, and yet this mighty rope subdued him. So they agreed that Sun could travel quickly six months out of the year, but the other six months he had to travel slowly. Ever since that day, we've had summer as well as winter. When the days grow long, people's hearts are filled with gratitude. Hina, Granny, and all of humankind can thank that rascal, Maui.

WINTER BLUES | LONGING FOR LIGHT: Sun-lovers who grow winter-weary have Maui to thank for the coming of spring and the long, bright days of summer. Like most tales on the origin of the seasons, "Maui Snares the Sun" provides a sympathetic mirror for those diagnosed with Seasonal Affective Disorder. Such tales are heartening reminders that "to everything there is a season," and "this too shall pass." (See also "Kore of Darkness Maiden of Light," "Amaterasu's Light," and "Raven Brings Light"). Myth tells us that light deprivation has effected human moods since time immemorial. Longing for light has not always been considered a "disorder," but part of the human condition. The action in this tale models active strategizing and never once implies winter weariness is "all in your head."

FAMILIAL COOPERATION | GENEROSITY | COOPERATION AND DEVOTION | MEN'S ESTEEM AND EMPOWERMENT | WOMEN'S ESTEEM AND EMPOWERMENT | YOUTH-ELDER ALLIANCE | INNOVATION | HELP FROM WISE ELDERS: I once took five minutes to paraphrase "Maui Snares the Sun," in family therapy with a single mother and her teenage son. I chose the tale because the mother suffered from seasonal depression. However, the most beneficial impact was to plant the notion of helpfulness into the mind of the son, for Maui's chief aim in this tale is to help his mother. The teenager was a well-meaning only child, doted on by his mother and grandparents. It had simply never occurred to him to pitch in and help. Though he didn't credit Maui for his new-found initiative, after he heard the tale, his mother noted that, "out of the blue he started doing laundry and dishes." His increased cooperation greatly improved the mood of the household. The beauty of it was, the son came to this on his own, without prodding or lecturing. When our ancestors employed storytelling as a way of teaching, they minimized shame and maximized inspiration.

In our culture cooperative males are sometimes characterized as cowed or tied to apron strings. This can discourage young men from exercising their innate cooperative tendencies. Maui's blend of bold innovation and familial cooperation make him more, not less a man. Maui tales enhance self esteem for both genders, since the women have influential powers of their own. Like other heroes of old, Maui takes counsel from the women in his life and his great deeds could not be accomplished without the help of his mother, grandmother, sister, and an ancestress from the world below.

TRICKS AND TRICKING | HUMOR: "Full of beans," is my mother's description for someone behaving just naughtily enough to be fun, without crossing over into defiance or vindictiveness. Maui's misdemeanors fall into this category. His motives are admirable and his tricks lead to positive results. Part of what's lovable about tricksters, is that they don't embody pure virtue, they are fallible like us. Some adults fear youngsters may think trickster tales condone mischief. If your listener is highly suggestible you may want to choose a tale which is morally explicit at every turn. With that said, remember most young people, even those full of excuses for acting out, are capable of ascertaining when they crossed the line from being "full of beans" to being malicious. This is precisely the type of discernment needed in youth-elder dialogues, if young people are to formulate a personal code. Well-chosen trickster tales, if told in the context of a good family, classroom, discussion group or treatment center, intrigue young people no end.

Young people love defining right and wrong, and often espouse loftier standards of conduct than you might expect.

ADVENTURESOME SPIRIT | MEN'S INITIATION | EMOTIONAL RESILIENCE | SACRED MASCULINE | ATHLETIC EXCELLENCE: This and the following tale, "Maui Fishes Up the Islands," attribute great deeds to the spirited exuberance of youth. Motivated not only by his adventuresome desire to exert himself in nature, but also by his desire to help others, Maui achieves great things. This heartens young men coming of age, as it suggests that properly directed, and with the right support, their innate caring and exuberance can lead to something good. When I told this tale in an adolescent boys group, a fifteen-year-old wrestler named Joey, asked, "So is Maui a god, or a hero, or a kid?"

"A bit of all three," I replied.

"Cool," he said, pleased to have a quick, strong, agile young hero to look up to.

THE MORE-THAN-HUMAN WORLD | REVERENCE FOR NATURE | HONORING THE EARTH: As in other Polynesian tales, the natural world pulsates with *mana* a vibrant, sacred essence, an invisible power which infuses all life, and all natural things. The wili wili tree, the seaweed used to craft the rope, and of course the sun, are infused with these marvelous powers. Maui's ability to creatively engage and direct the mana of the world makes him great.

Maui Fishes Up the Islands

POLYNESIA | (658 words)

(for background on Maui, see p. 191)

Maui wanted nothing more than to go fishing with his brothers. But they refused to take him along. They said he got in the way and never caught a thing. He had no fishhooks of his own. He borrowed theirs and lost them. One day Maui set out to turn things around.

In those days fishhooks were made of bone. Maui journeyed to the underworld to get a special bone which would outdo all others. There he met an ancestress who was half-dead and half-living. One side of her was nothing but bone. From this side Maui took the jaw. "You're welcome to it," said the ancestress. Her jawbone was perfectly shaped for catching fish, and it was loaded with ancestral powers to lure the fish with the meatiest flesh. Such fish would roast up deliciously, and please all the women, his grandmother, his mother, and his sister Hina-of-the-Sea. Some say Maui had a wife too, and it was she he most wanted to please. Others say he was just out to please himself. In any case, here's what happened:

His brothers went fishing without him. So he went to his mother and asked for one of her sacred birds. "Why do you need this bird?" she asked.

"I need powerful bait for my new hook," said Maui. His mother gave him one of her sacred birds. Maui went to the beach and waited for his brothers. They returned saying they hadn't caught a single fish. Maui saw his chance. He flashed his new hook and told them where to paddle. They went far out to sea and threw out their lines, but caught nothing. "Keep going," said Maui. "Farther out, that's where we must fish."

The brothers paddled and paddled. At last they got angry. "Maui, there are no fish to show for all your talk. And as for your clever hook, it hasn't even touched water. Why did we listen? We're going home!"

Then Maui let down his line. He lowered the magic hook made from the jawbone of his ancestress. Attached to it was the sacred bird his mother had given for bait. It went down through the depths, to the very bottom. There it passed in front of an ancient being called Old-One-Tooth. Old-One-Tooth holds down the land at the floor of the sea. When the hook came by with the bird on it, Old-One-Tooth took it into his mouth. Some say Maui's sister Hina-of-the-Sea was there at the time and it was she who secured the hook to Old-One-Tooth's jaw. In any case, Maui's line grew taut. He tied it to the canoe and told his brothers to paddle fiercely. They used all their might. They paddled as they'd never paddled before, but the weight of their catch grew heavier and heavier. Maui's paddle surged in the water, and he sang a magic chant that went something like this:

> *"Oh Sacred Lands beneath the Sea,*
> *arise, arise.*
> *Face the Sun.*
> *The Powers of Sea bid it!*
> *The Powers of Sky bid it!*

Sea foam shall dance around you.
Do not sulk below.
Arise! Face the Sun."

The brothers looked back to see a great island rise up out of the water. It was covered with mountains and trees. One of the brothers was so shocked he dropped his paddle. Just then the line broke. The great island stopped and stayed in place. A few smaller islands rose up and rested nearby. If the line had not broken, a whole continent might have emerged. As it was, there emerged a large island with smaller ones attached below the surface. These sacred islands were as hospitable as paradise. Colorful birds, flowers, and fruits abounded. The surrounding waters were abundant with delicious fish. Polynesian people who settled there are strong and proud. To this day those with devout hearts still give thanks for Maui's fishing up their sacred home from the floor of the sea.

EXCLUSION | COURAGE, INTEGRITY, RESILIENCE | CREATIVE COURAGE | FAMILIAL COOPERATION | YOUTH-ELDER ALLIANCE | EMOTIONAL RESILIENCE | INNOVATION | MALE INTUITION | SACRED MASCULINE | ATHLETIC EXCELLENCE | ADVENTURESOME SPIRIT | INITIATION | ECSTASY AND ELATION: Maui is akin to the younger brother in fairytales whose ingenuity is underestimated and overlooked. Maui's brothers consider him a nuisance and exclude him from fishing trips. But on this occasion he turns things around. As in the previous tale, "Maui Snares the Sun," he gets special assistance from the females in the family. From an ancestress, he secures a magic fish hook, and from his mother he obtains extraordinary bait. These items, used along with what could only be assumed to be Maui's intuition about where to fish, lead to the emergence of the islands themselves. With a whole new archipelago to show for his efforts, no longer can Little Brother be dismissed as a mere slacker. This tale is heartening to anyone who feels excluded or undervalued. Like the tale, "The Frog," it reminds us not to dismiss our youthful longing and enthusiasm. Our own Maui-like urges to be included and to strive for something wondrous, could lead us toward stunning adventures at any age. Maui's descent to the world below, his quest for mana-filled fishing gear, culminating in his extraordinary feat remind us not only of quintessential heroes' quests the world over, but also of our own persistence and creative courage, and those rare ecstatic moments when the results of our efforts far exceed our dreams.

THE MORE-THAN-HUMAN WORLD | HONORING THE EARTH | REVERENCE FOR NATURE | GRATITUDE: "Maui Fishes Up the Islands" bespeaks the sacred life of the earth and ocean, and provides us with delightful images for the origin of the islands. When indigenous people tell this tale it rollicks with exuberant humor at the same time it conveys great reverence and devotion for the land. Retelling the tale is a means for islanders to express their never-ending gratitude for their home. Told in mainland mainstream settings the tale encourages the protection of wildlife and the judicious use of the land.

Hina's Adventure
or
The First Coconut

POLYNESIA

(too sexually explicit for children)
(for background on Maui, see p. 191)

HINA'S ADVENTURE, BACKGROUND AND SOURCES: *My retelling here is based on the narration of Fariua-a-Makitua a chieftain from the Tuamotu Archipelago east of Tahiti. His tale, offered word-for-word in Joseph Campbell's* Primitive Mythology, *escaped the puritanical hand of colonial translators. It's the tale of a love triangle, and if it were a movie, it would be "R" rated because of sexually explicit language, nudity, and violence. The characters have dynamic personalities which defy stereotypes. Their accessibility and imperfections are refreshing and delightful. The rivals make ferocious threats, but veiled behind their braggadocio we glimpse hints of timidity and acquiescence. Hina's audacity in throwing herself at men is uproariously funny, especially when those men flee for cover.*

Long ago Hina lived with her husband, the eel god Te Tuna, in the land beneath the sea. It was a cold place and Hina wanted out. She said, "Husband, you stay here. I'm going to gather food for us."

Te Tuna asked, "Will you be gone long?"

"Yes," said Hina. "To get where I'm going, to gather and prepare the food, will take about three days."

"Go ahead then." Te Tuna replied, "Take as long as you need."

So off she went. Hina didn't stop to look for food at all, but foraged for a sweetheart instead. First she traveled to the home of the Tane clan. When she got there she called, "There must be an eel-shaped one among you—one who'll surge forth and satisfy a ready woman. The eel god Te Tuna, is but a limp stalk. Oh, men of the Tane clan, your passion is widely touted. I've come all this way without shame to copulate with the firmest among you."

The men of the Tane clan did not show themselves. They cried out from within their mothers' houses, "Hina, don't hang around here! Te Tuna will slay any man who touches you! Don't endanger us! Hit the road and keep going!"

Hina continued unruffled, until she came to the home of the Peka clan. There she called out, "Oh, Men of the Peka, surely there is a hot one among you, a man eager to plunge into my love patch and be gratified." But the men begged her to have pity and be gone. So on she went.

At the place of the Tu clan, she implored the men to please her, but they gave the same reaction. Hina traveled on to the Maui clan, and still her offer drew no takers. When Maui's mother saw Hina she said, "Maui, don't pass up this chance!"

So Maui took Hina as his wife, and they lived happily in Maui's mother's home. But people like to talk. The more they talked the more their minds stirred. At last they went to Te Tuna and said, "Maui has taken your wife."

"Oh, he can have her," replied Te Tuna who was willing to leave it at that. But people kept pressing. At last their talk annoyed him. "Who is this wife-stealer, this Maui? What does he look like?"

"Short of stature," they told him, "and with a misshapen penis at that."

"Wait 'til he sees his rival," said Te Tuna getting worked up. "One glance at my semen-stained loin-cloth will scare him to death! Tell him I'm out for vengeance." Then Te Tuna sang lamentations of loneliness for Hina.

People hurried to warn Maui, "Take heed, Maui. Your rival comes on a mission of vengeance."

"Let him come!" shouted Maui. But as an afterthought he asked, "This rival, this, Te Tuna, what sort of a monster is he?"

"An enormous monster," they replied.

"I suppose," ventured Maui, "he is as tall and upright as a tree."

"Perhaps he is like a bent tree," people said, trying to assuage Maui's fears.

"He's rather stooped, then?" said Maui, "rather weak?" To this people nodded, even though it was not true. Maui shouted, "One glimpse of my lopsided penis will send him running!"

Maui waited for his rival. Days passed. He and his family lived peacefully as usual. Then one day the sky grew dark and stormy. Lightning began to flash and thunder roared. The villagers hid, for they knew Te Tuna was coming. "Maui has caused our ruin!" they cried. "No man touches the wife of another! Now everyone will die!"

"Don't worry," said Maui. "If we stick close together we'll survive."

Te Tuna soon appeared flanked by four monstrous helpers. The eel god raised his semen-stained loin-cloth and waved it like a flag above his head. This summoned a huge frothy wave from far out at sea. It surged toward the village at great speed. "Maui, quick," said his mother, "show your power!" Maui showed the lopsided tip of his penis, and the wave swiftly retreated, carrying with it Te Tuna's helpers. It rolled farther and farther out to sea dashing the monsters upon the reef. Maui went out to finish them off, but spared the great Te Tuna.

Everyone returned to their homes and Te Tuna went to Maui's where he stayed as a guest for quite some time. It was a pleasant stay, but one day Te Tuna said to Maui, "The matter between us must be settled."

"Very well," said Maui. "What do you suggest?"

Te Tuna replied, "We shall do battle. Whoever survives shall be Hina's husband."

"All right," said Maui. "What sort of battle do you have in mind?"

"We'll say incantations enabling us to enter the body of the other," said Te Tuna. "Then I will kill you and take my woman home."

"As you wish," said Maui. "Would you like to go first?"

Te Tuna stood up and began chanting. His song boasted about his place of origin, his awesome moves, and his might. At last he cried, "I will enter you, Oh, Maui, and you will piss from fright!" At that Te Tuna grew smaller and smaller and entered completely into Maui's body. He stayed there for a long while, and then came out again.

Maui was not the least bit troubled. Now it was his turn to chant. He praised Te Tuna's moves as well as praising his own firm stance upon the land. Without Te Tuna knowing, Maui used a sprig of fern to bewitch him. Then he cried, "Monster Eel, you'll piss your loincloth from fright!" Maui grew smaller and smaller until he could barely be seen. Then he disappeared into Te Tuna's body. In no time at all the eel god's sinews broke apart. Soon the great Te Tuna fell lifeless to the ground. Maui sprang forth and cut off his head. His mother said, "Maui, My Son, bury the head near the corner post of the house." He did as she instructed and gave it no further thought.

Then the days went by as usual. Maui and his family went about their tasks as before. One day he noticed a green shoot sprouting forth near the corner post of the house. "What are you looking at?" his mother asked.

"The spot where I buried the Monster's head. Why does it sprout?"

"Because," his mother replied, "a new tree comes to us from the god below the sea. From his head will come a nourishing nut with a sea-green husk. Take care of this coconut tree, for it will provide the family with food." So Maui cared for the tree and when it offered ripe coconuts, he shared the meat with all. He took the shell and from it made two cups. He and Hina drank from them. Then Maui danced and sang boastfully, "Te Tuna, no more than a fleeing cockroach, was easily bewitched. His arts of enchantment were pitiful, and no match for Maui's!"

That is the tale of how Hina found and wedded Maui. It's a good thing she did, for people have enjoyed the coconut ever since.

ADVENTURESOME SPIRIT | LOVE AND ALCHEMICAL UNION | LOVE TRIANGLES | HUMOR | CREATION AND DESTRUCTION |POSTERITY: Like Finn and Saeva, and Rhiannon and Powel, Hina and Maui are an amorous, generative, destined-to-unite duo. From them we get a taste of the proud, uncensored Polynesian view of sexuality. Genitalia and generativity are openly bragged about and poetically praised, not unlike the way sexuality is celebrated in the Sumerian hymns to Inanna and in the Hebrew Song of Songs. With great pathos and humor Hina's lusty search for a lover unfolds, and with equal hilarity, Maui and Te Tuna battle it out to see who will prevail as Hina's mate. Their rivalry parallels the clash between cosmic contraries, day and night, summer and winter, the world above and the world below. This myth celebrates fertility, procreation, fruitfulness, and nourishment, and rejoices in these as earthy aspects of divinity. In the Polynesian storytelling tradition, lewd side-splitting trickster antics do not detract from the sacred, but add to its appeal.

This tale can enhance sexual self-esteem. It can inspire inhibited spouses to become more amorous and bold. It can be especially helpful to women who feel shut down and want to get in touch with their desires. It serves as an antidote to the old puritanical rule: "Women don't initiate sex." There is something admirable and endearing in the way Hina takes initiative and proclaims ardency without shame. There is a lesson for us in Maui's sexual pride as well, for despite his small stature and funny-looking penis, he's full of confidence. This tale can inspire anyone who feels inadequate about their physical allure. It reminds us that being sexy is an attitude, a feeling, a state of being, and does not require a flawless figure.

APPROPRIATE AUDIENCE: *This tale is not appropriate for children or for adults who struggle with sex addictions or have difficulty establishing sexual boundaries. Ancestral tellers upheld taboos regulating when and to whom a tale could be told. Today it's still important to choose stories carefully, based on respect for the story and for the listener.*

Wild Pony and Smoke

A JICARILLA APACHE STORY FROM NORTH AMERICA

(1,661 words)

Let's go back a long time ago, before there were cities, towns, or villages. Let's go back to the time when from one horizon to the next the earth was covered with mountains, plains, valleys, and rivers. At that time eagle roamed the sky and wild ponies meandered the earth. Trout swam the streams, and butterflies flitted from flower to flower, but never did these creatures see a rooftop or a road, a fence or a campfire, for the humans had not yet made their place on this earth.

At that time there was but one man and one woman. Her name was Wild Pony because her spirit was like that of the wild ponies running across the plain. His name was Smoke because his spirit was like that of smoke from a fire. Life was very hard for Wild Pony and Smoke. They found little to eat, and though they loved each other, they felt lonely, for they had no tribe.

One day Smoke and Wild Pony were walking along the plain and there appeared before them a powerful spirit called a hatsin. Whether the hatsin appeared as a butterfly, a snake, a rainbow, or a raven, I cannot say, for the shape of a hatsin is something secret. But according to the story, the hatsin said, "Greetings Wild Pony and Smoke. Listen closely, I'm here to tell you important things. You must learn to live well on this earth because you shall be the first parents of the Jicarilla Apache people. You will always be remembered as the original ancestors of this noble tribe. To show your nobility you must adorn yourselves with silver jewelry." The hatsin pointed to the distant mountains and told them where veins of shining silver could be found deep in the ground. Wild Pony and Smoke looked carefully, so they could remember where to dig for silver. When they turned back toward the hatsin, the spirit had disappeared. Wild Pony said, "Silver jewelry sounds beautiful, but how can we start a tribe without food in our bellies?" So they set out searching for food. Smoke and Wild Pony covered a lot of ground and grew very tired, but found no food to chase away their hunger.

Just when their hearts sank in despair the hatsin appeared once again. "The jewelry we spoke of," said the hatsin, "you can think about that later on. For now you must think about food. I want you to travel south. There you will find a sacred plant called corn. Learn to plant corn and you will never again suffer hunger." Smoke and Wild Pony went south. There they found a tall green plant with long flowing leaves which sang in the breeze. "This must be the corn!" said Wild Pony. They found its golden fruit was easy to harvest and sweet to the taste. Wild Pony and Smoke sang to each plant and made sure they each got plenty of water. After the harvest they saved the best seeds. Later when the time was right they tilled and planted, tended and harvested, all the while making prayers and giving thanks to the life-giving powers of Earth, Water, and Sun.

One day Wild Pony was alone tending the corn. She thought about the hatsin and to her surprise it appeared. "Come," the hatsin said, "I want to speak to you about the horses." Wild Pony walked with the hatsin to a rocky ledge which looked down upon a herd of wild ponies grazing below. "As you know," said the hatsin, "horses run fast and travel great distances. They have strong backs. You must learn how to befriend them. They will take you places and carry your burdens. With the help of the horse, you can travel far and plant corn in all four directions. And you can go north to obtain silver."

This time the hatsin did not disappear, but gestured for Wild Pony to keep walking. "Come," the hatsin said, "I will take you to a bank of red earth and show you how to make bowls out of clay." When they came to the spot the hatsin took a handful of red clay. It pressed the clay into Wild Pony's hand and encouraged her to shape it into a bowl. When Wild Pony discovered the skill of her own hands she was delighted. She sat down and made two bowls, one to hold corn and one to hold water. She wanted to show the hatsin, but it had vanished. Wild Pony so enjoyed making the bowls that she made two more, thinking all the while of the smile they would bring to Smoke's face when she returned home.

With so much excitement, Wild Pony felt tired. She lay down to rest briefly before the long walk home. She stretched out on the earth and found herself feeling very sleepy. "I'll just take a short nap," she thought to herself, and fell into a deep sleep. Soon Wild Pony was dreaming. This was the sort of dream in which every sound is real to the ears, every sight is clear and every smell lingers. Here she took the clay bowls to the edge of a stream. She knelt down and dipped one into the cool water. It began to fill, but before she could raise it out of the water, the clay softened and the bowl fell apart. Wild Pony felt so disheartened she wanted to cry. Just then, the hatsin joined her in the dream. "Don't be sad," said the spirit. "It will be all right. Let me tell you all about pottery. The hatsin told Wild Pony how to dry the bowls in the sun. "You must wrap them in pine bark," it said, "and seal them with pine tar." The hatsin went on to tell her how to make a hot fire and bake the bowls for three days. "Do as I say, Wild Pony," said the hatsin, "and your bowls will stay hard and strong. They will last a long time."

When Wild Pony awoke she remembered all the hatsin had told her. She went home and told Smoke about befriending horses and shaping clay. In the years to come they carried out all the hatsin had taught them. They found silver and hammered it into beautiful hoops to adorn their ankles, necks and wrists. They met and befriended horses, and those horses carried them everywhere they wished to go. Because of what they'd learned about corn, they never went hungry. Their life was happy and full and they had many children. Their children went on to have children, and their life on Earth was good.

Wild Pony had granddaughters, and great-granddaughters. They all loved her dearly and they believed Wild Pony and Smoke would live forever, but Wild Pony knew better. One day she took one of her granddaughters to the bank of red clay and tried to teach her to make bowls. "You must learn this work," Wild Pony said, "to carry on after I am gone." The granddaughter tried and tried, but her little hands remained clumsy. Her bowls were too thick here, and too thin there. They kept slumping over or caving in.

That night Wild Pony felt sad. When she dozed off to sleep the hatsin came to her once more through a dream. This time it said, "Remember when I first took you to the sacred red earth? I pressed the clay into your hand and encouraged you." Wild Pony remembered. "Always remember that day," said the hatsin. "Reenact it as a ceremony to help the young ones. It will bring skill to their hands, just as it did for you." The hatsin went on, "I have shown you the gifts of corn and silver, the gift of horses, and the gift of clay. Today I will give you a fifth and final gift. When I have told you, your knowledge will be complete." At this the hatsin went on to tell Wild Pony about the peace pipe and how to make it. The hatsin explained how there would be difficult times and times of war. The sacred pipe would be used to restore wisdom and peace. "This is the last time I shall guide you," said the hatsin. "Now you know everything the Jicarilla Apaches will need to live well." Wild Pony thanked the spirit being for the five gifts.

The next morning when she woke up, Wild Pony knew just what to do. She took her granddaughters to the bank of red earth. There, one at a time, she took each girl's hand in hers, and pressed into the palm a ball of red clay. To each girl she said, "Take heart, the skill of shaping bowls will come through you. It will be your gift to our people." Thus began the ceremony that would bless all Jicarilla Apache grand-daughters ever since. Then Wild Pony told the girls to sit down as she had done with the hatsin so many years before. However, they did not begin by making bowls for water and corn. They made the sacred peace pipe instead.

They baked the pipe in a hot fire for three days. When it was finished baking, they took it out to cool in the morning air. Wild Pony filled the pipe with herbs and drew four puffs. Then she passed it on to the granddaughters who each in turn drew four puffs. One of the granddaughters said, "Grandmother, would it be fitting for us to give our new clay pipe to Grandfather Smoke?"

"Yes," said Wild Pony, and thus began the tradition. Ever after, girls of a certain age were taken to the sacred place. Their hands were blessed and rubbed with clay. They always made peace pipes and out of respect gave them to the grandfathers. And with these special pipes, the grandfathers made prayers of peace.

DEPRIVATION | SCARCITY | FIGHTING POVERTY AND HUNGER | EMOTIONAL RESILIENCE | AGRICULTURE | POTTERY | THE ORIGINS OF HORSEMANSHIP | ANIMALS AS HELPERS AND TEACHERS | GUIDANCE FROM SPIRIT | SPIRIT AS THE SOURCE OF KNOWLEDGE | DREAM AND RITUAL | DREAM AS GUIDE | ELDER WISDOM | HELP FROM WISE ELDERS | YOUTH-ELDER ALLIANCES | MENTORSHIP | FAMILIAL COOPERATION | LOVING KINDNESS | SUSTAINABILITY | FAMILIAL COOPERATION | POSTERITY | EARTH AS SACRED | HONORING THE EARTH | THE MORE-THAN-HUMAN WORLD | COURAGE, INTEGRITY, RESILIENCE | COOPERATION AND DEVOTION | CREATIVE COURAGE | PASSION FOR LEARNING | PASSING ON THE TORCH: This wonderful origin tale resonates at so many levels, it is truly a touchstone tale for people of all ages and walks of life. For the Jicarilla Apache, it orients them to their ancestral beginnings, to the source of their sacred arts, and their place in the scheme of life. Their cultural wealth, from agriculture to the treasured peace pipe, came to them through Wild Pony and Smoke, from the hatsin, a representative of the spirit realm. The tale teaches the connection between the spirit world and the human family. It also teaches sustainability by showing that familial and intergenerational cooperation enables sacred arts to flourish down through the generations.

Like the Penobscot tale, "Corn Mother," this tale illustrates universal principals common to cultures the world over: such as spirit as the source of knowledge, the importance of dream and ritual, the role of the elders, the link between youths and elders, initiation for young women, the sacredness of the Earth, respect for animals, the value of persistence, and the necessity of passing on traditions and life skills. Today, stories like this one give meaning, credence, and depth to the life-sustaining values and practices of indigenous people.

WOMEN'S INITIATION | SACRED FEMININE | WOMEN'S ESTEEM AND EMPOWERMENT | WOMEN AND EDUCATION: Like many indigenous traditions, the Jicarilla holds an esteemed place for women. I have told this tale in gatherings for women of all ages, and it invariably evokes great emotion. It seems to strike that place where tears of joy flow simultaneously with tears of sorrow, and the weeper feels cleansed and renewed. In our culture today older women yearn for the opportunity to give something of themselves, and younger women long to receive. This tale evokes dialogues of grief for the kinds of communion that are missing in our society. It often acts as a catalyst, calling women to create new ways to share and connect. After I told it at a women's spiritual center, the participants were inspired to start a weekly group for women of all ages to gather and share their dreams.

How the Human Race Came to Be

A MODOC TALE FROM NORTH AMERICA | (772 words)

Long ago, before human beings made their home on this earth, Sky Spirit Chief and his family lived above the clouds. One day the sky spirit took his stick and began poking a hole through the clouds. As he poked, snow fell to the earth below. The hole got bigger and bigger, and so did the heap of snow beneath it. At last the hole was big enough to step through and the heap of snow had become a high mountain peak jutting up into the clouds. This peak would later come to be called Mount Shasta.

Sky Spirit Chief brought his family to live atop Mount Shasta in its crater. They always kept a fire going, so smoke and sparks often flew from the mountain top.

One day the wind blew wildly. Sky Spirit Chief feared it would blow their fire out, so he sent his young daughter out to plead with the wind. "Go up to the rim of the crater and ask the wind to blow more gently," he instructed, "but be sure to keep your head well below the rim."

The girl climbed up to a spot below the rim and cried, "Oh great wind spirit, please blow more gently," but the sound of her voice was drowned out by the howling of the wind. She called out many times, but the wind did not hear. She had never looked out to see the land below. She had always been curious, and she had once heard her father say that looking west, one could view the sea. Surely there would be no harm in taking one glimpse. Just as the top of her head rose to the height of the rim, a huge gust of wind came along. It snatched hold of her hair and pulled her right out of the crater. She tumbled down the snowy mountainside head over heels with her long red hair trailing behind her.

She tumbled and tumbled until she landed in the foothills against a great tree. She would have died there if Old Man Grizzly had not happened by. He picked her up and carried her home. Old Woman Grizzly had the knowledge of healing and she nursed the girl back to health. Old Woman Grizzly loved the girl's smooth skin and long fiery hair. She held the girl close and rocked and stroked her just like a mother. The girl grew well and strong, and stayed on with the grizzly family as one of their own.

When the Sky Spirit Girl reached a marrying age, it was only natural that she should take her favorite grizzly brother as her husband. They had many fine children. The grizzly bears loved the strange offspring which were half grizzly and half sky spirit. They built a special lodge for Sky Spirit Woman and her children. It would later be called Little Shasta.

Old Woman Grizzly had lived a long life and was coming to the end of her days. She had made peace with all the deeds of her life, except one. She felt badly that she had never gone to Sky Spirit Chief and told him his daughter was alive and living among the grizzlies. She thought to set things right before she died. She sent a messenger to the top of Mt. Shasta to tell the Sky Spirit Chief the whole story. Sky Spirit Chief flew into a rage. He stormed down the mountain and into the grizzly lodge. "I curse you for stealing my daughter! You grizzlies will never again have the gift of speech and you will never again walk upright!" From that moment on, the grizzlies walked on all fours. They grunted and growled, but they could not speak.

Then Sky Spirit Chief went to Little Shasta to claim his daughter. He grabbed her by the hair and pulled her out the door. "Father," she cried, "don't you want to meet your grandchildren?"

"I do not claim them!" was all he would say. He dragged his daughter up to the crater and told the rest of the family they were returning to the sky. After they left, the fire turned to ash and went cold. The mountain never again billowed smoke or threw sparks. The sky spirit poked his stick from time to time causing the snow to fall, but he never again returned to Earth. As for his daughter, she sometimes weeps for her children, and when she does the sky grows dark and the rain falls. As for her many children, they would later come to be called human beings. They wandered in all directions forming different tribes. To this day human beings sometimes feel lonesome for their original home. The Modoc people still remember their mother, the Sky Spirit Woman. They remember their father too, and to this day no Modoc has ever killed a grizzly bear.

HONORING THE EARTH | REVERENCE FOR NATURE | THE MORE-THAN-HUMAN WORLD | ANIMALS AS HELPERS AND TEACHERS | HEALING TOUCH | LOVING KINDNESS | HONORING TRUE ESSENCE | POSTERITY | SACRED FEMININE | SACRED MASCULINE: Mount Shasta, like the other volcanic peaks of the Cascade Range, dominates the skyline for hundreds of miles. The sight of it takes one's breath away and it's no surprise that the early inhabitants of Northern California and Southern Oregon saw this dazzling mountain as a place where sky spirits once resided. Stories like this one spring from a time when people lived in harmony with the natural world and felt great awe toward the cosmos. I've told this tale at Earth Day symposia to open discussions on indigenous perspectives which hold sacred the world around us. It makes people think twice about the role of us humans in the more-than-human-world. The grizzlies not only rescue and heal our heroine, they join her bloodline, to produce humankind, making living grizzlies our blood relatives, and early grizzlies our first earthly ancestors. This strikingly poetic schema of the origin of humankind evokes poignant discussion on human nature. When I told it to a graduate psychology class the students found the half-grizzly, half-spirit metaphor to be wonderfully apt in characterizing human nature. One student later wrote, "Born of this dichotomy, we humans are unable to escape our inner conflicts and our sense of exile from our original home. If we truly understood the Modoc perspective we might accept ourselves as half beast, half spirit. In accepting our essential nature, might we find a more harmonious way to live respectfully with the other peoples, and other species on this planet?"

LOSE-LOSE SITUATIONS | REVENGE AND RETRIBUTION: In this tale, the angry spirit chief feels betrayed, and curses the grizzlies to an eternity on all fours without the gift of speech. Ever after the humans are exiled from their original home. A woman named Beth was particularly struck by the finality of the curse, and its long-standing results. "It makes you stop and think," she said. "I've been in the middle of a family battle for a while now, and my temper runs hot. More than once I've been close to writing off my son's wife, but that would be cutting off my nose to spite my face, because I would lose contact with my grandkids. This story makes me think twice. There has to be a better way."

The Mouse Girls Outsmart Coyote

ADAPTED FROM ARAPAHO & KORYAK TALES
OF NORTH AMERICA

(967 words)

COYOTE, BACKGROUND AND SOURCES: *In her book* COYOTE STORIES, *Okanogan storyteller Mourning Dove, describes the "Animal People," the original beings who preceded us humans on this earth. The Animal People are full of wisdom and conscious intent. Among them, Eagle, Bear, Fox, Salmon, Beaver, and others are highly esteemed teachers from whom we humans have much to learn. Dove explains how Coyote the trickster, is the most important because he did the most "to make the world a good place in which to live." Dove describes Coyote as a shiftless trouble-maker when left to his own devices. Yet under the direction of "Spirit Chief," the Native American supreme being, Coyote's trickiness evolves into a kind of focused inventiveness, a dynamic blend of foresight and spontaneity which he uses to serve others. Coyote stops picking needless quarrels and redirects his gall toward truly monstrous foes. His petty egotism transforms into expansive altruism. Coyote stories appear deceptively simple, but their manner of teaching is exquisite and profound. From Coyote's low-down maneuvers we learn what the human shadow is made of. We get a clear view of our own lesser traits. His misadventures remind us that true respect is won through decency and right action, not bragging and bullying, and that true inner satisfaction comes from doing good. Through Coyote we gain insight into how each day is a chance to turn over a new leaf and culti-vate our nobler, more creative traits.*

Old Man Coyote was a hunter. Just before deer season the other hunters went searching for straight sticks to make arrows. Coyote slept late and went out at the last minute. He grabbed whatever sticks were close at hand. They bent this way and that. Crooked sticks make crooked arrows, and everyone knows crooked arrows don't shoot straight. Coyote knew it too, but he was careless.

His wife, Old Woman Coyote, was a Mole and a skilled a trapper. She carefully wove her traps and placed them in the bush. Then she waited. Later when she checked them they were full of small game for supper.

On the first day of the hunt, Coyote got up late. The other hunters had already gone into the mountains with their straight arrows and strong bows. Old Woman Coyote had already gone out to set her traps. Coyote took his old bow and crooked arrows and stomped off toward the hills. Wandering along, he caught sight of a big buck, not far off. He aimed his arrow and shot. The arrow veered to the left and hit a tree. Each time he took aim his arrows veered left or right, up or down. He kept missing the mark. At the end of the day he went home empty-handed.

The other hunters all brought home game. Everyone was happy to have large pieces of fresh meat to feed their families. Everyone was pleased to have hides for new clothes. Old Woman Coyote had caught a ptarmigan that day and she was cooking a savory stew. When she saw Coyote she asked, "How was the hunt?"

"I had bad luck," answered Coyote. "Someone must have sat on my arrows and bent them."

Old Woman Coyote was no fool. "No one sat on your arrows," she said. "They were crooked when you made them. You look hungry. Have some stew."

Coyote was angry. "I don't want any stew. It smells bad! Besides, I'm going on a long hunt! I'm leaving right now and might not be back for a long time! I'm serious, so don't try to stop me!"

"Have it your way," said Old Woman Coyote.

Coyote stomped out with his crooked arrows and bow. He walked until dark and then it began to rain. Leaving in such haste, he had forgotten to pack food and a blanket. He soon got soaking wet and shivering cold. Finally he lay down beneath a large tree and put some leaves over himself for warmth. The leaves were damp and full of bugs. Coyote did not sleep well.

In the morning he found a sunny spot to dry off and fell asleep. When he woke it was almost noon. He got up and walked along a nearby stream. After a while he heard some voices. He had come to the spot where the women from the next village came to bathe. Coyote knew the place was supposed to be private, but instead of turning back, he went closer. He hid behind a tree and peeked out to see what he could see.

The Mouse Girls were having a bath. After washing their hair they got out to dry off on a sunny bank. Coyote liked looking. After a while he wanted their attention and decided to trick them. He went over to the path and started crying as if in pain, "Oh help me! My eyes! My eyes! I cannot see! Where am I? Where am I?"

The girls wrapped up in their deerskins and ran over to help. "Uncle Coyote," they exclaimed, "you don't belong here. This is the women's bath."

Coyote rolled on the ground and writhed. He looked like he was really suffering. "There's something in my eye. Come help me. I might go blind."

The Mouse Girls inched toward him. "Hold still," they said. "How can we help you if you squirm all over?" Coyote held still and opened his eyes wide. The girls said, "There is nothing in your eyes, Uncle, and they do not look the least bit red or sore."

Coyote pretended to be blind. He groped around and touched their breasts. "Stop it, Uncle!" cried the eldest.

"Help me lie down and rest," said Coyote. The Mouse girls took his arms and helped him sit down. "I'm all full of sand," he said, "Won't you help me brush off?" The girls knelt down to brush his back and shoulders. At first Coyote acted helpless, then he grabbed their private parts.

"You're full of tricks!" the girls shouted. They jumped up and ran away.

Coyote grabbed for the youngest, so she threw sand in his eyes. "Now you've really hurt me!" he cried. Old Man tried to stand up, but he stumbled into the stickers instead.

The girls ran away, shouting, "Coyote's at the women's bath!" The more he thrashed about, the more stickers and burrs got knotted in his hair.

At last he lay still. He cried and the tears washed the sand out of his eyes. Then he used his flint knife to cut the burrs and stickers one by one out of his hair. When he was finished he had many ugly bald spots. He felt sulky and headed for home.

When she saw him, Old Woman Coyote asked, "What happened to your hair?" Old Man felt ashamed and tried to fool her, "Oh, my wife, I'm so glad to see you! I had to give up the hunt and come home! In the next village people told me you had died! I wept until my eyes were sore. Then I cut my hair in grief!"

Old Woman placed another log on the fire. "Someone gave you false news, My Husband." Coyote said no more. He took his knife and went out to look for straight sticks. He had to hurry. Hunting season was well underway.

SEXUAL ABUSE PREVENTION | DENIAL AND DECEPTION | CUNNING AND CON-NING | SCAMMING | HEALTHY SKEPTICISM: Today many parents, teachers, therapists and youth workers are working to prevent child sexual abuse. This tale sheds light on the dynamics of the problem with a focus on offender tricks, and child self-protection. It can be helpful in prevention education for children at risk. It can also be helpful to individuals and families whose lives have been shaken by sexual abuse. This includes children and their loved ones, as well as those who have committed offenses and truly want to stop. This tale shows Coyote in one of his more childish, self-centered, and low-down states. Luckily the Mouse Girls have healthy personal boundaries, self protective instincts, and the ability to teach Uncle Coyote a lesson. For children and those who would protect them, this tale models discernment, healthy skepticism, and the all-important abuse prevention maneuver, "go tell." The episode with the Mouse Girls is not enough to cure Coyote of lying, but the tone of his wife's final comment let's us know she is not fooled. It is crucial for non-offending spouses and other family members to practice healthy skepticism and not buy into offenders' deception and rationalization, no matter how sweetly contrived or touching these might be.

Because this tale illustrates several aspects of the "offender-cycle," it can be helpful to remorseful offenders seeking honest self-reflection. Howard was in a court ordered treatment program after having molested his granddaughter. He noted Coyote's attempts to overcome shame by manipulating, bullying, blaming, rejecting, and telling lies. He wrote in his therapy journal about his own tendency to do the same. "I've always felt cheated and told myself it was okay to cut corners, push people around, and bend the rules. When that didn't work I'd play the victim. Now I'm starting to realize what Coyote realizes, that to genuinely feel good, you have to do good. I'm fifty-seven, but Uncle Coyote is an old fart, too. It's never too late to learn."

Coyote and Mole

AN OKANOGAN TALE FROM NORTH AMERICA | (856 words)

(too frightening for small children)
(for background on Coyote see p. 210)

Old Man Coyote was shiftless and tricky, so no one wanted him around. Because of this he, his wife Mole, and their children lived far from the village. One winter they had little to eat. Coyote loafed around practicing war songs while Mole did all the work. She dug roots, gathered herbs and moss and collected dried rose hips so her children could survive. Coyote looked down on chores like gathering wood and hauling water, so Mole did it all.

One day Mole chopped away at a stump for firewood. While she was chopping a little fawn jumped right out of the stump. Mole knew it was a gift from the Deer People. They felt sad for Mole and wanted her to have meat for her children. She dropped her ax and grabbed the little deer. She called to her eldest son, "Tell your father to hurry with his knife! We shall have venison for supper!"

The boy ran as fast as he could and told his father what Mole had said. Coyote replied, "I am a hunter. I don't need your mother telling me what to do." Instead of hurrying to Mole with a knife, Coyote went out to find a piece of dogwood to make a bow. Then he went to a service berry bush and cut two branches for arrows. He feathered the arrows with feathers from his war bonnet. Since he had no sinew for a bowstring, he used his moccasin string instead. He fussed around getting weapons together as if going on a real hunt.

All the while Mole, who was rather small, struggled to hold the fawn. It kicked and fought. Mole cried out, "Husband, quick, get your knife." But Coyote wanted it to look like he had gone out and hunted the deer himself. He cleared away the snow so he could kneel and shoot. "Let go so I can shoot it," he cried. Exhausted, Mole let go. Coyote shot the first arrow and missed. Coyote aimed again and missed and the fawn disappeared into the woods.

Mole was disgusted. Now she would have to see what she could scrape together for supper. She looked around the lodge and discovered that while Coyote had been making his weapons he had eaten all the rose-hips and roots. There was nothing left. When Coyote came back Mole scolded him for having a full belly and making his family go hungry. Coyote didn't want to hear it. He was angry. He pulled out his flint knife and lunged at her. Mole ran out of the lodge and Coyote ran after. "I'll kill you!" he cried. Mole changed herself into a smaller Mole and Coyote stabbed again. She ran into a hole in the ground and Coyote knelt over the hole stabbing the earth over and over. Mole opened the little pouch she carried. She took a dab of red face paint and put it on the earth. When Coyote stabbed his knife came back red. It looked like blood and Coyote was satisfied he'd killed her off with the last blow.

He thought life would be better without Mole nagging him. But it was worse. He found out how hard it was to take care of the children. They could not live as before, so Coyote told his four eldest children to go find their Uncle Kingfisher. He was a good fisherman and had plenty to eat. Coyote took his youngest son, his favorite, and set out traveling. They went many days without food.

One day they came upon a large meadow. There they saw a woman dressed in red buckskin. She was digging bitter-root. The sight made Coyote miss his wife. He wished Mole were alive to dig roots and to cook for him. He took the little one down from his shoulders and told him to wait. Then he went over to the woman. In a friendly voice he said, "Greetings, Good Woman, tell me what's new?" The woman paid him no mind. She kept on digging. Then she brushed the dirt off the roots and placed them in her basket.

Coyote was forward with women. He walked closer. "I'm a traveler from far away. Talk to me, Woman, give me a smile."

The woman stopped her work and looked at Coyote. "I'll tell you a story," she said. "It is about Coyote, who tried to kill his wife and deserted his children." Suddenly Coyote recognized her. She had followed him to watch over her child. He grabbed for his knife and tried to stab her, but she changed herself into a smaller Mole and hid underground. Coyote went back to where his son was waiting. "Father, who was that woman?" he asked.

"No one," said Coyote. He lifted his son to his shoulder and started walking.

"Where are we going, Father," asked the little one.

"Far away," grumbled Coyote. "People around here don't respect me." Coyote wanted to find a place where his low-down ways were not known.

DOMESTIC VIOLENCE | THE FUTILITY OF VIOLENCE | FAMILIAL HOMICIDE | ONGOING QUARRELS | LOSE-LOSE SITUATIONS | SCAMMING: Like the previous tale, this Okanogan story highlights parts of human behavior we'd rather not see. The problem dynamics portrayed in "Coyote and Mole" reflect many aspects of domestic violence today. They include the danger of isolation, the problem of an overly compliant female paired with an overly aggressive male, and the shame and contempt that build when one spouse does all the menial work. Coyote tries twice to kill his wife. The theme of homicide is distressing, but pertinent. Today when a married woman is murdered, her husband becomes an automatic suspect. This is because such a large percentage of married female homicide victims were murdered by their husbands. The tale reminds us of the troubling fact that many women are not safe in their own homes. It also shows how difficult it is to nurture children in an abusive environment.

DENIAL AND DECEPTION | WORTHY USE OF DECEPTION: "Coyote and Mole" can be useful to anyone whose life is torn by domestic violence. This tale is especially good medicine for genuinely contrite batterers who want to gain insight and change old patterns of behavior. It's also helpful for women who've been battered, whether they are in denial, or simply trying to patch together their lives and move on.

Ellen suffered ongoing beatings from her husband who drank too much. He owned guns and threatened to kill her if she tried to leave. For years she refused to press charges. "Down deep he was a good man, and I believed things would get better if I could show him enough love." This level of denial is classic among battered wives. Ellen was covered with bruises when she went in for her annual pap smear. She remembered it had been the same the year before. She confided her troubles to the nurse practitioner, and the nurse shared this tale. Later Ellen said, "I went home and thought about Mole. I was living the same way. I realized things were not getting better, and I was responsible for what my sons were learning about life." Describing how she got out, Ellen said, "When Coyote tries to kill Mole, she saves herself by tricking him with red face paint. That's how I got out, too, by tricking him. The boys and I saved money on the sly. I said I was taking them to help me drop off some old clothes at Goodwill. Instead we took a few things, and rented an apartment. It was scary, but it was the best move I ever made."

Coyote's Name

AN OKANAGON TALE FROM NORTH AMERICA | (1,025 words)

(for background on Coyote see p. 210)

Spirit Chief called a meeting of all the Animal People. They came from far and wide and gathered together in one lodge. Spirit Chief told them a change was coming. A new kind of people would be joining them on the earth. Spirit Chief said, "These people will be called human beings. They will know very little and you will have to teach them. To help them learn better, you will have to have names. Many of you have names now, but some of you don't. Tomorrow you will receive your true names— names that will be kept by you and your descendants from now on. Come to my lodge at first light tomorrow. Whoever arrives first may choose any name he or she wants. The next person may choose any other name, and so on. Along with the name, you will each be given your own special task."

The Animal People grew excited. They hoped for proud names, and important tasks. They planned to get up before dawn and head straight for Spirit Chief's lodge. Old Man Coyote strode about boasting. He said he would be first. He didn't care for the name Coyote, which means "Imitator." People said the name suited him because he claimed he could do anything anyone else could do. He pretended to know all about everything. When he learned something new he always said, "I knew that. I don't need to be told." He bragged to the others, "After tomorrow I shall be Grizzly Bear, Chief of the Mountain. Or no, perhaps I will be Eagle, Chief of the Sky. Then again, maybe I'll be Salmon, Chief of the Waters."

Fox listened to Coyote. "Don't be so sure, Brother," he said. "You may have to keep your name. Nobody else wants it."

"I'm sick of the name," said Coyote. "Let some feeble person take it. I am a great warrior. You will look up to me when I am Grizzly Bear!"

"Big talk, as always," said Fox. "You better go home and get some rest, or you'll oversleep and wind up with no name at all."

Coyote stormed off. He vowed not to sleep, that way he could be first. When he got home his sons cried out, "Father, we are hungry." Coyote had brought them nothing to eat.

Coyote's wife, Mole sat near the door. After naming day Spirit Chief would give her the title, Mound Digger. She asked, "Can you bring us some supper? There are no roots left for me to dig."

Coyote replied, "I have important things on my mind. After tomorrow I will be a great chief, worthy of the name Grizzly Bear. I will tear my enemies to bits. I will be respected by all, and I will find myself a better wife."

Mole said nothing. She gathered together some old bones and boiled them over the fire. Coyote told her to bring in plenty of firewood so he could stay up all night. She did so, and then she and the children went off to bed. Coyote sat watching the fire. The night passed slowly. He grew sleepy and found it impossible to keep his eyes open. He picked up two sticks and propped them between his heavy lids. Soon he lay there snoring with his eyes wide open.

When he awoke, the sun was high in the sky. Mole called to him, "Coyote, wake up." She had just returned from Spirit Chief's lodge, with her new name, Mole, the Mound Digger. She had not awakened her husband earlier. She feared he might leave her if he received a powerful name. Coyote jumped up and rushed to Spirit Chief's lodge. There were no other Animal People in sight. Coyote laughed and wiped the sleep from his eyes. He was sure he was the first. He burst through the door and proclaimed, "Here I am, Grizzly Bear, ready to begin my great task."

Spirit Chief said, "The name Grizzly Bear was chosen at dawn."

"Very well, then," said Coyote, a little more softly, "Then I shall be Eagle."

"Eagle flew away at sunrise," answered Spirit Chief.

"Well," said Coyote, "then I will have to take the name Salmon."

"Salmon has already received his name," replied Spirit Chief. "No one tried to steal your name, Coyote. It is the only name left."

Coyote's legs weakened beneath him and he sank to the floor of Spirit Chief's lodge. Spirit Chief was touched. "Coyote, the name *Imitator* suits you. You must accept it. That is who you are. I made you sleep late because I wanted to see you last. I have special work for you. Terrible monsters prowl the earth, eating everyone in sight. This will be hard on the new people. They will not flourish as I wish unless these monsters are stopped. It will take a tricky rascal to do the job. That's why I've saved the task especially for you. You will be honored and praised for this. But remember, when you do foolish things, you will be laughed at and despised. That is the way it is. To help you succeed, I give you special powers. You will be able to change yourself into any form you wish. I will give Fox special powers to restore you if you are killed. All he will need to bring you back is a single hair from your hide. Now go forth, Coyote. Do not sulk. Get started on your work."

Coyote felt better. After that morning, his eyes took on a new look. Some say this came from being propped open all night. Others say

Spirit Chief changed him. The new people who came along had eyes a bit like his. To this very day, there is still a little of Coyote in the human beings. They look up to him for making good things happen. But when he is foolish they laugh. That is the way it is. Old Man doesn't sulk so much. Now he understands.

ENVY AND SELF IMAGE | JEALOUSY, ENVY, COMPETITION | UNSTABLE IDENTITY | HONORING TRUE ESSENCE | GUIDANCE FROM SPIRIT | HUMILITY | HUMOR | TAKING OURSELVES LESS SERIOUSLY | SACRED MASCULINE | THE ALCHEMY OF SELFHOOD: We use another mythic name, that of Narcissus, to discuss the complications that arise around questions of self and self image. As Narcissus was fixated on his reflection in still water, Coyote fixates on getting an image-enhancing name. In either case, there is a sense of lack at the core, and a misguided attempt to fill it. When the mask becomes more important than the essence, the narcissist becomes estranged, not only from the authentic self, but also from reality. Spirit Chief, the ultimate healer, helps Coyote find and embrace his true self. Through understanding his own unique nature and purpose, Coyote gains self-acceptance, genuine self-worth, humility, and interest in others.

Most people can identify with this tale, for it is part of the human experience to go astray from the authentic self. Most of us have tried out roles that do not suit us because it seemed they would bring status, power, affection, or security. This heartening tale gives us a nudge toward Spirit Chief's lodge, that place of reckoning where we are reminded that in human life, the most fulfilling possibility is to know and to be oneself. From that authentic place we can genuinely respond to others and engage in the adventure of life.

Oftentimes the wounded make the best teachers and healers, because they know what pain is about, and once they are truly healed, they have the gift of compassion for others. Coyote is the quintessential wounded healer. Once his narcissistic wound has been soothed, he sets out to teach us human beings about our role on the earth.

Coyote Creates Human Beings

A NEZ PERCE TALE FROM NORTH AMERICA | (516 words)

(for background on Coyote see p. 210)

*L*ong ago, before there were human beings on this earth, a terrible monster came down from the north. This enormous being traveled around the mountains and plains devouring all the Animal People in its path. It ate many of Coyote's small friends, Chipmunk, Mouse, and Raccoon. As it grew, it ate his large friends too, Deer, Elk, and Mountain Lion. It grew harder and harder for Coyote to find friends. He grew very angry, so angry he decided to go after the monster.

He crossed the river and climbed the tallest mountain peak. There he tied himself to a solid rock. When the monster came to the river for a drink Coyote cried out, "Hey Monster, why don't you try to eat me?"

The monster came crashing across the river and charged over to the mountain. His prickly lips parted, and his menacing tongue shot out. When he tried to suck Coyote into his mouth, Coyote's rope held firm. This confused the monster. Never before had he failed to slay a victim on the first bite. The monster took pause and tried again from another angle, and then another, but all his efforts failed. "Coyote has powerful medicine," thought the monster to himself. "Since I cannot slay him, I would be well off to become his ally." Then the monster asked, "Coyote, how would you like to stay at my camp for a while?"

Coyote agreed. They were sitting around one day and Coyote said, "You have a lot of people in your belly."

"Too many to count," said the monster.

"It must be an impressive lot," said Coyote, "I would very much like to see."

"Very well," said the monster, "you may go inside my belly." So Coyote went down the gullet and into the monster's belly. There he saw all sorts of friends. He was glad to see they were all right. He used his special fire starter to build a large fire in the monster's belly. He then took his flint knife and cut the monster's heart. The monster fell down dead. Then Coyote cut his belly open. One by one the Animal People began climbing out. Coyote made sure they all got out safely. Then he joined them.

Coyote remarked what a great event this was. He said he was going to commemorate the moment by creating a new kind of people, the human beings. With his flint knife, he chopped the monster into bits. He turned to each of the four directions, one by one, casting bits of monster flesh to each. Some landed to the north, some to the south, some to the east, and some to the west. Where the bits landed, tribes sprang up. This was how all the tribes came to be. Then it occurred to Coyote, there was nothing left for the spot on which they stood. A thought came to him. He washed the blood from his hands, and let the drops fall to the earth. Coyote said, "Here I make the Nez Perce. They will be few in number, but they will be fine and strong." This is the tale of how Coyote created human beings. Out of something bad, he made something good.

GREED AND ACQUISITIVENESS | CRAVINGS AND TROUBLESOME DESIRES | EMOTIONAL RESILIENCE | INNOVATION | LOSS, COURAGE, AND TRANSFORMATION | TRICKS AND TRICKING | WORTHY USE OF DECEPTION: I first encountered this beautiful Nez Perce tale twenty years ago in Barry Lopez's collection of Coyote tales. Its seemingly simple metaphors have as many lives as Coyote himself. A devouring monster goes around killing the Animal People. If you let your imagination roam free, this monster might remind you of some of the monstrous problems of our time such as epidemic diseases, environmental hazards, and corporate greed. The monster might also symbolize addictions that tear up families and eat up lives. Coyote gets mad and sets out to stop the monster. Before he can stop it, he has to get close and observe the nature of the beast. He befriends the monster and moves into its camp, then he tricks it in order to save lives. Coyote is outlandish and not afraid to be laughed at for trying new things. He reminds us of the importance of courageous innovation in an ever-changing world. The story encourages us not to sit helplessly while powerful forces destroy what is dear. He also reminds us that the spirit of genius pops up at surprising times and in unexpected places.

CREATIVE COURAGE | CHANGE AS AN OPPORTUNITY TO CREATE ANEW | HARDSHIP AS AN OPPORTUNITY | SELF DETERMINATION | SELF RELIANCE | CREATION AND DESTRUCTION | TRICKS AND TRICKING | SACRED MASCULINE | THE JOY OF LIFE-AFFIRMING WORK: Coyote's finest creation comes as an afterthought to slaying the monster. From the flesh of the vile thing, he creates human beings. He makes something essentially good out of something essentially foul. This is invention and creativity at its best. This story can be encouraging to anyone working to make a hardship into an opportunity. It works well in AIDS prevention programs to inspire folks to develop innovative ways to fight prejudice, stop the spread of disease, and create a loving community. It can also be used in substance abuse programs. It supports families in the difficult process of learning the "nature of the beast" we call addiction. It inspires grass-roots groups to stand up and fight for what's right, even when challenging a powerful foe. It can also be used to celebrate people's efforts at the end of a challenging project. It is truly a celebration of the creative spirit.

Coyote and the Frog People

A KALAPUYA TALE FROM NORTH AMERICA | (485 words)

(for background on Coyote see p. 210)

(for background on Coyote see p. 210)

One day Old Man Coyote was out loping through the yellow grass. He came upon the half decayed carcass of a dead deer. The skin had grown dry and leathery. One of the deer's rib bones poked out and it looked like a big dentalia shell. Coyote snapped it off like a dry stick and carried it along. He was growing thirsty, so he decided to pay a visit to the Frog People. The Frog People had water, more than their share of water. They knew how to make dams, and they had dammed up the river and made themselves a lake. They acted like they owned the water. Anyone who wanted to drink or wash had to go to the Frog People.

"Hey there, Frog People. I have here a fine dentalia shell. It's worth quite a bit. I would like to trade it for a drink, a very big drink."

"Give me that shell," said the Frog Chief looking it over. The Frog Chief did not realize it was just the rib of a dead deer. "All right, you can drink for as long as you like."

"Don't worry if I take a long time," said Coyote, walking toward the dam. "I'm very thirsty, and I like to drink slowly."

"Whatever," said the Frog People, snickering among themselves. Bear was capable of taking a big drink. Caribou could lap up great quantities of water, equal to the worth of a dentalia shell. But with a scrawny little fellow like Coyote, the Frog People were really making out.

Coyote went behind the dam where the water was kept in a deep lake. Out of sight from the Frog People, Coyote put his head down and lapped up a nice long drink. The Frog People joked among themselves. Time passed, more than enough time for Coyote to have taken a long, slow drink. The Frog People went to check. The only sign of Coyote was a ring of ripples and few bubbles, at the edge of the dam. He was under water. When he came up for air, Frog Chief called out, "Hey Coyote, you're taking a swim! That will cost you another shell."

"I'm not swimming," said Coyote, "I'm drinking the nice cool water from down deep. Just let me take one more swallow," he said, disappearing again. What the Frog People did not know was that deep under the water, Old Man Coyote was digging out the rocks at the base of the dam. All of a sudden the water started flowing, then gushing down into the valley. The whole dam caved in. The Frog People were furious. "Coyote, you have ruined our dam and stolen our water!"

Coyote cried, "It is not right for you Frogs to have all the water, just because you're good at making dams! Water is meant to be shared." After that the river flowed freely. Now anyone can go to the river to drink, to wash, or just to swim around.

GREED AND ACQUISITIVENESS | MISUSE OF POWER | SCAMMING | UNHEALTHY ENTITLEMENT | SUSTAINABILITY | WORTHY USE OF DECEPTION | RESPONSIBLE USE OF TECHNOLOGY | ANIMALS AS HELPERS AND TEACHERS: It seems a part of human nature to monopolize resources for one's own gain. In this tale the Frog People exploit their easy access to water. Like a big corporation with no conscience, they monopolize the resource to make big profits, and who suffers, but the land and the rest of the Animal People. As in the previous tale, when fighting a formidable foe, Coyote gets on the inside, and uses trickery and ingenuity to set things right. This tale encourages such "little guys" as employees, students, grass roots environmentalists, and farm laborers, to use their wiles and ingenuity in challenging corporate greed. Peaceful organizers have used this tale to encourage and inspire activists to insist on fair labor, fair trade, and fair use of resources.

Corn Mother

A PENOBSCOT TALE FROM NORTH AMERICA | (748 words)

(too spiritually sophisticated for young children)

Long ago, before there were human beings on this earth, the All-maker walked the earth alone. One morning he walked along the edge of the sea. Something was happening at the place where the water lapped upon the sand. There mounds of sea foam gathered. The wind nudged the mounds of foam and the waves gently lulled them back and forth. Sunshine poured down, warming the sea foam. Moisture, warmth, and motion, these are the stuff of life. And what should be born of the foam, but a young man? He stepped forward, fully formed and said to the All-Maker, "Uncle, I am here to help you." The young man moved in with the All-maker and together they created all manner of things.

Then one day there was a dew drop resting on a leaf. The breeze blew past, rocking the leaf, and the sun shone down brightly, warming the dew drop. And what should be born of that warmth, moisture, and motion, but a young woman? She said, "I am love. I am the strength-giver and nourisher, I am the provider."

The All-maker rejoiced and gave thanks to the Great Mystery. The young man and woman married and soon the woman was heavy with child. She became First Mother of the first people. The All-maker taught her children how to hunt so they could survive. They prospered for a long time, but as their numbers grew, they had to kill more and more game. There came a time when the game grew scarce. Hunters returned home empty-handed. Children went hungry. They howled, "Grandmother, feed us!" And she said, "Be patient little ones. I will find a way." First Mother wept and wept to see her children suffering so. She wondered if she would ever again see smiles on their faces. She prayed to the Great Mystery for a dream telling her what to do. When the dream came, she wept and wept some more.

Her husband said, "What can I do to make you smile again?"

She said, "One thing only will restore joy to me. I must ask you to do that which is most difficult. My body is to be seed for a new kind of food. The food will be called corn, and it will be the sacred nourishment of our children, our grandchildren, and all the children ever after. This food shall come, not from the flesh of animals, but from the earth. In order to plant it, you will have to kill me, for the first growth comes from First Mother's body. Our sons shall have to scatter my remains across the field. And the people will have to pray and wait patiently, for seven moons.

No thought could be more abhorrent to First Father, than what his wife requested, but she kept weeping and prodding, weeping and prodding. At last he went to All-maker, and asked for advice. All-maker saw the larger picture and knew that the Great Mystery was at work. He told First Father what he must do.

With a heavy heart and much weeping, First Father returned and slew his beloved wife. Then, with much weeping, her sons scattered her remains in the field. Then the people prayed and waited for seven moons, as First Mother had instructed. At the end of seven moons the field was full of beautiful music. It was the rustling of tall green plants in the breeze. These plants bore many fruits and these fruits bore tassels of long golden hair that sparkled in the warm sunlight. Dewdrops collected on the tassels, and there was moisture, motion, and warmth. The people could smell the essence of life waiting to nourish them. They harvested the corn just as First Mother had told them to, and they feasted until their bellies were full. Once again smiles came easily to the children's faces.

First Father called all the people together. He said, "From now on we will be nourished and sustained by First Mother's flesh. We must respect her body which feeds us. We must respect the soil in which her body grows. She is not dead. she lives in the green plants, in the little seeds, and in the smiles on the children's faces." The people understood. They feasted some more. Then they stored corn for the long winter. They saved the best seeds to plant again in spring. That is the story of First Mother, Corn Mother, and how her flesh brought sustenance to the people.

HONORING THE EARTH | EARTH AS SACRED | REVERENCE FOR NATURE | THE MORE-THAN-HUMAN WORLD | SACRIFICE | DREAM AS GUIDE | DREAM AND RITUAL | CREATION AND DESTRUCTION | GENEROSITY | GRATITUDE | AGRICULTURE | HELP FROM WISE ELDERS: Versions of this tale can be found among Native North American peoples from the Pueblo to the Penobscot. The tale reminds us of a time when people turned to dreams for guidance, lived close to the earth, partook of life-affirming rituals, and remained reverent and attentive to the growing season. The tale is a call to gratitude for the "simple things," like fertile soil, and life-giving sweet corn at harvest time, and yet it reminds us that the underlying force which animates the world is so beyond our comprehension that it can only be referred to as "The Great Mystery." The mind is not big enough to capture it, and yet at times we may be struck by an emotional or intuitive impression of it. This tale helps to awaken us at these levels. It reminds children of all ages that we would not be here, if not for the sustaining nourishment we've received from the gracious Earth, from the inexplicable sources of life, and from elder providers like Corn Mother. The tale should never be taken lightly, nor should we take it literally as a prescription for mindless self-sacrifice. It is more an expression of awe and gratitude for the life-death-rebirth cycle, so well regarded by indigenous peoples.

SCARCITY | DEPRIVATION | SUSTAINABILITY | POSTERITY: Today, the tale's message on sustainability could not be more apt: The more we prosper, the more we consume, the more other species disappear, the more precarious our foothold on this earth. The story's answer is one of sacrifice. First Mother gives her life so that others can be sustained. The people sacrifice their mainly carnivorous ways, to become farmers. What they get in return is a far greater reward: that of remaining a healthy part of the ongoing continuum of life. We humans have to take stock of our consumption and its long-term effects. To take steps toward conservation, requires sacrifice; cutting back on consumables, and choosing more sustainable ways of nourishing ourselves. What we sacrifice now will enable our children's children to sustain their children. That continuity is the greatest of all possible rewards.

FIGHTING POVERTY AND HUNGER | ADVOCACY FOR CHILDREN | YOUTH-ELDER ALLIANCE: This tale speaks to the problem of children and hunger, which plagues the world and our nation even in the most opulent of times. Told at fundraisers for food programs, this tale opens hearts and affirms convictions that all children must be fed.

HARDSHIP AS AN OPPORTUNITY | SACRIFICE | LIFE-DEATH-REBIRTH CYCLE | LOSS, COURAGE, TRANSFORMATION | GRIEF AND LOSS | SACRED FEMININE | SACRED MASCULINE | SPIRIT AS THE SOURCE OF KNOWLEDGE: Life is a mysterious adventure, born of moisture, motion, and warmth. In the course of a lifetime, we come across astounding beauty, as well as great hunger and unexpected loss. Sometimes the life-death-rebirth cycle seems unbearably cruel. Yet within life's losses lie possibilities for learning, deepening, and transforming. I find the images in this tale to be profoundly moving, particularly when held in a state of nonjudgmental contemplation. Through the image of corn mother we clearly see how our very bodies could not exist without the billions upon billions of lives which preceded us. These include not only our ancestors, but all the species who gave their lives so our ancestors could live.

People who have endured much loss, but still see themselves as part of a wondrous mystery knowingly identify with this tale. I shared it in bereavement therapy with a woman who suffered the tragic death of her husband and daughter and soon after, lost sixty per cent of her vision. "Sometimes I wonder, 'Why me?'" she said. "My surviving son says, 'Don't give up, Mom. Dad wouldn't want you to give up.' I realize for his sake, for my sake, and for my future grandchildren, I have to keep getting up in the morning. I have to keep planting my seeds of corn and watering them with my tears. My vision is very poor now, but I can still see the pink color of the sunrise, and I can surely hear the tassels rustling on the corn. My pleasures are pared down now, and in a funny way that makes it all the more clear: It's a blessing to be alive."

Another woman, a young mother who had a double mastectomy followed by radiation therapy said, "I feel very close to death now, and this story is a great comfort to me. My thoughts of death are not morbid. Anything but. I am more filled with light and love than ever before, because death is so near, it puts life into perspective. Every drink of water, ever kiss from my child, every chirp of a bird, and yes, the way the light hits a dew drop, all of that just makes me weep, not tears of sorrow, because I may lose it, no, these are tears of joy because it's so clear to me now, I am one with it."

Strong Wind the Mystic Warrior

AN ALGONQUIAN TALE FROM NORTH AMERICA | (1337 words)

Long ago on the Atlantic coast there lived a mystic warrior by the name of Strong Wind. Strong Wind could fly invisibly from place to place, floating over the mountain tops, through the trees, and across the sea. He lived with his sister in a lodge near the shore. One day while Strong Wind and his sister were talking Strong Wind said, "My Sister, I am lonely and I would like to find a wife."

Strong Wind's sister replied, "My Brother, it is easy to find a woman, but it is difficult to choose the right one to be your wife."

"What must I look for in choosing a wife?" he asked.

"You need to find out whether or not a woman is truthful," she answered.

Strong Wind thought silently for a while and then said, "We will put the women to a test. You will spread the word far and wide, that who ever is able to see my mystic form shall be my wife."

"But no one can see your mystic form," said the sister. "You are the wind."

"That's right," said Strong Wind. "but we will not be testing their vision, we will be testing their truthfulness."

So Strong Wind's sister spread the word, and soon young women came from every direction to see if they could win the heart and hand of Strong Wind. The sister was the only one who could see him. As he came around the point she would ask, "Do you see my brother, Strong Wind, do you see him?" The only thing the women could see was the branches blowing on the trees, but sooner or later a bold one would cry out, "I see him!"

Then the others would chime in, "I see him, too!"

Then the sister would test, "If you see him, tell me: Of what is his bow string made?"

The women would stammer and falter, and eventually one would shout, "It is made of a great raw-hide strap!" Then the others would chime in saying they saw the same. Strong Wind's sister would send them away, for not one of them admitted the simple truth. It went on like that for a long time and Strong Wind wondered if he would ever find a wife.

It happened that in a nearby village there lived a chief whose wife had long since died. The chief had three daughters and he did his best to raise them alone. The two eldest were lovely to look at, but the youngest was loved by all, for she had the kindest manner and the warmest heart. Her sisters were jealous of the affection others gave her. One day when their father was away on a hunt they yanked at her and tore her dress. When the chief returned and saw her dress he asked, "My Daughter, what happened?"

Before the youngest could reply, the two eldest said, "Father, our little sister is clumsy. She tore her dress. She is not worth the attention you give her."

Another time when the chief was away they told her they would comb her hair. But when she sat down they took a knife and chopped off her long beautiful braids. When the chief returned he asked, "My Daughter, what happened to your hair?"

Before she could reply her sisters answered, "Father, our sister is a fool. She chopped off her hair. She is not worth the affection you give her."

A third time when the chief was away they sneaked up on their young sister as she tended the fire. Then they pushed her face first into the hot coals. She cried out, "My Sisters, help me!" But the sisters ran away.

When their father came home and found his youngest daughter burnt and weeping, he cried, "What has happened?" Before the youngest could speak her sisters answered, "Father, we told her to be careful, but she can do nothing right. She stumbled into the fire and now look at her." The chief washed her face with cool water, but it was too late. Her face was badly scarred with bits of ash and coal embedded in her skin.

The chief's two eldest daughters wanted to win the heart and hand of Strong Wind. They went to the shore to meet Strong Wind's sister. When Strong Wind came around the point, they saw nothing except the branches blowing on the trees. But even so, the eldest cried out, "I see Strong Wind!"

The second sister joined in, "I see him too!"

Strong Wind's sister tested, "If you see him then tell me: With what does he draw his sled?"

The sisters paused and then one burst out, "He draws his sled with a great hemp rope!" Then Strong Wind's sister knew they lied, and she sent them home like all the rest.

The day came when the chief's youngest daughter, the scar-faced one, reached a marrying age. She decided to try and win the heart and hand of Strong Wind. She mended her dress and decorated it with white shells she had gathered on the shore. When her sisters saw what she was doing they scoffed, "You're wasting your time. Strong Wind does not want a scar-faced bride." But she paid them no mind.

When she walked through the village she held her head up high. The neighbors encouraged her saying, "We wish you well."

She went to the lodge where Strong Wind's sister was waiting. They went to the shore and when Strong Wind came around the point his sister said, "Do you see my brother Strong Wind?"

The chief's youngest daughter looked long and hard, but all she could see were the leaves moving on the trees. At last she replied, "I see nothing."

Strong Wind's sister was astonished, for out of dozens of women, here, at last, was one who told the truth. "Look again," she said, "and tell me if you see him."

The scar-faced one looked at the trees, and then her eyes grew wide with wonder. Her mouth opened and no sound came out. Strong Wind's sister said, "Tell me what you see."

"I do see him," said the chief's youngest daughter, "and he is marvelous!"

Then the sister tested, "If you see him tell me: Of what is his bowstring made?"

"It is made of the rainbow."

The sister was truly amazed, and she tested further, "Well, then, with what does he draw his sled?"

"He draws his sled," stammered the chief's youngest daughter, "with the milky way."

Then Strong Wind's sister understood. He had made himself visible to the scar-faced one, because she had told the truth. The sister led her to the women's side of the lodge. There she bathed her with fresh spring water and her skin grew radiant and smooth. She washed her hair and it shone black as a raven's wing. Then she gave her a white buckskin robe and seated her at the wife's seat at the table.

Through the door came Strong Wind in human form. He stood handsome, straight, and tall, and wore a buckskin shirt. He took the husband's seat at the table. The two shared a meal together and when they finished, they said wedding vows. The scar-faced one became known as a bringer of truth, and people came from far and wide to seek her counsel. She was loved by all, except her two sisters. They were jealous because she had won the hand of Strong Wind. They decided to take revenge. One day while she was baking at her oven, they crept up behind her, intending to push her face first into the fire. This time they would close the doors, and finish her off for good.

But it happened that Strong Wind was moving unseen through the forest that day. Before they could enact their plan, he changed them, on the spot, to aspen trees, rooted to the ground, so they could never again do their sister harm. And that is why, to this very day, when Strong Wind enters the forest, the aspen leaves tremble and quake.

INNER BEAUTY | HONORING TRUE ESSENCE | EXPANDING NARROW DEFINITIONS OF BEAUTY | MATE SELECTION | COURAGE, INTEGRITY, RESILIENCE | EMOTIONAL RESILIENCE: Like, "Maureen the Red," "The Goose Girl at the Spring," and "The Frog," this tale revisits the age-old theme of character and inner beauty, to remind us it's what's on the inside that counts. Young fiancees, Court and Doris took this tale to heart, when after a ski accident, Doris's lovely face was disfigured. Court's brothers told him that while going ahead with the marriage was the "right" thing to do, they would understand if he broke off the engagement. Doris herself broke it off to grieve the loss of her former face, and to free Court from his obligations. Court was left to search his soul. This tale gave him a means of reflection. "I admit in the beginning I was attracted to Doris for her looks. But when I got to know her I found she was way more than just pretty. She's the most honest, caring person I've ever met. I can't imagine having kids with anyone else. I've thought this through from a million angles, and they all point back to me and Doris getting through this together."

It was Doris who needed coaxing. After her release from the hospital, while she was still in physical therapy, Court gave her a written copy of this story, with a note saying, "You are my truth, my one-in-a-million woman." Doris was deeply moved, but she reflected that even after the plastic surgeons had completed their work, there was no magic spring water that would restore her previous looks. Court wasn't sure how to respond, other than to say, "It doesn't matter," which did not resolve it for Doris. Time went by and after the surgeries were completed, Doris had a permanently droopy eye, which teared up with the slightest hint of sorrow or joy. When she smiled or laughed she looked joyous on one side and sad on the other. With their wedding plans still suspended, Court one day whispered to her, "I love you more now than before. I especially love your sad eye." He told his brothers, "She is more beautiful to me now than ever."

They said, "Marry her, you idiot! Don't take no for an answer."

Court proposed again and Doris accepted, and the last I heard they were very happy. The old stories tell us that hardship can bring out the true self, deepen our connections with others, and illuminate us as to what matters in life. When the true self is seen and loved for its essence, petty jealousies cannot harm us, and the diamondness of true character draws others to us. This tale, and people like Doris and Court bear this out.

TRUTHFULNESS | MATE SELECTION: I've often told this tale to children and youths as a way to open discussion on the theme of truthfulness. The romantic intrigue rivets them, and their interest in inner goodness comes to life. Each girl who listens likes to think of herself as one who would have the courage to tell the truth. This is a healthy way to fantasize, for imagining oneself behaving with integrity when it counts, puts one on the path to actually doing so. Boys see themselves as gallant, discerning, truth-loving, and able to detect inner beauty. This is an important lesson for living. Looking beyond appearance to essence is a skill that serves not only in mate selection, but in everything we do. This tale gives us the call to go beyond the enticements of mere loveliness to something firmer, stronger, deeper, truer, and ultimately more radiant.

ENVY AND JEALOUSY | JEALOUSY, ENVY, AND COMPETITION: This tale helped a woman named Andrea get a handle on her jealousy toward other women. "Our dad favored my sister," Andrea explained. "She says it was no piece of cake to be Dad's favorite, that it just put pressure on her, but she definitely got more love and praise. I always feel jealous of other women when it seems like they get shown favor." With a bit of encouragement, Andrea was able to see that she gave herself short shrift, by presuming others would get more attention, and by not valuing her own inner qualities. "I know I have a great sense of humor, I'm smart and loyal, and people like me. But at work and in yoga class I'm always comparing myself to other women, and resenting it when they get attention. I mask it pretty well, but inwardly it gnaws at me, like the sisters nagging, 'Nobody wants *you* for a bride.'"

Andrea noticed that the cycle of jealousy played out within her similarly to the way it played out in the story. She hurt herself with condemning thoughts, which accentuated her emotional scar and had the effect of making her less attractive to others. "The scar-faced girl nurtures herself by mending her dress, and doing the best she can with her face and hair. I need to care for myself better, by doing the best I can, and giving myself credit for it. The scar-faced girl doesn't give a lot of power to harsh things her sisters say. For me that's the big one. I have to stop giving power to my own self-doubt. When her neighbors encourage her, she holds her head high, and listens. I need to be better at receiving compliments and encouragement from others. Lastly, I need to respect my own integrity. I spend too much time like all those wanna-be brides, trying to second guess what I should think and say, rather than respecting my inner self and my own truth."

WOMEN'S INITIATION | RITES OF PASSAGE | EMANCIPATION FROM HOME | HARDSHIP AS AN OPPORTUNITY | DISENFRANCHISEMENT: In this tale, as in wisdom traditions the world over, the young woman coming of age endures pressures and hardships which might break her, yet eventually, due to her inner strength she comes into her own. Oftentimes in reality as in the story, when one is truly gifted, and meant to develop a special gift, one is also scarred, and may carry more pain and experience greater rejection than others. This tale encourages us all to persist despite scars, and to move forward from a place of genuineness and truth. We cannot find out whether we truly merit fullness, wholeness, and excellence unless we try. And as this wisdom tale reveals, our highest destiny is not merely handed to us, we have to reach and aspire to it. Hardships are iniatory ordeals which test our strength and endurance and teach us how miraculously resourceful the human spirit can be.

DOMESTIC VIOLENCE | JEALOUSY, ENVY, AND COMPETITION | DENIAL AND DECEPTION| JUSTICE AND FAIRNESS | SIBLING RIVALRY | THE FUTILITY OF VIOLENCE: The scar-faced girl does not tell on her sisters, and they get away with denying and lying about their destructive behaviors. For those who have never been treated violently by loved ones, this sounds unlikely, but it is surprisingly common. The reasons are complex. Survivors of abuse do not want to rock the boat. They want to give loved ones the benefit of the doubt. They convince themselves it will never happen again, or they must have somehow deserved it. This tale is encouraging to survivors of all ages. It generally awakens in them a desire to tell their own truth, and to evaluate their own story. Occasionally it encourages survivors to tell, and to seek justice for abuses they have suffered.

REVERENCE FOR NATURE | THE MORE-THAN-HUMAN WORLD | INTUITION | SPIRIT AS A SOURCE OF KNOWLEDGE | GUIDANCE FROM SPIRIT | INITIATION | RITES OF PASSAGE | SACRED MASCULINE: In countless wisdom tales nature has consciousness and the desire to guide and to empower us. More-than-human beings befriend wounded heroines (or heroes), guide them through initiatory scenarios, and help bring about their rightful destinies. In this tale the wind itself is a mystical lover, a warrior who detects our heroine's integrity and chooses to wed her. The result is her becoming one who gives counsel. Lumi tribal elder, Gary Hillaire, said the tale illustrates "the way to wisdom." It shows that in order to learn we must unite with and emulate nature spirits such as totem animals, elements like water and earth, or in this case, the wind. As Gary explained it, one must first be called, either through a dream or an encounter in nature. Then one must be awake enough to recognize one has been called. Then one must work to identify the particular nature spirit, study its special qualities, and emulate them. This approach is enormously heartening, for it reminds us that the lessons we need to learn, and the abilities we need to develop reside in the things of the natural world. Our task is to be awake, to receive, and to learn from them. If we take this tale to heart, what ability might it call us to emulate?

Strong Wind moves swiftly and invisibly, to detect people's motives and plans. This resembles the gift of intuition, the ability to "see around corners," as Carl Jung said, and the ability to see into the hearts of others. The tale encourages gifted intuitives to honor the gift, and it encourages us all to develop our innate intuitive capacities. Parents, teachers, bosses, therapists, investigators, and physicians are among the many who might benefit from the swift insights of Strong Wind.

SACRED MASCULINE | MEN'S ESTEEM AND EMPOWERMENT: After telling this tale in a pre-teen youth group, I noticed Jasper, a talented introverted boy intently drawing comic book style sketches of Strong Wind. Jasper was a member of the Quinalt tribe. His avid concentration told me he was pleased to hear this native hero tale. His sketches were so striking I asked him to share them with the group the following week. By the end of the week he had illustrated each scene in the story. When I asked what he liked best he said, "Strong Wind. He's not really a guy he's a spirit. A spirit is cool because it protects you and helps you like he did for the scarred girl. In my bed at night I listen to the wind." Jasper's normally antsy peers listened intently, as if they understood that Strong Wind had become Jasper's own special protector.

Raven Didn't Look Back

A TLINGIT STORY FROM CANADA | (688 words)

RAVEN, BACKGROUND AND SOURCES: *Storytelling traditions of the Pacific Northwest including those of the Haida, the Tsimshian, and the Tlingit, are famous for their rousing mythic dramas made bigger than life with mesmerizing drums, extravagant dance, and full-body masks with moving parts. Central to these dramas is Raven, at once a beneficent creator, a favorite trickster, and a strong totem spirit. Like fellow tricksters, Coyote and Maui, Raven sometimes serves meaningful causes, and sometimes merely serves his appetites and whims. In any case, we learn from his actions. He is a mirror of human weakness and human potential, as well as an enigmatic near-divine shape-shifter, who overcomes the limits of matter, time, and space.*

Way up Eskimo way there lived a woman who had lots of young men waiting in line. She was beautiful and they all wanted to marry her, but she turned down each and every one.

Then one day along came an unusual guy. He was dressed to kill. He wore a ground-squirrel parka with wolverine trim. On his feet he wore the most deluxe pair of mukluks you ever saw. Nobody around there dressed like that. All of a sudden the woman was thinking about marriage and settling down.

The fancy dresser said, "Hey, fine woman, are you in love with me yet?" And she nodded, yes, quicker than you could snap your fingers.

She took him home to her father and said, "Father, I'm married."

The father eyed the fancy dresser and said, "Hmmm, can you hunt caribou?" The son-in-law didn't reply. He just looked down and scratched the ground with the toe of his fancy mukluk.

The father gave him a set of arrows. The fancy dresser kissed his new wife good-bye and went off to hunt caribou. A while later he returned empty-handed, all scraped up. The arrows were bent and broken. The young wife said, "My dear Husband, come rest, you look tired."

The father started sniffing. "Smells like raven around here," he said. Others noticed it too, and they began looking around. All through the night they searched the woods. The good-looking guy held the lamp. They all smelled raven, but they didn't find one.

Whenever the fancy dresser went hunting, he came back looking sorely battered. His beautiful wife cleaned his clothes. She cooked him delicious caribou meat which her father had brought back from the hunt. One day when he went hunting the father-in-law told a young tracker to follow and see what he could see. The handsome guy did not know he was being followed. After a while he stopped and sat on a rock. He took off his mukluks and pounded them into the dirt. The tracker watched as he took off his spiffy parka and rolled it in the mud. He stomped on the arrows until they were bent and broken. Then the fancy dresser took a sharp stone and scraped himself.

The tracker hurried back to the father to report what he had seen. That night the father called together the whole village. "There is somebody here," he said, "who has only three toes." Then the old man went 'round the group. Each of the men took off a mukluk, and held up their five toes for all to see.

As the beautiful woman's father neared his son-in-law, the younger man began whining, "What's so great about five toes, anyway?" He didn't want to take off his fancy mukluk. Everyone watched and waited. Finally he pulled it off. When everyone saw his raven toes, they knew where the smell had been coming from.

"Now there's proof, Daughter. You can't deny it. You've married Raven, who cannot do much but act tricky and eat other people's caribou meat." The young wife did not reply. The light was dim and she did not want to see what the others saw.

The next day she said to Raven, "Let's go to your village. Your parents will treat us better." They went to Raven's village and walked to the door of his parents' home. She could smell something, but she tried not to notice. They went inside and his parents invited them to a meal. It turned out, all they had to eat were caribou stomachs, scavenged from hunters' camps. "I cannot eat this," the beautiful bride sniffled. Throughout the whole village there was nothing to eat except entrails. "Your people are scavengers," said the young woman bitterly. She did not look so beautiful when she cried.

"That's how we get our food," said Raven. "Now eat and stop complaining."

"I'm going back," she said. And she did. As quickly as you could snap your fingers, she was gone.

"Have it your way," said Raven. He flew off, and didn't look back. He wasn't the sort to stay married long.

IMPRESSIONABILITY | HUMOR | HEALTHY SKEPTICISM | CRAVINGS AND TROUBLESOME DESIRES: No matter how pure and promising they may appear, most head-turning objects of desire have a down-side, a dark-side, or a hidden shadow. With great humor this tale illustrates just how readily the hopeful believer can be led astray. It goes over well in teen groups where prevention is the theme. Whether the topic is drug and alcohol dependency prevention, teen pregnancy prevention, or the prevention of sexually transmitted disease, this tale offers meaningful metaphors and drives home its point: tempting enticements have a backlash and a downside.

MATE SELECTION | DENIAL AND DECEPTION | UNSTABLE IDENTITY | INTUITION | MALE INTUITION | ELDER WISDOM | CUNNING AND CONNING | SCAMMING | OPPORTUNISM: Youngsters are not the only ones who ignore the shadow when they are smitten. A thirty-seven-year-old named Margaret took this story to heart when it began to dawn on her that her fiancee was not who he pretended to be. Her friends and family had tried for months to make her take stock of his half-truths, yet she refused to see. Then one day her fiancee's own son revealed to Margaret that he knew of at least two other "fiancees" waiting in the wings. Margaret could no longer ignore her lover's "three toes," and wised up. This tale reminds us of the importance of intuition and the ability to sniff out the subtle aromas of the ingenuous. As with many wisdom tales, it is the elder—the father figure—whose sagely old nose can be trusted.

Raven Brings Light

A HAIDA TALE FROM WESTERN CANADA | (882 words)

(for background on Raven see p. 234)

⟨ong ago the earth was covered in darkness. Neither the sun nor the moon shone in the sky. It was said that a powerful old chief living at the headwaters of the Nass River kept the sun and moon hidden away so he could hoard all the light for himself.

Raven wanted something better for the Haida People. He wanted moonlight so they could see to fish at night. He wanted sunlight so food could grow. He flew high in the sky making the long journey to the headwaters of the river. He carried with him some pebbles, one of which his father had given him. Each time he dropped one of the pebbles into the water it turned into an island where he could stop to rest.

At last Raven arrived at the chief's village. He wanted to enter the chief's house. Once inside he would find the sun and moon and devise a way to release them into the sky so everyone could enjoy their light. He went to the edge of the river and changed himself into a tiny seed. When the chief's daughter went to the river to drink, she swallowed the seed and became pregnant. When her child was born, she and her parents loved him dearly. He looked like any human infant, and they had no idea he was really Raven in human form.

As the infant learned to crawl about the lodge, his grandfather, the old chief, gave him everything he wanted. He crawled around every nook and corner, just like a curious baby. He saw baskets and bags everywhere. Whenever he pointed to one his grandfather gave it to him to play with. One day he pointed at a special bag and his grandfather gave it to him. He rolled the bag along the floor and then let it go. It floated up into the air, out through the smoke hole, and into the dark sky. It rose high up into the heavens. There it opened and what should float out of it, but the stars. They spread like sparkling seeds across the night sky.

Each day the boy wanted to play with a different basket or bag. One day he pointed to the one which held the moon. The chief gave it to him and he had great fun rolling it around on the floor. When he let it go, it floated up to the smoke hole and drifted out into the sky, just as the bag of stars had done. It went up into the heavens and opened. There it opened and released the moon to hang freely and brightly in the night sky.

Finally the day came when the boy pointed to a large box which held the sun. Grandfather took him into his arms and said, "This is my greatest treasure. I will let you play with it, but you must promise to be careful." Then the chief closed the smoke hole and brought the box out from the corner in which it was hidden. He opened the box and inside it was a second box nestled within a spider web. Within that was another box and within that was another. The chief kept opening smaller and smaller boxes until he reached the eighth box. When he lifted the lid a marvelous, glowing ball came out and filled the room with light. The boy was astonished and delighted. He played with it for hours, rolling it about the lodge, until at last he grew tired and fell asleep. Then Grandfather put the sun back into the smallest box and placed each box into the next until the sun was nestled away within the eight boxes.

Each day the boy asked to play with the sun, and each day the old chief took it out of the box for him, always closing the smoke hole so the sun would not escape. One day Grandfather grew lax and forgot to close the smoke hole. The boy saw his chance. He changed back into his Raven form, clutched the sun in his claw and flew out the smoke hole. He flew along with the sun tucked under his wing, and began to feel very hungry. Luckily he saw some people fishing in the dark water below. He perched in a nearby tree and called to them, "If you give me some fish, I will give you light." The people were skeptical. Everyone knew that light, if it existed at all, was securely hidden away. Raven was the sort to exaggerate, so why believe him?

Raven lifted his wing a little to prove he was telling the truth. The people saw light beam forth. They eagerly shared their fish with him, for in the light they would have an easy time catching more. Each day Raven came and offered light in exchange for part of their catch. This went on until one day when he grew tired of eating fish, he grasped the sun and hurled it high into the air. "Haida People," he cried, "Enjoy this light. It will help you fish and it will make things grow. Because of this light you will live well and prosper!" Ever since Raven's trip to the headwaters, the sun, moon, and stars have lit up the sky.

DEPRIVATION | SCARCITY | LONGING FOR LIGHT | WINTER BLUES | GREED AND ACQUISITIVENESS | ANIMALS AS HELPERS AND TEACHERS | TRICKS AND TRICKING | WORTHY USE OF DECEPTION | SACRED MASCULINE: Ancestors around the globe told myths of original darkness, light deprivation, and the greedy hoarding of light. In many myths hero-tricksters such as Maui and Raven, through their cunning ingenuity, secure sunlight for all. These tales celebrate the life-giving force of the sun, and the triumph over the forces of darkness and deprivation. They give us marvelous metaphors of illumination, and help us pass the long winter nights. This Raven tale provides the theme for solstice gatherings which bring tribal people together to honor the seasonal transition from dark to light.

In contrast to the Northwest tribal traditions from which this story arises, mainstream society has become increasingly out of touch with seasonal cycles. We function at a continuously rapid pace, and expect year-round high yield production. People who slow down in winter, those who become less motivated to achieve, who yearn for more sleep, and prefer to curl up beside the fire are often diagnosed as having Seasonal Affective Disorder. But these tendencies sometimes indicate natural rhythms taking hold, for when we look at the natural world we see that no earthly beings are designed to rev full speed through all four seasons. For thousands of years our ancestors have looked forward to putting away food for the winter, nestling close to the fire, catching up on their mending, and delving into stories. Perhaps from nature's point of view, there is more "disorder" in the obsession with year-round productivity, than in our winter resistance to it. As long as Earth circles around the sun, seasons will influence our lives, our energy levels, and our moods. Winter solstice tales help us appreciate winter as a slower more interior season.

IxChel and the Dragonflies

ADAPTED FROM MAYA AND QUICHE MYTHS OF GUATEMALA
(1,568 words)

IXCHEL, BACKGROUND AND SOURCES: *Sometimes known as Lady Rainbow, IxChel is the principal Moon Goddess of Mayan lore in Campeche, Yucatan, and Guatemala. Among her many forms are the solitary virgin, the enchanting seductress with multiple lovers, the nurturing mother of all life, and the grandmother-healer. Being the moon, it is her nature to wax and wane. In several stories, like this one, she is struck down, nearly defeated, and then miraculously restored to her former brilliance. IxChel is credited with being the weaver of fate, the guardian of erotic love, the protector of women's fertile cycles, childbirth and children, and the matron of medicine and the healing arts. This episode is part of a longer tale told to me in 1975 by two Cakchiquel brothers, Ateca and Alena. They pieced together the tale in a casual manner, recalling what they could from their grandfather's telling.*

Long ago in the land of the wandering jaguar, the sacred deer, the soaring quetzal, the ant, and the butterfly, beneath the jade mountain, alongside the turquoise sea, in the land of the Mayan people, the moon was said to be the most beautiful of all heavenly bodies. People spent hours on clear nights gazing up at the sky, awed by that lustrous pearl, that white gardenia which could drop billions of shimmering petals on the sea, and still remain in full bloom. "The moon" they said, "is a radiant queen, who lives and breathes, laughs and cries," and they called her by name, IxChel, Moon Woman.

IxChel had everything a queen might want, her own moon palace with walled gardens laden with cascading pink bougainvillea and dancing yellow nicotiana blooms. She had her own variety of bees to produce heavenly honey. Green capped hummingbirds flit here and there in her garden. Lest you think her frivolous, let me make clear, her duties kept her fully occupied. She watched over the tides of the great oceans, steadily guiding them in and out. No one's timing was more reliable. IxChel held sway over the pulse of life itself, including women's fertile cycles which still flow today in accord with the moon. She watched over midwives and healers, and was known to be their guiding light.

IxChel's favorite pastime was traversing the cosmic stream in her dugout canoe. She would paddle along the milky way, and admire the swirling eddies of stars. She would sometimes shine boldly and fully, wearing a rainbow crown. Other times she was partially hidden beneath her silken rebozo shawl. Other times she would wrap herself entirely so not even a sliver of her luminous cheek showed as she glided silently across the sky.

The sun secretly admired her and watched her as much as he could. During her dark times he strained to catch a glimpse of her. Then, her shawl would open slightly. Her white earlobe would shine at first like a tiny pearl, and then her shoulder would shine like an abalone shell. Then Sun could not take his eyes off her. The harder he stared, the brighter she shone, until she began wrapping up in her rebozo again. This waiting, watching, and shining went on for eons, so say the Mayan people.

In the land of the Mayan people there is a calm season and a stormy one, and the storms are created by a storm maker called Chak. During the calm season the storm maker grew very bored. One day to pass the time Chak paid a visit to the moon palace while IxChel was away in her canoe. Chak spoke with IxChel's guardian, her grandfather. Chak liked nothing better than to stir things up. He said,

"Grandfather, you are an observant sort. Do you see that glint in Sun's eye when he looks upon IxChel?"

Grandfather replied, "I see nothing out of the ordinary, for it is Sun's place to see and to watch over all."

"Well," said Chak, "he looks at IxChel differently. His brightest rays shoot across the sky to her like arrows. Surely these are arrows of desire."

"Hmmm," said Grandfather. "I had not noticed." After Chak departed Grandfather could not get the thought out of his mind: *the sun warming IxChel with rays of desire?* This was not right. IxChel's domain was that of the night, the tides, health, and healing. Sun ruled over the day and the nourishing crops that grow upon the land. If they should come together all manner of confusion would result. If they ran away together, the world would be engulfed in floods and darkness. It was unthinkable.

For the next few days, the sea was as smooth as glass and the sky was cloudless and blue. An excruciating boredom came over Chak and he decided to assuage it by visiting Vulture at the top of Jade Mountain. "You know," he said to Vulture, "whoever marries IxChel will be the king of the sky." After Chak departed Vulture could not stop hearing that phrase, *king of the sky.* Being a scavenger who always made do with leftovers, the thought of being king intrigued him. Vulture was a meek fellow, but very persistent. He began flying toward IxChel each day before dawn. "Good morning, Jewel of the Sky," he would call. "How radiantly you glowed upon the clouds last night." These morning visits were not lost on Sun and he grew jealous.

The calm season was nearly over. Storm Maker Chak went to Grandfather and said, "It is plain to see: Sun and Vulture are rivals for IxChel's love. I've heard Vulture plans to elope with her, and to prevent it, Sun plans to kidnap her. But why am I telling you? You are IxChel's guardian. Surely these things do not escape your watchful eye."

Grandfather did not wish to appear negligent. "I'm aware of the problem," he said, "but I'm still deliberating what to do."

"I have a plan," said Chak. "Tonight when IxChel paddles upstream, I will follow, staying a good distance behind so she does not see me. When morning dawns, and her suitors come to claim her,

I will seethe and churn and produce the greatest of all storms to block their way. Grandfather thanked Chak and encouraged him to be strong.

Whether Vulture truly planned to elope with IxChel, and whether Sun truly intended to kidnap her, no one can say for sure. But it is known that both Vulture and Sun moved toward IxChel that dawn, as was their invariable habit every dawn before.

What was special this day, is that Storm Maker Chak was poised upon the sea. His clouds darkened the sky. His fierce winds began to howl. His thunder-claps roared so violently they nearly jolted the morning star loose from its place in the sky. His lightening bolts cracked wildly. One of them struck IxChel and knocked her into the sea. She sank down, down, and fearing for her life, she changed herself into a red crab that she might survive the depths. She thought deep below the waves she would be safe from Chak's lightening, but no. Chak raged blindly. His wild spears of lightening pierced the water and struck her again and again. IxChel was tossed about in the sea until Chak grew tired and his storm gave way to calm. IxChel's lifeless body floated in the water alongside her canoe.

Do you think that was the end of IxChel? Was her strength, precision, and beauty snuffed out forever? No. Fortunately, she had friends who came in search of her, the dragonflies. Dragonflies appear dainty and frail, but in truth they hold great power. They crossed the seas and continents in gale force winds to come to IxChel's aid. They came in ones and in twos, in tens and in twenties, until they were four-hundred strong. They righted the canoe, and placed IxChel in it. Then they returned her to the moon palace.

Grandfather wept, and said since she had so loved her dugout canoe, it would serve as her coffin on her journey to the other world. Grandfather also said since she had so loved the dragonflies they would be the singers at her funeral. For many days and nights Grandfather mourned. All four hundred dragonflies covered her coffin. Their iridescent bodies shone like mother of pearl, like shimmering turquoise, and jade. For many days the dragonflies hummed. Grandfather thought they were humming funeral songs, but in truth they were filling her with their life force. They were bringing IxChel back to life.

Imagine Grandfather's joy when he saw her stirring, when she rose up for all to see her radiance once again. She thanked her friends and soon resumed her rightful place in the sky. She still paddles her canoe in the cosmic waters. She still rules over the tides and the cycles of new life. She still bestows blessings on the healing arts.

And if the story I've told is not a lie then it's the truth, the whole truth as known in the land of the wandering jaguar, the sacred deer, the soaring quetzal, the ant, and the butterfly, beneath the jade mountain, alongside the turquoise sea, in the land of the Mayan people, where the moon is still said to be the most beautiful of all heavenly bodies. And now, My Friends you understand why the Mayans say, "Never underestimate the power of a dragonfly." One dragonfly is steadfast and strong, four hundred make miracles occur.

WOMEN'S INITIATION | THE LIFE-DEATH-REBIRTH CYCLE | WOMEN'S ESTEEM AND EMPOWERMENT | INSPIRATION LOST AND REGAINED | CHANGE AS AN OPPORTUNITY TO CREATE ANEW | CREATION AND DESTRUCTION | THE JOY OF LIFE-AFFIRMING WORK | SACRED FEMININE | WOUNDED HEALER | REVERENCE FOR NATURE | ANIMALS AS HELPERS AND TEACHERS | THE MORE-THAN-HUMAN WORLD: Because of the moon's steady cycle, her waxing and waning, and its influence on the tides and fertility cycles, ancestral stories the world over have depicted the moon as a female source of inspiration, transformation, and change. IxChel's journey into darkness and her return from the otherworld make her a model initiate into the mysteries of the life-death-rebirth cycle. In her we see a soothing pattern of continuity which contains within it unceasing flux and change.

IxChel is a wonderful example of the wounded healer who is herself healed. The care she receives from the dragonflies reminds healers of times when they must be still and put their trust in others. The tale imparts great dignity and encouragement to all who are trying to make changes, including those who have been struck down by illness or loss. Like Storm Maker Chak, life delivers unexpected blows and devastating falls. Accidents, illness, and interpersonal strife, send us into unforeseen ordeals of darkness. Survivors of breast and uterine cancer, as well as survivors of divorce and bereavement have been among the many to draw courage from this tale.

FALSE WORDS AND INSTIGATING TROUBLE | MISUSE OF POWER | IMPRESSIONABILITY: Sharing secrets, speaking in confidence, passing on observations and interpretations about others will always be a rich part of human communication. Speculating on the motives and intentions of others is one of the more intriguing occupations, one which is entirely necessary to many disciplines including criminal justice, literature, and psychology. But Storm Maker Chak's speculations cross the boundary from useful to meddlesome. Bored during the calm season, he gads about spreading gossip, planting the seeds of trouble. Were Grandfather wiser, he could mitigate the trouble, but instead he is highly impressionable, and directs his support toward the wrong end. Even though this tale is more about the great forces of creation and destruction than it is about human morality, it still nicely illustrates the destructive power of false words. It can be instructive in family, classroom, workplace, and social situations where someone is stirring up conflict by spreading lies, or inducing needless strife between others with slyly chosen words.

HEALING TOUCH | LOVING KINDNESS | COOPERATION AND DEVOTION | DEVOTION | GENEROSITY: I like to think of the dragonflies as the conveyors of chi, reike, prana, Shakti, the life force. Wise ones and hands-on-healers tell us this energy flows throughout the universe, and can readily be channeled through breathing exercises and light touch. IxChel herself is the patron of healing and the healing arts. Her story reminds healing practitioners of the sacred source of their craft.

Acknowledgments

Heartfelt thanks to my editor, Kerri Mommer at Open Court. It is a joy to know and to work with her.

This book was blessed by colleagues and friends whose comments, critiques, suggestions, and encouragement helped it take shape. They include David Abram, Robert and Ruth Bly, George Callan, John and Carolyn Candy, Allison Cox, Catherine Goetsch, Elaine Hanowell, James Hillman, Merna Ann Hecht, Diane Hillaire, Gary Hillaire, Grietje Laga, Donald Lawn, Fionn Meade, Bill Montgomery, Randy Morris, Charlie Murphy, Susan Plum, Miguel Rivera, Stephanie Franz Rivera, Vicki Robin, Farouk Seif, Stephen Silha, Rick Simonson, Sobonfu Somé, Barbara Thomas, Rebecca Wells, Gertrude Wemhoff, and Cristy West.

Much gratitude to all the clients and listeners who have over the years drunk deeply of these tales and shared their personal and family reflections. They keep storytelling alive and have been delightful teachers.

Many thanks to the Brimstone Fund for a grant which aided in the completion of this book.

Bibliography

Abram, David. THE SPELL OF THE SENSUOUS: PERCEPTION AND LANGUAGE IN A MORE THAN HUMAN WORLD. New York: Random House, 1986.

Aman, S.D.B. FOLK TALES FROM INDONESIA. Jakarta: P.T. Penerbit Djambatan, 1986

Arbuthnot, Mary Hill. THE ARBUTHNOT ANTHOLOGY OF CHILDREN'S LITERATURE. Chicago: Scott, Foresman, 1961.

Baker, Ian A. THE DALAI LAMA'S SECRET TEMPLE. New York: Harper Collins, Thames and Hudson, 2000

Barks, Coleman, with John Moyne. THE ESSENTIAL RUMI. San Francisco: Harper Collins, 1995.

Beane, W. C., and Doty, W.G. MYTHS, RITES, SYMBOLS. A MIRCEA ELIADE READER. New York: Harper and Row, 1976.

Beckwith, Martha. HAWAIIAN MYTHOLOGY. Honolulu: University of Hawaii Press, 1970.

Birkhäuser-Oeri, Sibylle. THE MOTHER: ARCHETYPAL IMAGE IN FAIRY TALES. Toronto: Inner City Books, 1988.

Bond, D. Stevenson. LIVING MYTH: PERSONAL MEANING AS A WAY OF LIFE. Boston and London: Shambhala, 1993.

Bonheim, Jalaja. GODDESS: A CELEBRATION IN ART AND LITERATURE. Stewart, Tabori and Chang, 1997.

Campbell, Joseph. ORIENTAL MYTHOLOGY: THE MASKS OF GOD. Arkana: Penguin, 1991.

_____. PRIMITIVE MYTHOLOGY: THE MASKS OF GOD. Arkana: Penguin, 1991.

_____. THE HERO WITH THE THOUSAND FACES. Princeton University Press, 1973.

_____. THE MYTHIC IMAGE. Bollingen Series C. Princeton University Press, 1974.

Carlson, Richard, and Benjamin Shield. HEALERS ON HEALING. Los Angeles: Tarcher, 1989.

Clark, Ella E. INDIAN LEGENDS OF THE PACIFIC NORTHWEST. University of California Press, 1973.

Coe, Michael D. THE MAYA. New York: Thames and Hudson, 1987.

Cole, Joanna. BEST LOVED FOLKTALES OF THE WORLD. New York: Anchor Press/Doubleday, 1983.

Colum, Padraic. LEGENDS OF HAWAII. Yale University Press, 1924.

Cooper, J. C. FAIRY TALES: ALLEGORIES OF THE INNER LIFE. Northhamptonshire, England: The Aquarian Press.

Courlander, Harold. THE TIGER'S WHISKER AND OTHER TALES AND LEGENDS FROM ASIA AND THE PACIFIC. New York: Harcourt, Brace and Company 1959.

Cross, Tom P., and Slover, Clark H. ANCIENT IRISH TALES. Henry Holt and Co. Inc., 1936

Dorson, Richard M. FOLKTALES TOLD AROUND THE WORLD. The University of Chicago Press, 1975.

Dove, Mourning (Humishuma). COYOTE STORIES. Lincoln and London: University of Nebraska Press, 1990.

Dzielska, Maria. HYPATIA OF ALEXANDRIA. Harvard University Press, 1995.

El-Shamy, Hasan M. FOLKTALES OF EGYPT. Chicago: The University of Chicago Press, 1980.

Elgin, Duane. PROMISE AHEAD: A VISION OF HOPE AND ACTION FOR HUMANITY'S FUTURE. William Morrow and Company, 2000.

Eliade, Mircea. RITES AND SYMBOLS OF INITIATION: THE MYSTERIES OF BIRTH AND REBIRTH. Dallas: Spring Publications, 1994.

_____. THE FORGE AND THE CRUCIBLE: THE ORIGINS AND STRUCTURES OF ALCHEMY. Chicago: University of Chicago Press, 1978.

Erdoes, Richard, and Alfonso Ortiz. AMERICAN INDIAN MYTHS AND LEGENDS. New York: Pantheon, 1984.

Feldmann, Susan. AFRICAN MYTHS AND TALES. New York: Dell Publishing Co., 1963.

Fraser, Richard McIlwaine. THE POEMS OF HESIOD. University of Oklahoma Press, 1984.

Futehally, Shama. IN THE DARK OF THE HEART: SONGS OF MEERA. San Francisco: HarperCollins,1994.

Gantz, Jeffrey. THE MABINOGION. New York: Penguin Books, 1977.

Geer Kelsey, Alice. ONCE THE HODJA. New York and Toronto: Longmans, Green and Company, 1958.

Gose, Elliott B., Jr. THE WORLD OF THE IRISH WONDER TALE: AN INTRODUCTION TO THE STUDY OF FAIRY TALES. University of Toronto Press, 1985.

Graves, Robert. THE SONG OF SONGS. New York: Clarkson N. Potter, Inc., 1973.

Gray, Ann and Cusick, Edmund. GRONW'S STONE: VOICES FROM THE MABINOGION. Great Britain: Headland, 1997.

Gregory, Lady Augusta. GODS AND FIGHTING MEN: THE STORY OF THE TUATHA DE DANAAN AND THE FIANNA OF IRELAND. London: John Murray, 1913.

Guest, Lady Charlotte. THE MABINOGION. Chicago: Academy Press Limited, 1977.

Harrison, Jim. THE BEAST GOD FORGOT TO INVENT. New York: Atlantic Monthly Press, 2000.

Haviland, Virginia. NORTH AMERICAN LEGENDS. New York and Cleveland: Collins, 1979.

Hillman, James. THE SOUL'S CODE: IN SEARCH OF CHARACTER AND CALLING. New York: Random House, 1996.

Ho, Mae Wan. THE RAINBOW AND THE WORM: THE PHYSICS OF ORGANISMS. London: World Scientific Publishing Company, 1993.

Hogan, Linda; Metzger Deena; and Peterson, Brenda. INTIMATE NATURE: THE BOND BETWEEN WOMEN AND ANIMALS. New York: Ballantine Publishing Group, 1998.

Hyde-Chambers, Fredrick and Audrey. TIBETAN FOLKTALES. Boston: Shambhala, 1981.

James, Grace. GREEN WILLOW AND OTHER JAPANESE FAIRY TALES. New York: Avenel Books, 1987.

Jordan, Michael. ENCYCLOPEDIA OF GODS: OVER 2500 DEITIES OF THE WORLD. New York: Facts on File, Inc., 1993.

Jung, C. G. MYSTERIUM CONIUNCTIONIS: AN INQUIRY INTO THE SEPARA-TION AND SYNTHESIS OF PSYCHIC OPPOSITES IN ALCHEMY. Princeton University Press, 1977.

———. SYMBOLS OF TRANSFORMATION. Princeton University Press, 1976.

Kane, Sean. WISDOM OF THE MYTHTELLERS. Ontario: Broadview Press, 1994.

Kinsella, Thomas. THE TAIN. Oxford University Press, 1985.

Knappert, Jan. PACIFIC MYTHOLOGY: AN ENCYCLOPEDIA OF MYTH AND LEGEND. London: HarperCollins, 1992.

Leach, Maria. FUNK AND WAGNALLS STANDARD DICTIONARY OF FOLKLORE, MYTHOLOGY AND LEGEND. Harper and Row, 1972.

Lopez, Barry Holstun. GIVING BIRTH TO THUNDER, SLEEPING WITH HIS DAUGHTER: COYOTE BUILDS NORTH AMERICA. Kansas City: Universal Press Syndicate, 1977.

Lüthi, Max. ONCE UPON A TIME: ON THE NATURE OF FAIRY TALES. Indiana University Press, 1970.

MacCana, Proinsias. CELTIC MYTHOLOGY. London: Hamlyn Publishing Group, 1970.

Macmillan, Cyrus. CANADIAN WONDER TALES. New York and London: Dodd, 1922.

Manheim, Ralph. GRIMMS' TALES FOR YOUNG AND OLD: THE COMPLETE STORIES. New York: Anchor Press Doubleday, 1977.

Markman, Roberta H. and Peter T. THE FLAYED GOD: THE MYTHOLOGY OF MESOAMERICA: SACRED TEXTS AND IMAGES FROM PRE-COLUMBIAN MEXICO AND CENTRAL AMERICA. HarperSanFrancisco, 1992.

Marlan, Stanton, ed. SALT AND THE ALCHEMICAL SOUL: THREE ESSAYS BYERNEST JONES, C.G. JUNG, AND JAMES HILLMAN. Woodstock, Connecticut: Spring Publications, 1995.

Meade, Erica Helm. TELL IT BY HEART: WOMEN AND THE HEALING POWER OF STORY. Chicago: Open Court Publishing Company, 1995.

Mellon, Nancy. THE ART OF STORYTELLING. Elements Books, 1998.

Minard, Rosemary.WOMENFOLK AND FAIRY TALES. Boston: Houghton Mifflin Company, 1975.

Moyers, Bill. HEALING AND THE MIND. New York: Doubleday, 1993.

Murray, Henry A. MYTH AND MYTHMAKING, Beacon Press, Boston, 1960

Norman, Howard, NORTHERN TALES: TRADITIONAL STORIES OF ESKIMO AND INDIAN PEOPLES. New York: Pantheon Books, 1990.

O'Sullivan, Sean. FOLKTALES OF IRELAND. Chicago: University of Chicago Press, 1966.

Paris, Ginette. PAGAN GRACE: DIONYSOS, HERMES, AND GODDESS MEMORY IN DAILY LIFE. Dallas: Spring Publications, 1990.

Paz, Octavio. SOR JUANA, OR THE TRAPS OF FAITH. Cambridge, Mass.: Harvard University Press, 1988.

Pearson, Clara. NEHALEM TILLAMOOK TALES. Corvallis: Oregon State University Press, 1990.

Peseschkian, Nossrat. ORIENTAL STORIES AS TOOLS IN PSYCHOTHERAPY. New Delhi: Sterling Publishers, 1985.

Radin, Paul. AFRICAN FOLKTALES. New York: Random House, 1983.

———. THE TRICKSTER: A STUDY IN AMERICAN INDIAN MYTHOLOGY. NewYork: Schocken Books, 1976

Rank, Otto. ART AND ARTIST: CREATIVE URGE AND PERSONALITY DEVELOPMENT. New York and London: Norton, 1989.

Rees, Alwy, and Brinley. CELTIC HERITAGE: AN ANCIENT TRADITION IN IRELAND AND WALES. Thames and Hudson, 1990.

Rifkin, Jeremy. THE BIOTECH CENTURY: HARNESSING THE GENE AND REMAKING THE WORLD. J. P. Tarcher, 1999.

Riordan, James. THE SUN MAIDEN AND THE CRESCENT MOON: Siberian Folktales. New York: Interlink Books, 1991.

Roheim, Geza. FIRE IN THE DRAGON AND OTHER PSYCHOANALYTIC ESSAYS ON FOLKLORE. Edited and Introduced by Alan Dundes. New Jersey: Princeton University Press, 1992.

Rosenberg, Donna. WORLD MYTHOLOGY: AN ANTHOLOGY OF THE GREAT MYTHS AND EPICS. Second Edition. Chicago: NTC Publishing Group, 1994.

Segaller, Stephen and Merrill Berger. THE WISDOM OF THE DREAM: THE WORLD OF C.G. JUNG. Boston: Shambhala, 1989.

Sexton, James D. MAYAN FOLKTALES: FOLKLORE FROM LAKE ATITLAN. GUATEMALA. New York: Doubleday, 1992.

Shah, Indries. THE INCOMPARABLE EXPLOITS OF NASREDDIN MULLA. New York: Dutton.

Sheehan, Ethna. FOLK AND FAIRYTALES FROM AROUND THE WORLD. New York: Dodd, 1970.

Shiva, Vandana. BIOPIRACY: THE PLUNDER OF NATURE AND KNOWLEDGE. Boulder: University of Colorado, April 29, 1997.

Spence, Lewis. THE MYTHS OF THE NORTH AMERICAN INDIANS. New York: Dover, 1989.

Squire, Charles. CELTIC MYTH AND LEGEND POETRY AND ROMANCE. U.S.A.: Newcastle Publishing Co., 1975.

Stephens, James. IRISH FAIRY TALES. Dublin: Gill & Macmillan, Ltd., 1995.

Stone, Merlin. ANCIENT MIRRORS OF WOMANHOOD: A TREASURY OF GODDESS AND HEROINE LORE FROM AROUND THE WORLD. Boston: Beacon Press, 1984.

Stone, Richard. THE HEALING ART OF STORYTELLING: A SACRED JOURNEY OF PERSONAL DISCOVERY. New York: Hyperion, 1996.

Thompson, Stith. TALES OF THE NORTH AMERICAN INDIANS. Bloomington and London: Indiana University Press, 1971.

Townsend, George Fyler. AESOP'S FABLES. Doubleday & Company Inc., New York: 1968.

von Franz, Marie-Louise. ALCHEMICAL ACTIVE IMAGINATION. Dallas: Spring Publications, 1987.

_____. ALCHEMY: AN INTRODUCTION TO THE SYMBOLISM AND PSYCHOL-OGY. Toronto: Inner City Books, 1980.

_____. AN INTRODUCTION TO THE INTERPRETATION OF FAIRY TALES. Dallas: Spring Publications, 1970.

_____. CREATION MYTHS. Zurich: Spring Publications, 1972.

_____. INDIVIDUATION IN FAIRYTALES. Zurich: Spring Publications, 1977.

_____. INTERPRETATION OF FAIRYTALES. Dallas: Spring Publications,1987.

_____. NUMBER AND TIME: REFLECTIONS LEADING TOWARD A UNIFICA-TION OF DEPTH PSYCHOLOGY AND PHYSICS. Evanston: Northwestern University Press, 1974.

von Grunebaum, G. E. and Roger Caillios. THE DREAM AND HUMAN SOCI-ETIES. Berkeley: University of California Press, and London: Cambridge University Press, 1966.

Ward, Candace. AESOP'S FABLES. New York: Dover, 1994.

Wheatley, Margaret J. and Myron Kellner-Rogers. A SIMPLER WAY. San Francisco: Berrett-Koehler Publishers, 1996.

Wolkstein, Diane, and Kramer, Samuel Noah. INANNA, QUEEN OF HEAVEN AND EARTH: HER STORIES AND HYMNS FROM SUMER. New York: Harper and Rowe, 1983.

Wolkstein, Diane. FIRST LOVE STORIES, FROM ISIS AND OSIRIS TO TRISTAN AND ISEULT. New York: Harper Collins, 1991.

Yates, Frances A. THE ART OF MEMORY. Chicago: University of Chicago Press, 1966.

Yeats, William Butler. THE COLLECTED POEMS OF WILLIAM BUTLER YEATS. New York: Macmillan Publishing Company,1956.

Theme Index

the Human Race Came to Be (207), Coyote Creates Human Beings (219), Corn Mother (223), Strong Wind the Mystic Warrior (227), IxChel and the Dragonflies (239)

MORTALITY, ACCEPTING: Why Death Is Like the Banana Tree (141), How Death Came to Humankind (143), Queen Hyena's Funeral (145), How Death Came to Be Feared (151)

MOTHER WOUNDS, HEALING: Gold Tree and Silver Tree (84), Rapunzel (109)

NATURE, REVERENCE FOR: (The majority of the tales convey great respect for nature. The following are especially poignant.) Finn McCoul Learns to Run (25), Finn and the Salmon of Wisdom (30), The Farmer's Hidden Treasure (117), Pythagoras and the White Beans (127), Three Scholars and a Lion (149), The Boy and the Tiger (157), Whale Boy (161), Grandfather Ape (174), Amaterasu's Light (187), Maui Snares the Sun (191), Maui Fishes Up the Islands (195), Wild Pony and Smoke (202), How the Human Race Came to Be (207), Corn Mother (223), IxChel and the Dragonflies (239)

NUMBERS AND THE SACRED: Pythagoras and the White Beans (127), Hypatia's Gift (136)

NURTURING FATHERS: Finn and Saeva (36), Hypatia's Gift (136), Grandfather Ape (174)

OLD AGE AND DEATH, THE INEVITABILITY OF: How Diarmuid Got the Love Spot (45), Why Death Is Like the Banana Tree (141), How Death Came to Humankind (143), How Death Came to Be Feared (151)

ONGOING QUARRELS: Diarmuid and Grania (48), The Horse, the Stag and the Man (121), Whale Boy (161), Coyote and Mole (213)

OPPORTUNISM: The Love of Powel and Rhiannon (67), Rumpelstiltskin (113), The Horse and the Lion (119), Fair Pay (134), Raven Didn't Look Back (234)

PASSAGE, RITES OF: Finn and the Salmon of Wisdom (30), Maureen the Red (58), The Love of Powel and Rhiannon (67), The Goose Girl at the Spring (93), Snow White and Rose Red (102), The Boy and the Tiger (157), The Frog (167), Grandfather Ape (174), Mero's Bride (184), Maui Fishes Up the Islands (195), Strong Wind the Mystic Warrior (227)

PASSING ON THE TORCH: Finn and the Salmon of Wisdom (30), Wild Pony and Smoke (202)

PASSION FOR LEARNING: Finn and the Salmon of Wisdom (30), Pythagoras and the White Beans (127), Hypatia's Gift (136), Kuan Yin's Vows (179), Mero's Bride (184), Wild Pony and Smoke (202)

PEAK EXPERIENCE: The Key Flower (64), Three Scholars and a Lion (149), Mero's Bride (184)

PERFECTIONISM: Rumpelstiltskin (113), The Potter's Wish (153)

POSTERITY: The Farmer's Hidden Treasure (117), Why Death Is Like the Banana Tree (141), The Twisted Message (144), Grandfather Ape (174), Hina's

White and Rose Red (102), The Boy and the Tiger (157), Why Hares Have Long Ears (160), Whale Boy (161), The Frog (167), Coyote's Name (216), Raven Didn't Look Back (234)

VIOLENCE, DOMESTIC: Finn and Saeva (36), Gold Tree and Silver Tree (84), Coyote and Mole (213), Strong Wind the Mystic Warrior (227)

VIOLENCE, THE FUTILITY OF: Diarmuid and Grania (48), Gold Tree and Silver Tree (84), Hypatia's Gift (136), Whale Boy (161), Coyote and Mole (213), Strong Wind the Mystic Warrior (227)

WALKING ONE'S TALK: The Farmer's Hidden Treasure (117), The Mother Crab and Her Child (122), Fair Pay (134)

WINTER BLUES: Kore, Queen of Darkness, Maiden of Light (124), Amaterasu's Light (187), Maui Snares the Sun (191), Raven Brings Light (236)

WISDOM OF COMMON PEOPLE: Choosing a Bride (108), The Sesame Seed (138), Not All at Once (147), Three Scholars and a Lion (149)

WISDOM, KOWLEDGE TEMPERED BY: Not All at Once (147), Three Scholars and a Lion (149)

WISE ELDERS, HELP FROM: Finn McCoul Learns to Run (25), Finn and the Salmon of Wisdom (30), The Stolen Child (78), The Goose Girl at the Spring (93), The Farmer's Hidden Treasure (117), The Sesame Seed (138), Grandfather Ape (174), Maui Snares the Sun (191), Wild Pony and Smoke (202), Corn Mother (223)

WOMEN'S ESTEEM AND EMPOWERMENT: How Brigit Got Lands for the Poor (23), Finn McCoul Learns to Run (25), Finn and the Salmon of Wisdom (30), Maureen the Red (58), The Love of Powel and Rhiannon (67), The Stolen Child (78), Amaterasu's Light (187), Wild Pony and Smoke (202)

WOMEN'S INITIATION: The Stolen Child (78), The Goose Girl at the Spring (93), Whale Boy (161), Grandfather Ape (174), Wild Pony and Smoke (202), IxChel and the Dragonflies (239)

WOMEN AND EDUCATION: Finn McCoul Learns to Run (25), Hypatia's Gift (136), Kuan Yin's Vows (179), Wild Pony and Smoke (202)

WORTHY USE OF DECEPTION: The Love of Powel and Rhiannon (67), The Farmer's Hidden Treasure (117), The Horse and the Lion (119), Kuan Yin's Vows (179), Mero's Bride (184), Coyote and Mole (213), Coyote Creates Human Beings (219), Coyote and the Frog People (222), Raven Brings Light (236)

WOUNDED HEALER: Finn and Saeva (36), Diarmuid and Grania (48), Kuan Yin's Vows (179), Coyote's Name (216), IxChel and the Dragonflies (239)

YOUTH-ELDER ALLIANCE: Finn McCoul Learns to Run (25), Finn and the Salmon of Wisdom (30), The Goose Girl at the Spring (93), The Frog (167), Grandfather Ape (174), Kuan Yin's Vows (179), Maui Snares the Sun (191), Maui Fishes Up the Islands (195), Wild Pony and Smoke (202), Corn Mother (223)